AF522637

# Ambedkar in London

# Ambedkar in London

EDITED BY **WILLIAM GOULD, SANTOSH DASS** AND **CHRISTOPHE JAFFRELOT**

RUPA

First published in India by
Rupa Publications India Pvt. Ltd 2024
7/16, Ansari Road, Daryaganj
New Delhi 110002

*Sales centres:*
Bengaluru Chennai
Hyderabad Jaipur Kathmandu
Kolkata Mumbai Prayagraj



Originally published in Great Britain in 2023 by C. Hurst & Co. (Publishers) London



P-ISBN: 978-93-6156-079-8
E-ISBN: 978-93-6156-636-3

Second impression 2025

10 9 8 7 6 5 4 3 2



Printed in India

# CONTENTS

# LIST OF ILLUSTRATIONS

# AMBEDKARITE ORGANISATIONS IN BRITAIN SINCE THE 1960s

Ambedkar Centenary Celebration Committee, UK

Ambedkar International Mission UK

Ambedkar Mission Society, Bedford

Babasaheb Ambedkar Buddhist Association

Babasaheb Dr Ambedkar Buddhist Association

Bhartiya Buddhist Cultural Association

Buddha Dhamma Association

Dr Ambedkar Buddhist Association

Dr Ambedkar Memorial Trust, London

Dr Ambedkar Memorial Committee of Great Britain

Dr Ambedkar Mission Society, Glasgow

Federation of Ambedkarite and Buddhist Organisations UK

Indian Buddhist Society London

Punjab Buddhist Society UK

Republican Group of Great Britain

The Indian Welfare Association

# FOREWORD

*Suraj Milind Yengde*

One of the earliest curiosities that lingered in my mind when embarking on studying Dr B. R. Ambedkar concerned his international presence. Was Ambedkar confined solely to one geography behind the barbed wire fences of South Asia? Or was he available to the rest of the world? And if so, how much?

This curiosity took me to places and into archives that one would not regularly visit to find the cues and clues. Having been prompted, seven years ago, I started excavating Ambedkar's internationalism. Relatively little had been studied, researched or published concerning his international politics and internationalism. The research findings led to the publication of an article which profiled Ambedkar and his global presence. Admittedly, that article, published in 2018, referenced various sites that Ambedkar had been to, but it couldn't detail much owing to lacunae in research. The two international cities that Ambedkar carried lifelong with him were New York and London.

On the New York front, there are new documents unearthed in recent years. Indeed, his association with Columbia University is the highlight; therefore, files regarding his student days exist. Ambedkar's mammoth intellect comes to light after perusing the list of courses he took in three years. However, outside of that, there is not much to salvage. After departing from Columbia, he kept in touch with his advisor Seligman who went back and forth regarding the progress of his dissertation or recommendation letters. In 1952, his alma mater called on its illustrious alumni to accept the honorary doctorate LL.D. bestowed upon him and there are official missives concerning Ambedkar and Columbia. This and other records of Ambedkar are preserved with honour by the Columbia University archives under the title 'Notable Columbians'. To further Ambedkar's importance, an *Ambedkar Initiative* has been launched under the stewardship of Anupama Rao, a scholar of caste. However, there is relatively little original documentation referring to New York City, even though scholars such as Eleanor Zelliot (1926–2016) tried to decipher Ambedkar's presence in Harlem and New York. But that is not the case with London—a site of political ground where Ambedkar demonstrated his serious statesmanship. Newspaper archives and official records show Ambedkar's importance during and after his periods there.

Some have sought to describe Ambedkar's engagement and negotiation with the British Empire as that of a colonialist handler or suchlike. Detractors have done this through nationalist and proto-post-colonialist perspectives, wherein qualifiers for a developed nationality are identified with bloodshed and rebellion. Another charge against Ambedkar places his scholarship within the Orientalist canon. The latter might be contestable, but what defeats that argument is the 'historicity of knowledge'. In other words, what Ambedkar had at his disposal were the tools and sources available to him then, without hindsight. What he used was vetted to the standards of the highest scholarship available. If his interpretations or discourses appear to lack historical perspective or context through the prism of today, that is because his methodology was historical. That is why through that prism Ambedkar's discourse might appear Eurocentric in nature or wedded to European notions of modernity. But his theses were a culmination of sophisticated rhetoric and heterodox theorisation.

### *Londoner!*

London became the symbolic and tangible centre of extracted riches from near and far, masterminded by elites through exploitation, slavery and colonisation. The imperial metropolis therefore had a seat at the table of world affairs. Each competing faction in civilised liberalism vied for their rights. Ambedkar was among the many to have walked on this land to rally and harness support for their cause or movement. However, he was different in that in his homeland he was viewed as the lowest of the low. The nearest modern European comparison might be the plight of serfdom in Russia before the Emancipation Reforms of 1861.

To correct the prejudices and misunderstandings of the caste system in the subcontinent, Ambedkar chose London as a place to secure rights for his people. In many ways, his people still enjoy those rights in modified form. Ambedkar repeatedly switched between various positions, from trying to persuade and challenge caste Hindus for reform, and making demands for joint and then separate electorates, to finally entering the Constituent Assembly. His objective was to find ways that could benefit his struggle. Ambedkar had material interests at hand. As demonstrated in this volume, the various satyagrahas that he launched were aimed at creating a momentum and uniting Dalits for a cause. He used such movements as a pivot to then claim social and political equality. Ambedkar wanted politics and education for Dalits—a reflection of his own best assets—to challenge Hindu oppression.

With India acting as a centre for the empire's activities, and indeed the crown jewel of the British Empire directed from London, many inferences were drawn quickly by the examples set in India. The Sanskritist and philologist Max Müller, known in India as Max Mueller, famously preached to the British Association for the Advancement of Science convening in 1847, asking them to adopt the policies they had been practising in India across Britain's expanding African colonies. He wanted them to use the caste system as a template for a colonising mission. India had long shone out as an important cultural wellspring, drawn on for fresh intellectual ideas and insights for use by the European world.

*Ambedkar in London* is an interface of multiple disciplines criss-crossing diverse topics. Spatiality has always been one hallmark of caste society. The outcastes are doomed to the filthier and inhospitable contexts of village society. Thus, space as an arbiter of Dalit prospects remains a subject for critical interlocution. Space in the archive of Dalit memory occupies a significant place. Henri Lefebvre thinks of space as both mind and physical. For Dalits, space is always imaginative in that it produces the identity of the unissued, and the Dalit thus becomes a marginal native in the identity of the domestic nation. However, when one among them goes to the capital where power is brokered and bangs on the tables of those denying their rights, space here becomes a logic of optimism. Thus, focusing on the cityscape and the urban geolocations surrounding Ambedkar's work is certainly a novel approach to understanding Ambedkar better. Urban studies and geography discipline have not looked at Ambedkar or Dalit politics satisfactorily enough. By focusing on the city lives and the afterlives of the archives, these domains of investigation can proffer a commendable insight into the studies of communities, capitalism and global mobility.

### *Ambedkar's Scholarship*

Ambedkar's presence was vast, and the shadow he cast was even longer. The Commonwealth of Nations, due to its past commonality of empire, shared resources across its network and propagated knowledge within its ambit. One of the questions that remain with us is the possibility of Ambedkar's literature reaching out to these nations. One can undoubtedly attest to the fact that Ambedkar was a well-known name. Not least for his leadership but also his submissions to various committees in pre- and post-independence India, which at times acted as a guide to those committees' reports. At other times, for example in the areas of currency reform and the franchise, it served as an educational dossier for members of committees and the state.

Ambedkar's pathbreaking interventions in finance and monetary policies concerned the empire. He wrote three theses in his early career—one each for Columbia and the London School of Economics (LSE). The third was originally a Columbia thesis, which was lost along with other books. Accordingly, he wrote a new dissertation entitled *The Stabilization of the Indian Exchange: Problem of the Rupee*. He communicated this to his teacher Edwin Seligman in 1922, but eventually submitted it for his DSc degree in London, which was awarded to him in November 1923. He published his thesis right away in December 1923, entitled *The Problem of the Rupee*. For Columbia, he subsequently submitted *The Evolution of Provincial Finance in India: A Study in the Provincial Decentralisation of Imperial Finance* as a requirement for his doctoral degree. This monograph was first published in book form in 1923 in London. He had started working on this after his MSc degree. The dissertation was entitled *Provincial Decentralization of Imperial Finance in India* (1921). A survey of this is covered by William Gould in his probing essay. In addition to this, Gould has altered our view of 'F' seen in Ambedkar's life. Consulting the census records and verifying it with the registers of tenants, Gould has questioned the identity of Fanny Fitzgerald.

What remains striking is Dr Ambedkar's serious interest in the economic and financial affairs of the political economy of the state. His dissertations abroad concerned the history of agriculture examined through commerce, finance, and the administration of the imperial economy through the East India Company. He also wrote on the relationship between the federal and provincial decentralisation of finance. His two texts published as books introduced Ambedkar to an international network, a small tribe of finance and economics scholars. Indeed, the endorsement of Edwin Seligman, an authority on public finance, would have introduced him to the networks of policymakers and scholars.

Dr Ambedkar's work centred around mercantile interests and regulation of exchange value set by gold standards as opposed to silver. The Indian rupee was widely used in East Africa, southern parts of Arabia, and the Persian Gulf, and was travelling through the south coast of Mozambique up to the northern tip, looking eastwards in Africa. Would his research, *The Problem of the Rupee: Its origin and its solution*, be taken up in devising economic policies in India and abroad? By 1921 the rupee was replaced with the shilling in East Africa, so that possibility became academic. However, his influence among policymakers remained, in the formation of the reserve board that formed the Reserve Bank of India and in the management of reserves tabulated in gold standards as opposed to silver. One of the limitations within the Ambedkarite tradition, as with this text, is delineating the economic or financial aspects of Ambedkar's early thinking. His statement on the Indian rupee, discussed in this volume by William Gould, was a bone of contention. Why and how his economic interventions were not appreciated and later accepted by the professors at LSE is a question of scholarly significance. A further thorough, dedicated examination of this topic remains to be carried out. A scholar at Columbia University told me that Ambedkar was toggling between Keynesian and Smithian models of classical and non-classical economics. Yet, we do not get a clear picture of Ambedkar's doctoral theses' thick, discipline-oriented texts. Some say those theories are worn out, and thus they have lost their significance. Can the methodology or style of investigation merit any interest?

Ambedkar's books were written and reported widely in the English-speaking world. In my research, I came across Ambedkar's influential presence in the Australian, British, Canadian and American media. The people reviewing his books were ministers, high-ranking bureaucrats, noted journalists and writers. This means Ambedkar became a name not confined within the boundaries of India. His was a more prominent presence that people are now coming to terms with, and in a much more refined and beautiful form. A key element of this presence, through his early work, is presented in *Ambedkar in London* as an interface of multiple disciplines criss-crossing diverse topics.

Alongside its many other facets, London now has another addition in its extensive *résumé*: *Ambedkar in London*, carved in the able hands of its editors. Santosh Dass, a seasoned British bureaucrat and a descendant of proud Punjabi Dalits, first proposed this project several years ago. Since then, she has championed Ambedkar's legacy in London, notably at the Ambedkar Museum on King Henry's Road at Primrose Hill, and at Gray's Inn, where he was called to the Bar. She has also been leading the struggle in the parliamentary chambers in Westminster, along with other stellar Ambedkarites of Britain, against caste discrimination. William Gould is an expert historian of twentieth- and twenty-first-century India, who acted as an expert witness in the Public inquiry surrounding Ambedkar House, which is covered in this volume. Christophe Jaffrelot is an ace scholar of South Asian studies who also authored the first non-

Indian biography of Ambedkar. They joined forces to produce this brilliant milestone.

*Ambedkarite Internationalism*

*Ambedkar in London* promises to be a meeting point for scholarly exchange, discussion and public memory. The pages ring with many of the authentic names associated with different fields in which Ambedkar excelled. The present volume emerged out of the struggle by Ambedkar's followers to foreground their status as equals in the face of a colour- and caste-dominated country. The subcontinent's diaspora communities are among Britain's largest ethnic minorities. Dalits come across as peace-loving, democratically invested groups fronting dignity and fraternity as a core principle. From leading the struggle to outlaw caste from Britain to lobbying for the purchase of the house in which Ambedkar lived in north London, this has been a long, noteworthy and illuminating struggle. These are stories to inspire present and future generations.

The book emphatically inserts London in Ambedkar's oeuvre. In the absence of plentiful direct sources, the authors have brought together personal experience, expert sleuthing and original, oral testimony, in order to create an extensive account of Ambedkar's time in London, as both a student and political leader. To this, the book adds an account of his legacy woven in a community history of Dalits and Ambedkarites in British society.

There are two locations that any Dalit in India would recite in the same breath: New York and London. These two names are related to Ambedkar's stay. These cities helped forge one of the most brilliant thinkers and political minds in history. That is why both have a special resonance for Dalit people.

Unlike New York, where Ambedkar only nourished himself in intellectual activities and academic growth, London was where he began to put his ideas into action. The cities that made him who he was didn't just carry his name in their archival registers, but remain active hotspots for the Ambedkarite discourse led by his ardent followers decades later. Figuratively speaking, Ambedkar wrestled on the streets of London. He did this not only while getting through his poverty-stricken times as a DPhil student at LSE, as Sue Donnelly and Daniel Payne illustrate in this volume, or interning as a barrister at Gray's Inn (Steven Gasztowicz, Chapter 3), but also later, importantly, at conventions fighting for the rights of the muzzled, to make them heroes. For example, entering the world of the Marathi-language press, he founded the newspaper *Mooknayak* ('The Leader of Voiceless') at the beginning of his journey to London.

In all of this work, Ambedkar's conduct was feisty. He held himself high. He certainly didn't think of himself as any lesser, nor did he treat his opponents as devilish. Ambedkar elevated statesmanship to a level which required Britain's bureaucrats and aristocratic political classes to sit up and pay attention.

### *Ambedkar's Sojourns*

Ambedkar swung easily, like a dervish, in many directions while contesting the rights of his people. He shifted gear from social (Bahishkrit Hitakarni Sabha) to political (Independent Labour Party) to spiritual (Buddhism) as possible means of emancipation or, as he called it, 'salvation' of the outcastes. While doing this, he attracted the attention of state and non-state players. The British secret service had a file on Ambedkar from the moment he disembarked on the island. The archive of the British Library gives a hint as to the reports and duty memos of the police and secret service. One would guess that such information is either still classified or destroyed. On the public record, there is an impressive amount of information preserved in the official letters of exchanges between the Secretary of State in India and both the Viceroy and the Prime Minister's office in London while seeking to find a way to sway Ambedkar on various matters. One such exchange concerns the politics of the London Round Table Conferences held between 1930 and 1933, discussed with great insight by Jesús Cháirez-Garza and by Christophe Jaffrelot in this volume.

Archival records show that the government was increasingly concerned about his next moves, even leading up to the Government of India Act 1935. It proves that Ambedkar was a vital element in the national life of India. Ambedkar's statements and scholarly texts were read with great interest and referred to in both houses of the UK Parliament during debates—an official record of which is available in *Hansard*. Did Ambedkar then look for possible connections to strengthen his cause and compensate for the lack of representation in international bodies?

Ambedkar's insistence on foreign intervention in the cause of Dalits was grit in the eye of the caste elites. The newly independent India did not want Ambedkar to embarrass the freedom agenda propagated by the Indian government. Ambedkar played on this fear to gain concessions (albeit limited) for his cause. He would often invoke the United Nations as a threat but later 'rein in' his demands in order to negotiate something in return—for example, his election to the Constituent Assembly. After that tenure, seeing that progress had not been made, a frustrated Ambedkar started exploring international options, towards the end of his life even considering communism over the Congress Party's hegemony in parliamentary democracy. He observed that the kind of parliamentary democracy promoted by the Congress Party was proving ineffective in providing the required representation and justice.

Ambedkar was one of the most travelled Indian politicians (distance-wise) of his time. Looking at his busy itinerary and the many places he reached by bullock cart, railway, road, air and/or water, the possibility arises that travel and mobility played a strong role in shaping and broadening Ambedkar's mind. As I travel with a busy itinerary, I reckon that travelling to places is a move towards something that is not clearly defined. Perhaps Ambedkar's physical mobility granted him the space to explore the elasticity of the mind? Yet, as a busy man, he could hardly personally respond to all the requests he received. That was why he had to send lieutenants to address gatherings on his behalf. Travelling overseas, thousands of miles away, and keeping it straight can therefore be added as one of Ambedkar's qualities. *Ambedkar in London* is a collection which invites readers to experience and fulfil their desire to walk a little in Ambedkar's shoes. One can't travel to all the places he went, but *Ambedkar in London* is a five-star tour into the lifeworld of Ambedkar's time in London.

*Global Agendas*

The chapters of this volume are written with the general public in mind, yet make available lines of further research for scholars to pursue. They provide us with a catalogued story and timeline of the Ambedkarite history of the UK. Important national and international events concerning Dalit and backward castes have the name of British Ambedkarites. The implementation of the 1980 'Mandal Commission' report in India a decade later during the V. P. Singh government also has a story in the UK. Singh was a witness to the Ambedkarite organising in the UK as a guest of the Ambedkar Centenary Celebrations. His work in social justice could be partly inspired by the initiatives undertaken by Dalits in the UK. The United Nations World Conference Against Racism had representation from the country's Ambedkarite organisations. The blockbuster film *Dr Babasaheb Ambedkar*, directed by Jabbar Patel, was cut short for reasons of budget. The UK Ambedkarites, under the auspices of the Federation of Ambedkarite and Buddhist Organisations UK (FABO UK), facilitated the shooting as well as offering logistical support on the ground.

Reading about the Dalit movement in the UK and some of its recent developments felt nostalgic for me. Many of the names mentioned are known to me personally. Their incredible work over many decades has now been etched into the history and legacy of the Ambedkarite movement. I was fortunate to witness, participate in and lobby in some of the activities mentioned in the book, having been introduced to the Ambedkarite movement in the UK in 2011 when I arrived there as a student. Ever since then I have been an ardent follower of its activities. I briefly volunteered with some organisations. My role was to develop alliances with other groups who could be potential partners in the campaign for caste legislation. My primary geography was Southall, and it is here that I had a brush with grassroots Ambedkarite politics. I was introduced to various Dalit temples, Buddhist viharas, gurudwaras and social, cultural and religious organisations. I was also introduced to cooperative sector organisations, churches and gurudwaras concerned about caste discrimination in the UK.

UK Ambedkarites have been at the forefront of influencing significant movements across the world. That is why Santosh Dass and Arun Kumar's long-overdue, comprehensive introduction to 'The Ambedkarite Movement in Britain' makes for rewarding reading. This chapter is a first-person account infused with originality and passion. The idea of donating the busts to the US universities, which I supported as a member of a local group in Boston, emanated from FABO-like organisations' strategies. These have included having a hand in drafting the Vancouver Conference declaration, recording essential milestones, such as donating busts to LSE and the Indian High Commission in London, portraits at Gray's Inn, championing the purchase of the property for the Ambedkar Museum in London, input into 2019 Public Inquiry (discussed by Jamie Sullivan), and replicating similar works at Columbia University, the University of British Columbia, Vancouver, and Simon Fraser University in Canada.

Many of these important milestone events and episodes are vital in fathoming the struggles of Dalits in the UK. Many of the actual participants of these struggles have written about what brought us to this day, narrating in detail the events and explaining their historical significance. Enriched with empirical insights and first-person experiences, these chapters, with the added perspective of Kevin Brown's insights into Ambedkar's relevance for the African-American community, make for highly original source material. *Ambedkar in London* will be desirable reading for general readers of history or biography, activists and scholars interested in knowing more about the times of Ambedkar, whose London days could only be imagined from a faraway land. His importance as a social reformer remains of the highest order.

Oxford and Cambridge, MA.
July 2022

Register No. 11520 Ambedkar Bhimrao R. Ticket No. 9249

22nd Yr Lent Term 1916-17 22nd Yr Summer Term 1916-17

The London School of Economics and Political Science.

**APPLICATION FOR ADMISSION.**

All fees must be paid in advance, if possible two clear days before the first meeting of the class which the student desires to join. Fees may be paid in the office or sent by post, in which latter case the remittance must be accompanied by a form of application for admission properly filled in and addressed to THE DIRECTOR, the London School of Economics, Clare Market, W.C.

Cheques, &c., must be made payable to the Hon. W. P. REEVES, and crossed London County and Westminster Bank, Ltd.

The office is open from 10 a.m. to 5 p.m.; on Saturdays from 10 a.m. to 12 noon; and during term, for the convenience of students, from 5.30 to 8 p.m.

PLEASE WRITE DISTINCTLY. NAME IN FULL.

| SURNAME. | CHRISTIAN NAME OR NAMES IN FULL. | Mr., ~~Mrs., Miss, etc.~~ |
| --- | --- | --- |
| Ambedkar | Bhimrao. R. | |

| LONDON ADDRESS. | PERMANENT ADDRESS. (If London Address is not permanent.) |
| --- | --- |
| 21 Cromwell Rd. SW. London | Bombay India |

| OCCUPATION. | ACADEMIC STATUS. |
| --- | --- |
| If in the Public Service, or in the service of a Railway, Bank, Insurance Company, or other semi-public body, please state Department or Office. | DATE OF BIRTH IF UNDER 21 ___<br>UNIVERSITY OF COLLEGE Bombay & Columbia<br>DEGREE OF STANDING M.A.<br>Undergraduates of London University are requested to state month and year of matriculation. |

| NUMBER IN CALENDAR | COURSES THE APPLICANT DESIRES TO TAKE. | FEES PAID. £ | s. | d. |
| --- | --- | --- | --- | --- |
| | Full Course. | 10 | 10 | |

Usual Signature ___

Date ___ 19 ___

*Top*: Ambedkar's application form to study a master's degree at LSE, 1916.
*Bottom*: Interior of the main building at LSE.

To
Prof. Edwin Cannan.
As a token of sincere regards and gratitude from his pupil the Author.
29.1.24.

THE PROBLEM OF THE RUPEE

*Top*: (Left) Professor Edwin Cannan (Ambedkar's supervisor), c. 1920. (Right) Ambedkar's signed dedication to Professor Edwin Cannan in *The Problem of the Rupee*, 29 January 1924.

*Bottom*: The presentation of Ambedkar's portrait by the Dr Ambedkar Memorial Committee of Great Britain, 25 September 1973, in the presence of Sir Walter Adam, Director of LSE.

*Top*: The Ambedkar bust in situ, donated by the Federation of Ambedkarite and Buddhist Organisations UK (FABO UK) and unveiled by Dr John Ashworth, Director of LSE, on 14 April 1994.
*Bottom*: Dr Ambedkar as a barrister in 1922.

*Top*: Master Treasurer Ali Malek QC unveiling the new portrait of Ambedkar by David Newens (third from the right), donated by FABO UK for the Ambedkar Room at Gray's Inn. Sujat Ambedkar (Ambedkar's great-grandson) far right, Santosh Dass second from the right, and Lord David Alton of Liverpool fourth from the right.
*Bottom*: Ambedkarites and academics outside Gray's Inn after the unveiling of the portrait on 30 June 2021.

## DIKSHA CEREMONY

*The ex-untouchables convert to Buddhism on Lord Buddha JAYANTI DAY, 1973 in West Bromwich Town Hall, Birmingham.*

DR. BHADANT ANAND KAUSALYAYAN — VEN. KASSAPA — MR. D. C. AHIR

DR. D. R. JATAVA — MR. BHAGWAN DAS — MR. K. C. LEAL

49

Diksha ceremony (a conversion to Buddhism) in West Bromwich, 1973. From the *Babasaheb Ambedkar, A Birth Centenary Commemoration Vol II*, p. 49.

*Top*: Great Hall, Gray's Inn, 21 February 1991, marking the birth centenary of Dr Ambedkar. In the front row, from left to right: Countess Mountbatten of Burma, Bhagwan Das, Lord Goff of Chieveley, Philip Cox QC, Master Treasurer at Gray's Inn (fourth from the right), Baroness Shreela Flather, and Chanan Chahal (furthest right). Office bearers of the Dr Ambedkar Centenary Celebration Committee (standing) include, from left to right, Sohan Lal Gindha (fourth), C. Gautam (fifth), Harbans Virdee (fifteenth) and M. S. Bahal (sixteenth).

*Bottom*: Ambedkar Jayanti, House of Lords, 28 April 2017. Left to right, C. Gautam (second), Arun Kumar, Lord Bhikhu Parekh (fifth), Lord Richard Harries, Baroness Flather, Santosh Dass, Rajesh Dabre, Lord David Alton (eleventh), Adam Orsulik, David Orsulik, Rob Marris MP (tallest, behind David Orsulik). To the right of Marris, Siddharth Mahanandia, Eugene Culas, Harbans Virdee (behind the Buddhist monk).

*Top*: Ambedkar Jayanti, Westminster Hall, House of Lords, 11 May 2022. Attendees included, starting from fourth from the left in the front row, Steven Gasztowicz KC, Lord Harries of Pentregarth, Sushant Singh, Santosh Dass, Raj Mohinder Sidhu, Arun Kumar. Second row: Raj Bangar (second from the left), Councillor Ram Lakha (third from the left), Nigel Planer (third from the right), Ken Hunt (far right). Third row: Sue Donnelly (far right).
*Bottom*: Dr Ambedkar International Convention, Paris, July 2014. Raju Kamble in the back row, fourth from the left.

*Top*: FABO UK Conference at LSE, 16 June 2016. From left to right: Amartya Sen, Anand Teltumbde, Radha D’Souza, Santosh Dass.
*Bottom*: Ambedkar in London with Scheduled Caste students on 2 November 1946 at 4 Downside Crescent, London.

*Top*: King Henry's Road, Chalk Farm. Commemorative blue plaque unveiling, 6 December 1991. Rt Hon Roy Hattersley MP (front row, third from the left), Glenda Jackson (right of Hattersley), acting High Commissioner Krishna Rajan (right of Jackson), Sohan Lal Gindha (front right). Second row, on the right, Councillor Jim Turner (Mayor of Camden) in Mayoral Chains of Office, and top left, furthest back, C. Gautam.
*Bottom*: Inside 10 King Henry's Road, 4 September 2014.

*Top*: Outside the Ambedkar Museum, 26 September 2022.
*Bottom*: Inside the Ambedkar Museum, 26 September 2022.

*Top*: Inside the Ambedkar Museum, 26 September 2022.
*Bottom*: Inside 10 King Henry's Road, 14 April 2018.

Back garden of 10 King Henry's Road, 14 April 2018. This life-sized statue of Dr Ambedkar was donated to the Ambedkar Museum by the Federation of Ambedkarite and Buddhist Organisations UK in 2018.

*Top*: At the Public Inquiry into the Ambedkar Museum, from the left: William Gould, Santosh Dass, Steven Gasztowicz QC (now KC), Jamie Sullivan, 11 October 2019.
*Bottom*: Caste law protest on Parliament Square, 2013.

*Top*: ACDA meeting in the House of Lords with Navi Pillay (UN Commissioner for Human Rights) as Chief Guest, 6 November 2013. Seated left to right: Dr Raj Chand (ACDA Chair), Navi Pillay, Lord Avebury and Jeremy Corbyn MP. Standing left to right: Desraj Bunger, Sam Kalyan, Santosh Dass, Sat Paul, Sat Pal Muman, Ravi Kumar, unknown, Pirthi Kaeley, Ram Kishan Mehmi.
*Bottom*: Kevin Brown (standing) lecturing at 10 King Henry's Road, 12 August 2019.

# INTRODUCTION

*Santosh Dass and William Gould*

Dr Bhimrao Ramji Ambedkar (14 April 1891–6 December 1956) is one of India's greatest intellectuals and social reformers, whose political ideas continue to inspire and mobilise some of the world's poorest and most socially disadvantaged men and women in both India and the Indian diaspora worldwide. Although mostly associated with India, Ambedkar's outlook was global, and the ideas on which he drew, including (but not limited to) subjects such as labour, legal rights, women's rights, education, caste, political representation and the economy, were international in significance. Most writings on the political thought (and career) of Ambedkar focus on the mature phase of his politics in India—the 1930s to 1950s. Yet some of the roots of Ambedkar's thinking in key texts such as *Annihilation of Caste*, and in the central constitutional position of Scheduled Castes or Dalits, were rooted in his earlier work around caste, labour, governance, the economy and representation from his time in London as a PhD/law student in the early 1920s. Equally, Ambedkarite ideas continue to inspire important sections of India's huge Indian diaspora—the UK's largest ethnic minority by nationality.

The idea for this book came to us soon after we had both given evidence at the Public Inquiry (PI) in 2019 into the Government of Maharashtra's (GOM) appeal against Camden Council's refusal to allow 10 King Henry's Road, in North London (hereafter 10KHR) to have museum status. The circumstances surrounding the appeal hearing captured the contribution of Ambedkar's life as a student and intellectual in the city to his later career. The process of gathering our evidence together for this allowed us to both become reacquainted with his earlier life and to begin to see anew the significant ways in which it formed, as well as how it connected to his later political movements and thought.

In most of the existing biographical literature, Ambedkar's life in London has been set out as an educational prelude to the man's intellectual and political career, or as a place that he later revisited in the larger projects of constitutional reform and shaping a free India. But in the process of doing this work for the Museum, it became clear that the relationship between his relatively brief time in London and the larger dynamics of Ambedkar's public and political significance in the UK were momentous and necessitated a different kind of analysis. We felt that the events around the Museum and the organisations responsible for it required us to bring historical work into conversation with the contemporary, as happened in the PI itself. In a very direct form, it turned out that new historical research and evidence helped to confirm the centrality of 10KHR itself to Ambedkar's life in the capital. This research was one of a few factors which helped to sway the case, and as such it features in our narrative. The book therefore contains new material on the contemporary legal battle for the Museum from first-hand experience and the campaign to save 10KHR from new private ownership when it came on the market in 2014.

But there are other perhaps more far-reaching reasons why we connect detailed historical research on this phase of Ambedkar's life with the longer-term Dalit movement in the UK. The PI demonstrated the emotional importance of Ambedkar to Britain's Ambedkarite and Dalit communities, which is now enshrined in material form in a new museum. The significance of that contemporary politics of remembrance and action requires us to explore the processes of how Ambedkar's connections to London empowered particular ideas about Dalit education and internationalism. Equally, it necessitates a sense of how Ambedkar's life and approach to activism and rights have shaped the specific moves for Dalit political organisation and legal campaigning in the UK. In this way, we draw direct connections between the histories and contemporary characteristics of Ambedkar's influence in London and the UK, as we will explain in more detail below. This interaction between Ambedkar's early career and his contemporary significance in the UK has therefore shaped the organisation and structure of the book. At the same time, the book does not set out to present an exhaustive account of Ambedkar's career in London, but intends to open up some of the key areas of his connection to the UK's capital. It also does not aim to explore the significance of Ambedkar in India's contemporary politics, although some of the chapters in Part One do deal with his early career in India.

We begin *Ambedkar in London* with contributions from international historians of Ambedkar and the late colonial politics of caste. This crucial phase of Ambedkar's life in London is set out in Part One of the book and draws on extensive archival and observational research, some of which has never been used or published before. Rather than simply being a footnote to his later career, we argue that Ambedkar's oeuvre and political experiences were shaped, both directly and inadvertently, by his time in London and by his connections to the city. In direct ways, some of the latest research on Ambedkar's politics has shown that we need to explore the strategic ways in which he made use of a number of international networks and spaces.[1] In the late colonial struggle for the recognition of legal and political rights for Untouchables (or Dalits, as they started to be referred to in the 1930s), Ambedkar was always keenly aware of the need to leverage negotiations in non-Indian contexts, especially in the UK and USA. Indirectly too—as we show in this book—Ambedkar's political thought and political praxis were subtly shaped by interwar political theory on governance, the economy, labour and political representation, ideas which were also channelled through London's intellectual milieu.

What is less known than these developments in Ambedkar's thought and action, and what this book attempts to show in its thematic juxtapositions is how Ambedkar's international career in the 1920s also shaped approaches to Dalit rights in the UK and internationally. This history of Ambedkar's global connections and his specific links to London, as the chapters in Part Two of this book explore, has a powerful afterlife in London and the UK more generally. Most prominently, this has taken place in the movements to establish legal protections for citizens subject to caste discrimination outside India. But the connections to Ambedkar are also socially deep and emotional: 10KHR—one of the last focal points for those who wish to remember and learn from Ambedkar—has already become a site of powerful and affective connection between Dalits in the UK, helping to make sense of their ideas of belonging and their continued need to defend and promote their rights.

Although historians have explored the exceptional scholarship of Ambedkar during the early phase of his career, there has so far been little detailed treatment of his life in London during the late 1910s and 1920s. In the opening chapter, William Gould explores Ambedkar's time as a student, from his period of study at Columbia University in New York in 1913–16 to his interrupted sojourn in London in 1916–1917, and then his longer period of study in the early 1920s. He argues that the comparative experiences of Ambedkar as a student in the USA, India and London help us to understand the nature of his early political writings and movements. Ambedkar's key contributions to the ideologies and organisation of the nascent Dalit movement in the 1930s and 1940s were partly formed by two interrelated themes from his early 1920s London experiences: first was his work on governance—an area that he explored in his research on the financial crises arising from India's contemporary fiscal and currency policy. The second, interrelated area was the implications of these forms of governance for income inequalities and, by extension, social and legal inequality, and representation. The chapter further suggests that the experiences of Ambedkar in London laid the base for his later global agendas and ideas, including the idea of the mutability of caste into different environments. This theme is then taken up by other authors in Part Two of the book, especially in relation to the caste law campaign in Britain. Drawing on personal correspondence, archival research from the India Office collections on student life in London, sources from the archive of the London School of Economics and Political Science (LSE), and some never before published documents, the chapter explores the relationships Ambedkar developed, the intellectual influences he nurtured and the interactions he had with a range of London-based intellectuals. Finally, William explores the specific significance of 10KHR to Ambedkar's everyday lived experiences while living in the city, and their larger bearing on his work. This included Ambedkar's close friendship with a widow living at the property—Frances or Fanny—about whom William reveals completely new information.

As part of this book, we wanted to look at Ambedkar's time at the two most important London institutions with which he had an association—LSE and Gray's Inn. Sue Donnelly and Daniel Payne, of LSE, and Steven Gasztowicz KC, a member of Gray's Inn, are uniquely positioned to explore these areas, as people with careers centred in the institutions that were important to Ambedkar, while being relative newcomers to Ambedkar's politics. Donnelly and Payne have been responsible for much of the work on the LSE exhibitions about Ambedkar, and in Chapter 2 they explore his time and studies at LSE. With access to LSE's rich archive, including Ambedkar's student file (and those of his contemporaries), they have explored his probable networks of staff and students, the developing academic and cultural life of the university in the 1920s and its connections with India. In this environment, Ambedkar was able to develop a range of intellectual contacts at LSE that came to be important in both his early writings and the nature of his longer-term international connections in interwar and 1940s India. Donnelly and Payne also consider LSE's continuing links with Ambedkar and the Ambedkarite movement in the UK from the 1930s and the acquisition in 1973 and 1994 of a portrait and bust of Ambedkar, which remain on display there. In this sense, the chapter connects the institutional history of LSE to some of the themes explored in Part Two—the Ambedkarite movement in the UK, and the PI, in which the LSE connection was an important consideration in the case.

Ambedkar was training to be a barrister at Gray's Inn at the same time as studying at LSE. With a few exceptions, there is very little treatment in published work to date on Ambedkar's legal training.[2] There is next to nothing on what being a student member of Gray's Inn (one of the four great Inns of Court in London) involved, and how it probably equipped and affected him, directly and indirectly, first in practice as a lawyer and then in more direct political contexts back in India. In Chapter 3, Steven Gasztowicz, who was part of the legal team at the 2019 PI, and also an alumnus of Gray's Inn, explores Ambedkar's formal legal training and the other aspects of being a student barrister at Gray's Inn in the 1920s. Drawing on personal experience, he discusses how being a student barrister would have brought Ambedkar into contact with those with experience of how the legal system operated on the ground, and with the code of ethics governing the Bar. He explores the experience for an outsider coming into the law with no family contacts, and the nature of social contacts with fellow students, practising lawyers and judges. This was not just possible but compulsory, with the requirement to eat a required number of formal dinners in The Hall with them, with its associated customs, which was as much a condition of the Call to the Bar as passing the law exams. Gasztowicz writes with direct experience of this informal and formal learning and contact system within Gray's Inn, as a member of it himself, and as someone who has entered into it as an outsider. Some of the requirements and customs have not changed much compared to when Gasztowicz was called to the Bar in the early 1980s, and his own experience is related to that of Ambedkar. The chapter is also a unique reflection on what it means for a practising barrister in the UK to come across the work and life of B. R. Ambedkar, again reflecting the longer-term and contemporary themes taken up in Part Two of the book.

We can only make sense of Ambedkar's time in London as a student by further exploring its immediate aftermath from the mid-1920s to mid-1930s and his continued reference to London's international spaces in the articulation of an anti-caste politics. The next two chapters by leading scholars of Ambedkar, Christophe Jaffrelot and Dr Jesús Cháirez-Garza, cover these themes and time period. After securing an MSc and doctorate in science from LSE and Bar-at-law in 1922, as well as a network of contacts, Ambedkar returned to India to practise law and develop his social activism. In Chapter 4, Christophe Jaffrelot explores his reformism in the late 1920s. In the early part of the decade, as a student, Ambedkar moved towards ideas and practices which would become the trademarks of Ambedkarism.

Jaffrelot shows, however, that this did not happen precipitately but via a gradual shift from reformism to outright demands for separate electorates for Untouchables, as the decade progressed. While the *Bahishkrit Hitakarini Sabha* that he created after coming back from England in 1924,[3] displayed some features of a Sanskritisation drive, including for example a temple entry movement, by the 1927 Mahad satyagraha, Ambedkar had moved towards a complete rejection of Hinduism. Politically, if Ambedkar hesitated between reserved seats and a separate electorate for the Dalits, from the Southborough Committee to the Simon Commission, by 1930 he had opted for the latter, even though he was eager not to appear as a separatist (something that changed again in the following decade). The 1920s in London and thereafter can be seen then as a formative decade in which earlier ideas formed the basis for political experimentation as Ambedkar adapted to India's changing contexts.

Ambedkar returned to London in 1930, this time as part of the delegation to provide a voice to the Depressed Classes at the Round Table Conferences (RTCs) in London, which were tasked with the exercise of carving out a plan for India's new constitutional arrangements. In Chapter 5, Jesús Cháirez-Garza explores and analyses the early attempts of Ambedkar to internationalise the problem of untouchability by looking at his participation in the first of these conferences during the winter months of late 1930 and early 1931. The first RTC was boycotted by Congress but allowed Ambedkar access to British political figures that had an important say about the future of the Depressed Classes (another term for Dalits). London also became a space where the rules of caste could be relaxed and where he could interact with Indian politicians face to face and on relatively equal terms. The second RTC, from the autumn of 1931 to 1932, was the scene for one of Ambedkar's biggest political battles—his contest with Gandhi over the voting rights of Dalits, about which much has already been written. Finally, closer to the independence of India in 1946, Cháirez-Garza discusses how Ambedkar would visit London once more to speak at Westminster and meet Winston Churchill. At this time, Ambedkar aimed to secure constitutional rights for Dalits before the British left India, something he was unable to do. By looking at these key moments, Cháirez-Garza rethinks the importance of London as a political centre of power which at times helped Ambedkar's cause but equally, at other times, damaged his endeavours to support the rights of Dalits. There are also extended implications to this history. Santosh Dass's Chapter 8 in Part Two takes up some of the key strategies of Ambedkar in exploring their wider and longer-term resonance for the caste law movement.

Ambedkar chaired the drafting committee of India's Constitution, which came into force on 26 January 1950. It outlawed untouchability and in theory granted equal rights and protections to all Indians under the law. This gave many Dalits in India the confidence, with some legal safeguards, to potentially build new lives and assert their political and everyday rights.[4] Not all stayed in India though. There was both a colonial and post-colonial global diaspora, including many that arrived in Britain from the 1950s onwards as economic migrants looking for a brighter future.[5] Later, their families joined them. Arun Kumar, who has been in the Ambedkarite movement in the UK for over four decades, and Santosh Dass, President of the Federation of Ambedkarite and Buddhist Organisations UK (FABO UK), discuss the vibrant and energetic Ambedkarite movement in the Britain that developed out of this historical context. With the exception of one very recent article,[6] relatively little has been written about this specific group of movements beyond specific Ambedkarite-led articles and commemorative brochures.[7] In Chapter 6, Kumar and Dass catalogue the history of the Ambedkarite movement in Britain, the key early pioneers, the Ambedkarite organisations that formed, their work, and how they have adapted over time.

The campaign led by Ambedkarites to secure funding from the GOM to buy 10KHR, the house where Ambedkar lodged in the 1920s, began with a written proposal from FABO UK in September 2014. A year later, setting up the Museum involved contestations of different kinds, and a PI followed in 2019 to secure it museum status. In Chapter 6, Dass has created an account of the campaign, based on letters, email exchanges and media stories related to the key actions that were taken and the main players involved. This gives a sense of the drive and determination required to secure an expenditure of over £4 million by the State of Maharashtra in India for the first memorial outside of India dedicated to Ambedkar at a place where he lodged. The narrative sets out the obstructions and obfuscations faced by the campaign, how these were overcome, and the challenges going forward for the Museum. In the same chapter, Jamie Sullivan discusses in detail the application for museum status for 10KHR and preparation for the subsequent PI that led to permission being granted for the Museum. This chapter brings us back squarely into some of the reflections of Part One of the book—from the reflections of Steven Gasztowicz, who acted as the appellant's barrister, to the LSE connections (Donnelly and Payne) and the detailed historical connection between Ambedkar and this most important house in London, as explored by Gould. Sullivan provides an insight into wider issues in the London property market that made the application for museum status unique in more ways than one. The final decision was made at the highest levels of government, with India watching. The Public Inquiry uncovered huge support from many corners for the new museum, and Sullivan discusses the colourful cast of characters not normally involved in the planning process and how they eloquently made the case for the proposal.

As Indian migrants from the Dalit community made new lives for themselves in Britain from the 1950s onwards, and the communities grew, they were soon to find caste and untouchability had followed them. Although Cháirez-Garza's chapter in Part One of this volume argues that Ambedkar's internationalisation of anti-caste politics afforded him, for a time, some freedom of manoeuvre outside the confines of caste in London, it is well known that caste has not disappeared over time, but is also transported to other global spaces, often assuming different discriminatory forms.[8] The campaign to highlight examples of caste discrimination began in the 1970s with some far-sighted, committed and politically savvy Ambedkarites. In Chapter 8, Dass, who has been in the campaign to outlaw caste discrimination in the UK for over two decades as a founding member of CasteWatchUK and the Anti Caste Discrimination Alliance, describes with personal insights the ongoing campaign to outlaw caste-based discrimination in Britain. She discusses the campaign's notable successes; the resistance from other organisations; and the key

Dalit and Ambedkarite movements and British politicians involved in the campaign. Chapter 8 also connects us back to Cháirez-Garza's chapter in Part One, and Dass reflects on the deeper significance of Ambedkar's own lobbying and political strategies for Dalit rights for the contemporary campaigns.

The book ends in an exploration of a different international trajectory in Ambedkar's movements, albeit one that relates in important ways to the London experiences. Professor Kevin Brown, from Maurer School of Law in Bloomington, Indiana—a friend of the Ambedkarites in Britain—delivered the talk 'Common Struggles: The Benefits for African-Americans and Dalits from Comparing their Struggles' at the Ambedkar Museum in 2019 at FABO UK's invitation. Brown has long been interested in the knowledge that African-Americans have about Ambedkar. In Chapter 9 of this volume, Brown discusses W. E. B. Du Bois's article in the most significant media publication of the Black community at the time, *The Crisis*. In the article, Du Bois stresses Ambedkar's statement that the British did nothing to improve the conditions of the Dalits. This became an important piece in the understanding of the Black press about the liberation struggles in India. To the Black community, who have viewed their oppression as derived from white supremacy, it meant that the white British were not the supporters of Dalits. Rather, they were using Dalits to maintain their control of India and delay independence. Black people in the US supported India's freedom fighters because they understood them as seeking a dual victory: both the end of British colonialism and the end of discrimination based on untouchability. The latter would not occur as long as the British were colonising India. Brown explores the larger goal that Ambedkar pursued, not only for an independent India, but also one where the Dalits had some relief from untouchability as a precursor to social progression.

Finally, we were honoured to have Dr Suraj Yengde write the Foreword for this book. Yengde came to London in 2021 to join the Faculty of History at Oxford University after many years at Harvard. We both met Suraj at the inauguration of the Ambedkar Room at Gray's Inn on 30 June and the unveiling of the new portrait of Ambedkar donated by FABO UK for that room. His infectious energy and intellect have continued to inspire some of the same trends that we see today in the contemporary Ambedkarite movement, and its many and varied supporters and spin-offs. Looking back on how the idea for this book came to life, we never imagined we would be discussing, all in one volume, the musicians Bonnie Dobson and Jackson Browne, the actors Glenda Jackson and Nigel Planer, politicians such as Jeremy Corbyn MP and Lord Eric Avebury, the Bahujan Samaj Party's Kanshi Ram and Mayawati, Phoolan Devi, the Indian bandit queen, and Václav Havel, the last President of Czechoslovakia and the first of the Czech Republic. These individuals are part and parcel of the colourful narratives that surround Ambedkar and the movements which have been inspired by him in India, the UK and beyond.

# PART ONE

1

# AMBEDKAR THE ACTIVIST RESEARCH SCHOLAR IN 1920s LONDON

*William Gould*

Dr Ambedkar's life as a student in London has been relatively under-researched in existing biographies, and his work and life from this period typically serve as a footnote to his later, more radical critiques of caste, or is separated out as his 'economics' phase and treated separately.[1] Part of the reason for this is that the archives do not contain a very full picture of Ambedkar's personal journey in this period, although we can gain a good sense of what he must have experienced by exploring London and its academic milieu at this time. As well as attempting the latter, this chapter will explore how Ambedkar's key contributions to the ideologies and organisation of the nascent Dalit movement in the 1930s and 1940s were shaped by twin and interrelated themes rooted in his early 1920s London experiences: first was the political economy of governance—an area that he explored in depth via his LSE work, which researched the financial crises arising from India's contemporary fiscal and currency policy. The works that explored these problems of governance were among the most well-evidenced and logically argued critiques of the system of colonialism of their time. The second, interrelated area was the implications of these forms of governance for income inequalities and, by extension, social and legal inequality, and representation. It was in these two areas that Ambedkar further developed new forms of self-conscious 'Untouchable' mobilisation, which both used and embraced concepts of education and leadership. In terms of Ambedkar's own political praxis, this later equipped him to forcefully direct and develop the 'Depressed Classes' cause back in India from the late 1920s and early 1930s, as later chapters in this volume go on to address. Ambedkar's milieu in London—the conditions of his domestic arrangements, research experiences and wider intellectual circle at LSE—also played a part in these experiences. Finally, the chapter will look at how Ambedkar's earliest published works on the political economy of colonialism and the nature of India's currency also bring insights into the inherent internationalism of his political thought and influence.

### *Between USA, London and India*

Simply exploring B. R. Ambedkar's early career and his life as a student is in many respects disorienting and overwhelming. In these early years, he set up publishing and educational initiatives, managed multiple qualifications, intellectual outcomes and networks, seemingly spinning at least three plates in connecting London with the USA and India. He was also under pressure in attempting to support, from a distance, his extended family back home in India. In some respects, Ambedkar was caught up in a whirlwind not of his own making: his postgraduate education and early career were characterised by quite frantic and unanticipated international travel and financial uncertainties. This situation of disorientation alongside extraordinary intellectual and political focus was, however, the central theme of his early career and it was productive in often unanticipated ways.

Before commencing his studies in London, Ambedkar had started to carry out a PhD at Columbia University. This was financed by a scholarship from the State of Baroda, which Ambedkar had applied for following Maharaj Sayajirao's suggestion and which ran from June 1914 to June 1917 (following an extension of one year). A condition of the award was that he should serve the State of Baroda for ten years after the completion of his education. Ambedkar's Columbia PhD, which he started following his arrival on 20 July 1913, started the pattern of his student life which came to extend into his London sojourn: long working days, collecting of books and documents, and an emerging interest in contemporary political economy. Ambedkar majored in economics with sociology, history, philosophy, anthropology and political science as additional studies. The Columbia PhD, 'The National Dividend of India—A Historical and Analytical Study', was replaced by a second work which was subsequently published under the title *The Evolution of Provincial Finance in India*: *A Study in the Provincial Decentralisation of Imperial Finance* (1925). This was carried out under the supervision of Edwin Seligman, who later became a correspondent of 'Bhim' during his subsequent time in London. This period of time was not without misfortune for Ambedkar, as the eventual PhD submitted to Columbia was a replacement for lost doctoral work that was destroyed during a torpedo attack on a ship carrying his books and belongings in 1917.[2]

US contacts spawned other networks: Seligman being a friend of Sidney Webb was probably instrumental in advising the young Ambedkar on the choice of LSE as a point of contact for his initial London research. On 23 May 1914, he wrote to Webb asking him to guide Ambedkar following his departure from the USA at around the same time.[3] While in the USA, he made contact with John Dewey, the historians James Shotwell and James Harvey Robinson, the sociologist Franklin Giddings and the anthropologist Alexander Goldenweiser.[4] Such interactions were to become extremely important in Ambedkar's later anthropological work and thinking, which informed his ideas on the sociology of caste. Although not the main focus of this chapter, these formulations of caste (like his work in London) developed via intellectual interactions outside India as much as inside, and, as Jesús Cháirez-Garza has argued, eventually became important to Ambedkar's central critiques of those proposing the immutability of caste.[5]

Ambedkar arrived in England in the autumn of 1916,[6] and his first admission to LSE took place in October 1916 under the supervision of Edwin Cannan. Sidney Webb, meanwhile, helped Ambedkar to get access to the India Office library. On 11 November of the same year he was admitted to Gray's Inn. In this year, Ambedkar took courses in political ideas, social evolution, geography and social theory.[7] However, he interrupted his study from August 1917 due to the expiration of his scholarship, and LSE granted him permission to return within a space of four years. In the period between returning to India in August 1917 and his commencement of study in July 1920, Ambedkar worked as Professor of Political Economy at Sydenham College of Commerce, Bombay (now Mumbai). More important than this employment was his political work, which would also develop into further networks in London from 1920. As well as providing evidence to the Southborough Committee from late 1918 to January 1919, he established his first periodical, *Mooknayak*, in January 1920[8] and the 'Depressed Classes' organisation the Bahishkrit Hitkarini Sabha in February 1920. Ambedkar was a leading figure in two large-scale Dalit conferences before his early 1920s stay in London. These took place at Mangaon (Kolhapur), which involved a dinner with the Maharaja, and at Nagpur—the First All-India Depressed Classes Conference—in which Ambedkar was the principal speaker.

Such conferences had begun to develop from the late nineteenth century, with a strong focus on the promotion of 'Depressed Class' education, and in western India they were led by the likes of the Gaikwad of Baroda, Karmaveer Bhaurao Patil, Vitthal Ramchandra Shinde, who fell out of favour with the more radical Ambedkar, and the Maharaja of Kolhapur.[9] The latter helped to finance Ambedkar's studies and career through his second phase in London (which started in 1920). He considered Ambedkar to be a representative of the non-Brahman cause in England and urged him to speak in that capacity. The Maharaja, who probably first met Ambedkar in 1919, was himself a keen advocate of the anti-Brahman cause, following the refusal of local Brahmans to grant Marathas *kshatriya* status. As such, he viewed Ambedkar as a kind of ambassador, suggesting to his friend Sir Alfred Pease that he might educate British opinion on the Brahmanical bias within the freedom movement in India.[10]

The three to four years that Ambedkar spent in London in this period appear at first glance to be a relatively insignificant prelude to his later career, and historians have generally passed over his London experiences in brief. Studying in England was to be treading a similar path to many other nationalists and publicists of his and a younger generation: M. K. Gandhi, Mohammad Ali Jinnah, Jawaharlal Nehru and a host of other figures in Indian politics made their way through London or Oxford and Cambridge. However, Ambedkar was both challenging the notion that such international educational sojourns were the preserve of the privileged and conducting a trip that was more focused and deliberate. The writings and publications that emerged from these early years, although less developed, are nevertheless consistent with (and, as I will argue later, shaped) his later formulations of 'Depressed Classes' politics and civil rights, although as Christophe Jaffrelot in Chapter 5 shows, they had not at this point reached their full maturity. As such, they form a crucial background to his later intellectual moves. These intellectual and academic formulations also took place via a particular range of international experiences, which rooted his thinking—at least from his own perception—in certain notions of its universal applicability.

There is no doubt either that study in London was part of a larger agenda of preparation for political leadership. Ambedkar's interlude between his two periods of study in London had occupied him with specific campaigns to further the interests of 'Depressed Classes'—not just the speeches and programmes of mass meetings and journals, but also the deliberate demand to the Southborough Committee for nine reserved places for Untouchables on the Bombay Legislative Council.[11] This direct, constitutional approach to 'Depressed Classes' rights also shaped the focus of Ambedkar's studies. Like previous students, Ambedkar followed the path of the law. But he also deliberately developed his study of specific social science fields—principally, economics and sociology or social anthropology. In this sense, as we will see below, his choice of LSE was also significant.

### *A House in Primrose Hill*

It seems inconceivable that Ambedkar would have enjoyed much time to pursue other interests outside of his studies, political networking and correspondence with contacts in India. Yet it is also quite likely that the events of this formative period in his thinking and writing would have made an impact on what he went on to publish and in how his later career developed. In 1920, the relationship between Britain and India was changing at an unprecedented rate following the end of the First World War. New constitutional arrangements had reorganised India's provincial and financial governance (discussed more below), and there were new radical challenges to British colonial power both in India and elsewhere: the Khilafat movement protested against Britain's post-war control of the Muslim holy places following the disintegration of the Ottoman Empire and was being connected to an India-based protest led by M. K. Gandhi; protests were developing against the post-war repressive Rowlatt Bill that extended the wartime security measures of the Raj; and uprisings against Britain were also taking place (or had recently occurred) against British imperial interests in Egypt, Iraq and Ireland. Ambedkar's thinking about Indian governance took place, then, in an era of rapid political transformation and rebellion. Britain was also dramatically changed by the war, and Ambedkar would have been reading and hearing about these effects in papers and lecture theatres: the post-war economic crisis, industrial unrest, the effects of Spanish influenza, and the changing patterns of employment as more young women took up vacancies created by the massive number of casualties of the war. Ambedkar was keenly interested in political representation and the rights of the under-represented. This was another new preoccupation of Indian governments following the 1919 Government of India Act. But it was also forming part of the political milieu of Britain, following the 1918 Representation of the People Act, which created universal male suffrage, and the more radical transformation of the women's suffragette movement in post-war Britain. Certainly, as we will see below, Ambedkar would have experienced first-hand women's new admission into higher education, the law and professions, and their more direct engagement in the political life of the country.

But how did this context affect Ambedkar's everyday experiences in London? The archival record for Ambedkar's time in the city, especially around his accommodation and personal life, is thin. We do know for certain that he stayed at two other addresses before arriving at 10KHR, and that in at least one case (if not both) his experience was an unhappy one. On first arrival in London, he lodged at 21 Cromwell Road for around two weeks. This was student accommodation under the auspices of the Bureau of Information—a body initially set up to gather intelligence and help to divert Indian political extremism in the wake of the ideas that had emerged out of Shyamaji Krishnavarma's India House radicals.[12] At the time of Ambedkar's visit it was subject to a report on conditions for Indian students, set up by an official Committee for Indian Students. Most damning was the suspicion in the minds of residents that the landlady of the house, a Miss Beck, was a spy employed by the British government to monitor Indian students' political activities. The Committee of Indian Students strenuously denied the allegations.[13] A second address in 95 Brook Green, Hammersmith provided a room for Ambedkar between July 1920 and toward the end of the year, and it is likely that at this address Ambedkar's stay was not successful. He wrote to Prabhakar Padhye that the food was wholly inadequate, with supper often only consisting of a 'cup of Bovril, biscuits and butter'. According to Ambedkar, 'The landlady was a terrible woman. I am always praying for her soul; but I am sure she will go to perdition'.[14] The experiences of Indian students finding accommodation on their first arrival in the UK was not just hindered by financial considerations. Research just a year prior to Ambedkar's arrival suggested there was 'evidence that there is some reluctance on the part of some landladies to admit Indian students'. They were sometimes asked to pay high prices and their food requirements were typically not taken into consideration.[15] This situation reflected a wider problem of student segregation and racism in interwar Britain that pervaded both universities and wider social interactions among young people.[16]

Ambedkar moved to 10KHR before 5 January 1921, which is the first evidence we have from correspondence with his old PhD supervisor from Columbia, Edwin Seligman, that he was definitely resident at the house. It is therefore likely that he was there in late 1920.[17] We also know from correspondence with Seligman that he was still there at the end of February 1922. A letter was written by Ambedkar from the house on 12 May 1921 and another on 27 June 1921,[18] but he does not appear at all in the 1921 UK census of population which took place on 19 June 1921 although two other student boarders are listed for 10KHR, Rustom C Vakeel and Becharbhai P Desai.[19] Since he does not appear at any other address in the census, it is highly likely that he was out of the country, most probably in Bonn, Germany, exploring the possibility of study there, where he had signed up in April 1921.[20] 10KHR, as the last known address for B. R. Ambedkar in London, was therefore almost certainly the lodging where he spent most of his time while in the capital. As Chapter 7 in this volume describes, the detailed process of establishing these connections to the house turned out to be pivotal in securing success for the Museum in the Public Inquiry in 2019. Therefore, although somewhat incidental in their details, the effect on the overall public and historical memory of Ambedkar's connections to London has turned out to be momentous. Biographers agree that during his London years, his main pastime was to read and research in the British Library.[21] But later correspondence suggests that Ambedkar maintained contact with a resident of the house following his return to India, which is additional evidence that this is likely to have been his most important residence as a student.

It is clear from collected correspondence received by Ambedkar that a woman who signed herself as 'F', 'Fx' or 'Little Pal' subsequently wrote to him from 10KHR from a date shortly following his arrival back in India.[22] This has led biographers to suggest the name of 'Fanny Fitzgerald', whose romantic connection to Ambedkar is written up as axiomatic. The existence and even character of 'F' has assumed a form, however, largely via historians' reformulation rather than hard evidence. Despite the fact that Ambedkar himself dedicated his book *What Gandhi and the Congress Have Done to the Untouchables* (1945) to 'F', with the biblical line 'In Thy Presence Is The Fullness of Joy',[23] there is very little information or direct evidence on the person in question, although as we will see below, much of what was apparently recorded about 'F' could be incorrect in some crucial details. Two letters from 10KHR which appeared in a 1993 volume suggest a very close or even intimate relationship, but there is no correspondence available from Ambedkar's side.[24] Other texts suggest that the 'F' in question was the daughter of the landlady in the house,[25] had no children,[26] or that she worked at the India Office.[27]

The rate books, the yearly records of occupiers and owners of properties, and electoral registers held at Camden Local Studies and Archives Centre suggest no evidence of a person by the name of Fanny Fitzgerald living at 10KHR in the 20 years either side of his time in London. In April 1917, just a few years before Ambedkar's arrival, Gaston Amedee Proust took over the property as the ratepayer, and he passed away on 17 June 1918.[28] In October 1918, his wife, a Mrs Frances Proust (née Brooks)[29] took over as ratepayer and continued to live at the property until April 1941.[30] Frances Proust is one possible candidate for the 'F' who appears in letters written to Ambedkar. However, this woman was not a childless widow living with her mother as depicted in Jabbar Patel's film *Dr Babasaheb Ambedkar* (2000), and there is no evidence that she worked at the India Office. During 1921–22, while Ambedkar was at 10KHR, she was the head of the household, and census records show her occupation in 1939 as 'unpaid domestic duties'. Also at the address were her four children—Frances Edwina Proust (born 28 September 1911), Roy Eric Proust (born 12 June 1913), Dolores E. Proust (born 11 October 1915) and Gaston Albert Proust (born 23 March 1918).[31] In other words, far from being a childless widow, if Frances Proust was the 'F' in question writing from 10KHR, she would have been heavily occupied in caring for her four young children. This situation makes the hitherto suggested nature of the relationship of Ambedkar somewhat more complicated. Frances Proust left the house in April 1941 to live in Westbury Grove, Finchley, and passed away on 20 April 1946.[32] The earlier given date of 'F's death does not clearly connect to this date in existing accounts either. A second woman by the name of Florence Ballard appears at 10KHR, listed as a separate householder to Frances Proust, in the 1921 census. She is listed as a clerk and with a birth date of 1892 (one year younger than Ambedkar). Again, this person could have been the 'F' in question as her stay corresponds to that of Ambedkar. However, she does not appear in the list of residents at 10KHR from 1923,[33] and the letters of 'F' to Ambedkar from the address were also sent in 1925.

To gain a fuller and more complex picture of Ambedkar's politics as a whole, this domestic situation is important, but it is not productive to speculate about the full nature of his relationship to 'F'. It was possibly significant in explaining the habitus of Ambedkar: faced with a double situation of alienation—as both an Indian in Europe and a Dalit among Indians—the forms of solace that Ambedkar sought out are as important as his public engagements. It is also quite possible, given the later correspondence, that Ambedkar's decision to move to 10KHR was motivated by her assistance and friendship, as well as his financial stringency. In other ways, the ongoing relationship with 'F', rooted in his association with 10KHR, provides an antidote to the sometimes two-dimensional representations of Ambedkar as Dalit icon *par excellence*. We are tempted to treat Ambedkar's intellectualism and rationalism as a defining feature of his character. But in seeing him as a rounded human being, we perhaps gain a clearer sense of what motivated his strongly held positions on a whole range of social and political subjects over the ensuing decades, and the human experiences in which that rationalism was situated.

*Ambedkar's London Contemporaries*

In many respects, Ambedkar could not have chosen a better institution to base himself for his second doctoral study. LSE was significant from its foundation by the Webbs as an institution that naturally nurtured thinkers who promoted anti-colonial ideas. Studying economics at LSE in the 1920s brought Ambedkar into regular contact with a wide range of intellectuals, among them Edwin Cannan, who acted as his PhD supervisor. By the time Cannan was supervising Ambedkar in the early 1920s, he had turned firmly to neoclassicism in economics, so Ambedkar's radicalism was at this time more aligned with Harold Laski, well known as a promoter of Indian leftism and anti-colonialism.[34] In LSE and London, Ambedkar really began to develop his critique of the ultimately exploitative nature of colonial finance—an intellectual theme that would later underpin his work in the Constituent Assembly, as he backed the principles of the planned economy after 1947.[35] At LSE, a range of nascent public intellectuals and political figures from colonial and other international contexts experienced relative freedom to ruminate on the absence of similar rights in their home countries (see Chapter 3 in this volume for more details). They were also exposed to comparative national contexts and even (unusually for the 1920s) different racial and gender-based perspectives, especially given the cultural diversity of the college. Foreign students in the 1920s made up about twenty to twenty-five per cent of the population. Records at LSE also show that the highly influential Harold Laski had set up a forum for international students in 1922.[36] Eventually, this body of international students was to include, over this interwar to 1950s period, some of the most important figures in post-colonial international politics: Pierre Trudeau, Moshe Sharett, Joseph Kennedy Jr, Jomo Kenyatta, Kwame Nkrumah, and V. K. Krishna Menon.[37]

In exploring the possible intellectual environment that Ambedkar would have moved within in the city, we can also explore his direct student contemporaries. During Ambedkar's time in London in the early 1920s, there was a disproportionately large number of students from India studying at LSE. Three significant postgraduate student contemporaries from India studying economics were Chandulal Nagindas Vakil, Mithan Ardeshir Tata and Jaikrishna Nagardas Varma. Vakil's research, undertaken between 1919 and 1921, related closely to Ambedkar's PhD on finance and monetary policy, but in his case focused on fiscal policy. Moreover, like Ambedkar, he was supervised by Cannan. This PhD, not unlike Ambedkar's work, was sharply critical of the hypocrisies underlying Indian fiscal policy, especially in relation to the forcible connection of India to 'free trade' and lack of protective tariffs on industrial goods.[38] Vakil's later studies brought him more clearly into the area of planning and development, and the economic consequences of Partition.[39] Mithan Tata was the daughter of the women's activist Herabai Tata, and was herself active in speaking to public bodies, including the House of Commons about women's suffrage, while in London in the early 1920s. Like Ambedkar, she simultaneously worked for an MSc and studied at the Bar—in her case, Lincoln's Inn. On her return to India, again like Ambedkar, she turned her legal work towards social and political causes, in this case as a member of the All-India Women's Conference and as the editor of *Stri Dharma*.[40] Tata, whose married name was Lam from 1933, was not only the first Indian woman to be called to the Bar but also became the first woman to practise at the Bombay Bar.[41] Finally, there was J. N. Varma, who graduated from LSE six months after Ambedkar and also went on to publish on the constitutional law of India. Three of the five students graduating in the two years prior to Ambedkar were of Indian origin and included Ratan Chand Rawlley, an economist of the silk industry and later author of a fictional critique of British rule.[42] During Ambedkar's time in London up to 1924, a number of other Indian students followed him to postgraduate study in economics at LSE, including the historian of Indian transport Hira Metharam Jagtiani,[43] Rajaram Narayan Vaidya and Moreshwar Narayan Asnodkar.[44]

Other non-Indian postgraduate contemporaries of Ambedkar at LSE also composed this intellectual milieu, undertaking research in law and the effects of the economy on social justice and labour. Many shared Ambedkar's approaches to society and the state, although in some cases from quite different political perspectives. The number of women in this cohort (four out of twelve students between mid-1920 and mid-1922) was significant for the interwar period: Edith How-Martyn, who graduated six months after Ambedkar, was a well-known suffragette;[45] Mildred Wretts-Smith, who graduated a year before Ambedkar, became an accomplished economic historian;[46] and the Australian Persia Campbell, who studied about and published on the exploitation of indentured labourers from China, continued to promote Fabian and feminist causes as well as consumer rights.[47]

Graduating with a PhD in economics at the same time as Ambedkar was the Romanian-born Fabian political scientist Herman Finer, who lectured on public administration and became an important figure in the Labour movement. One of the pioneers of comparative politics, Finer went on to be Professor of Politics at the University of Chicago. Like Ambedkar, he was a defender of planned economic development and welfare and wrote against the theories of Hayek.[48] William Aylott Orton, who graduated in the same month as Ambedkar, served as a staff officer in industrial relations in the Ministry of Labour following military service in the war, and completed a thesis on 'British Industrial History Since 1914'.[49] He also published on concepts of liberalism and on the economic role of the state.[50] Graduating just before Ambedkar, Robert MacGregor Dawson became one of Canada's leading political scientists, publishing the influential 1947 textbook *The Government of Canada*.[51]

This international atmosphere, above all, would have allowed Ambedkar to situate many of his nascent ideas and approaches within a wider theoretical context, which also built on his earlier studies at Columbia. The intellectual cosmopolitanism of interwar London provided an alternative basis for building a more adaptable and expansive approach to the problems of caste discrimination in India, and, in some ways, the funding of his studies was also directed to that end. In other ways, it probably sharpened Ambedkar's sense of larger questions of comparative legal rights and structures of governance. Just as those around him had done, Ambedkar would have been exploring, albeit in early stages, the possible direct applications of his research and erudition in the practical fields of social and political rights. LSE and Gray's Inn also permitted different kinds of experimentation, exemplified by his early, and at this stage subtle, critiques of colonial rule and its association with forms of Indian social dominance.

On the other hand, as Christophe Jaffrelot suggests in this volume, we should not attempt to find, fully formed, the radicalism of *The Annihilation of Caste* in these experimental years. According to one biographer, Ambedkar built a reputation as a political radical after a presentation attended by Laski in April 1921, entitled 'Responsibilities of a Responsible Government'. This talk, according to Keer, was considered by Laski to be 'frankly of a revolutionary nature'.[52] However, most of Ambedkar's thinking at this stage was of a more constructive and reformist nature, as exemplified by his PhD thesis—'The Indian Rupee', which while critical of British policy in India, nevertheless was comparable to the work of his contemporaries also working with Cannan, such as C. N. Vakil.

### *Ambedkar's Work on the Colonial Economy and Its Social Effects*

It would perhaps seem improbable to many not familiar with Ambedkar's early intellectual career that his second PhD thesis was not only in the discipline of economics, but also explored the technical subject of currency policy. Naturally concerned with his approaches to caste, we associate Ambedkarite thought more clearly with law and sociology. But India's interwar public intellectuals were using the tools of economists to sharpen the most influential critiques of colonial power. Equally, the study of 'economics' in Ambedkar's case at LSE was not as a form of pure subject as we might understand it today. Ambedkar also studied a range of other subjects during his time there, as will be explored in more detail in Chapter 2, among them anthropology, sociology and political theory. This holism or interdisciplinary drive in the social sciences was typical of the 1920s academy, especially as it related to India: the first anthropology departments in India, for example, drew strong connections between anthropology and sociology, and certainly by the late 1940s the Planning Commission was connecting the research of economists with that of sociologists and anthropologists.[53]

In the 1920s, there were other contemporary justifications for the study of economics. Critiques of British rule had for a long time focused on the issue of economic and fiscal policy as the central pillar of colonial governance.[54] In order to understand the workings and thereby critique the colonial state, Indian leaders explored how its financial structures knitted onto mechanisms of political control. Following the 1919 Government of India Act, the structures of colonial finance had taken on a new significance, given the changed fiscal responsibilities of the provinces after the introduction of dyarchy. This followed from a larger readjustment of colonial finance, which was gradually shifting away from reliance on traditional forms of revenue to new taxable subjects.[55] It is likely, therefore, that the subject of financial and fiscal policy in India was in vogue in interwar London, and a vital subject of political discussion.

Most crucially, Ambedkar's economics work at Columbia and in London was principally about exploring the material bases of social justice, the relationship between the economy and the rights of labour, and the interconnections between a state's financial and fiscal policy and larger questions of social change. His Columbia PhD, published in 1925 as *The Evolution of Provincial Finance*, provided one of the best and most thorough critiques of the ultimate fallibility of the new system of provincial dyarchy that had been introduced immediately following the 1919 Government of India Act.[56] In his MSc thesis for LSE, 'Evolution of Provincial Finance', he further argued that the Raj's 1909 Councils Act 'besmeared the Indian statute book with a set of repressive laws hardly paralleled in other parts of the world'. He condemned the ruling bureaucracy as repressive, irresponsible and conservative, and discussed how the British in India had, through reforms, attempted to make legislature independent, but effectively muzzled it. For one of his biographers, Gail Omvedt, 'It showed how British fiscal policy had impoverished India through irrational taxation methods, through a land tax that prevented agricultural prosperity, and heavy customs and internal excise duties that injured its industry'.[57]

Further, in *Evolution of Provincial Finance,* Ambedkar struck at the root of the financial inadequacies of the new system of dyarchy after 1919, suggesting that provincial governments were bound to continue with unsound finance while the revenue policy of the Government of India failed to make more of elastic sources, such as customs revenues. The latter, Ambedkar made clear, were hindered by the requirements of the colonial system itself: 'India has been subjected to a pernicious limitation on its fiscal powers which prevents it from using a source of revenue which has everywhere else proved to be more elastic and abundant ...'.[58] The social dangers in this system were not straightforward, but were closely tied into a more nuanced sense of India's social differentiation: 'owing to the inveterate social prejudices of the educated classes there is a great danger of their abusing the political power to exploit the masses'. Ambedkar finished the text with the most telling and powerful sentence: 'Thus in India the political problem is entirely a social problem, and a postponement of its solution virtually postpones the day when India can have a free government subject to the mandate of none but her own people.'[59] These social and economic commentaries in *Provincial Finance* were significant in Ambedkar's later work, not least in his evidence to the Simon Commission in 1928, when he argued that provincial finance should attend to the problems of untouchable education.[60]

Like his earlier work on the political implications of colonial financial and economic policy, his LSE PhD, which resulted in *The Problem of the Rupee: Its origin and its solution*, was squarely targeted at critiquing British currency policy. But the most telling argument of Ambedkar's text surrounded the distributional consequences of exchange rate management—the effects respectively on business groups and earners. Congress leaders, for example, who were largely supportive of Indian business, wanted a sharp devaluation of the rupee.[61] But Ambedkar rightly identified the disadvantages for wage earners in such a proposal, and argued instead for a limited devaluation, which promoted a gold standard rather than a gold exchange standard. The demand for a rapid devaluation would potentially create steep inflation which would disproportionately affect labour. Ambedkar argued to the Royal Commission on Indian Currency and Finance that the gain of rapid devaluation and an larger export trade, as well as promoting price stability, 'is not a gain coming to the nation from outside, but is a gain from one class at the cost of another class in the country'.[62] Ambedkar arrived at this argument about distribution via a more theoretical argument that sharply differed from that proposed by J. M. Keynes, in suggesting a 'gold exchange standard'.[63] Ambedkar argued that the latter did not create a situation of price stability.[64]

Alongside these connections between money and its social distribution in Ambedkar's thinking about the economy and the state, it is revealing to explore the dynamics of style and approach in *The Problem of the Rupee* as a text. From the outset, Ambedkar pointed out that he had written at length and in detail because he wanted to write 'primarily for the benefit of the Indian public, and, as their grasp of currency principles does not seem to be as good as one would wish it to be, an over-statement, it will be agreed, is better than an under-statement of the argument on which I have based my conclusions'.[65] To this end, the text is historical in its first four chapters, bringing the reader right back to basic principles and social contexts for the development of India's unique currency systems. This ranged from the history of bimetallism and local currency variations as the Mughal Empire declined to the early provincial experiments in creating a monometallic standard, and from the development of a pan-Indian common currency to the (inadequate) adoption of a silver standard as India moved into being a cash economy. This latter development was rooted in an analysis of colonial finance and revenue requirements, and the creation of a precipitate cash-based economy and associated polity.

In exploring the defectiveness of the silver-based rupee (and then the later gold exchange standard), Ambedkar weaved in social, non-monetary uses of currency, the popular use of gold ingots in reaction to poor silver supply, the introduction of part paper currency and the problem of India not fully adopting the gold standard in the late nineteenth century.[66] Its most powerful historical arguments explored the problems of the irregularity of money supply in a country where fluctuation in demand for currency was so dependent on seasonal and temporally shifting economic activity and social customs. The inability of currency to meet these changing public demands created convulsions in money markets, compounded by the weakness of the banking system and its remoteness from the general population. The latter, in turn, Ambedkar showed, was caused by inelasticity of the credit system, as the most important cash reserves were held by the government in an independent treasury and not released at the appropriate times. This astute commentary on Indian conditions was also punctuated in the text by an extensive exploration of global changes in currency policy up to the 1910s. For Ambedkar, there were some terrible effects for India being tied into a rupee–sterling exchange when (after 1873) it was one of the few global economies using a silver standard, but still had bills to pay for the colonial establishment in gold.[67] By this means, as well as establishing arguments contemporary to his own times, Ambedkar anticipated the perverse and adverse effects of the colonial monetary system on economic and business crises. In relation to the problems of credit, he wrote: 'Such fluctuations [in credit supply] increase business risks, lead to higher business expenses and a greater cost to the consumer. They bring about swings in prices, promote speculation, and prepare for panics.'[68] In the area of the post-1870s exchange crisis, Ambedkar exposed the real reason for the Indianisation of the bureaucracy to be about financial stringency, as the Government of India faced budgetary difficulties on account of the sterling demands,[69] and he set out the problems of funding infrastructure, alleviating famine and providing for capital investment at the end of the nineteenth century—all of which fell as a heavy burden on the Indian population.[70]

One important reason for the socially differentiated effects of exchange rate problems was the impact of rising product prices for wage earners, whose wages did not rise in tandem. But the most crucial point Ambedkar made in *Problem* was India's exchange rate instability, given its silver standard (and its continued use of silver while using a 'gold exchange' system) concurrent with Britain's use of gold.[71] This instability of value created a whole host of further crises. For Ambedkar, while low exchange value may have aided Indian trade, 'the [trade] bounty was a mulcting of the Indian labourer, whose wages did not rise as fast as prices.'[72] It also created a dangerous currency instability in the period of 1917–20, when the value of silver expanded quickly, and then fell again. Ambedkar also showed that the failure of the gold exchange system was caused in large part by falls in the general purchasing power of the rupee, and not (as Keynes argued) as a result of an adverse balance of trade. In the final part of his thesis, Ambedkar exposed the largely disingenuous arguments of the Government of India in its currency policy, which were in reality focused on meeting the commitments of its 'Home Charges' (i.e. payments of salaries and establishments) in the context of the new system of dyarchy in 1920.[73] It therefore represented an extensive and deeply researched criticism of the schemes of Alexander Lindsay (of the Bank of Bengal) in particular, and of the hypocrisies contained within early twentieth-century colonial financial policy in general.[74]

*The Problem of the Rupee* was quickly published in 1923 in England at a time when a larger political battle raged around currency. The text and Ambedkar's work was later acknowledged, in Ambedkar's invited presentation to the Royal Commission on Indian Currency in 1925.[75] The deliberations of the latter eventually led to the establishment of the Reserve Bank of India.[76] But the larger significance of this work, like that of *Evolution of Provincial Finance*, lies in a consideration of the wider and, most crucially, combined intellectual interests that occupied Ambedkar in the early 1920s. Throughout all of his work in the field of economics, alongside a sharp use of theory, Ambedkar continually came back to two interconnected themes: first were the problems of governance that were thrown up by the financial crises arising from fiscal and currency policy. These considerations, although seemingly subtle, were among the most well-evidenced and logically argued critiques of the system of colonialism of their time. Secondly, these critiques clearly only made sense throughout all of these early writings when explained through the lens of social inequality, the problems of income inequalities and the politics of representation.

### *Ambedkar's London Studies: Research, Books and Education*

The sheer ambition of Ambedkar's London PhD, as the only work at the time, aside from that of Keynes, to fully explore India's gold exchange standard, was also reflected in the style of research he must have undertaken. The text is punctuated throughout with long and detailed quotations from official reports, India Office archival materials and published sources from contemporary economists. The archetypal image of B. R Ambedkar sitting for hours on end in archives and the British Library, hunched over texts, is perhaps supported by this style. It is likely, for example, that unless he had assistance in the process,[77] he would have needed to hand-copy long sections of text. The laborious nature of Ambedkar's research method was also set out in his own Preface to *The Evolution of Provincial Finance in British India,* in which as well as thanking 'Mr. Robinson the Financial Secretary and the India Office, for many valuable suggestions and for the loan of many important documents bearing on the subject', Ambedkar added: 'Not very seldom does it happen that a pioneer student is jubilant over his find of his material bearing on his subject, but it is not without a long and wearisome search that he is able to sift the grain from the chaff. Again, sources sometimes prove false guides, so that a perusal of them only ends in a considerable waste of time and energy.'[78] Reading these early 1920s works, it is difficult not to be struck by the research intensity of the prose too. Close readings of contemporary economic theory are weaved into an almost prescient analysis of governance, political change and the wider social milieu of his subject. The use of documentary analysis is consistently rigorous and logically argued to the point that the reader can almost feel Ambedkar's urge to grapple with argumentation jumping off the page.

Given the concentration of research and writing in this period, which resulted in two published texts from postgraduate study in the USA and London, the achievement of a legal education, and an aborted plan to study in Germany, it is clear that Ambedkar lived in a world of texts and books. According to one study, he had probably purchased around 2,000 books in New York.[79] In correspondence with his wife in the early 1920s, it appeared, according to one cited letter, that the safety of these books in India was uppermost in his mind, as he asked her to not let anyone touch them while he was away.[80] The Siddhartha College, which holds the largest collection of Ambedkar's books, is illustrative of the immense range of Ambedkar's life as a bibliophile. The collection covers, among other disciplines, a large number of texts in law, history, philosophy, economics, ethics, politics and government. Many of these books date back to purchases in the 1910s and 1920s, although clearly his later 1940s interests in the politics of labour movements, unions and socialism had its roots in his earlier readings. No doubt his interest in Fabianism, with its attendant concepts of social and economic justice, also dated back to his US and London collections. These, in their turn, contributed to Ambedkar's later ideas around the connection between property and the delinking of occupation from caste.[81]

Clearly, books and research were of lifelong importance to Ambedkar, and in this period of his life we get the sense that he must have been moving rapidly between different archives and collections. While still completing his work at Columbia in May 1916, for example, he was already planning to travel and explore archives in London.[82] Once in London, he probably spent a good deal of his time gathering research materials, both in the applications he made for access to archives,[83] and also in terms of the written output—two full-length PhDs apparently researched from UK-based materials and then published between 1916 and 1924, in which time Ambedkar spent less than four years in total in London. According to one biographer, he had collected a complete run of East India Company records that he had purchased while in London too.[84] These, as well as other texts that eventually made their way into his vast collection, were annotated heavily in some cases, suggesting that in key areas he integrated them closely into his own work. It is likely that Ambedkar also would have made full and urgent use of other libraries in the capital, and according to one text, he moved between the British Museum Library, Goldsmiths Library of Economic Literature and the India Office library.[85] But this research was carried on with a constant eye on developments in India—something that is clearly evident in the published dissertations themselves, which explored the most pressing Indian political issue of the time—the working of the new system of dyarchy and its financial implications. It is also suggested in some of his cited correspondence: writing to Shahu Maharaj of Kolhapur on 3 February 1921 from 10 King Henry's Road, he pointed out that he had arranged to meet with Edwin Montagu, the Secretary of State for India, and had become despondent about the lack of knowledge in England around the nuances in the non-Brahman movements.[86]

Given this extraordinary commitment to education and training, exploring Ambedkar's life in London also suggests new ways of thinking about the significance of the principles underlying education for Ambedkar's larger projects of activism. The centrality of education for many Ambedkarites is rooted in the idea that freedom for Dalits would only come once they are able to engender their own intellectuals. In the case of Ambedkar, there is little doubt that his own education was never principally personal and career-oriented, but was self-consciously directed towards the ends of a larger community and political agenda.[87] This was, in time, articulated in the parts of India's Constitution for which Ambedkar was responsible. Article 46 of the Indian Constitution, drafted specifically by Ambedkar, specifies that 'The State shall promote with special care the educational and economic interests of the weaker section of the people, and in particular, of the Scheduled Castes and the Scheduled Tribes, and shall protect them from social injustice and all forms of exploitation.' For Ambedkar, the ability of Dalits to gain political power (*sattaa*) rested on their skilfulness in occupying 'effective positions in the government' (*maaranyachya jaagaa*) as a result and fulfilment of successful education, something pushed by Ambedkar in the drive for common schools. This, in turn, underpinned self-respect (*svaabhimaan*) and self-reliance (*svaavalamban*), which have since become tenets of the Dalit movement. These principles have been a central part of agendas for Dalit women's education, too, although not without ambiguities and contradictions, given their male-centred origins.[88]

We might reflect on these longer-term educational agendas of Ambedkar through the lens of his experiences in London in a more direct sense. There is no doubt that John Dewey was one of the key intellectual influences on Ambedkar, following his work at Columbia around the time he moved to London. His personal copy of Dewey's *Democracy and Education* appears from its annotations to have been more important than any other, the text being marked and annotated in grey, blue and red pencil. For example, he underlined in red Dewey's sentence: 'Society exists through a process of transmission quite as much as biological life' since this process 'makes possible through transmission of ideas and practices the constant renewing of the social fabric'.[89] Response to, and development of, the work of theorists like Dewey were forming and shaping in Ambedkar's own work in early 1920s London, given their focus on social justice through education. There is little doubt about Ambedkar's views on the deeper political extension of his own education. He directly viewed his studies in London, he stated to Kohlapur in February 1921, as a necessary delay in the launching of a political career, since his degrees and intellectual contacts would better equip him to represent the non-Brahman cause.[90] Ambedkar's research and personal development was, as we noted above, rooted in the twin and interconnected themes of the political economy of governance and its implications for social and legal equality and representation. And it was these two areas that, in terms of Ambedkar's political praxis, later equipped him to most forcefully direct and develop a Dalit cause back in India.

There were both instrumental and more complex reasons why education, and specifically the use of education in these areas of systems of governance, was of material importance to leaders of the Dalit movement in India, especially in the 1920s–30s. Ambedkar's education was pivotal in his positioning both in relation to the state and for 'Depressed Classes' leadership in the Bombay Presidency. At the instrumental level, given the importance of Ambedkar's establishment as a Dalit leader in the phase between his US and UK studies, and given the nature of his intellectual work in London, he was quickly immersed in areas of public life relating to India's colonial status in the early 1920s. Writing to the Maharaja of Kolhapur on 3 February 1921, he narrated his meeting with Edwin Montagu, the Secretary of State for India.[91] His main concern, he wrote, was the absence of a large-scale non-Brahman movement in intervening in discussions around the Montagu–Chelmsford reforms. Although the discussions were already concluded, Montagu reportedly advised him to approach the Viceroy and Governor of Bombay, and perhaps to explore the possibility of representation in the Legislative Council. He also pointed out that he was taking his role as a spokesperson very seriously: 'I take every opportunity possible to put every important English man I meet into a right frame of mind,' he wrote, 'regarding the inter-relations of social and political problems in India'.[92] Some of the principles and ideas surrounding the economy and systems of education that formed the basis of his thinking while in London appeared again in direct form following Ambedkar's return to India, especially in his larger social and political movements. For example, Ambedkar set up the Bahishkrit Hitakarini Sabha (BHS) (The Council of Excluded Peoples) on 20 July 1924. The objective of the BHS was the development of an entrepreneurial ecology among the oppressed masses. It was dedicated to welfare measures and activities such as setting up schools for agricultural and industrial entrepreneurial skill development programmes, and also aimed at establishing cooperative societies.

But more interesting is to explore how his early work and research had a bearing on the kinds of approaches and arguments he made in these fora. Here we can look at two examples that straddled his period of stay in London—one in 1919 and one in 1928. In the former, Ambedkar appeared before the Southborough Committee on the Franchise, which at one level illustrated his stress on the necessities of constitutional protections in forms of governance.[93] The deeper implications of this stance and approach to social and political problems surrounding representation appear directly throughout his London work, especially in its focus on rational bases (i.e. arguments that explicitly rejected preconceived notions of social authority) as solutions to social inequality. He made the argument to Southborough, for example, that Untouchables should not make this claim as 'Adi-Hindus' but because of social isolation: 'British rule in India was meant to provide equal opportunities for all, and that in transferring a large share of the power to popular assemblies, arrangements should be made whereby the hardships and disabilities entailed by the social system should not be reproduced and perpetuated in political institutions.'[94]

Further, when we look at his evidence before the Simon Commission in 1928, it is clear that his approaches to Depressed Classes representation were directed, shaped and contextualised in terms of spaces and jurisdictions of governance. A great deal of focus by historians has been placed on his evidence relating directly to Dalit representation. But Ambedkar also framed this evidence against a wider and detailed exploration of the problems of dyarchy, divisions of powers, executive and legislative authority, and financial structures as a way of more fully and forcefully making a case for the legal and jurisdictional problems of protecting minority rights.[95] This spatial governance context was particularly important since in his evidence to the Simon Commission in October 1928, Ambedkar's central claim for separate Depressed Classes representation, depended upon arguments that set up their minority rights as comparable to those of Muslims. In addition, his arguments in this evidence were also shaped around different levels and scales of governance, from the injustices faced by Untouchables ill-treated by legal processes and courts to municipal governance, Depressed Classes representation in public services, and the connections of these local concerns to provincial politics.[96]

### *Conclusion: London and Ambedkar's Internationalism*

When we situate Ambedkar in London, we cannot forget that although Ambedkar was writing and thinking consistently with India in his mind, the other key space of his work was international. In their prefaces to his early books, his two PhD supervisors, Edwin Seligman and Edwin Cannan, pointed to the wider applications of his work to other contexts of decentralised governance or currency management.[97] They were perhaps beholden to do so. But in writing about the financial functions of government, the balance between centralisation and decentralisation, and, most importantly, the social consequences of fiscal policy and changing structures of governance, Ambedkar was drawing on larger themes in interwar politics. Relevant to most emerging democratic regimes were questions of redistributive justice, social welfare, the concept of the minimum wage and how to establish a capitalist welfare state. All of these themes became important to post-colonial developmental agendas by the middle of the twentieth century, and Ambedkar was very much at the centre of them as India drafted its 1950 Constitution. Reading Ambedkar's 1920s works we are struck by a self-conscious awareness of universalism in his concepts. With ease, for example, he narrated the specific consequences of India's colonial currency arrangements, the so-called 'gold exchange standard', as inherently tied into the constant ebb and flow of international policies on currency.

In some ways, Ambedkar stood out as one of the only 'Untouchable' students in London to have achieved the privilege typically granted to caste Hindu or wealthy cosmopolitan Indians. In other ways, in the LSE of the early 1920s, he fitted right in: truly international in character, idiosyncratic in its student body, whose often radical political views led them into dazzling intellectual careers, the Webbs' college suited Ambedkar's academic ambitions well. Although there is little direct evidence about his social interactions in the city, it is likely that the cosmopolitan anonymity of the metropolis, with its international research libraries, must have shaped his critical outlook, not least in his strategies for applying research and education to activism. It is possible that the city also allowed for other kinds of personal freedoms that may have altered the kinds of friendships he was to later maintain by correspondence, and especially those that connected him to 10KHR.

The overall significance of Ambedkar's time in London, then, is not easily reduced, but there is no doubt that while it was not a time when he set out his fully formed radical critique of caste, it created many of the intellectual contexts for that move. As Chapter 5 in this volume shows, on his return to India, Ambedkar was still somewhat concerned with promoting a reformist agenda, exemplified by the protests around temple entry and a residual hesitancy about full separate electorates for 'Untouchables'. Some of the roots of his thinking were in place: in 1917, in between his two periods of stay in London, Ambedkar published his first article, 'Castes in India: Their Mechanism, Genesis and Development', which appeared in the *Journal of Indian Antiquary*. Arguing that caste was rooted in the endogamy of Brahmans in a culturally unified region, the article's approach was important to later work on caste, which related the phenomenon not to differences of race or culture, but disabilities incurred via social isolation—Brahmanical ideas of exclusion/excommunication.[98] But perhaps the key contribution of Ambedkar's early 1920s intellectual experiences lay in his ability to tease out and strategise the larger spatial and political frames for his later activism—from a comprehensive understanding of the powers of the state to the financial structures of colonial authority and governance. It was these areas which provided the key bases for setting out the conditions for Depressed Classes representation and social justice and welfare.

## 2

# A STUDENT IN LONDON

## AMBEDKAR AT THE LONDON SCHOOL OF ECONOMICS AND POLITICAL SCIENCE

*Sue Donnelly and Daniel Payne*

An instantly recognisable name in India, Ambedkar's significance as an alumnus of LSE has often been overlooked. Although the many who come to study, research and work at LSE from India have no doubt been influenced by Ambedkar's legacy (with evidence of at least one Indian student coming to study at LSE on a scholarship personally organised by Ambedkar), his recognition from the School and the wider LSE community has fluctuated over the hundred years since his studies. In part, this may be because the surviving archival record provides little direct evidence of Ambedkar's personal experience of studying at LSE. The administrative records, including his student file, are rich in factual details but poor in recording Ambedkar's daily life as an LSE student. Nevertheless, it is possible to piece together a picture of what Ambedkar's likely academic experiences would have been at LSE, from the wider context of his contemporaries' lives and the academic community overall. From its earliest years, LSE had attracted students from the Indian subcontinent, and Ambedkar was part of a cohort of students travelling to London to continue their education. An investigation into his experience of studying at LSE can also shed some light on the experience of this wider community of students.

Bhimrao Ramji Ambedkar arrived in London in October 1916 after obtaining a master's and working on his PhD at Columbia University in New York. This PhD would be formally awarded in 1927. He enrolled at LSE to study for an MSc in economics, alongside studying for the Bar at Gray's Inn, a short walk from LSE.

Ambedkar was twenty-five years old when he arrived at LSE, four years older than the School itself. LSE opened its doors to students in October 1895 at 9 John Adam Street, close to Charing Cross Station. The first prospectus declared that:

> The special aim of the School will be, from the first, the study and investigation of the concrete facts of industrial life and the actual working of economic and political relations as they exist or have existed, in the United Kingdom and in foreign countries.[1]

Initially, the School focused on teaching nine subjects: economics, statistics, commerce, commercial geography, commercial history, commercial and industrial law, currency and banking, taxation and finance, and political science. The prospectus also emphasised the importance of research in the life of LSE.[2]

LSE's key founders were Sidney and Beatrice Webb, Graham Wallas and George Bernard Shaw—all members of the Fabian Society, Britain's oldest political think tank which aimed to advance democratic socialism through gradual reform. Sidney and Beatrice Webb, who married in 1892, were both active in Fabian and Labour politics. Sidney Webb (1849–1947) would be MP for Seaham Harbour from 1922 until 1929, and in 1929 entered the House of Lords as Baron Passfield, serving as both Secretary of State for the Colonies and as Secretary of State for Dominion Affairs. Beatrice Webb (1848–1943) served on the Royal Commission on the Poor Law and was the main author of the Minority Report of 1909, viewed as a precursor to the post-1945 development of the welfare state. The political scientist Graham Wallas (1858–1932) taught at LSE from 1895, becoming Professor of Political Science in 1914.[3] George Bernard Shaw (1856–1950), writer, journalist and political activist, was a close friend of Sidney Webb and an active Fabian. His wife, the Irish heiress Charlotte Shaw (née Payne-Townshend), was a significant donor in LSE's early years.[4]

LSE's first Director, the economic historian William Hewins, was not a Fabian, and in 1912 he became a Unionist MP for Hereford. However, all those involved in managing LSE's foundation years were united in a commitment to providing a modern education particularly relevant to those wishing to work in politics, the civil service, local government, business or welfare work. LSE initially existed outside the university system, and thus did not prepare students for examinations, but its approach was rewarded in 1900 when it joined the University of London. In the same year, it moved to its own premises on Clare Market, near the Kingsway and Lincoln's Inn Fields, where it remains to the present day.[5]

The years leading up to Ambedkar's arrival were a period of significant development for LSE. In 1909 William Pember-Reeves (1857–1932) was appointed as the third Director. A New Zealand journalist and politician, he had been New Zealand High Commissioner in London before his appointment. His wife, Maud Pember-Reeves, was an active member of the Fabian Society, and in 1913 published *Round About a Pound a Week*.[6] His daughter, Amber Reeves, had been at the centre of a scandal in 1909 following an affair with the writer H. G. Wells and the birth of their daughter, Anna-Jane. In 1917 Pember-Reeves' son, Fabian, a Flight Lieutenant in the Royal Navy Air Service was killed in action, going down behind enemy lines. Following Fabian's death, Pember-Reeves withdrew from public life, leaving LSE's management to the School Secretary, Christian Mactaggart. In 1919 he was replaced by William Beveridge.

On the eve of the First World War, LSE was established as a small, specialist college of the University of London. Its focus was social science research and support for vocational training. It also provided evening teaching for students in employment, allowing students to support themselves during study, a practice which continued until the 1960s. In 1913–1914 there were 1,681 students, with 368 listed as attending the School to undertake postgraduate studies. Seventy-nine postgraduate students (twenty-two per cent) were listed as having completed first degrees outside of the UK.[7] Despite the arrival of refugees from Belgium and Russia, the First World War saw student numbers fall. Two hundred staff and students undertook military service and eighty-one were lost in the conflict. The reduction in students meant fee income fell and the School struggled to find replacement teachers.

This was the context for Ambedkar's first period of study at LSE. In 1916 his studies were supported by the Baroda State Scholarship he had received in 1913. His student file, the core record maintained by the School recording a student's academic career, allows us to trace his studies. After the appointment of William Beveridge as Director in 1919 and Janet Mair as School Secretary in 1920, LSE's administrative system was overhauled, and the creation and retention of student files was standardised and improved. LSE has retained its series of student files, and these can be consulted by researchers within the legal requirements of data protection. Files for students prior to the Second World War provide a wealth of information on individual students, though they vary in size and detail. Files can include application forms and enquiry letters, attendance cards, and correspondence with tutors and other School staff relating to their studies. Sometimes files contain material that post-dates attendance at the School, shedding light on continuing relationships between the former student and LSE.[8]

Ambedkar's file opens with his arrival at LSE in 1916, but is fuller for his time in London during the 1920s. On his arrival in London, Ambedkar registered for an MSc in economics under Statute 113 of the University of London which permitted graduates of other universities to register for postgraduate degrees. There was a minimum of two years of study and the degree was examined by thesis; in addition, 'candidates may be tested orally with reference both to the special subject selected by him and to the thesis'.[9] Examinations took place in December and June, and candidates had to provide the examiners with four copies of their thesis. Students were encouraged to attend lecture series that might support their studies.

Ambedkar's attendance card indicates that he registered for four courses during his first year at LSE: 'The History of Political Ideas',

'Geography', 'Social Evolution' and 'Social Theory'. Ambedkar attended the courses during the Michaelmas Term, focusing on the research for his thesis in Lent and Summer Terms. His attendance was very regular at the social evolution and social theory lectures, and for the first half of the term he attended the geography lectures but was then marked as absent. He only attended two of the lectures in the political ideas course.[10]

'The History of Political Ideas in connection with the History of Europe and of the United States' was a series of thirty lectures given over three terms at 5 p.m. on a Monday by Goldsworthy Lowes Dickinson (1862–1932). The first term was devoted to the political thought of the ancient world, including Plato and Aristotle and the political thought of Rome. Dickinson, a graduate of King's College, Cambridge, taught at LSE from 1896, and in 1911 joined the permanent staff as a lecturer in political science. He resigned in 1920 but returned from 1924 to give a short course on the causes of the First World War. In 1916 he published *The European Anarchy*[11] on the causes of war and in 1926 *The International Anarchy.*[12] He died in 1932.[13]

Geography was another course of thirty lectures taught over three terms. The School's calendar describes the course by saying 'the treatment of each division of the world will be physical from the regional point of view, with economic applications'. The first term was devoted to the study of India 'which country will be treated as a type for the explanation of fundamental principles'.[14] The focus on India may explain why Ambedkar felt the course was not a priority for his time. The course teacher was the eminent geographer Halford Mackinder (1861–1947), often hailed as the founder of geopolitics and geostrategy. His 1904 paper 'The Geographical Pivot of History' was significant in highlighting the importance of Eastern Europe in relations between the world powers. Mackinder was listed in LSE's first prospectus as teaching commercial geography, and in 1903 became LSE's second Director. After his resignation in 1908 he combined political and academic careers, continuing to teach at LSE while serving as the Liberal Unionist MP for the Glasgow Division of Camlachie, and in 1923 he became Professor of Geography in the University of London.

In contrast, Ambedkar appears to have attended all the lectures in the courses on 'social evolution' and 'social theory' in the Michaelmas Term. 'Social theory', a course of twenty lectures, taught over the Michaelmas and Lent Terms on Wednesday afternoons, covered both analytical and comparative methods in sociology, looking at the nature of the social union, law and justice, class relations, the family, and ideas of property. 'Social evolution' ran over ten lectures in the Michaelmas Term and included investigation of the theories of social evolution and the impact of biology on sociological thinking.[15] Both courses were taught by Professor L. T. Hobhouse (1864–1929).

Leonard Trelawney Hobhouse had a long association with LSE, becoming a teacher in 1896 while still a full fellow at Corpus Christi College, Oxford. He left academic life to work as a journalist for the *Manchester Guardian* and as the secretary to a trade union. In 1907 he became the first Professor of Sociology in Britain on his appointment to the newly created Martin White Chair in Sociology in the University of London, based at LSE. Hobhouse's inaugural lecture pointed to the origins of sociology in political philosophy, the philosophy of history and developments in the sciences—particularly biology.[16]

Hobhouse had read greats at Oxford and had become a familiar part of radical Oxford, although he never identified with socialism and never joined the Fabian Society. He could, nevertheless, be seen as a radical Liberal whose book *Liberalism*, published in 1911, provided intellectual support for the Liberal Party's social policies, including the provision of pensions and progressive use of taxation.[17] Hobhouse played an important role in the establishment of the Ratan Tata Department of Social Administration at LSE, supporting the development of the applied social sciences. Hobhouse had opposed the Boer War and his anti-imperialist views may have been of interest to Ambedkar.[18]

In 1917 Ambedkar was recalled to India, with the removal of his scholarship, to serve as the Military Secretary in Baroda. Later correspondence from the 1950s between the University of London and LSE, in Ambedkar's student file, reports that Ambedkar was permitted to interrupt his course for not more than four years. His return trip to India, made during the height of the First World

War, was a dangerous one. Sending his luggage, personal library and academic work in a separate boat, Ambedkar took a train to Marseille and then boarded the *SS Kaiser-I-Hind*. Whilst Ambedkar made it home safely to the relief of his family, the ship carrying his personal belongings was torpedoed and sunk by a German submarine, losing Ambedkar's luggage forever.[19]

Ambedkar was to return to LSE in 1920 using his own funds and the support of the Maharaja of Kolhapur, who shared Ambedkar's opposition to the Hindu caste system. He returned to LSE in a moment of change. The most obvious change was the leadership of a new Director, William Beveridge (1879–1963), who had replaced William Pember Reeves in 1919 and whose family had connections to India. Beveridge was born in Rangpur City (now in Bangladesh) where his father, Henry Beveridge (1837–1929), was a judge. His mother, Annette Beveridge (1842–1929), was a translator and supporter of women's education in India. William Beveridge returned to England as a child, and after studying at Oxford, he joined the community at Toynbee Hall in the East End of London, established in 1884 by Samuel and Henrietta Barnett to inspire future leaders to develop practical solutions in the fight against poverty by learning from the direct experience of living alongside working people. The experience gave Beveridge a lifelong interest in employment policy and brought him into contact with Beatrice and Sidney Webb. After a brief period as a journalist, Beveridge joined the Board of Trade, implementing a national system of labour exchanges, moving on to the Ministry of Munitions and Ministry of Food during the First World War.

Beveridge never joined the Labour Party, and in 1905 described himself as only a 'little bit socialist'—but he was a social reformer genuinely concerned about poverty and its causes, partly because he believed that national prosperity was impossible when a significant portion of the population were destitute, badly educated and in poor health. He also believed that reform should be based on research and knowledge. His views made him an appropriate choice for the role of Director.[20] Beveridge was not Sidney Webb's first choice in 1919, but after the economist J. M. Keynes had declined the post, it was offered to Beveridge and the post was confirmed by the Senate of the University of London in July 1919. He was to remain at LSE until 1937. Beveridge joined an institution firmly established in the social sciences, but his ambition was to transform the School from a small college into a major institution, recognisable as a university.[21]

Beveridge's annual address to students illustrates his commitment to the importance of the social sciences and the benefits of studying at LSE. In his notes for 1924–25 he writes:

> The School again is not a place of technical education fitting you for one and only one profession. It makes you better for every occupation, it does help you get on in life ... But you will lose most of the value of the School if you regard it solely as a means of getting on in life. Regard it as a means of learning, to advance science and civilization.[22]

Beveridge's annual address to students in 1935 encapsulates his thinking on the importance of undertaking the study of society, and his ideas behind the application of research compare well to Ambedkar's own views on the subject:

> A belief that reason applied to human affairs might make it possible for us ultimately to manage them better, as reason applied to nature has enabled us to master so much of nature. Their general idea was a belief in the possibility and the need for a Science of Society. But it's not enough to have a general idea. You must know how to put it into practice.[23]

Beveridge was joined at LSE by Janet Mair (1876–1959) who was appointed Business Secretary in 1919 and became School Secretary and Dean in 1920. Janet Mair had studied mathematics at St Andrews University and married David Mair, William Beveridge's cousin. David Mair was a civil servant, and the family settled in London in 1913 close to Beveridge's home in Bedford Gardens. The marriage was not successful, and in 1915 Janet Mair joined the Ministry of Munitions as a volunteer and then as Beveridge's private secretary. Mair was involved in all aspects of LSE life from the selection of a coat of arms and motto to support for students. Ultimately, her close relationship with Beveridge (the couple eventually married in 1942) led to friction with senior staff members.[24]

At LSE, Ambedkar was studying in the heart of London. By 1916 LSE was based in Passmore Edwards Hall on Clare Market, tucked between Aldwych, Kingsway and Lincoln's Inn Fields. LSE had begun in three rooms in John Adam Street, near Charing Cross Station, in 1895, moving to 10 Adelphi Terrace, overlooking the Thames, in 1896. In 1900 LSE joined the University of London and required its own accommodation. London County Council's slum clearance programme around Clare Market and the construction of Kingsway allowed LSE to obtain 4,300 square feet on Clare Market 'on permanent loan' on a peppercorn rent. Construction work was funded by the publishing philanthropist John Passmore Edwards (1823–1911) and donations from the City of London and Lord Rothschild. The building was finished in 1902, and LSE was settled on the site it has occupied to the present day.

By the start of the First World War the School was desperately overcrowded, but any expansion was blocked by the war when student numbers fell. In 1919 the situation worsened, with the School having to use former YMCA huts based on Aldwych. But on 28 May 1920 George V and Queen Mary laid the foundation stone for a new building funded by the introduction of a new University of London degree, the Bachelor of Commerce (BCom), which was based at LSE. On that day, one of the students selected to meet the King and Queen was Mithan Tata, another LSE student from India (see more below and Chapter 1). Beveridge continued to expand the LSE campus throughout the 1920s and 1930s, and throughout Ambedkar's time at LSE it was in a state of constant development. In his 1924–25 Director's Report, Beveridge declared that a colleague had described LSE as being the 'empire on which the cement never set'.[25] The new building, designed by the architects Trehearne and Norman, who designed many buildings in the Kingsway area, contained two floors of teaching rooms, an imposing arched entrance on Houghton Street and the School's first large lecture theatre, still in use today and now known as the Old Theatre. The new building also provided some additional space for the library, where it is likely that Ambedkar spent time studying.

Beveridge was keen that LSE's intellectual development should match its physical growth, so alongside new buildings there were new members of faculty and areas of study. Harold Laski arrived in 1920 and was appointed Professor of Government in 1926. Laski taught many generations of Indian students, and was a high-profile supporter of Indian independence and socialism in India and other countries. Laski hosted an international study circle with students, with the student journal *Clare Market Review* reporting his presence there in 1922.[26] Unfortunately, there is no direct evidence of any interaction between Ambedkar and Laski. However, we know that Laski regularly invited international students to Sunday afternoon social gatherings at his home, and it is likely that his presence at LSE fed into the range of socialist influences in Ambedkar's education.[27] For example, in his later work, such as *States and Minorities*, his views were seemingly influenced by the state socialism model of Laski, mediated via parliamentary democracy.[28]

Other significant figures around the School included Arthur Bowley, Professor of Statistics, the economic historian R. H. Tawney and economist Theodore Gregory, who left LSE in 1937 to become an adviser to the Indian government. Lilian Knowles, who had achieved a double first in history and law at Cambridge (while being unable to take her degree), in 1921 became both LSE's first female professor and its first Professor of Economic History. Women were represented on the staff at LSE, but it did not appoint its first black academic until 1938 when the future Nobel Prize-winner, Arthur Lewis was appointed to an assistant lectureship.[29]

In 1921 former LSE student Vera Anstey was appointed assistant lecturer in economic history. Anstey was known to Ambedkar from India, where her husband, Percy Anstey, another LSE alumnus, had been Principal of Sydenham College of Commerce and Economics in Bombay. While there, Vera Anstey had worked as an examiner in economic theory for Sydenham College's BCom degree while Ambedkar had been Professor of Commerce and Economics from 1917 to 1919. Anstey returned to England following the death of her husband and youngest child from cholera in 1920, in desperate need of a job. Lilian Knowles recommended her to the Director. Anstey had a lifelong interest in the economy of India, writing on the subject, and was also supportive of Indian students studying at the School until her retirement in 1964.[30]

Ambedkar completed his new LSE registration form on 30 September 1920. His London address at that time was given as 95 Brook Green, Hammersmith, and his occupation as ex-Professor of Economics, following his employment as Professor of Political Economy at Sydenham College, part of Bombay University. He was continuing his registration for the MSc (Economics) and would be working towards the completion of his thesis, 'The Evolution of Provincial Finance in British India'. The fee paid was £11 11 shillings.[31]

A few days earlier, Professor Edwin Seligman, the American economist who had taught Ambedkar at Columbia, had written to Professor Herbert Foxwell of London University to introduce Ambedkar. Seligman wrote that 'Ambedkar was a student with us for several years at Columbia and passed his examination for the Doctor's degree with considerable distinction. He has been filling the chair of Commerce and Economics at the Sydenham College of Commerce in Body, and he is now proposing to spend about two years in Great Britain to finish a piece of research work in which he is interested'.[32] Ambedkar had asked Seligman to write a letter of introduction:

> This I am very glad indeed to give him, as he is not only a very able, but an exceedingly pleasant fellow, and I am sure that you will do for him what you can.[33]

Foxwell was clearly bemused by Ambedkar's intention to study at LSE as he had already completed a thesis at Columbia. On 19 November 1920 he wrote to the School Secretary, Janet Mair, unaware that Ambedkar had returned and registered at the School:

> I find he has already taken his doctor's degree, & has only come here to finish his research. I had forgotten this. I am sorry that we cannot identify him with the School—but there are no more worlds here for him to conquer.[34]

Despite Foxwell's pessimism, Ambedkar would go on to complete his MSc and a DSc at LSE.

Ambedkar provides no contemporary accounts on his time at LSE, but the *Clare Market Review*, one of the oldest student-run journals in the UK, published pieces about student life which convey the atmosphere of the time. In one article,[35] the Students' Union discusses the influx of students to the school, with the Union now reaching 500 members. They lament the lack of engagement that students had with the Student Union. There were few social events beyond a regular Wednesday evening meeting, and it was felt that 'the students are widely scattered'. At this time, many LSE students worked full time and the student body was split into day and evening students. Research students appear to have found the situation particularly isolating and disjointed.

> A research student works alone on a subject which usually has no personal interest for any other student. He pursues his studies mostly at that intellectual quarantine known as the Reading Room of the British Museum.... It is admitted that many research students come from abroad and that most have graduated in a university other than London. Their opportunities for identifying themselves wholeheartedly with the common interests of the school are not numerous, and placed as they are they soon lose the desire to do so. The most they achieve is to hover on the fringe of social activity in the School.[36]

The article proceeds to call for a Director of Research to help address the neglect of research students by the School. Sadly this development was too late for Ambedkar's studies. An India Society was founded in the Summer Term of 1922 but there is no evidence that Ambedkar was or was not involved with it. It was founded to 'promote knowledge of India and her culture and to act as a social centre for all interested in India'.[37]

It is possible that Ambedkar did not greatly engage with the social side of School life as completing his studies in three years would have required him to spend most of his time studying. He is not pictured in any photographs or mentioned in the *Clare Market Review*. This is in contrast to Krishna Menon (1896–1974) who obtained a first-class BSc (Economics) in 1927, specialising in the history of political ideas. Menon features in several photographs of tennis parties held at the School's sports ground in New Malden.[38]

Ambedkar aimed to submit his thesis for examination in June 1921, but administrative letters in his student file show that he failed to complete the appropriate forms. In April 1921 the School Secretary had to write to the University of London Academic Registrar on Ambedkar's behalf:

> Another case has just come to light in which a candidate for the June Examination for the MSc (Econ) has failed to send in his entry form at the proper time. He states that he went to the University in February to make enquiries, and that he gathered the impression that he need not submit his entry form before April 15th. The probability is that he was confusing the sending in of the entry form with the actual submission of his thesis; but however that may be, he certainly seems to have misunderstood the information given to him. Having pointed out to him his responsibility for acquainting himself with the printed regulations, I have promised to submit the entry form to you with a request that the university will, under the circumstances, permit the student to take the June Examination, if it is at all possible.[39]

The School Secretary explained to Ambedkar that he had sent the wrong form for the MSc (Economics) examination as he had not specified the faculty for which he proposed to take the degree. Ambedkar now had to complete a new form, send it to Edwin Cannan, the Professor of Economics, for his signature and then return it to the School. The correct form was finally forwarded to the Academic Registrar by Eve Evans, LSE's Registrar, on 13 April. Fortunately, the University of London was happy to accept the revised application.

The *LSE Calendar 1922–1923*[40] lists Bhimrao Ramji Ambedkar as being awarded the MSc (Economics) in 1921 alongside seven other students. These were Robert Macgregor Dawson, a Canadian who was later Professor of Political Science at the University of Saskatchewan, William Aylott Orton, who emigrated to the USA and worked at the University of California and Amherst College, the economic historian Mildred Wretts-Smith, Chandulal Nagindas Vakil, later Professor of Economics at the University of Bombay,

Persia Crawford Campbell, an Australian-born economist who completed her PhD at Columbia and taught at Queens College, City University of New York until 1965, William George Henry Cook, who became a barrister and legal writer, and Herman Finer, who was to obtain his DSc alongside Ambedkar in 1923. Vakil, like Ambedkar, was a graduate of the University of Bombay and went on to be University Professor of Economics there. In 1922 two Indian students were awarded the MSc (Economics)—Mithan Ardeshir Tata and Jaikrishna Nagardas Varma.[41]

Ambedkar immediately began work on his doctorate, probably registering for the DSc as he had already undertaken PhD-level research at Columbia. The LSE Calendar for 1920–21 notes that LSE is 'one of the largest centres of post-graduate study in the United Kingdom' and was therefore a logical place for Ambedkar to continue his research and studies for a doctorate. But the research degree in the UK was a relatively recent development prompted in part by a desire to attract students from the empire who might otherwise study in the USA or Germany, where undertaking research led to a qualification. The Doctor of Science degree was first awarded by the University of London in 1860 based on research undertaken, and the University of London finally approved the introduction of a PhD degree on 22 October 1919.[42]

Research students had individual supervision, seminars and special classes plus access to both the LSE Library and the British Library. They were assigned a supervisor who would support them in critiquing their research methods and results. Research students could begin their research work at any time during the year and it was possible to undertake research without studying for a degree. Students studying for a DSc in economics were required to obtain a MSc or PhD unless they had a specific exemption on the grounds of previous work undertaken, either published or unpublished, being of the character and standard of an MSc. Doctorates were examined by thesis, and candidates would have an oral examination and could be asked to submit a reasoned report on a subject prescribed by the examiners.[43] Ambedkar's DSc thesis, 'The Problem of the Rupee', analysed the impact of the development of Indian currency throughout the nineteenth and early twentieth century with a move away from a silver standard, the introduction of paper currency and a gold exchange standard which was seen as detrimental to Indian commerce by many Indian nationalists. The thesis is discussed in more detail in Chapter 1.

Ambedkar's student file does not cover the process of undertaking the research for the DSc or include any correspondence with his supervisor, Edwin Cannan, about the development of the thesis. Later in the file, a letter from the University of London Academic Department dated 12 December 1950 reported that Ambedkar submitted his DSc (Economics) thesis in October 1922 and it was examined in March 1923. The award of the degree was not recommended but the candidate was allowed to revise and resubmit the thesis. Ambedkar resubmitted in August 1923 and his degree was conferred in November 1923. Some accounts claim that the thesis was initially rejected for its anti-British or anti-imperial content—but neither the student file nor the correspondence with the University of London provide evidence for or against this claim.[44] The regulations permitted the examiners to recommend to Senate that a candidate be permitted to resubmit their thesis after a six-month period but within one year where the thesis was of sufficient merit, and this was done in Ambedkar's case. Candidates were required to publish their thesis.

In the preface to the thesis, Ambedkar thanked his supervisor, Edwin Cannan, for his support:

> His sympathy towards me and his keen interest in my undertaking has placed me under obligations which I can never repay. I feel happy to be able to say that this work has undergone close supervision at his hands, and although he is in no way responsible for the views I have expressed, I can say that his severe examination of my theoretical discussions has saved me from many an error.[45]

Cannan had taught at LSE since 1895, beginning with a series of lectures on local government taxation. He had studied at Balliol College, Oxford, where his ill health meant he took a pass rather than an honours degree in 1884. He then spent ten years researching and writing on economic subjects. The teaching of economics at Oxford took a historical view of the subject arguing for the inclusion of historical and institutional as well as theoretical factors in its development, a view of economics that appealed to LSE's founders, including Sidney Webb. Ambedkar may have met Sidney Webb when Webb gave a paper to the Fabian Society on economics and socialism in 1889. After the School joined the University of London in 1900, Cannan became Dean of the Faculty of Economics. In 1907 he became Professor of Political Economy in the University of London. First-year students at LSE attended Cannan's sixty-lecture series on the principles of economics, which formed the foundation of economic study at the School. The lectures formed the basis of Cannan's introductory textbook *Wealth*, published in 1914.[46] His lectures to second- and third-year students were published as *A Review of Economic Theory* after his retirement in 1929.[47] Cannan was also an expert on the eighteenth-century economist Adam Smith, and his critical edition of Smith's *Wealth of Nations* was published in 1904.[48] Although students were frequently unimpressed by Cannan's teaching, his support for free markets and liberalism influenced later LSE economists including Lionel Robbins and Arnold Plant. Cannan contributed a foreword to the published version of Ambedkar's PhD which indicated that though he was not in complete agreement with its conclusions he respected Ambedkar's arguments.

Ambedkar was part of a strong cohort of overseas students who came to study at LSE as both undergraduates and postgraduates. LSE's first prospectus included within its institutional aims a desire to support students and researchers from overseas:

> ...the special aim of the School will be, from the first, the study and investigation of the concrete facts of industrial life and the actual working of economic and political relations as they exist or have existed in the United Kingdom and in foreign countries. With this object in view the school will provide scientific training in methods of investigation and research, and will afford facilities to British and foreign students to undertake special studies of industrial life and original work in economics and political science.[49]

The LSE Register indicates that between 1895 and 1932, 130 students from the Indian subcontinent completed degrees and certificated courses.[50] Others may have attended as occasional students attending lectures but not completing a formal course of study. In 1912 the LSE Students' Union elected its first Indian Chairman, Nandlal Maneklal Muzumdar, who was studying for the BSc (Economics), with Public Administration as his special subject.[51] While the majority of the students were men, some Indian women did graduate from LSE. Mithan Tata was awarded an MSc (Economics) in 1922[52] as well as training for the Bar, and a surviving student file[53] indicates that her mother, Herabai Tata, attended the Social Science course and lectures in economics. Like Ambedkar, Mithan Tata was an alumnus of Elphinstone College, Bombay. Both women were in England to present a petition supporting women's suffrage in India.

During Ambedkar's time at LSE between 1916 and 1923, forty-four Indian students completed courses. Twenty-seven were undergraduates studying for a BSc (Economics) or the BCom degree, a practical course intended for those wishing to enter business. A further two students took the Social Science Certificate (providing practical training in welfare work) and the diploma in journalism. There were fifteen postgraduates studying for MSc (Economics), PhD or a DSc, and thirty-five students are known to have previously studied at Indian universities, including Bombay, Patna, Allahabad and Calcutta. Two of the PhD students had also studied outside India: Hans Raj Soni came to LSE from the University of Edinburgh whereas Nanak Batukram Mehta had studied at Harvard University after completing his undergraduate degree at the University of Bombay.[54]

Most of the theses written by Indian students were in the broad subject area of economics, including banking in India, commercial relations between India and England between 1758 and 1857, Indian railways, Indian tariffs, industrial conditions in India, and the wealth and welfare of the Bengal Delta. Satyashraya Gopal Panandikar, who was awarded his PhD in 1921 and a DSc in 1926 for his work on the Bengal Delta, was also supervised by Professor Edwin Cannan.

Four PhDs were awarded in 1923. Santibhusan Datta (Dutt) was awared a PhD that year for 'A Critical Exposition of Indian

Constitutional Reforms'. He was called to the Bar at Gray's Inn and practised as an advocate in the Calcutta High Court from 1923. Purushottama Padmanabha Pillai, whose study was on 'Industrial conditions in Modern India', was a member of the Economic and Financial Section of the League of Nations in Geneva, a member of the diplomatic division of the International Labour Organisation (ILO), and from 1928 the ILO's representative in Geneva. Naginchand Jagjivandas Shah, an alumnus of Bombay University, wrote his thesis on 'The History of Indian Tariffs' and applied to join the Indian Educational Service, seeking an appointment in an Indian university. Sadly, by 1932, when the *LSE Register* was produced, he had died. The three Indian students were joined by Kiyoshi Ogata, a graduate of the University of Tokyo. His PhD thesis, 'The Co-operative Movement in Japan',[55] was published in 1923 by P. S. King, who also published Ambedkar's DSc thesis. There was one other DSc awarded in 1923 alongside Ambedkar, which went to Herman Finer. Finer had been born in Romania but came to England with his parents as a child. He had undertaken all his university studies at LSE, with a BSc (Economics) specialising in Public Administration in 1919, an MSc in 1922 and his DSc in 1923. He was a lecturer on public administration at LSE from 1920 to 1942, later moving to the University of Chicago as Professor of Political Science.

Ambedkar returned to London in 1930 to attend the Round Table Conference—a series of peace conferences to discuss constitutional reforms in India. There is evidence that during this time, Ambedkar paid a visit to his former colleagues at LSE, in 1931 and 1932. In a letter from his PhD supervisor, Edwin Cannan wrote to then Director of LSE William Beveridge encouraging him to meet with Ambedkar during the visit:

> ...the School might offer Ambedkar some politeness while he is here. I always said he was by far the ablest Indian we ever had in my time, and lately when I read in the papers that the Brahmins were hoping to persuade (or that Gandhi was, I forget which) Dr Ambedkar to modify his demands, I chuckled, remember the obstinacy with which he used to hold out even when quite wrong—so unlike most of the Indians who would say black was

> white to please their supervisor. I saw him in September last year and he was extremely interesting.[56]

Beveridge replied that Ambedkar had already been invited to LSE by John Coatman who was Professor of Imperial Economic Relations at the University of London. Coatman had arranged for Ambedkar to meet Professor Theodore Gregory, whose work on banking Ambedkar admired.[57]

Returning to India, Ambedkar maintained a relationship with LSE, and there is evidence that he was heavily involved in financing students from Dalit communities to be able to study abroad, including at LSE, in the 1950s (see Chapter 6 in this volume). This was achieved through his role as chairman of the People's Education Society, whose remit was to spread higher education amongst 'the Untouchables and the Backward classes'.[58]

Previously unknown letters from Ambedkar found in the file of Vithal Bayajee Kadam, born in 1926 in the Karjat District of Bombay, illustrate Ambedkar's personal involvement in this work. After completing several degrees in India, including a Master of Commerce and an LLB, Kadam began a PhD as a student at Sydenham Commerce College, having previously worked as a tutor in economics at Siddharth College, Bombay. In Kadam's student file, Ambedkar writes to then Chancellor of the Exchequer Richard Austen Butler in 1952:

> My dear Butler, I need your help; that is why I am troubling you with this letter.
>
> Some five years ago, I started a Society called the People's Education Society for spreading higher education among the Untouchables and the Backward Classes. The Society is running a College in Bombay in which facilities are given to boys from these classes.
>
> The Society has gone a step further and has undertaken the responsibility to finance the education of boys from the Untouchable Classes in foreign countries as and when finances permit.
>
> This year the Society proposes to send one student to the London School of Economics for the B.Sc. (Econ) degree. They have selected Mr V. B. Kadam.[59]

Ambedkar went on to explain that there was no use sending the student without guaranteed acceptance at LSE, despite admission being notoriously difficult. Ambedkar was aware of Butler's role on the Court of Governors at LSE from looking this up in the LSE calendars, and hoped Butler would be able to help. Despite LSE's usually strict rules on late applications, Ambedkar's influence enabled the student to be accepted on the course. As well as Butler, he also contacted Vera Anstey, an economist who also chaired admissions and was Chair of the Overseas Students Committee. In this letter, Ambedkar refers to knowing Anstey personally:

> I hope you remember me. I was a Professor at the Sydenham College of Commerce and Economics when your husband was Principal. I need your help; that is why I am troubling you with this letter.[60]

Ambedkar describes the high quality of Kadam's academic work, and confirms the financial support that the People's Education Society will provide:

> Mr. Kadam is being financed for the three year duration of the course by the People's Education Society which I founded six years ago. The Society is giving Mr. Kadam adequate sums of money to pay his tuition fees, to buy the necessary books and to defray his living expenses. He will thus have sufficient financial resources to cover the three year course of study.'[61]

Although Vithal graduated from LSE, his return to India was an unhappy one. He subsequently wrote to Lionel Robbins, Professor of Economics, speaking of the difficult working conditions at Siddharth College of Commerce and Economics, where he was employed as a tutor.

> Ever since I was told by the successor to Dr B. R. Ambedkar as chairman, People's Education Society that I had better leave the Society's employ, I have been feeling very low—and anxious to get some other employment.[62]

He was waiting for Ambedkar's visit to Bombay to discuss the difficulties with him, but unfortunately Ambedkar did not live to make the visit. It seems likely that there were other students Ambedkar arranged to support at LSE, in keeping with the mission of the People's Education Society, but only this case could be traced through individual student files.

The association of Ambedkar with LSE has continued to be marked and memorialised in contemporary times. In 1994 the Federation of Ambedkarite and Buddhist Organisations UK (FABO UK) gifted to LSE a bust of Ambedkar, sculpted by Brahmesh V. Wagh and cast in bronze. The Wagh firm of sculptors in Mumbai were renowned for their sculptures of significant figures in twentieth-century Indian politics. At the time of writing (2022), the bust, unveiled on 14 April 1994 by LSE Director John Ashworth, is housed in the LSE Atrium Gallery. Many visitors come to see the bust and often garland the figure. The student newspaper *The Beaver* reported an event where Professor Amartya Sen garlanded the statue during India Week.[63]

The School also received a portrait of Ambedkar in 1972 which was gifted by the Dr Ambedkar Memorial Committee of Great Britain. The portrait depicts Ambedkar wearing a white suit and holding a copy of the Indian constitution in a book-lined interior, signed by G. S. Nagdeve on 23 October 1970. The portrait was presented to the School on 25 September 1973 by the Dr Ambedkar Memorial Committee of Great Britain. The event in the Old Theatre was attended by Mr M. Rasgotra, Acting Indian High Commissioner, and the Venerable Dr H. Saddatissa, Head of London Buddhist Vihara. The portrait was accepted by the School's Director, Sir Walter Adams, who said that 'by his work as a scholar and as a man of action, he [Ambedkar] helped decisively to shape the development of India in this century'.[64]

This interest in Ambedkar has also resulted in the opening up of more archival materials around his life in London. The LSE Library recently produced an online exhibition of Ambedkar's student file celebrating his time at the School, and released the entirety of the student file for the first time to the general public.[65] It was the Library's most viewed online exhibition,[66] reflecting the global impact of Ambedkar and interest in his life at the School. An associated round-table event[67] exploring Ambedkar's contemporary relationship to studies in caste, constitution and gender received nearly 2,000 views, LSE Library's highest viewed event online at the time of writing.

Ambedkar's LSE career and links with the School are both an example of the impact and experience of an exceptional student as well as an illustration of the experiences of many of his contemporaries seeking their education beyond India in the interwar period. He shared their experience of pursuing an education in Britain to establish and develop a career in India. Several of his contemporaries would go on to have significant political or academic careers, though few to the same extent as Ambedkar. Ambedkar's student file indicates that he maintained his connection with the School during his political and campaigning career, but his early death in 1956 perhaps led to his influence and importance to LSE being forgotten, at least until a few decades later. The renewed connection with FABO UK and recent physical and online exhibitions have revived interest in the School's Ambedkar connections, and his bust now stands on one of the School's busiest thoroughfares. He was neither the first nor the last Indian student to study at LSE, but he was among those who have made the greatest impact on the world.

3

# AMBEDKAR AS LAWYER

## FROM LONDON TO INDIA IN THE 1920s

*Steven Gasztowicz KC*

Many people may think it possible to imagine what it was like for an ordinary citizen to live in England, and indeed London, in the 1920s, when B. R. Ambedkar was studying to be a barrister there. Some idea of this can be formed from TV, films, books or documentaries. But what was it like for someone like Ambedkar to study for the Bar at that time, and what did that, and becoming a barrister, actually involve? And how did it then shape him, the legal and other work that he did, and his achievements? Ambedkar's legal training and the effect it had on him seem never to have been examined in any detail by historians, though there is valuable learning available in relation to his early career in the law in India.[1] This chapter looks at Ambedkar's legal training and his subsequent achievements from the perspective of a barrister belonging to the same Inn of Court, who came to know about his extraordinary career unexpectedly, in a way that Ambedkar himself would have approved of—as the result of a legal case.

Ambedkar was completely unknown to me when I took on the case relating to 10KHR. The history we learn is inevitably only that which we are exposed to. My previous lack of knowledge of him is a matter of regret to me, not only because of my ignorance, but because I feel he would have been a source of inspiration, in particular when I was thinking of embarking on, and then actually commencing, a career at the Bar. My sense of history has always helped me as a barrister. When starting off, I always preferred appearing in the old courtrooms—with their poor acoustics, cramped seats, dark wood and cavernous rooms—rather than in the modern purpose-built courtrooms. This may seem very strange. However, as a barrister, you have not only to solve the legal problems of your cases but to deal with other worries as well—such as how you are going to manage before a difficult judge, whether there was a question you should have asked a witness but may have missed, whether the judge, or jury if there is one, will simply go wrong, and so on. The old courtrooms provided reassurance in my early days because I knew that so many barristers before me had sat in what was now my seat, looked at the same panelled bench, and faced similar problems or worse, and got through them, often with great success.

Knowing of B. R. Ambedkar and the enormous obstacles he overcame, and the achievements he had despite them, would have offered even greater reassurance and inspiration. At every unexpected turn of the 10KHR case itself, and subsequently, I have thought back to Ambedkar and the minuscule nature of my own problems as a lawyer compared to the challenges he faced. Having learnt about him, I was also determined to win the case for him, if humanly possible, whatever the difficulties. Looking at the legal training and experiences of Ambedkar should provide not just reassurance but great inspiration, not only for lawyers but for people in a whole array of other occupations and ways of life.

### *Legal Training*

I will begin by considering what it was like training for the Bar in the 1920s, and in particular what it was like for Ambedkar as a student doing so. This was, of course, an instrumental stage in the formation of his views, and in the development and sharpening of the skills he needed subsequently. Ambedkar was admitted as a student at Gray's Inn in 1916. Every student and every qualified barrister must be a member of an Inn of Court. The name 'Inn of Court' goes back to ancient times—when the novice learnt the law and procedure from practising barristers over meals in the Inn to which they belonged. There are (and were in the 1920s) four Inns of Court—Inner Temple, Middle Temple, Lincoln's Inn and Gray's Inn. These are all clustered around the area of the law courts in the Strand in London. Gray's Inn itself is just off the street known as Holborn at the top of Chancery Lane—the most northern of the four Inns of Court, and closest therefore to 10KHR, where Ambedkar lived during his time studying the law.

By the 1920s the four Inns had combined to establish the Council of Legal Education as an entity to run lecture courses for students of all of them, with examinations at the end, as one would expect. Membership of an Inn of Court remained an essential requirement, however, and, as well as studying for their exams, it remained necessary for students to 'keep Terms' by eating a certain number of formal dinners in their Inn, as I shall explain shortly. The decision as to which Inn to join has always been entirely a matter for the aspiring barrister. Ambedkar chose to become a member of Gray's Inn, which I naturally think is the best, as it is also my own Inn! Inevitably, everyone thinks their own Inn of Court is the best, though in truth each differs only in minor respects in strengths and weaknesses, most of which are not apparent when you join. I chose Gray's Inn for the simple reason that a friend of mine at university told me her father was a member of that Inn. She had already joined it, and it seemed to me as good a choice as any other and, having no contacts of my own at the Bar, it meant we could go there together to dine.

It is not known why Ambedkar chose Gray's Inn, but it was probably for similarly insignificant reasons. Many of the records of Gray's Inn were destroyed in bombing in the Second World War, which has made much of his journey to becoming a barrister difficult to piece together. Any missing records would not have been likely to have given any clue as to why he joined the Inn, however. It has never been necessary to state a reason, other than wanting to become a barrister, and there is no indication from any source that he received any financial assistance from the Inn. The likelihood is that Gray's Inn was either recommended to Ambedkar by someone in India or in America, where he was studying prior to joining it, or he chose it simply because it seemed as good as any other.

The records the Inn does retain show that Ambedkar was admitted as a student member in 1916. The entry from the *Index of Admissions* reads as follows:

> Nov. 1916, Ambedkar, Bhimrao Ramji, B.A. Bombay, M.A. Columbia; of Baroda State, India; the youngest son of Ramji Ambedkar of Bombay, deceased.

It is of note that the Inn recorded the name of the father of the person admitted. Nowadays, no relevance would be seen in the identity of the father. At the time, however, it would have been expected that those admitted were the 'right sort', namely gentlemen proud of their backgrounds. And I mean 'men', as no women were at that time admitted by any of the Inns (and so women were unable to become barristers). I shall return to this below.

When Ambedkar applied for admission to the Inn he provided a letter from the Secretary for Indian Students at the India Office in Whitehall. This is dated 8 November 1916 and confirms that he had at that time just arrived from America, where he had obtained his MA from Columbia University.[2] He was only able to be admitted after being certified by the Secretary to be a 'gentleman of respectability' suitable for admission as a student of the Inn, as required by the Consolidated Regulations of the Inns of Court then in force.[3] What the records of the Inn do not reveal is that when in 1916 Ambedkar wanted to train as a barrister in London, he also proposed to study for, and obtain, a higher degree in economics from LSE at the same time. This was because—aside from his interest in economics—the scholarship he had obtained from the State of Baroda in order to go to America was on the basis of undertaking such study.

They also do not reveal that upon completion of his studies at Columbia, the Baroda Diwan had refused a requested extension of two years to his scholarship to enable this to be done. Ambedkar had appealed to the Maharaja. However, before the Diwan could reply, Ambedkar had left for London with very little money, and as one biographer states, travelled 'ticketless on the train, convincing the people with whom he had arranged to stay to pay for the carriage that brought his luggage'.[4] This was not the normal route by which a gentleman came to Gray's Inn as a student barrister in 1916—either physically or economically.

Happily, a couple of days after Ambedkar's arrival in England he was awarded a one-year extension to his scholarship. It was with the benefit of this that he registered at LSE to study for an MSc in economics and registered at the same time at Gray's Inn as a student member. However, a further extension of his scholarship was refused and he was forced to return to India, unqualified. After an unhappy period of service for the Baroda Government (a requirement of his scholarship) and work in an academic post in Bombay, by scrimping and saving, and with the benefit of a small gift from the Maharaja of Kolhapur, he managed through his determination to return to London in July 1920.[5] He therefore returned to his legal studies at Gray's Inn by this further unconventional route.

Where he lived in England following his return is not completely known, but was pieced together as far as possible for the 10KHR Inquiry. He stayed initially at an Indian Government hostel at 21 Cromwell Road in South Kensington (which is now the French Consulate) before moving briefly to 95 Brook Green. From correspondence used by some biographers, he does not appear to have enjoyed his time in at least one of these places.[6] By February 1921 at the latest, however—and probably earlier—he was living in a room at 10KHR in North London, which he continued to do during 1921 and 1922 while he was studying for the Bar, walking the three miles to Gray's Inn from this modest house in the suburbs.

As I have mentioned, in order to be called to the Bar (i.e. to qualify as a barrister), Ambedkar had not only to pass the required legal examinations but also to 'keep Terms' in Gray's Inn, which meant eating a certain number of dinners in its wood-panelled Hall. This may seem a bizarre notion to modern readers, but is neither so bizarre nor so archaic as may be thought. The requirement to eat a certain number of dinners in the student's Inn of Court, in addition to passing the exams, was a requirement of eligibility to be called to the Bar, and continued until 2016, though reduced in extent. The advantages of it will, I hope, become apparent shortly.

In the early 1920s, Ambedkar, as a member at the same time of LSE—which was part of the University of London—was required to 'keep Terms' by dining in Gray's Inn Hall at least three days during each of twelve legal terms (which broadly coincided with the university terms). These were formal dinners held on specified days, presided over by the 'Masters of the Bench', or 'Benchers'—judges or senior barristers who were members of the Inn elected by the existing Benchers to join their number as Governors of the Inn. Dinners were eaten at long oak tables (forty or fifty feet in length), seated on benches either side of them, with four or five rows of such tables running in parallel down the length of the hall. Students and barristers dined together, and each group of four members (two opposite two) constituted a mess and were expected to toast each other. The judges and senior barristers who were Masters of the Bench dined on the Bench table running horizontally across the head of the rows of longer tables at the top of the Hall, often mixing after dinner.

The Consolidated Regulations of the Inns of Court of the 1920s required that, in order for a dinner to qualify, the student had to be present 'at the grace before dinner, during the whole of the dinner, and until the concluding grace shall have been said'. Otherwise the dinner would not count. Missing one of the dinners would have meant their Call to the Bar having to be deferred by a term, until the required number of 'Terms' had been kept—in other words, another three dinners eaten in Hall (or six if the applicant was no longer a member of one of the specified universities by then).

What Ambedkar thought of this requirement is not known. As an outsider seeking to come into the profession, I myself initially faced these dinners with some trepidation, even in the company of my friend, in the 1980s. It is likely, therefore, that Ambedkar, more worldly wise though he already was, would also have done so. For someone like Ambedkar, however, as for myself, these dinners would probably have been invaluable in certain respects despite any initial feelings of discomfort. Only at the Bar did students from the very beginning, whatever their background, have the opportunity to mix with senior members of the profession informally in a setting where they were not just able, but compelled, to talk to them. They would also meet their own contemporaries, wherever they might be from, over a meal, with a resulting exchange of information and views.[7]

Even in the 1980s, when I was studying, and since that time, though dining in an ancient hall was perceived in some quarters as elitist, it in fact had some value in levelling out the advantages some may have had from knowing members of the profession, and knowing the way things were done, which others did not have. It meant being required to mix with people very different from oneself and enabled students to learn informally from barristers, judges and fellow students. There was no requirement to discuss any particular things, but, aside from other subjects—helpful in life and to the formation of ideas—legal talk would invariably take place, ranging from how things were done in practice (rather than in the books) to what difficulties people had faced in their careers and how they had dealt with them, and what the best and worst parts of the English legal system currently were.

Dining (the 'keeping of Terms') also fostered a collegiate atmosphere and the ethos of 'doing the right thing' when practising—learning the best traditions of the Bar, which the students were expected to follow. Though there were obviously severe racial and other prejudices in England at the time, members of the Inn from the colonies who were training in the law in order to return to their own countries to practise were commonplace in the 1920s and probably faced less prejudice there than elsewhere. An Indian member of the Inn would have been known to have been certified a 'gentleman' and the collegiate atmosphere seems likely to have generated greater acceptance by other members than in many institutions.

Ambedkar obviously needed to gain a sound knowledge of the principles of the law itself, which he would have learnt from the Council of Legal Education's lectures. However, he may have learnt almost as much from the dinner table as from the lecture hall, about the best and worst aspects of the English legal system as it operated in practice. It seems unlikely that someone who was to be the architect of the Indian Constitution and one of its law officers should not have benefited from knowing what was going on in practice in the English legal system, and to judge what the best and worst aspects of it were. It also seems unlikely that—as the person who enabled the 'Untouchables' to enter important positions in Indian society—he would not also have been encouraged by the sort of 'levelling up', as we may now call it, that the dinners offered. Finally, the meals themselves would also have been welcome to Ambedkar who was otherwise living a frugal life.[8] They were cheap, even though they were substantial, and in the 1920s included both wine (with a decanter for each 'mess' of four members) and a silver tankard of beer for any member who wanted it. Those who did want it benefited from that, and even those who did not drink took the tankard so that they were then very popular to sit with during dinner, when their allocation could be utilised by the rest of the mess.

In terms of Ambedkar's formal studies, in the early 1920s the Bar student needed to attend the Council of Legal Education's lectures on the following subjects:

I: Roman Law, Jurisprudence, International Law, and the Conflict of Laws
II: Constitutional Law (English and Colonial) and Legal History
III: English Law (Civil and Criminal) and Equity.

Examinations were then required to be passed in each of the following papers (as set out in the *Consolidated Regulations of the Inns of Court* of the Council of Legal Education):[9]

Part I
Section I. Roman Law
Section II. Constitutional Law (English and Colonial) and Legal History
Section III. Criminal Law and Procedure, and
Section IV. Real Property and Conveyancing
*or*
Hindu and Mohammedan Law
*or*
Roman-Dutch Law
(student to choose ONE of the options in Section IV)

Part II
(The Final Examination)
Section I. Common Law
Section II. Equity
Section III. The Law of Evidence and Civil Procedure
Section IV. A General Paper on the subjects of I, II and III of this Part.

It is not actually known which of the optional parts Ambedkar chose, though it obviously seems likely to have been 'Hindu and Mohammedan Law'.

Lectures on Hindu law, as set out in the early 1920s Calendars of the Council of Legal Education, covered:

> Its Application, Sources and Works of Authority—Marriage-Adoption-Duties and Right of Father, Guardianship, Maintenance—The Joint Family—Partition—Inheritance—Stridhan, and Women's Property—Right of Reversioners—Religious Endowments.

Lectures on Mohammedan Law covered the following:

> History and Sources—Marriage and Divorce—Guardianship—Maintenance—Inheritance—Wills—Alienations *inter vivos*—Religious and Charitable Endowments—*Wakf*—Pre-emption.

In addition, it was necessary to study 'Customary law: Its effects on Hindu and Mohammedan Law'. That these were part of the courses offered shows that the Inns were accustomed to having students from India, and took into account the particular needs of those intending to practise there.

### *Ambedkar's Contemporaries*

In the period of 1880 to the 1920s, when Ambedkar studied law, the National Indian Association census of students showed that Law was the most popular course of study among Indians in Britain.[10] In contrast to Ambedkar, however, the social background of nearly all other Indian students studying for the Bar was cosmopolitan and/or high caste.[11] The Lee Warner Committee Report reinforced a policy of government surveillance of Indian students in the first two decades of the twentieth century. It seems that in contrast to what may be termed the earlier India House radicals, Ambedkar may in consequence have kept his head below the parapet during the period of his legal training. Shyamaji Krishnavarma, founder of the radical Indian House in Highgate, was himself a Barrister of the Inner Temple. However, there is no evidence that Ambedkar took part in such organisations, and he seems likely not to have done so because of his personal circumstances, although it is known that he continued to develop his own political activities around the early Dalit movement and his journal, *Mooknayak*.

Ambedkar's predecessors in the Inns of Court included early Congress notables and social reformers from elite backgrounds such as Behari Lal Gupta, Syed Hasan Imam, Womesh Chunder Bonnerjee, Sarat Chadra Bose and Feroz Khan Noon. Figures from India who preceded him at Gray's Inn included Snehansu Kanta Acharya, a son of the Maharaja of Mymensingh who went on to become a leading communist despite his family wealth,[12] and Gurusaday Dutt, the illustrious social reformer and founder of the *Volkisch* Bratachari Movement.[13]

Mithan Tata joined Lincoln's Inn on 13 April 1919 and was called to the Bar on 26 January 1923, and was therefore an immediate contemporary.[14] Like Ambedkar, in 1919 Tata gave evidence before the Southborough Commission on Indian Reforms. While Ambedkar was keen to see better representation for 'Untouchables', Tata and her mother pushed against the apparent exclusion of women from the franchise. Like Ambedkar, she promoted the rights of disadvantaged Indian subjects—in this case women. And not unlike Ambedkar, once she returned to India, she made use of her training and experiences in London to advance her cause (in her case promoting education and social legislation through the Tata Institute of Social Work).[15]

### *Call to the Bar*

Following the necessary dining and successful completion of his examinations, Ambedkar was called to the Bar by Gray's Inn on 28

June 1922. Volume XXV of the *Order Books* of the Inn, which relates to this period, contains the following entry:

> June 21, 1922, upon the Petition of Bhimrao Ramji Ambedkar to be called to the Bar, it is moved by Master Keogh and seconded by Master Wilson that he be called to the Bar.

Then, on 28 June 1922, it recorded that:

> It is ordered that ... Bhimrao Ramji Ambedkar [amongst others] ... be called to the Bar and they are hereby published Barristers accordingly.[16]

This would have been a moment of great pride for Ambedkar. He was then entitled to call himself a barrister, or, to give the fuller title in common use then, barrister-at-law. This achievement should also be seen in the context of other social barriers to legal training at this time. Just over two months before this, on 10 May 1922, the very first woman, Ivy Williams, was in fact called to the Bar by the Inner Temple. In the same period, as Chapters 1 and 2 in this volume show, the first Indian woman to study at LSE, Mithan Ardeshir Tata, was also admitted to Lincoln's Inn and was called to the Bar in 1923. In 1918 the Bar Council had at its Annual General Meeting voted 178 to 22 against allowing women to become barristers. This further confirms the narrowness of the Bar at that time. It took an Act of Parliament—the Sex Disqualification (Removal) Act 1919 (which also gave wider rights to women in relation to such things as jury service) to bring about change.[17]

Ivy Williams and Mithan Tata were admitted as students by their Inns in 1920 after the change in the law made by the Act. Though they were members of different Inns of Court (the first woman was not called to the Bar by Gray's Inn until June 1923),[18] the students from all the Inns attended the same Council of Legal Education lectures. Ambedkar would therefore undoubtedly have known of Williams, Tata and their few female compatriots, who for the first time were able as women to enter this profession, even if he did not actually discuss things with them, as he may well have done. Again, it seems likely that this only encouraged Ambedkar in his work on equality in India, and in considering how participation in both the law and society was not preordained and could be changed, whatever the initial resistance. Following his call to the Bar, Ambedkar went on to receive his doctorate in economics from LSE the following year, 1923.

### *From Gray's Inn to India*

Ambedkar then returned to India and set up in practice in a small office of the Social Service League in Bombay. It took him a long time to then get cases because of his caste, and it is likely that he faced more prejudice there than in Gray's Inn.[19] So far as political life in India was concerned, it was from the late nineteenth century onwards dominated by qualified lawyers. There is nothing particularly surprising in this. The Bar attracted, and attracts, those interested in public speaking and trains them in how laws are both made and changed, as well as applied. Indeed, in this, India largely mirrored Britain and other parts of Europe. Leading politicians were often barristers, and notable among them in the 1920s were people such as F. E. Smith (a Conservative), Patrick Hastings (Labour) and Edward Carson (an Irish Unionist).

What was different about Ambedkar, however, was that unlike most of his Indian lawyer-politician contemporaries, or British equivalents, he came from a low-caste family unexperienced in legal or governmental matters, with no capital behind him. This was in sharp contrast to others—most famously, Gandhi (who had gone to Inner Temple), Jinnah (of Lincoln's Inn) and Nehru (of Inner Temple). Nehru, for example, was born to a wealthy and politically powerful high-caste family.[20] The high social background of most Indian students reading for the Bar has been referred to above. In contrast, Ambedkar, with no contacts, took a brave decision to train as a lawyer, obtaining his own funding and employment to finally achieve this, with it being speculative as to whether he would actually succeed in a legal or similar career.

In several speeches Ambedkar later gave, he said that what attracted him to qualifying and practising as a lawyer was that it was the only profession in colonial India in which a person could be completely independent of the state.[21] Perhaps unsurprisingly, given the prejudices against his caste and lack of connections, he found it hard to get a practice going. This difficulty in establishing a legal practice was not exclusive to Ambedkar, and many would-be advocates in India had to wait a long time for their first briefs, as indeed many young barristers in England did. However, the difficulties were increased by reason of his 'Untouchable' status and lack of connections.[22] In comparison, Jinnah got going through his connections, with his first case being to represent his uncle, a businessman, in a commercial dispute. Gandhi, though he was considered to have poor oral advocacy skills, also drew upon family networks for legal work in Bombay. Ambedkar's cases were low in both volume and in value in the 1920s. Towards the end of the decade, the *Times of India* reported, in the same edition on 29 January 1929, on Jinnah's appearance in a high-value commercial case and on a low-value breach of trust case (for just twenty-four rupees) brought by a retired schoolteacher who was represented by Ambedkar.[23]

However, Ambedkar clearly had considerable legal skills and it was soon apparent that he was a man of principle. He turned down appointment as a district judge, with promised promotion to the Bombay High Court thereafter, even when he was living in straightened circumstances in a single room. As he later explained in a speech in 1951, he did so because this would have meant an end to carrying things forward in India by independent practice and political activity.[24] He also later turned down a lucrative offer from the Nizam of Hyderabad to become the Chief Justice of that state.[25] His cases inevitably being low value meant that he was encouraged to take 'political' and 'public law' cases which, though generally low paying, were of interest to him, and effectively led to him becoming one of India's first civil rights lawyers. He became a law professor at the same time. In addition to giving him a steady income, this would have kept him clearly focused on legal principles and thinking about how the law might develop.

Ambedkar's first high-profile appearance was as junior defence counsel (the second barrister in a case, who assists 'leading counsel' in the preparation and presentation of it) in the case of Philip Spratt in 1927—a figure who was later involved in the famous Meerut conspiracy case.[26] Spratt, one of the founders of the Communist

Party of India, was charged with the crime of sedition as a result of a pamphlet he had written entitled 'India and China'. In it, Spratt argued that Indians should follow the example of the Chinese and overthrow their foreign masters, who were described as murderers. Perhaps unsurprisingly, this was alleged to cause hatred and incite disaffection with the Government of India. Leading counsel for the defence was F. S. Taleyarkhan. The defence was rather technical in suggesting the pamphlet challenged 'British Imperialism' rather than the 'Government of India', and demanded freedom from foreign rule rather than from the specific legal authorities established by the Government of India Act.[27] With large-scale public support creating a 'sympathy vote' combining with the technical argument, Spratt was ultimately acquitted, to thunderous applause in the courtroom.[28]

It is easy when one starts off in practice to focus just on the technical legal arguments there are in a case, building on knowledge from the legal courses studied and examinations taken. Some—though not all—become aware sooner or later that there is always the human element involved in decision-making as well. No one wants to decide a case in favour of the unsympathetic if they can avoid it, and in India there was a clearly developing political background. His involvement in the Spratt case would have emphasised these things to Ambedkar. He quickly established himself as a 'public law' or 'civil rights' barrister, exemplified in his work as junior defence counsel in this case.[29] In the political arena, Ambedkar was critical of the Communist Party of India, of which Spratt was leader, as being upper-caste dominated and advocating violence, notwithstanding that he agreed with aspects of its economic policy. What he showed in the Spratt case was a willingness to support civil rights regardless of his personal views about those involved or their organisations (for example, in this case, being dominated by high-caste Hindus). In this, he was following the best traditions and ethos of the English Bar in which he had been trained at Gray's Inn, which involved—and involves—taking on cases regardless of one's own personal views of those involved or their organisations.

Ambedkar went on to deal with several other high-profile public law cases, building no doubt on what he had learnt as junior counsel in the Spratt case, where he had also watched the case 'leaders' at work, as part of their legal team. In 1934 he took on the defence of the leaders of the trade union known as The All-India Textile Workers Conference, many of whom were also communists.[30] His success here led to him having a strong relationship with trade unionists, and he came to be seen as one of the main lawyers for trade union leaders, whatever their political affiliations.[31] It was also an area where, in the future, his legal skills and political approaches would intersect: for example, in 1938 Ambedkar opposed the Bombay Congress Government's Industrial Disputes Act by leading a strike of Dalit workers as part of the Independent Labour Party.[32]

Ambedkar's legal skills were not confined to aiding defined sections of the community such as trade unionists, however. In the 'Samaj Swasthya' case, Ambedkar defended Professor R. D. Karve in relation to charges of obscenity resulting from his publication of the journal of this name. Karve was the son of Maharshi Karvem, a famous social reformer who had established India's first birth control clinic. The journal considered sexual questions in an open way. Ambedkar argued that under the Indian Penal Code the test for obscenity was that the publication would 'tend to deprave or corrupt a person who may in ordinary circumstances come to read it', and that no one would be likely to come to read this publication other than those concerned with sexual hygiene and that there was no law against dealing with such issues. This was a classic case on freedom to address taboo topics. Although the defence failed, both at first instance and on appeal, the fact that Ambedkar undertook it—and was chosen to do so—further demonstrates his promotion of civil liberties by egalitarian argument in the courts.[33]

Interestingly, in England the legal test for obscenity was then similar, and it took until the 'Lady Chatterley's Lover' case in 1960 for freedom of expression for legitimate purposes to be accepted by courts to outweigh perceived damage to public morals. This followed a specific defence on the grounds of publication 'in the interests of science, literature, art or learning' being introduced by the Obscene Publications Act 1959.[34] Both of the defence barristers prepared to take on that case were also active politically. One—Jeremy Hutchinson—became a very prominent civil rights barrister. The other—Gerald Gardiner—a near-contemporary of Ambedkar, who was called to the Bar by Inner Temple in 1925, went on to became Lord Chancellor, the politician responsible for the English legal system. Though from very different backgrounds to that of Ambedkar,[35] and living in a country in many respects very different from colonial India, obvious parallels can be seen, though neither faced the challenges or had the constitutional achievements that Ambedkar did.

Departing from his role as a courtroom lawyer, Ambedkar nevertheless made use of his legal skills in more direct political activities. One of the most famous examples of this was his early leadership of a satyagraha group in accessing water from the Chavdar tank in 1927. A right to these public resources was in theory guaranteed by the Bombay legislature but was rarely enforced. They were met by force, and upper-caste Hindus filed a court action on the basis that the tank was private property. Ambedkar was this time himself a defendant. In response, he publicly burned the *Manusmiriti* (one of the Hindu religious books), indicating he would obey the laws of the secular state whilst condemning Brahminical Hindu law. The Bombay High Court determined that merely because the plaintiffs could show there was a long-standing custom of excluding Dalits from the use of the tank did not mean there was no legal right for those of the lower caste to use it. This was now a rights victory for those of lower caste, following Ambedkar's own involvement in direct political action.[36]

In such instances, Dr Ambedkar's legal learning and abilities were used by him in support of, and combined with, his political activity for Dalits. He identified legal bases on which he and others could and did take practical action to advance their situation. Subsequently, he became part of a movement to open up the Brahmin-run Bhuleshwar temple which had a tank attached to it. In the resultant court case, it was held that the temple and its priest were maintained by gifts from the public and communal funds, and it was ordered that the temple be placed in the receivership of the court until the state organised its administration. However, the trustees of the temple then failed to take action to open up the temple to Dalits, using the judgment to say that the state was now responsible for matters, not them, and nothing was actually done.[37] Ambedkar realised that here the use of the law alone had not resulted in practical gains, and he advocated direct action. Had the Dalits then taken control of the temple, it may have meant that the slow-acting state processes would have resulted in a new status quo—in practice a result that would be no better than that of the recalcitrant trustees, until a properly organised administration of the temple had been achieved. This showed the combination of Ambedkar's legal training and strategic thinking.

However, whilst a number of Dalit organisations took up Ambedkar's call for direct action following legal success, and attempted to force their way into the temple, they were met by violence and were unsuccessful. By 1932, just three years later, the combination of events on the streets and legislative compromises led to five major temples, including Bhuleshwar, being opened up to everyone.[38] Ambedkar's skills as a lawyer led to successful legal action, which led to political action, which led to the achievement of his aim of securing an improvement in the position of the Dalits. In both the Chavdar and Bhuleshwar cases, Ambedkar was now active directly in the political arena as a result of using the law as a tool. Later, he was to be one of the great influences in extending this theme of legal access to religious sites and specifically water bodies in the Fundamental Rights of the 1950 Constitution: Article 15 (2b), which specifically bans untouchability in relation to tanks and bathing ghats.[39]

As well as his legal work on high-profile cases, Ambedkar obviously undertook a large number of low-profile cases, such as claims for workmen's compensation. Although of little general interest, it would be of great importance to his clients, to whose lives such work could make a great difference. He gave advice or representation for a low fee, or pro bono where necessary, and he allowed clients who came to Bombay for court hearings to stay with him in his own small apartment where necessary. He also undertook appeals in cases involving the death penalty, going on to advocate the abolition of it in the Constituent Assembly.

It is not for his day-to-day work as a lawyer that Ambedkar is most remembered. This was, however, work of importance, making a difference on the ground, both in individual cases and in helping, encouraging and achieving the advancement of what we would now call civil rights and equality, and correcting both legal and social injustices. It no doubt gave him strengthened purpose in endeavouring by legislative means to achieve greater equality and social justice.

Later in his career, Ambedkar was clearly able to build on these experiences both in his undertaking of high-level political roles and by infusing them with his sense of legal rights and social justice. In 1942 Ambedkar became a member of the Executive Council of the Governor-General of India, at the invitation of the Governor-General, Lord Linlithgow. This was noted with pride by Gray's Inn. The Treasurer of the Inn, Noel Middleton KC, wrote to Ambedkar on 14 October 1942 (addressing him by surname alone, as was then customary between members of the Bar), saying:

> Dear Ambedkar,
>
> The Masters of the Bench have observed with great pleasure that you have become a member of the Executive Council of the Governor-General of India. They desire me to congratulate you upon this appointment and to express to you their gratification that so high an office had been assumed by a Member of Gray's Inn.
>
> Yours sincerely,
> Noel Middleton.

Despite the rush of official matters and the delay that their resolution inevitably caused, Ambedkar, ever polite, did not overlook to reply, and wrote asking the Treasurer to 'convey my sincere thanks to the Bench'. As a member of the Council, and of the Constituent Assembly to which he was elected, he drew up plans for social security and labour reforms, drawing no doubt on his learning and beliefs as an economist as well as a lawyer. Following Indian independence in August 1947, Ambedkar was appointed by Nehru as India's first Minister for Law and Justice and was elected chairman of the committee drafting the Indian Constitution.

The committee led by Ambedkar had the difficult task of producing a coherent and robust constitution suitable for such a vast and demographically complex nation state. Ambedkar dedicated himself to the task and spent many long hours working on it. Though he had to navigate political waters, the Constitution of Free India, as it became, is to this day considered to be heavily influenced by his approach as one of the principal legal minds of India.

Ambedkar had been trained in the principles of the English Constitution at the Council of Legal Education, though he also, of course, had experience of living and studying economics in America. The Constitution he drafted provided for a parliamentary system of government on the British model—in preference to the American presidential form—and with a single judiciary. This was not purely his idea; it was building on India's own past, and there were political considerations in favour of it. However, he argued that even though it may mean less stability, such a system provided a greater degree of responsibility and accountability.[40]

Perhaps most important in his work on the Constitution was his realisation that social justice for everyone could not be secured unless it was enshrined in the Constitution. The latter could be designed with the aim of eliminating inequality, and ensuring that the State was subject to the rule of law as declared by an independent judiciary. He realised—as no one who had been involved in the Bhuleshwar temple case could have failed to have realised—that rights without effective remedies were of no use, and he ensured the Constitution would not just be a set of academic words. The members of the drafting committee were of course not entirely free agents. They had to work with other agencies, and Nehru as first Prime Minister and Sardar Vallabhbhai Patel as Home Minister had the final word on matters. However, under Ambedkar's influence fundamental rights were more comprehensively set out and safeguarded in the Indian Constitution than in any other Constitution in the world. He considered this necessary to ensure not only security and equality of citizenship, but also to maintain basic standards of conduct, justice and fairness. These were all qualities which would have been reinforced by his time at Gray's Inn and his study of the English legal system.

In connection with his work on constitutional matters and legal rights, Ambedkar subsequently worked on bills to give greater rights to women and collectively made up the Hindu Code Bills. However, he faced staunch opposition, and Nehru, who initially supported him, failed to press reforms through at that time. As a result of this, coupled with refusals to take class reform further and other matters, Ambedkar, a man of principle, resigned. He said in his resignation letter that 'To leave inequality between class and class, between sex and sex, which is the heart of Hindu Society untouched [and] to go on passing legislation relating to economic problems is to make a farce of the Constitution and to build a palace on a dung heap'.[41]

The economist in him seems by this time to have been subservient to the lawyer and social rights worker, but in truth both economics and the law were for him the means of achieving social justice. It is tempting to think that on this occasion he had failed, and this was true so far as immediate reform to give women rights was concerned. However, his work laid the foundation for a series of Acts which eventually secured passage in 1955 and 1956, including the Hindu Marriage Act 1955 and the Hindu Succession Act 1956.

### *Acknowledgment of Achievements and Inspiration for Lawyers*

Obviously, Ambedkar has so many more aspects to his work and achievements than those I have referred to in this chapter, but his legal training and work was at the heart of, and enabled, much of what he did in other spheres of work. Though Ambedkar's achievements deserve greater publicity in Britain (although he would himself have shied away from it), Gray's Inn remains rightly proud of him—as should lawyers everywhere, as he demonstrates the best of their profession. Since 1974 a portrait of Ambedkar (showing him seated alongside a copy of the Indian Constitution) has hung in Gray's Inn, for most of the time on the Treasury (i.e. executive office) staircase. Over the years the Inn has received many requests by Indian students to view this work. It seems they, like me, found inspiration and encouragement from others before them in the law—in this case from a great figure, who worked so hard, in such difficult circumstances, to achieve so much by use of his legal training and the law.

In 1997, at the north end of the Walks (as the gardens of Gray's Inn are known) a catalpa tree was planted in Ambedkar's memory by Lord Bingham, the Lord Chief Justice. In December 2016, to mark the centenary of Dr Ambedkar's admission to the Inn as a student, an evening event was held in Gray's Inn Hall. After an opening by the Treasurer (senior Bencher), and an address by the Indian Minister of State for Social Justice, a lecture was delivered by the acting Indian High Commissioner, HE Mr Dinesh K. Patnaik, entitled 'The Power of Change'. In it, the High Commissioner noted that the Constitution Ambedkar had drafted had been described by another great civil libertarian, Nelson Mandela, as 'the greatest safeguard of human liberty'. He went on—in the presence of Lady Hale, a member of Gray's Inn and the first female Supreme Court Justice (and later its first female president)—to quote Ambedkar's statement that 'one can measure the progress of a community by the progress of its women'.[42]

Following the lecture, a new portrait of Ambedkar—a gift from the Indian government—was unveiled, which now hangs proudly in the Large Pension Room, where the Benchers gather before and after dinner in Hall and when conducting the Inn's business. In June 2021 a further portrait was unveiled—to hang in the newly named Ambedkar Room in the Inn. The name of the room prominently listed on the board outside the door of the building may cause more people to enquire about him.[43]

More lawyers, and, more particularly law students, wherever they study (and indeed people everywhere), should know of Ambedkar's life and achievements, as a source of help, inspiration and courage to them, particularly in their early years. I am so grateful and honoured to have been involved in preparing and presenting the appeal for a permanent memorial/museum to Ambedkar at the house in London where he lodged whilst studying for the Bar. Without it, I may never even have heard of Ambedkar, who has, since I have learnt about him, been a source of inspiration to me, as he has been to others for all the reasons set out in this book; but in particular, for me, as a lawyer whose trials, tribulations and achievements were so very great. I have no greater pride in the success of any case I have dealt with than in the success of this one.

4

# AMBEDKAR, LONDON AND THE FIRST ROUND TABLE CONFERENCE

*Jesús F. Cháirez-Garza*

This chapter analyses the early attempts of B. R. Ambedkar to internationalise the problem of untouchability, by looking at his participation in the first session of the Indian Round Table Conference (RTC) held in London during the winter months of late 1930 and early 1931. The RTC was a series of encounters, over three years, between Indian and British politicians to discuss the future constitutional structure of this colony, including aspects such as federalism, the distribution of political representation, and the division of powers between the central government and the provinces.[1] Of course, while the RTCs were not strictly international events due to the imperial entanglement between Britain and India, I will argue that Ambedkar used these gatherings as a stage to present the plight of Dalits to an international audience beyond the subcontinent. In particular, Ambedkar used the political structures and technologies in place to sustain London as an imperial capital and centre of power to move the question of untouchability from being considered a socio-religious issue into a political question. Such structures secured Ambedkar's status as an 'All-India' political leader and permitted him to present his ideas to the international press, particularly newspapers based in the US.

For Ambedkar, London not only represented access to British political figures who had an important say about the future of Dalits, but the city also became a space where the rules of caste could be relaxed and where he could interact with Indian politicians face to face, on relatively equal terms. It is in this spatial context where we can observe Ambedkar's exchanges with people such as the British Prime Minister Ramsay MacDonald, Winston Churchill, the Aga Khan, M. A. Jinnah, B. S. Moonje and Gandhi, among many others. Equally, it is in this context that Ambedkar was able to gain unprecedented electoral concessions for the Depressed Classes in the form of the Communal Award of 1932. Despite all of this, it would be naive to idealise London as a place purely enabling the Dalit cause. The doors which opened to Ambedkar in the city came at a cost. The debate about Dalits being a minority in need of political protection was allowed to take place only because it justified the colonial government's presence in India. When the Dalit question stopped being a useful argument to delay independence, it was abandoned by the colonial government. This chapter uses Ambedkar's time in London as a metaphor reflecting his relationship with the imperial government. London and the empire seemed to represent access to the inner circles of political power to a future away from caste discrimination for Dalits. Yet, in crucial political moments, London and the empire would turn their back on Dalits and Ambedkar.

This chapter has four main sections. First, I begin with an explanation on the importance of looking at the concept of the international as an analytical tool to understand Ambedkar's political thought. Throughout his career, Ambedkar continuously made calls to international actors hoping to make untouchability more visible. With this, Ambedkar hoped international organisations such as the League of Nations would help Dalits to secure political protections due to their status as a minority. While Ambedkar's political orientation was quite fluid and changed dramatically over time, his wish of making untouchability a matter of international concern was a constant. The second section offers a brief political contextualisation of the late 1920s and early 1930s colonial India. This was a time of constant political experimentation and transformation. New debates and theories about what or who constituted a political minority in India were a feature of this period. In the same way, the constitutional structure of India was changing constantly and a number of options seemed possible whether it was dyarchy, a federation or dominion status. Such debates forced political groups to imagine their future through multiple scenarios and complicated political alliances. Such debates allowed Ambedkar to present his ideas about the political representation of Dalits to a wider audience.

The third section looks at London as place that permitted Ambedkar to move in a political circle relatively free of caste limits. This is done through an exploration of Ambedkar's letter to Bhaurao Gaikwad,[2] one of his close associates at this time, and through an examination of a series of articles published by *The New York Times* about Ambedkar's involvement in the first RTCs. Both sets of sources underscore the importance of London's space in Ambedkar's quest to present untouchability as a problem of an international character. The fourth section focuses on Ambedkar's intervention in the RTC, which came in the form of a written memorandum establishing his vision about the constitutional and electoral protections Dalits should be awarded in a future constitution in India. This was an ingenious and interesting document, drawing from multiple countries' constitutions, in which Ambedkar established a tangible plan for the abolition of untouchability and the recognition of Dalits as an independent political minority. While Ambedkar's role in the first RTC would be overshadowed by Gandhi a year later, this essay shows how the former was relatively successful in embedding untouchability as an international problem and in instituting Dalits as a separate political community.

### *The Importance of Internationalism*

In recent years, there have been numerous studies attempting to historicise India in a global context. Such efforts have been quite diverse and have included histories of labour, global revolutions and intellectual history. This turn towards the global, and to some extent the international, has offered us new insights into the lives of indentured workers and the lives of the Indian diaspora across the world, whether this was in Africa, Asia or the United States. Similarly, scholars such as Kris Manjapra, Maia Ramnath and Benjamin Zachariah have recovered life stories of peripatetic Indians attempting to bring the revolution to the subcontinent from beyond.[3] Through these works, a new and crisp perspective has emerged about how the different experiments of Indians with anarchism and Marxism, and consolidated movements such as *Ghadar*, are an important strand of Indian communism. Similarly, global intellectual histories led by the work of Chris Bayly, Shruti Kapila, Faisal Devji and Andrew Sartori unveiled Indian interventions on transforming global understandings of liberalism, violence, fraternity and labour.[4] This trend towards the global reflects the impossibility of studying India in isolation. India as a centre of capital, as a political idea and as a new nation state was to some extent a global and an international creation.

While the global origins, legacies and connections of India are now becoming common ground, the international element of such history is not as easily accepted, particularly in regard to the formation of the nation state. The common view is that India could not have international connections due largely to its colonial past. This resulted in the adoption and survival of many structures of governance implemented during the British Raj, such as governmental institutions and constitutional arrangements. Since India, as a colony, was subordinate to Britain when it came to its relationship with other nation states (for example, India's participation in the First and Second World Wars), the 'international' aspect of its history has usually been ignored.[5] However, such views are being questioned by new studies focusing on the creation of international spaces of the political, of international technologies, and of the international rights of Indian minorities, which show how imperialism and internationalism often intersected with one another.

The interactions between imperialism and internationalism may be observed in the recent work of scholars such as Luis Cabrera, Suraj Yengde and Stephen Legg. Cabrera and Yengde have followed Ambedkar's move towards internationalism by examining the latter's effort to present the Dalit plight to the United Nations.[6] Both Cabrera and Yengde emphasise the importance of international organisations as a 'third party' that could intercede for the rights of Dalits in an uncertain political future. In the same way, Ambedkar's correspondence with people like W. E. B. Du Bois is also interpreted by Cabrera and Yengde as evidence of Ambedkar's cosmopolitanism/internationalist outlook which, regardless of its material success, became a set of instructions for contemporary Dalit activists appealing their case to the United Nations. While I agree with the main arguments of Cabrera and Yengde, it is important to note that Ambedkar's internationalism was quite complicated as conservative and imperialist individuals like Churchill and Jan Smuts were also interested in the Dalit cause, something that had less to do with solidarity than with the preservation of imperialism. More importantly, I would like to extend Ambedkar's dealings with internationalism to include his role in the RTCs held in London as they set an important precedent in the way Ambedkar framed his discourse around the question of minority rights and interventionism.

It is here where Legg's work becomes relevant. In his recent major study about the geographies of the international, Stephen Legg, drawing on Fred Halliday, has shown the hybridity of what may be considered India's history of internationalism. Focusing on the RTCs, Legg shows how different approaches towards internationalism (liberal, imperial and radical/national) mixed and interacted in London during these meetings between Indian and British leaders. Legg does not deny the imperial element of these reunions, but he makes a very strong case to show how the RTCs mimicked the structure and format of international conventions of the time, particularly those organised by the League of Nations. Legg unveils how the RTCs were supported by what he calls new 'technologies of state-making' which 'allowed an internally divided sovereign body to function in the international sphere as if it were a singular and coherent form'.[7] In the conferences, India acted both as part of the British Empire and as a state in the making trying to define its internal and external politics, including the relationship between the state and the minorities within it. Apart from such technologies of state-making, the RTCs may also be considered international due to the structures supporting the proceedings of the conferences, including the coverage of the foreign press which treated these meetings as an international affair. In short, Legg shows how the RTCs transformed London into a space for internationalist politics even when such discussion occurred at the heart of the empire, and pre-empted the rise of Indian mass nationalism.

Following Legg, I consider the RTCs as an international event too. Yet, I complement his views in two ways. First, I analyse how the transformation of London as an international space allowed Ambedkar to present his case to a foreign audience and to circumvent the observation of caste rules observed in India. This permitted Ambedkar to enter the highest circles of political power in India and Britain. Second, I examine the discourse used by Ambedkar during the RTCs to imbue the Dalit struggle with an internationalist language. Specifically, I provide a close reading of Ambedkar's memorandum presented in the first iteration of the RTCs entitled 'A Scheme of Political Safeguards for the Protection of the Depressed Classes in the Future Constitution of a Self-governing India'. This scheme was written in London and its content is an amalgam of laws coming from different countries, repurposed by Ambedkar to protect the rights of Dalits. Even at this early stage, Ambedkar wanted to establish untouchability as a problem of international importance. It was through such language and by occupying the international space of the RTCs that Ambedkar emerged as a politician of national stature.

### *Political Context*

Before moving forward, a brief contextualisation is needed to comprehend how Ambedkar became the representative of the Depressed Classes in the RTCs. During this time, Ambedkar was still on the rise as a political figure, and his invitation was not entirely expected as there were other Dalit leaders, such as M. C. Rajah, who had a longer trajectory in the fight for the rights of Dalits.[8] In the same way, to have a Dalit representative at these reunions was not certain as Dalits were often represented by people outside their own community, ranging from colonial officials to high-caste leaders looking to reform Hinduism. However, Ambedkar's inclusion in the RTCs is explained by the combination of the political environment at the time and his qualities as a political leader. First, there was a significant change in the political discourse associated with the rights of Dalits during the 1920s and early 1930s. After the Montagu–Chelmsford reforms of 1919, the Depressed Classes were granted political (indirect) representation, albeit minimal, in the form of nomination. This was an important change as it legally established that this group, which had been previously neglected, had some political interests to defend. After this, the political potential of the Depressed Classes continued to grow as rights were periodically conceded to them. In addition, other groups used the political representation of Dalits to challenge Congress's claims of being the true representatives of all Indians. It was not uncommon for Muslim leaders, non-Brahmins and colonial officials to argue that Dalits were not truly Hindus or supporters of Congress. When Ambedkar arrived on the scene, being somewhat critical of the nationalist movement, he found a receptive audience across the different political groups in Bombay. After Congress's protest against the all-white Simon Commission of 1928, minority leaders, including Ambedkar, found themselves welcomed to the RTCs once Lord Irwin, the Viceroy of India, announced the holding of the conference.[9]

The second element explaining Ambedkar's inclusion in the RTCs relates to his personal qualities and politics. After receiving a PhD from Columbia University and a DSc from LSE, and becoming a barrister at Gray's Inn, Ambedkar became perhaps the Indian with most degrees from western universities of his era, which made him an ideal candidate to participate in a conference covering the constitutional future of India. As I have argued elsewhere, his foreign education illustrates how leaving India, a space organised through caste hierarchies, allowed Ambedkar to surpass the traditional role and status associated with Mahars, something that occurred once again in London during the RTCs. However, Ambedkar's educational credentials and legal expertise were not the only things that made him attractive for the British Raj. His personal politics also played a part. In particular, and despite not being an anti-nationalist, Ambedkar kept his distance from revolutionary individuals abroad, and the nationalist movement in general. Even though Ambedkar moved in some circles frequented by radical nationalists, both in New York and London, his main objective was to complete his education.[10]

He also did not shy away from highlighting the problems within the Congress leadership, particularly the conservative elements dominating Bombay's politics. For instance, after 1927 Ambedkar and his lieutenants began a series of long-term protests against the exclusion of Dalits from Hindu temples in Western India, which gained the attention of the colonial government (see Chapter 5, by Christophe Jaffrelot, in this volume). Ambedkar used this protest to appeal to the British audience in the RTCs. This attitude was noted by the colonial government, and after his participation in the Southborough (Franchise) Committee of 1919, Ambedkar became a frequent attendee and witness for Dalits in a range of central and provincial governmental commissions studying economic, educational, political and constitutional Indian affairs.[11] While he was critical of it, Ambedkar was willing to work with the colonial government if this meant improving the status of his community. As one may expect, the colonial government was happy to entertain Ambedkar too. In what follows, I move to an analysis of Ambedkar's experience in London during the RTCs.

### *London and the Space of the International*

This section looks at the way London's space during the RTCs provided an outlet where Ambedkar was able to present untouchability to an international audience. This segment unveils important information about Ambedkar's hopes for the first conference session based on his letters and private papers. While this first conference has been barely covered, as most of the studies about the RTCs focus on Gandhi's participation in 1931, analysing this event is vital as it illustrates Ambedkar's initial enthusiasm for change and his vision for an optimal type of political representation for Dalits. Indeed, Ambedkar travelled to London believing a positive change was on the horizon. His mission was to make untouchability known throughout the world, and he used the international press coverage surrounding the conference to achieve this. Aware of the time constraints to present his case, Ambedkar began establishing political alliances for his cause from the moment he left Indian soil.

Ambedkar travelled to London on board the RMS *Viceroy of India*. Travelling by sea was already a change of pace and space on how politics were played, for fellow attendees of the RTCs were also on the ship. Ambedkar noted this change while writing to his lieutenant, Bhaurao Gaikwad, explaining how 'the delegates of the R.T.C. are holding meetings to discuss various questions' and that he was 'glad to say that they are very sympathetic to the demands of the D.C. [Depressed Classes]'.[12] At the time Ambedkar was writing this letter, he was not only aiming to gain political representation for the Depressed Classes, he was also in the midst of the Nasik satyagraha, where Gaikwad was taking the lead. Ambedkar's demands were pressing, and establishing political alliances even before the conferences started was crucial. Thus, being confined to the space of the ship, a space somewhat removed of caste observation, allowed Ambedkar to get to know other Indian politicians and present his case extensively.

Once in London, the centrality of the imperial capital and the technologies of state-making allowed Ambedkar to present his ideas to a variety of British politicians. Ambedkar had two priorities: the political representation of Dalits, and securing their entry in the army. To achieve this, he set up a series of meetings and hearings with important personalities in Indian and English politics. First, Ambedkar met with the Secretary and the Under Secretary of State of India, and with George Lansbury, at the time one of the senior leaders of the Labour Party and acting First Commissioner of Works. Ambedkar had lunch with Lansbury and agreed to a meeting with other Labour and Liberal MPs. Ambedkar described these meetings as 'the work of influencing members of Parliament' in order 'to get their support for adult suffrage'. As Labour was in power in Britain at this time, having their support was vital to gain electoral rights for Dalits. Second, Ambedkar was not only interested in electoral rights; his letters to Gaikwad tells us that he 'was working on how best to promote the entry of the D.C. in the military'. For this, Ambedkar prepared a 'memorial' and contacted retired military officers who knew his community. He 'had a long talk ... on the questions of the employment of the D.C. [Depressed Classes] in the Indian Army' with Sir Philip Chetwode, the new Commander in Chief who gave Ambedkar 'a very sympathetic hearing'. Dalit recruitment in the armed forces served as a social mobility strategy for this community and Ambedkar was aware of it. In fact, a great deal of his political supporters were former army soldiers, just like Ambedkar's father. The concentration of power in London allowed Ambedkar to establish new political networks. In the same way, it allowed the international press to follow the activities of a young, active and politically ambitious Ambedkar.[13]

The RTC was covered extensively by the international press. The fate of the biggest colony of the British Empire was at stake, and the outcome of such negotiations could affect the global political order. The press followed the conference attendants through hotels in London trying to get the latest scoop of potential political deals. It was here where Ambedkar's story captured the attention of several newspapers, such as *The New York Times*. Several articles reported the significance of 'the inclusion of the delegate from the "untouchables" in the London conference', as this represented a 'new day for India's 60,000,000 Outcastes'.[14] American journalists were baffled about Ambedkar's educational and professional achievement despite his Dalit background. Indeed, *The New York Times* ran a long piece on Ambedkar where he 'tells of [his] own sufferings' and explains how 'he braved ostracism by teacher and pupils and won degrees at two universities'.[15] Of course, *The New York Times* emphasised that Ambedkar was partly a product of the US due to his education at Columbia. Ambedkar declared to the newspaper that 'The best friends I have had in my life ... were some of my classmates at Columbia and my great professors, John Dewey, James Shotwell, Edwin Seligman and James Harvey Robinson'.[16] The articles also underscored how New York City represented a significant social change in the life of Ambedkar as 'the difference between his physical surroundings on Morningside Heights and his "untouchable" quarters in Bombay was no greater than that between his new social environment and that from which he had come'.[17] Such details not only point to the importance of space as a transformative element in the life of Ambedkar, but also to its significance in transcending caste barriers. While the article portrays New York as an educational haven beyond the scope of untouchability, London became the place where such stories could be recovered and amplified.

To an extent, London became a state of exception where caste norms did not have to be observed religiously and where Dalit politics could emerge. *The New York Times* was particularly interested in how London's spatial features and the RTCs were able to affect ancient caste practices, even in contradictory terms. For instance, the newspaper reported how an orthodox Brahmin, who performed his daily ablutions with 'the waters of the sacred Ganges which have been carried so far from their source', decided to break 'the age-old ban against crossing the dark waters of the ocean' for the sake of India. Not only that, 'sitting in the same conference with Brahmins of princely rank [was] a delegate from the "untouchables"', who in India were 'condemned to menial and degrading occupations, denied access to the interior of temples, compelled to live apart from the rest of the village, who are often excluded from the schools ... whose presence and whose very shadow is regarded as pollution by the high-caste Brahmin'.[18] Similarly, the newspaper reported the details about the dinner party where the Maharajah of Baroda hosted Rao Bahadur Annepu Patro and Ambedkar, and claimed that 'if Indian correspondents had telegraphed it to their home papers it would have been one of the biggest pieces of news coming out of the conference'.[19] Being aware that the Maharaja of Baroda financed Ambedkar's education in the United States, the paper emphasised that this type of public dinner was possible only in London because caste practices were not as strict. Indeed, the paper claims that the Maharaja's financial support to pay for Ambedkar's education in the USA and in England was established discreetly to avoid a backlash due to a breach of caste rules.

> In the meantime the Maharajah of Baroda had heard of [Ambedkar's] scholarship and offered to finance his education abroad. It was the same Maharajah who invited him to dinner the other night at the Hyde Park Hotel in London. But no such hospitality was possible in India, and the news of the Prince's benefaction had to be conveyed to the 'Untouchable' Ambedkar through an intermediary.[20]

In other words, apart from the political changes that the RTCs could bring, the way London's space distorted caste practices was what journalists found most unusual. As the writer and poet Beatrice Barmby put it, 'Of all the wonders that may come out of this gathering this is the greatest'.[21] Aware that he had gained the attention of *The New York Times*, Ambedkar used the platform to convey his goals regarding his fight against untouchability.

Ambedkar's statement to *The New York Times* unveils some of his early views about the implications of untouchability and the best way to resolve it. At this time, Ambedkar was still committed to the project of breaking down 'the barriers against intermarriage and interdining between caste and no-caste'.[22] These efforts were part of Ambedkar's Samaj Samata Sangh (Social Equality League) and reflected a 'traditional' approach towards untouchability focusing on social interaction rather than political power. Interdining and intermarriage were common reform methods endorsed widely in India, even by Congress. While later in his life Ambedkar abandoned this method, especially after the publication of *Annihilation of Caste*,[23] his words to the newspaper show other initial understandings of caste discrimination that remained with him throughout his career, such as establishing untouchability as an international political problem.

Placing untouchability under the international limelight was a key part of Ambedkar's political project. We observe this at different points of his trajectory, such as the RTCs, during the eve of Partition, and even through his search for a religion with a global audience that Dalits could embrace as their own, such as Buddhism. This is why analysing Ambedkar's participation in the RTCs under the scope of the international is important as they offer one of his first sketches on how to imagine untouchability as a problem beyond the borders of India. Ambedkar's first argument related to the sheer quantity of his community. According to Ambedkar, the number of people suffering from this type of discrimination made untouchability a matter of global relevance which could only be resolved with 'nothing less than the aroused opinion of the world'.[24] He then emphasised the importance of international organisations to resolve this issue, noting that 'the plight of our 43,000,000 depressed people is not the problem of India alone. *It should be international, for it affects the economic and social welfare of the entire world and it is a case for the League of Nations just as slavery or the drug traffic is* [emphasis added].'[25]

Ambedkar's comparison of untouchability with slavery and drug trafficking is key. His intention was to disassociate untouchability from religion and to place it into a legal-political spectrum where interventionism was an option. This type of interventionism by foreign organisations in the political life of India was justified by Ambedkar as there were no guarantees that the rights of Dalits would be respected once the British left the subcontinent. He knew that whatever happened in London was subject to change and that any progress 'on the part of the Hindus' could have been a 'temporary political expedient for the sake of proving to Great Britain that all Indians have a common cause and are unanimous in their demand for self-government'.[26] Indian independence then posed a dilemma for Ambedkar as there was not a direct relationship between political freedom for the many and political freedom for Dalits. Young Ambedkar was afraid that 'If they win [independence], perhaps the Hindus will forget again that we "Untouchables" are human beings and will see no reason for removing caste slavery because they have gained political freedom'.[27] In sum, Ambedkar used the foreign press available to him in London to galvanise international support for Dalits while attempting to establish untouchability not as a religious issue, but as a strictly political problem. While international support was important for his objectives, Ambedkar still needed to convince other attendees to the RTCs that political protections were the best method to resolve the inequality caused by untouchability.

### *The RTCs and the Claim for Adequate Representation*

Despite his reservations of having Dalits living as a political minority in a new independent country dominated by a Hindu majority, Ambedkar knew that any political safeguards required a show of faith on his part. Thus, Ambedkar used his time in London to write the minimum conditions he envisioned for Dalits to become part of a new independent India. Ambedkar presented his case about the situation of untouchability to the attendees of the RTC in a succinct memorandum entitled 'A Scheme of Political Safeguards for the

Protection of the Depressed Classes in the Future Constitution of a Self-governing India'. In a letter to Gaikwad, Ambedkar described the memorandum as 'a very elaborate document drawn up in a legal language and if I may say so paints the case of the Depressed Classes clearly and thoroughly'.[28] The document was written and printed in London and 2,000 copies were produced for circulation in Britain and India. Once the memorandum arrived in India, under Ambedkar's instructions, Gaikwad was to telegraph the Chairman of the Minorities Committee of the RTC in London saying that the 'D.C. regard what is stated therein [the memorandum] as their irreducible minimum'.[29] More importantly, Ambedkar had to show he was a Dalit leader beyond his province, thus telegrams supporting his scheme were to 'come in plenty and should come from all Provinces of India'.[30] This shows Ambedkar's awareness of how important political strategies were and how he attempted to stir attention toward his memorandum.

Ambedkar's memorandum is instructive on what he considered to be the best methods to abolish untouchability. The memorandum reads as a legal document with a 'blue-skies' vision of achievable protections for Dalits. I focus my analysis in two main aspects: the legal influences of the document and the electoral protections suggested by Ambedkar. First, the memorandum reflected Ambedkar's legal ingenuity to use a heterogeneous cluster of imperial, national and civil legislations to defend the rights of Dalits across the subcontinent. The 'safeguards scheme' is clear about its purpose and lists 'the terms and conditions on which the Depressed Classes will consent to place themselves under a majority rule in a self-governing India'.[31] The conditions listed by Ambedkar were the following:

a) Equal Citizenship
b) Free enjoyment of equal rights
c) Protection against discrimination
d) Adequate representation in the legislatures
e) Adequate representation in the services
f) Redress against prejudicial action or neglect of interests
g) The establishment of Special Departmental Care
h) Representation of the Depressed Classes in the Cabinet

Each of these items were followed by an explanation of terms used in the scheme detailing the way Ambedkar planned to secure such conditions. It is here where Ambedkar's legal creativity comes to light.

Indeed, Ambedkar would tweak a number of laws to suit his purposes of defending the rights of Dalits. While some of these were created to defend civil rights, some of the laws Ambedkar took inspiration from were created to suppress political protests. This is particularly evident in the conditions regarding equal citizenship and free enjoyment of equal rights. Both of these conditions were inspired by US legislation directed to secure the rights of African-Americans after the abolition of slavery. Specifically, Ambedkar's vision of equal citizenship had to be accompanied by a fundamental right establishing that any sort of discrimination ceased to have any effect as 'All subjects of the State in India are equal before the law and possess equal civil rights'.[32] This fundamental right was built on the values proposed in the Fourteenth Amendment of the United States Constitution, which established equal protection for citizens before the law to protect former slaves from any passing or enforcement of discriminatory legislation.

Of course, there was a difference between pronouncing fundamental rights in law and being able to enjoy such rights freely. This is why Ambedkar's second condition in his scheme covered what he saw as the 'adequate pains and penalties' to prevent 'interference in the enjoyment of these declared [fundamental] rights'.[33] Basically, he wanted to criminalise the practice of untouchability or any infringement to the citizenship of Dalits with a fine and imprisonment. Ambedkar's definition of the infringement of the citizenship of Dalits drew heavily on the US Civil Rights Acts of 9 April 1866, and of 1 March 1875. This is interesting as these acts were created to protect African-Americans from discriminatory labour laws, or 'Black codes', and to prevent their exclusion from public spaces, including public transportation. The main difference is that Ambedkar adapted these infringements to cover actions associated with untouchability more so than with racial segregation, although both practices share spatial exclusion:

> Whoever denies to any person except for reasons by law applicable to persons of all classes and regardless of any previous condition of untouchability the full enjoyment of any of the accommodations, advantages, facilities, privileges of inns, educational institutions, roads, paths, streets, tanks, wells and other watering places, public conveyances on land, air or water, theatres of other places of public amusement, resort or convenience whether they are dedicated to or maintained or licensed for the use of the public shall be punished with imprisonment of either description for a term which may extend to five years and shall also be liable to a fine.[34]

From the paragraph above, the influence of ideas coming from the US civil rights movement is clear. In the same way, the lines above show how Ambedkar saw spatial exclusion as a key characteristic of untouchability. As I have argued elsewhere, throughout his life, Ambedkar experienced the spatial discrimination he described in the RTC's scheme—whether it was being seated outside of a classroom as a child; being denied water on a trip; or being denied accommodation in a hostel due to his status as a Mahar. The emphasis on access to roads, tanks, wells and water also reflected the simultaneous battle in the Nasik satyagraha in which Ambedkar was involved during his time in London. The fight against untouchability was a spatial one, and being in London allowed Ambedkar to present arguments that might have been too controversial in India.

Ambedkar knew that overt discrimination was not the only way untouchability was practised in India. He argued there were many times in which discrimination connected to untouchability could pass as 'freedom of contract,' or as the freedom of choice people have to not engage with someone if they don't wish to. This was quite problematic in villages where Dalits fighting for rights were often met with the unwillingness of the whole village to interact with them in all aspects of life, including social interactions or commercial transactions. Ambedkar called this type of reprisal 'social boycott', and considered that this was the most dangerous weapon Hindus had against Dalits, precisely because it passed as free will. In using it, people could claim they were free to engage with anyone they deemed fit and that their decision of not interacting with Dalits had nothing to do with untouchability.

Ambedkar's next step was to propose a solution on how to stop social boycott, but instead of getting inspiration from legislation used to defend civil rights, he would base his solution on punitive laws created to supress nationalist political protest against the British Empire, in particular the Burma Anti-Boycott Act of 1922. The reason for this relates to the fact that this was not the first time Ambedkar had to deal with the issue of social boycott. From 1928 to 1930, Ambedkar was part of a committee (Starte) looking into the conditions of the Depressed Classes and aboriginal tribes in the Bombay Presidency. This committee also identified social boycott as one of the major obstacles in ameliorating the life of Dalits.[35] However, in their report the Committee only recommended that 'social boycott, which operates against the Depressed Classes should be checked by propaganda and compromise and in the last resort by legislation'.[36] Such recommendations were lightweight and based on the good will of individuals to change their practices. This solution was probably a negotiated agreement between Ambedkar's progressive views to tackle untouchability, and the ones put forward by conservative members of the Starte Committee, who even published a note of dissent along with the report. In contrast, during the RTCs, Ambedkar's answer to social boycott was drastic and punitive. He began by giving boycott a very wide definition, which included abstaining from social, professional or business relations and even annoying or interfering with the lawful rights of another person. The only exception to this were bona fide labour disputes and ordinary business completion. Ambedkar continued to argue that 'In the opinion of the Depressed Classes the only way to overcome this kind of menace in their rights and liberties is to make social boycott an offence punishable by law.'[37] Thus, he proposed monetary fines and prison sentences of up to seven years for boycotting, instigating or promoting boycott, and even for threatening a boycott against Dalits.

The scheme also shows that being outside the spatial confines of India allowed him to present harsher methods to resolve untouchability. As his recommendations to resolve social boycott suggest, using legislation to quench nationalist protest in Burma was probably out of the question in India. However, he was comfortable enough to pursue this path in London. In sum, the scheme reflects Ambedkar's legal creativity and knowledge. He was comfortable using legislation that may have seemed contradictory if this could be of help to the Dalit cause. Now I turn to Ambedkar's demands for the political representation of Dalits presented in his scheme.

The question of political representation for any minority in India was a controversial one, and this was no exception. In the case of the Depressed Classes, a big part of the issue was that there was no certainty that Dalits were a minority at all. In India, political protections for minorities were based on religious differences; this excluded Dalits as they were traditionally considered to be Hindus. Ambedkar's first objective was not to get special political representation but to establish that Dalits were a minority in their own right, independent from the larger Hindu community.

The political representation of Dalits was not formally discussed in India until the twentieth century. The notion of universal franchise was not very popular, and most types of representation were based on the qualifications of being male, and on having political interests to protect. Such interests were often related to land tenure, although in India there were also exceptions made for people with certain educational backgrounds. This created quite a limited electorate in the subcontinent, a population that was largely rural with a large number of landless peasants, and where a large majority of the population was illiterate. Such conditions to access political representation were a great obstacle for Dalits. Whenever the question of their electoral rights came to the fore, the subject was dismissed with the argument that this group did not have any interests to protect. Even if certain Dalits were able to surpass these types of restrictions, there were so few of them that their political power was negligible.[38]

The conversation about Dalit rights was to change not because of the efforts of the community but because other religious communities began to question the amount of representation the general (that is, Hindu) constituency was given. Since 1906, when the question of Muslim representation was on the table for debate, it had been the

Aga Khan and other Muslim leaders who argued that the amount of representation Hindus were receiving was incorrect as the percentage took into consideration the Depressed Classes. The Aga Khan's point was that Dalits were not part of the Hindu community, they were excluded from the social life of Hindus, and that having Hindus as their representatives was therefore nonsensical. While the Aga Khan's claim did not bring immediate change, it did plant a doubt in the minds of both colonial and Indian politicians about who should represent Dalits. Their numbers were too important to be denied, but their condition, according to the standards of the time, did not warrant them any political representation.[39]

It was in this context that Ambedkar presented his vision for the political representation of Dalits. The first session of the RTC is important because Congress, one of the main groups claiming Dalits were Hindus, was not attending the meeting. Thus, Ambedkar was able to present his ideal view of what the voting safeguards should be for Dalits. As is widely known, the attendance of Gandhi at the second session of the RTC transformed the political dynamics of the conference. Gandhi became the centre of attention of the whole conference; he claimed to be the true representative of Dalits and opposed the electoral protections demanded by Ambedkar. Gandhi even accused Ambedkar of wanting to keep Dalits in an eternal state of oppression, arguing that granting political protection for certain communities would discourage the social advancement of Dalits. While the feud between Gandhi and Ambedkar has been the subject of a number of studies, Ambedkar's electoral demands in the first RTC have not been carefully analysed. However, taking a careful look at this shows that the political protections Ambedkar was asking for were only temporary—he never thought of them as permanent fixtures.

The impermanence of the electoral safeguards Ambedkar was asking for is evident in the demands for the representation of Dalits in the legislatures and in the executive Cabinet. He made it clear that these demands were necessary because 'the Majority rule of the future will be the rule of the orthodox, the Depressed Classes fear that such a Majority Rule will not be sympathetic to them and that the probability of prejudice to their interest and neglect of their vital needs cannot be overlooked'.[40] Due to this reason, Dalits were to be given 'sufficient political power to influence legislative and executive action of the purpose for securing their welfare'.[41] Thus, for Ambedkar, Dalits required political representation in all the legislatures of the country—provincial and central—for ten years. Specifically, he wanted Dalits to have the 'right to elect their own men as their representatives'.[42] This was to be done by introducing adult suffrage and by providing Dalits with 'separate electorates for *the first ten years* and thereafter by joint electorates and reserved seats' with the caveat that 'joint electorates shall not be forced upon the Depressed Classes against their will unless such joint electorates are accompanied by adult suffrage'.[43] In other words, Ambedkar's demands were limited to a decade and eventually would lead to a joint electorate. His demands for adult suffrage were not even that radical as this was a view which was growing in popularity at the time, particularly within Congress circles. The most controversial part of Ambedkar's view was precisely his conception of Dalits as a political minority in their own right rather than a subsection of the Hindu community.

In contrast to Gandhi's suggestion that separate electorates for Dalits would create a schism in Hinduism, I argue that Ambedkar's demands in the first RTC were quite optimistic. First, unlike Muslims a few years later, Ambedkar was not claiming that Dalits were a nation that could live independently from the rest of India. His plan at this stage, and for most of his career, usually aimed at the incorporation of Dalits to the social and political life of the country. This is what Ambedkar was striving for with his demands for adequate representation in the services and for the creation of a governmental department specialising in Dalit welfare. It was his contention that Dalits had suffered a great deal due to the monopolisation of the public services by 'high caste officers' who abused the law at their discretion 'to the prejudice of the Depressed Classes and to the advantage of the caste Hindus without any regard to justice, equity or good conscience'.[44] To avoid this, Ambedkar suggested regulating the recruitment to public services in a manner 'that *all* communities including the Depressed will have an adequate share in them'.[45] In the same way, Ambedkar's plea for the creation of a department for

Dalit welfare was not intended to establish an advantage for this group over the rest of the Indian population. Rather, the department would make sure the new legislation and safeguards created to protect Dalits were respected by everyone in the country. Ambedkar was aware that prejudices did not disappear overnight; thus, certain mechanisms were to be in place to secure social change. What is important to note is that at this time, Ambedkar did believe change in Hindu society was possible as his demands were only temporary. His proposals did not suggest a new civil code for Dalits either; all of these proposed measures were aimed at the integration of Dalits into the mainstream of Indian society.

This last point requires some expansion. Despite Ambedkar's intention to internationalise untouchability and to establish Dalits as a separate political community, he still believed that independence was the main objective at this time. He even surprised the attendees of the conference when he declared that the colonial government seemed to defend the cause of untouchability only when it suited them. Ambedkar claimed Dalits 'have had no friend. The Government has all along used them only as an excuse for its continued existence.' Of course, Ambedkar also had similar words for Hindus and Muslims, yet he made it clear that the new constitution could not be forcefully imposed: 'I am afraid it is not sufficiently realised that in the present temper of this country, no constitution will be workable, which is not acceptable to the majority of the people. The time when you were to choose and India was to accept is gone, never to return.'[46] In other words, even when Ambedkar was proposing important constitutional protections for his community, at this point in time he was not antagonistic to the nationalist cause.

## *Conclusion*

Ambedkar's participation in the first RTC had mixed results. On the one hand, he was able to publicise untouchability through the international coverage of important newspapers such as *The New York Times*. In these ways, London and the RTCs allowed Ambedkar to position himself in a confined circle of power where he emerged as the leading voice of Dalits in the years to come. On the other hand, while his memorandum received some positive attention, and some of the claims presented about the perilous state of Dalits in India were accepted by the RTC, these did not translate into consolidated agreements. For instance, the Minorities Committee of the RTC accepted Ambedkar's proposal of including in the future constitution a 'declaration of fundamental rights safeguarding the cultural and religious life of the various communities ... without discrimination as to race, caste, creed or sex, the free exercise of economic, social and civil rights'. However, his suggestion of enforcing or penalising a violation of such rights was only noted. Likewise, when it came to electoral protections, the Minorities Committee agreed that representation for minorities should not be less than their proportion in the population; but, once more, there was no consensus about what kind of representation Dalits would have. Regardless of these drawbacks, Ambedkar's cause had one important victory in the recognition of Dalits as a separate and independent political community. Indeed, the Minorities Committee concluded that Dalits 'should be deducted from the Hindu population and be regarded, for electoral purposes, as a separate community'.[47] This was perhaps Ambedkar's greatest achievement during the conference as it would transform the political debate about Dalits in India.

This, however, was not an easy ride, as a turbulent episode between Ambedkar and Gandhi would unfold just a year later, when the latter refused to recognised Dalits' existence outside Hinduism. During the second meeting of the RTCs, Gandhi opposed Ambedkar on the question regarding the creation of separate electorates for Dalits. This disagreement culminated in the usually forgotten Communal Award, a solution proposed by Ramsay MacDonald, the British Prime Minister at the time, which granted separate electorates for the Depressed Classes. While most of the attendants in London sided with Ambedkar, Gandhi refused to accept any of the agreements about the political representation of Dalits, claiming that Hinduism would be destroyed. However, Ambedkar's political achievements in London were not to last. On his return to the subcontinent, Ambedkar found that the caste boundaries he was able to defy in Britain were reinstated into the political debate about Dalit representation. At this stage, Gandhi, an upper-caste man sitting in jail, would make the Communal Award void by announcing a 'fast unto death' if Dalits did not return to the general (i.e. Hindu) electoral constituency. This type of incident taught Ambedkar that the space where politics is played matters a great deal. Finding international support for Dalits was key for Ambedkar, and he would continue to pursue this throughout his life, such as his appeal to the United Nations in 1946 or his attempt to make Dalits part of a global Buddhist community. Thus, this chapter has shown why looking at Ambedkar's participation in the first RTC held in London is vital in understanding the origin of his efforts to place untouchability as a problem of international relevance.

5

# DR AMBEDKAR IN THE 1920s

## THE TRANSITIONAL DECADE

*Christophe Jaffrelot*

The 1920s represent a transitional decade for B. R. Ambedkar from two points of view. First, while he had spent quite some time in the West in the 1910s and in the early 1920s, travelling back and forth between India, the USA, the UK and even Germany, he settled down in Bombay in the mid-1920s. Second, intellectually, while he had started to analyse caste in New York and London, as a student he started in the 1920s to also fight against caste. This fight oscillated between two poles—within the existing order or against it—and he finally moved from one pole to the other. This tension and evolution were evident from Ambedkar's political thinking as well as from his social reform agenda. On the one hand, he was in favour of reserved seats for Dalits, but attracted by the separate electorate formula—which was to become his official stand in the early 1930s. On the other, he moved away from the legacy of Sanskritisation and mobilised all his energy in the name of equality. In parallel, he also stopped asking for temple entry. Ambedkar spent quite some time in London during the 1920s, and this informed his later work once he returned to India. In this chapter, however, I will focus on his changing thought process and action after his return, in the course of this transitional decade.

*Reserved Seats or Separate Electorate?*

In 1924, in his famous speech of Barshi Takli, Ambedkar envisaged all the possible strategies for emancipating Dalits from the oppression they were subjected to, ranging from emigration to changing of name, through conversion; but he came to the conclusion that the obtaining of political rights was finally the most important issue.[1] Nevertheless, until the beginning of the 1930s, he favoured social reform at least as much as the struggle for such rights, and did not, in any case, come down in the political arena—except to be heard by the British as the representative of the Untouchables when the Raj organised rounds of consultations. And in this context, he hesitated between two political strategies: separate electorate or reserved seats—a formula he favoured until the 1930s.

Reserved seats were already requested by the few upper-caste reformers who catered to the needs of the Dalits, including the Depressed Classes Mission in Bombay, which had been founded in 1916 by a Brahmin reformer close to the Congress, Narayan Rao Chandavarkar. On 11 November 1917, Chandavarkar held a meeting in which he demanded that the Untouchables be granted a number of reserved seats in the legislative councils in proportion to their demographic weight.[2] Two years later, Ambedkar was consulted by the Southborough Committee, the body which had been entrusted with redefining the electoral franchise within the framework of the constitutional reforms initiated by Montagu and Chelmsford. In his testimony, he explained that the real line of cleavage among the Hindus was set between the 'touchables' and Untouchables. He thus rejected an electoral system which would be based on territorial constituencies because the latter would then be in a minority and therefore deprived of representation; all the more so as the criteria on which basis the franchise had been defined were not in their favour. He adduced in support of this reasoning figures from the local authorities of five districts of the Bombay Presidency, where the Brahmins represented 9,077 voters, Marathas 4,741, Muslims 1,830 and Mahars 55.[3]

To mitigate this imbalance, Ambedkar suggested, first of all, the lowering of the taxable rating level applied to the Untouchables. This would allow them to vote in larger numbers and would improve their political education by accelerating their integration in the electoral process. Above all, he recommended 'either to reserve seats ... for those minorities that cannot, otherwise, secure personal representation or grant communal electorates'.[4] The two options then seemed equally valid to him. It was only in an appended document that Ambedkar emphasised the need for a 'community electorate'[5] for the Untouchables.[6] Finally, the Untouchables obtained, within the framework of the 1919 reform, only one representative in the Legislative Council of Bombay Presidency; an additional representative was appointed later in 1924. Ambedkar was to join the Council this way in 1927.

The political system of India was expected to be revised every ten years, and therefore the British began in 1928 to consult once again representatives of the various political and social groups to work out a new reform. The Simon Commission (named after its president) charged with these consultations, however, consisted only of British men. Shocked to see the Indians excluded from it, the Congress decided to boycott its meetings. But organisations of minorities (Muslims, Sikhs, etc.) and Dalit associations took part in them. Ambedkar submitted a memorandum on behalf of the Bahishkrit Hitakarini Sabha, set up immediately after his return from London. He argued in favour of a quota of seats for the Untouchables rather than for separate electorates.[7] He asked for twenty-two seats in the Bombay assembly which counted for 140 (fifteen seats only would have been granted on the basis of their demographic weight) and the right to vote for every Untouchable adult.[8] He explained, during his speech before a delegation of the Simon Commission at Poona, that in the case of universal suffrage not being granted for the Dalits, then he would campaign for separate electorates.[9] He justified this position by resorting to arguments which he was not to use any more in the future—arguments which are clear indications that he still nurtured great hopes towards the upper castes and that he still had scruples which prevented him from severing his links with the social and political mainstream:

> At any rate, this must be said with certainty that a minority gets a larger advantage under joint electorates than it does under a system of separate electorates. With separate electorates the minority gets its own quota of representation and no more. The rest of the house owes no allegiance to it and is therefore not influenced by the desire to meet the wishes of the minority. The minority is thus thrown on its own resources and as no system of representation can convert a minority into a majority, it is bound to be overwhelmed. On the other hand, under a system of joint electorates and reserved seats the minority not only gets its quota of representation but something more. For, every member of the majority who has partly succeeded on the strength of the votes of the minority if not a member of the minority will certainly be a member for the minority.[10]

Ambedkar's reservations about separate electorates stem also here from his fears that such a reform would divide the Indian nation: 'I do contemplate and I do desire, the time when India shall be one; and I believe that a time will come when, for instance, all these things will not be necessary; but all that would depend upon the attitude of the majority towards the minority'.[11] Thus, the choice of joint electorate with reserved seats was a compromise aiming to reconcile the defence of a minority and the desire to strengthen the Indian nation. Ambedkar's preference was not, however, very firm. When, during the hearing, the Bengali Muslim leader Suhrawardy asked him whether the system of separate electorates would not be better to protect the Untouchables around the polling booth, against pressures of the upper castes at the time of voting, Ambedkar gladly agreed with him.[12]

Thus, in 1928 Ambedkar was not yet positive about what was the best formula for improving Dalits' political representation—an issue that he had also been mulling over while in London. But what seems to be quite sure was his conviction that 'political power is the only solvent'[13] of the problem of untouchability. This is why he became so critical of the proposals of the Nehru Committee. This committee had been set up by the Congress in reaction to the appointment of the Simon Commission. It had been entrusted with the task of preparing a counter project to the Constitution under the supervision of

Motilal Nehru. While the committee had consulted organisations of Muslims, Sikhs, Christians, Parsis, Anglo-Indians and non-Brahmins, the Dalit movements had been ignored. Above all, the final report of the Nehru committee did not, in the name of national integration, make provisions for the protection of the Untouchables and the Muslims. Its authors, drawing their inspiration from western liberal values, defined the nation as a collection of individuals. Ambedkar, in principle, followed the same line of reasoning, yet he could not accept that the Untouchables should be deprived of guarantees such as reserved seats.

The report of the Simon Commission finally granted reserved seats to the Depressed Classes, but it remained a dead letter since the main political force of the country—the Congress—had not been involved in its making. To get out of this deadlock, a Conference was held in London.

The first Round Table Conference (RTC) organised from autumn 1930 was again boycotted by the Congress although representatives of the Muslims, Sikhs, Christians, Untouchables and the Hindu Mahasabha participated in it, besides the traditional supporters of the British within the Liberal Party. Ambedkar was invited to attend it as a representative of the Depressed Classes (as Jesús Cháirez-Garza has discussed in Chapter 4). In August 1930, the All-India Depressed Classes Congress at Nagpur had committed itself to the same scheme as the one defended by Ambedkar before the Simon Commission, which combined reserved seats and universal suffrage.[14] In London, Ambedkar repeated this demand but the Conference did not bear any fruit given the absence of the Congress representatives. The British, therefore, organised a second RTC, to which Gandhi himself was invited. He was still hesitant to participate in it when—apparently for the first time—he met Ambedkar, who was about to embark for London, on 14 August 1931 in Bombay. When Ambedkar asked Gandhi what he thought of the debates of the first RTC, the Mahatma replied that he was 'against the political separation of the Untouchables from the Hindus'.[15]

Confrontation between the two personalities took on a more acute form during the second RTC in London, to which Gandhi went eventually. They were both members of the Minorities Committee, which was entrusted with the task of discussing the thorny problem of the place of the Muslims and the Untouchables within the new institutions which the British wished to set up. On 1 October 1931, Gandhi asked for a suspension of the meeting as to be able to discuss with the leaders of the minorities in order to persuade them not to indulge in any form of separatism. The debates started again on 8 October and Gandhi recognised then that he had not succeeded in getting a compromise, because, according to him, of the behaviour of the leaders with whom he had to deal and whose representativity seemed to him doubtful. Gandhi disputed, for example, Ambedkar's claim to be the spokesperson of the Untouchables, of whom the Congress, the spearhead of the national movement, was Gandhi's natural organ.[16]

Ambedkar had got closer to the Muslim, Anglo-Indian and European Christian representatives within the Minorities Committee. They drafted a memorandum together. Ambedkar put down on it the demand for a separate electorate with reserved seats for the Untouchables, a scheme that was planned to be subject to referendum within twenty years, but which would come to an end earlier if suffrage became universal. Gandhi opposed this scheme, but the Communal Award, announced on 16 August 1932, recognised the right of the Untouchables to have a separate electorate. Henceforth they were given the right to vote at the same moment within the framework of general constituencies and within seventy-one separate constituencies which could only be filled by Dalit candidates. Immediately, Gandhi, who was then imprisoned at Poona for having revived the Civil Disobedience movement, went on a fast.

The way Ambedkar shifted from reserved seats to separate electorates ran parallel to his estrangement vis-à-vis Gandhi. Ambedkar and Gandhi did not meet until the early 1930s, but the Mahatma's action had aroused the interest of Untouchable leaders, including Ambedkar, as early as the 1920s. Ambedkar's first comment about Gandhi dates back to 1925 and concerns the Vaikam satyagraha. On the occasion of the Depressed Classes Conference of the Bombay Presidency organized this year, Ambedkar declared:

> Before Mahatma Gandhi, no politician in this country maintained that it is necessary to remove social injustice here in order to do away with tension and conflict, and that every Indian should consider it his sacred duty to do so .... However, if one looks closely, one finds there is a slight disharmony ... for he does not insist on the removal of untouchability as much as he insists on the propagation of Khaddar [home-spun cloth] or the Hindu-Muslim unity. If he had he would have made the removal of untouchability a precondition of voting in the party. Well, be that as it may, when one is spurned by everyone, even the sympathy shown by Mahatma Gandhi is of no little importance.[17]

Ambedkar was also attracted by Gandhi's non-violent modus operandi. During the 1927 Mahad movement (see below), not only did a photo of the Mahatma adorn the pandal but Ambedkar explicitly adopted the technique of satyagraha, which he defined as 'affirmation of the right and duty to fight for truth'.[18] The Mahad movement indeed resembled to a large extent a satyagraha, like the second mobilisation for the opening of the Parvati temple to the Untouchables, at Poona in 1929. This movement did not, however, receive Gandhi's approval. A delegation of the Anti-Untouchability Sub-Committee of the Congress had led an inquiry on the spot and concluded that the satyagraha created an 'atmosphere of bitterness and distrust'.[19] This satyagraha failed—the Parvati temple would be opened to the Untouchables only in 1947. The attitude of the Congress and Gandhi aroused Ambedkar's animosity all the more, as a similar episode was repeated in 1930 during the movement for the opening of the Nasik temple to the Untouchables. By then, Ambedkar had lost all hope vis-à-vis Gandhi's Congress and opted for the separate electorates formula, something that was to result in the famous 1932 Ambedkar–Gandhi confrontation after the Communal Award was made public.

### *How to Fight Caste, Sanskritisation and Dalits' Divisions?*

Ambedkar achieved a similar transition in the domain of social reform. The first caste associations created by Mahars complied with the logic of Sanskritisation. The oldest one, the Anarya Dosh

Pariharak Mandal, had been founded in 1886 by a retired soldier, G. V. Walangkar, who had been initiated into social reform by Phule.[20] Walangkar wanted to destroy the caste system but, at the same time, he claimed—like Phule—that Mahars were former Kshatriyas.[21] Besides, Walangkar tried to challenge Brahminism by emphasising the vitality of the bhakti tradition of Maharashtra—what Constable calls 'bhakti egalitarianism'. It was not principally broad-based Dalit caste associations that followed the ethos of Sanskritisation, but specific jatis. The Mahar Sabha (Mahar Association) was a case in point. Founded in Nagpur in 1906, its main objective was to unify the Mahars. In this regard, it promoted their education and tried to purify their social practices.[22] But many Mahar leaders did not even take part in Mahar associations: they joined movements initiated by upper-caste social reformers who claimed that Untouchables should simply get Sanskritised to erase the stigma they were suffering from. Kisan Fagoji Bansode (1879–1946), inspired by the values of the bhakti cult in 1910,[23] adhered to the Prarthana Samaj and called upon the Mahars not to eat meat and not to drink, to educate themselves, and to pressurise the British to give them more posts in the government.[24] His main partner, a Mahar of Amraoti, Ganesh Akkaji Gavai (1888–1974), also a member of the Prarthana Samaj,[25] was to become the main rival of Ambedkar in the region. In 1919, the movement created by Bansode and Gavai, the Antyaja Samaj ('Society of Those Born Last', otherwise known as the 'Untouchables') was also imbued with the Sanskritisation ethos, as evident from its recommendations:

> We should not eat meat, drink, or sell cows to butchers. We should not read books of other religions. We should appoint a Hindu teacher and educate our children. We should not raise pigs—caste Hindus hold us untouchable because of this. Our women should not go to tamashas [public scenes of rejoicing which sometimes implied more or less indecent dances or trances]. We should take part in religious observances.[26]

To begin with, Ambedkar was also influenced by Prarthana Samaj leaders, including Vitthal Ramji Shinde,[27] one of the Kunbi co-founders of the Samaj, and, in 1906, of the Depressed Classes

Mission.[28] Shinde, as an historian, reflected at length upon the origins of untouchability. He was one of the first non-Brahmin ideologues to propose the thesis according to which the Untouchables had formerly been Buddhists reigning over Maharashtra before being conquered by upper-caste invaders.[29] He was also attracted by Bansode and Gavai, and joined the organisation they had created, the Akhil Bharatiya Bahishkrit Parishad (All-India Conference for the Victims of Social Ostracism), in 1920. In the first years of the 1920s, however, Ambedkar distanced himself from Shinde, rejected the upper castes reformism,[30] and reproached Bansode and Gavai and the way they tended to identify themselves with no other Dalit groups but the Mahars. In 1924, they organised a Mahar Conference which gave evidence of the particular interest which they continued to show for this caste.[31]

### *The Bahishkrit Hitakarini Sabha and the Mahad Satyagraha*

In 1924, soon after his definitive return from England, Ambedkar founded the Bahishkrit Hitakarini Sabha (Association for the Improvement of the Condition of the Victims of Social Ostracism) whose English name was 'Depressed Classes Institute'. This organisation had among its objectives the abolition by law of the *baluta* system.[32] Correlatively, it aimed to help the Mahars assert their rights as *vatandars*.[33] *Bahishkrit Bharat*, the newspaper founded by Ambedkar in 1927 in place of his early 1920s paper *Mooknayak*, subsequently campaigned also for the abolition of the *vatan*.[34] The Bahishkrit Hitakarini Sabha is therefore revealing of a certain tension between Ambedkar's will to defend the Mahars and his 'pan-Dalit' agenda: the question of vatan concerned primarily the Mahars and, indeed, Mahars were over-represented in the ranks of the Sabha;[35] but it was more than a caste association as it aimed, as its name indicated, to serve all Untouchables—and Chambhars as well as Dhors were represented in it.[36]

Another kind of tension pertains to Ambedkar's attitude vis-à-vis the upper castes. The constitution of the Depressed Classes Institute points out that 'without the cooperation and sympathy of [the upper classes], it would not be possible for the Depressed Classes to work out their salvation'.[37] The organisation concentrated first on one demand aiming to better integrate Untouchables into the Hindu world: their entry into temples, from which they were often excluded, as mentioned above.[38]

However, Ambedkar also asked for access to wells. This issue was at the centre of the famous conference of Mahad in 1927. This conference had been organised in reaction to a local conflict due to the passing of the Bole Resolution in the Legislative Council of Bombay on 4 August 1923. Introduced by S. K. Bole, a social reformer turned politician, it stipulated that the Untouchables were authorised to use water sources, *dharmashalas* (lodging places for pilgrims, or even inns), schools, courts, and offices of the administration and public dispensaries. This resolution not having been followed by tangible effects, on 5 August 1926 Bole introduced a new resolution asking the Government of India not to give any subsidy to the municipalities and other local organisations which would refuse to apply these measures. Many town councils then obeyed, but their orders were rarely carried out because of the hostility of the upper castes. It was notably the case at Mahad, a small town of Kolaba district (today a part of Pune district, formerly Poona) where the Untouchables could never get to certain wells. A conference was organized in this town, on 19 and 20 March 1927. Swapna H. Samel explains that:

> Two separate organisations were responsible for directing this movement. One was The Kokanastha Mahar Samaj Seva Sangh which had been established in 1926 in Bombay by R. B. More and Subedar V. G. Sawadkar. The organisation was dominated by Konkan dwelling Mahars and military and ex-military men. The second group which initiated the Mahad Satyagraha was the 'Sarnata Sangh' (Equality League) founded by Ambedkar in 1926–27. The leadership of the Samaj Sangh was largely in the hands of the upper-caste Hindus [including Brahmins and Kayasths] although it included some leaders of the non-Brahmin movement in Maharashtra.[39]

Ambedkar's March 1927 Mahad address was in tune with the principles of Sanskritisation: 'No lasting progress can be achieved unless we put ourselves through a three-fold process of purification. We must improve the general tone of our demeanour, re-tone our pronunciations and revitalise our thoughts. I, therefore, ask you now to take a vow from this moment to renounce eating carrion.'[40] Then, Ambedkar addressed the Mahars in particular, asking them to abandon their activity of *vatandar*. He exhorted them to clear a piece of land and to become farmers themselves. Soon afterwards, Ambedkar led a procession, starting from the stand from where he had spoken, up to a water source—the Chavdar tank—open, in theory, to the Untouchables, but to which access in fact had been denied. In a symbolic and solemn way, he drank from the tank.[41] This transgression was perceived as a provocation by the upper-caste Hindus who attacked the demonstrators when they returned to the meeting stand. Furthermore, in the following days, Mahad's upper castes ostracised the Untouchables and sometimes even deprived them of their jobs and expelled them from their tenancy rights.

Then, the orthodox Hindus of Mahad considered the possibility of the purification of the Chavdar lake. Accordingly, 'water in 108 earthen pots was taken out from the tank and mixed with curd [yoghurt], cow dung, cow milk and cow urine. The pots were then dipped in the tank and the water was declared pure and fit for use by the caste Hindus'.[42] Even more than physical violence, this ritual precipitated a radicalisation of Ambedkar and his followers: this purification ritual dissuaded them from following the purification/Sanskritisation path themselves: 'On hearing of the so-called purification ceremony, the marchers grew angrier. It hurt them deeply. Their touch was considered more polluting than cow-dung and cow urine. There cannot be a worse insult to any human being. Dr Ambedkar decided to launch a satyagraha struggle for the vindication of his people's rights.'[43]

Above all, on 4 August 1927, the Mahad municipality revoked the decision which it had taken in 1924 in favour of access of the Untouchables to the Chavdar tank. Ambedkar prepared then a second meeting which marked his transition towards a more radical fight against caste.

The second conference of Mahad took place on 25 December 1927. Ambedkar gave a speech where he called for a pure and simple abolition of the caste system. Because of its importance as a turning point in Ambedkar's career, it is worth quoting at length:[44]

> We are not going to the Chavadar Lake [sic] merely to drink its water. We are going to the Lake to assert that we too are human beings like others. It must be clear that this meeting has been called to set up the norm of equality. I am certain that no one who thinks of this meeting in this light will doubt that it is unprecedented. I feel that no parallel to it can be found in the history of India. If we seek for another meeting in the past to equal this, we shall have to go to the history of France on the continent of Europe. A hundred and thirty-eight years ago, on 24 January 1789, King Louis XVI had convened, by royal command, an assembly of deputies to represent the people of the kingdom. ... If European nations enjoy peace and prosperity today, it is for one reason: the revolutionary French National Assembly convened in 1789 set new principles for the organisation of society before the disorganized and decadent French nation of its time, and the same principles have been accepted and followed by Europe. ... That Assembly of the French people was convened to reorganize French society. Our meeting today too has been convened to reorganize Hindu society. Hence, before discussing on what principles our society should be reorganized, we should all pay heed to the principles on which the French Assembly relied and the policy it adopted. ... We need to pull away the nails which hold the framework of caste-bound Hindu society together, such as those of the prohibition of intermarriage down to the prohibition of social intercourse so that Hindu society becomes all of one caste. Otherwise untouchability cannot be removed nor can equality be established.
>
> Some of you may feel that since we are Untouchables, it is enough if we are set free from the prohibitions of inter-drinking and social intercourse. That we need not concern ourselves with the caste system; how does it matter if it remains? In my opinion this is a total error. ... If untouchability alone is removed, we may change from Atishudras to Shudras; but can we say that this radically removes untouchability? If such puny reforms as the removal of restrictions on social intercourse etc., were enough

> for the eradication of untouchability, I would not have suggested that the caste system itself must go. … If we want to remove untouchability in the home as well as outside, we must break down the prohibition against intermarriage. … The task of removing untouchability and establishing equality that we have undertaken, we must carry out ourselves. Others will not do it. Our life will gain its true meaning if we consider that we are born to carry out this task and set to work in earnest.

Excerpts of the last paragraphs of this speech also need to be cited at length, when Ambedkar says:

> Hence, if Hindu society is to be strengthened, we must uproot the four-castes system and untouchability, and set the society on the foundations of the two principles of one caste only and of equality. … Our work has been begun to bring about a real social revolution. … I pray to God that the social revolution which begins here today may fulfil itself by peaceful means. … Whether this social revolution will work peacefully or violently will depend wholly on the conduct of the caste Hindus. … We say to our opponents too: please do not oppose us. Put away the orthodox scriptures. Follow justice. And we assure you that we shall carry out our programme peacefully.

The values that Ambedkar here invokes are those of the French Revolution. He even compared the Mahar conference to the 'Etats Généraux de Versailles', where, for the first time, the Third Estate had expressed its revolt in a collective and formal fashion. This speech was followed by a vote via show of hands in favour of the statement of human rights and a resolution on the inalienable equality of the individual. Two other resolutions asked, first, for the reduction of internal divisions in Hindu society so that it eventually contained only one category of people, and, second, for the opening of the profession of priests to all those who would like to practise it. Finally, several speakers attacked the Laws of Manu.

In the speech he gave in the evening of 27 December, Ambedkar 'called Manusmriti as the Bible of slavery to the Shudras, the Hindu women and the Untouchables' and one of his lieutenants, Sahasrabuddhe, a Chitpavan Brahmin, 'suggested to set the Manusmriti on fire. At 9 p.m. a copy of Manusmriti was placed on the pyre in a specially dug pit in front of the *pendal* and was ceremoniously burnt at the hands of the untouchable hermits.'[45] The next day, Ambedkar launched a satyagraha[46] to obtain a restriction-free entry to the Chavdar tank. About 4,000 people came forward as volunteers to participate in this movement. The District Magistrate called upon them to maintain peace, arguing that the case had been taken to the courts by upper-caste Hindus claiming that it was a matter of private property; it was therefore advisable to wait for the judgement. The DM warned that any breach of legality would expose the Dalit demonstrators to police repression. Finally, Ambedkar decided to postpone the satyagraha and to replace it, for the time being, by a procession around the water source. This approach reflected a line of action to which he would adhere in similar circumstances in the future: his inclination to leave matters to the courts would generally override his determination to settle the disputes in the streets. This attitude also reflected Ambedkar's legalism, even his constitutionalism—a trait that was consistent through the decade, as shown in Chapters 1 and 3 of this volume. In this particular case, courts would uphold his stand in a judgment given in 1937.[47]

### *How to Break with Hinduism?*

By the late 1920s, Ambedkar had firmly emancipated himself from the logic of Sanskritisation and embraced a complete rejection of the caste system. He had even gone further and rejected too the path offered by the bhakti tradition. *Mooknayak*, the newspaper started by Ambedkar in 1920 just before his arrival in London, carried in its motto, under its heading, verses of Tukaram, a bhakti saint, about the contempt in which the ordinary people, those without say, have been held. But Ambedkar rose very fast against the debilitating impact of saints' worshipping. On the occasion of big festivals, he went to places of pilgrimage for meetings and dissuaded the Untouchables from playing ball with the Hindus. He even opposed his wife's journey to Pandharpur for paying homage to Chokhaba by standing on the steps of Vithoba's temple, since she would be refused access to the temple itself. He told her: 'We have to create another Pandharpur by a virtuous life, a selfless service and a sacrifice without any stains for the cause of the oppressed'.[48]

Ambedkar increasingly attacked Untouchables who continued to go on pilgrimages. He declared thus on the day of the big festival of Khandoba:

> How many generations of ours have worn themselves out by rubbing their foreheads on the steps of the god? But when did the god take pity on you? What big thing has he done for you? Generation after generation, you have been used to clean the village of its garbage and god gave you the dead animals to eat. In spite of all that, god did not show you any pity. It is not this god that you worship, it is your ignorance.[49]

Thus, Ambedkar consummated his break with Hinduism by rejecting all types of religious practice. Although invited, in January 1928, to chair a meeting of the Depressed Classes at Trymbak, near Nasik, where the construction of a temple dedicated to Chokhamela, the great Dalit saint of fifteenth century, was to be discussed, Ambedkar opposed the project. For, in his opinion, the saints and their spiritual legacy could promote only equality, not between a Brahmin and a Shudra, but between a Brahmin and a Shudra considered from the sole viewpoint of their spiritual practice:

> Yet from the viewpoint of the annihilation of caste ... the struggle of the saints did not have any effect on society. The value of man is axiomatic, self-evident; it does not come to him as a result of the gilding of Bhakti. The saints did not struggle to establish this point. On the contrary, their struggle had a very unhealthy effect on the Depressed Classes. It provided the Brahmins with an excuse to silence them by telling [them] that they would be respected if they also attained the status of Chokhamela.[50]

Ambedkar therefore disqualified the diversion advocated by men of religion as a path to equality: he did not want an equality limited to the spiritual sphere. What he asked for was social equality. Arguably, some of this logic around social justice was inherent in his early 1920s publications researched in London, as set out in Chapter 1 of this volume, but it was not until two years after his return that the concept was fully formed. He followed the same logic regarding the problem of entry to temples.

### *Demanding Access to Temples—or Not!*

In the first editorial of *Mooknayak* in 1920, Ambedkar hesitated between two possibilities. He wondered whether Untouchables should have their own temples or try to enter the Hindu temples.[51] In the mid-1920s, he still paid attention to the opening of the temples. Hence his interest in the Vaikam movement in 1924. In this city of the Travancore State (today's Kerala), Untouchables had launched a satyagraha to obtain the right to enter a local temple or, at least, to take the road in front of it, which was forbidden to them by the Brahmins. This confrontation benefited from wide publicity because Gandhi sided with those following the satyagraha and joined them. In 1925, while the conflict continued, Ambedkar declared: 'For us, the most important event in the country today, is satyagraha at Vaikam.'[52] The road was finally made accessible to the Untouchables, but the temple was not opened to them before 1936, a rather early date compared to what happened in other regions of India.

Meanwhile, the Mahars launched their first movement to reach a temple at Amraoti in 1927. G. A. Gavai was its main leader. Ambedkar supported it but was not able to join it personally because his brother died around that time. The movement failed quickly. The satyagraha aimed at the Parvati temple, at Poona, in 1929, was of quite another dimension. Shivram Janba Kamble led the operations and Brahmin reformers participated in it. But Ambedkar's role in this affair was even more limited than at Amraoti. The movement fizzled out rather fast, and this temple was not opened to the Untouchables before 1947. The most important attempt finally took place in 1930 at Nasik.[53] From the beginning, Ambedkar was directly involved. He saw this action as an instrument of social change, and not as an end in itself, as his first speech on the spot testifies: 'Your problems will not be solved by temple entry. Politics, economics, education, religion—all are part of the problem. Today's satyagraha is a challenge to the Hindu mind. Are the Hindus ready to consider us men or not; we will discover this today. ... We know that the god in the temple is of stone. Darsan and puja will not solve our problems. But we will start out, and try to make a change in the minds of the Hindus.'[54]

Sporadic acts of violence occurred between the demonstrators and members of the upper castes. Then the latter, contrary to a newly reached agreement, prevented certain Mahars from pulling the processional chariot during the annual festival of the temple. This incident reinforced Ambedkar in his determination. He eventually dissociated himself from the movement in 1934, lest his supporters should attach too great an importance to a non-priority, religious issue:

> I did not launch the temple entry movement because I wanted the Depressed Class to become worshippers of idols which they were prevented from worshipping or because I believed that temple entry would make them equal members in and an integral part of the Hindu society. So far as this aspect of the case is concerned I would advise the Depressed Class to insist upon a complete overhauling of Hindu society and Hindu theology before they consent to become an integral part of Hindu Society. I started temple entry Satyagraha only because I felt that was the best way of energising the Depressed Class and making them conscious of their position. As I believe I have achieved that therefore I have no more use for temple entry. I want the Depressed Class to concentrate their energy and resources on politics and education and I hope that they will realize the importance of both.[55]

For Ambedkar, even though it had been a relevant device to mobilise the Untouchables, to claim for them an entry to temples meant asking that they were given a place in Hinduism whose caste system condemned them to a subordinate position regardless. But in the end, he preferred to reject this society in its entirety—including the temple entry issue. Doubtless, he was also disappointed by the incapacity of the upper-caste representatives in the assemblies to pass laws legalising the entry of the Untouchables to temples. In 1934, Ranga Iyer thus had his Temple Entry Bill rejected by a majority of the members of the Central Assembly based in Delhi.

*Conclusion*

The 1920s saw the transition of Ambedkar from rather limited demands to the making of a program based on equality and liberty. If, in the early years of the decade, he was content with reserved seats and complied with some of the mainstays of Sanskritisation, including demands to access temples, by the late 1920s–early 1930s he demanded a separate electorate as well as access to tanks for Dalits, and rejected temple entry. This evolution, which was due to the lack of responsiveness to Dalits' moderate demands by upper castes, translated into the making of a new ideology: Ambedkarism, whose main pillar was the quest for equality.

The fact that Ambedkar now relied on a complete and coherent worldview did not mean that he would opt for a revolutionary agenda and that he would avoid all hesitation. First, he would oscillate between opposition to and collaboration with the rulers of India—be they British or Congressmen—but opposition and collaboration did not reflect any form of opportunism; these stands would always be determined by the quest for equality, and Ambedkar would pragmatically decide from which tactic the Dalits might benefit more.

Secondly, the ideology known as Ambedkarism offered the basis of a praxis which was to focus on the making of the political unity of the Dalits. Giving evidence in front of the Simon Commission on 23 October 1928, Ambedkar stated with bitterness that 'the caste Hindus have spread their poison to the rest'.[56] He was especially disturbed by the fact that the Mahars and Mangs in Maharashtra did not marry among themselves. Moreover, he was to meet the worst difficulties when he represented others than his own caste in the public sphere. Neither the Mangs nor Chambhars would support him, for instance. For Ambedkar, the caste system thus incorporated its own mechanism of self-preservation and he had to fight this evil. He did it in many ways, but the making of parties—the Independent Labour Party, the Scheduled Castes Federation and the Republican Party of India—were to be among his main instruments.

Thirdly, in the 1920s, Ambedkar broke with Hinduism after realising that not only caste hierarchies were inherent in

Hinduism—which he had known since the 1910s—but that upper-caste reformers, including Gandhi, would never go far enough to meet his point of view. Breaking with Hinduism had no immediate implication but in the following decade, in parallel to the building of the Independent Labour Party, Ambedkar said that he would not die a Hindu—and he did not.

# PART TWO

*Introduction – Santosh Dass and William Gould*

Part One of this book explored the experiences, intellectual development, political ambitions and mobilisations of B. R. Ambedkar in interwar London. We argued that these formative experiences and activities had a wider and longer-term significance both in India and globally. Existing work on his political career has typically narrated the building of institutions, movements and legal frameworks for the recognition of Dalit rights from the early to mid-1930s into the 1950s. But there were other elements to the London influence. As the final chapter of Part One suggested, the immediate aftermath of Ambedkar's experiences in London were a transitional moment in his changing advocacy of caste reform, towards his better-known radical break with Hinduism. In Part Two of the volume, we continue to locate Ambedkar's influences in London and the UK later in time, developing these wider political trajectories through the institutions and movements he inspired in Britain: from the Ambedkarite movements themselves among the UK's Dalit diaspora, to the campaign to establish the Ambedkar Museum at 10 King Henry's Road and the movements to include caste discrimination in UK equality law. The book therefore connects the ideas and foundations explored via Ambedkar's early career in the opening chapters to his later international influence in matters of caste, society, discrimination and law, including, in the final chapter, in the

USA. Reflecting this movement in time and space, the book also moves in style: from the approaches and research of historians and political scientists to the hitherto unheard personal testimonies and institutional histories of Ambedkarite and legal activists. The book therefore juxtaposes the historical Ambedkar with the contemporary Ambedkar, as he is located in London and further afield in the UK. In this sense, building on Part One's narratives, Part Two further develops the symbolic, emotional but also material and institutional impact of Ambedkar on Britain's Dalit diaspora.

6

# THE AMBEDKARITE MOVEMENT IN BRITAIN

*Santosh Dass and Arun Kumar*

Dr Ambedkar chaired the drafting committee of India's Constitution, which came into force on 26 January 1950. This outlawed untouchability and granted equal rights and protections to all Indian citizens under the law, and gave many Dalits and followers of Ambedkar the confidence, with some legal safeguards, to potentially build new lives and assert their political and everyday rights. Not all stayed in India though, and some migrated abroad looking for a brighter future away from the confines of the caste system. Many arrived in Britain as economic migrants in the 1950s and 1960s onwards. With the exception of one very recent article, relatively little has been written in detail about the vibrant Ambedkarite movement and organisations in Britain beyond specific Ambedkarite-led articles and commemorative brochures.[1] The movement has seen considerable progress in Britain since the 1960s. The Ambedkarites revere Ambedkar in their everyday lives and have converted to his reinterpreted Buddhism—Navayana. Ambedkar followers, for example from the Ravidassia and Valmiki diaspora, are increasingly valuing and admiring his social reforms, and celebrate Ambedkar Jayanti (birth anniversary) in their places of worship including bhavans, gurdwaras and temples.[2]

Using personal insights and community records, this chapter discusses the key early Ambedkarite pioneers, some of whom had direct links with Ambedkar, and the organisations that emerged and adapted over time through their activism in the UK. We look at the extensive work of the Ambedkar Centenary Celebrations Committee UK under the auspices of the Federation of Ambedkarite and Buddhist Organisations UK from 1989 to 1992. We explore British Ambedkarites' participation on the global stage and their activism against atrocities their community continues to face in India. Finally, we discuss Ambedkarites' contribution to the campaign to outlaw discrimination in the UK and recent developments in the Ambedkarite movement as a new generation of people begin to understand the importance of Ambedkar and his extraordinary achievements on the global stage. The chapter aims to explore Ambedkar's legacy in the UK both via the organisations and movements that continued his politics, and in terms of their larger campaigns that relate to the struggles for social justice that he himself initiated. Through a detailed exploration of the individual and collective endeavours of some of the key organisations, the chapter also shows how Dalit and Ambedkarite movements in the UK have mapped onto particular regions and cities of the country, and how a larger movement has managed to sustain and then expand itself.

### *The Early Ambedkarite Pioneers in Britain*

Displayed on one of the walls at the Ambedkar Museum in London, NW3 is a black-and-white photograph from 1946 of a seated Ambedkar surrounded by sixteen smartly dressed Indian men. Fourteen of them were the first of two batches of students sent by Ambedkar to the UK because he believed they would benefit from exposure to a further education in the West, just as he had. This photograph, taken on 2 November 1946 at 4 Downside Crescent, London, marks Ambedkar's meeting with these students in London at a reception they had organised in his honour.[3] We don't know if any of these students settled in Britain, but we do know Shyam Khobragade, the brother of one of these students, Advocate Bhaurao Dewaji Khobragade, did and that he was active in the Ambedkarite movement. Another student, Narayan Gomaji Uke—who preferred to be called N. G. Uke—and Khobragade 'took up the Ambedkarite movement in India after their return' to India.[4] Almost seven decades later, Uke's son Ujjwal Uke played an important part in 2015 in helping secure the Ambedkar Museum London when he worked as the Private Secretary to Minister Raj Kumar Badole in the Government of Maharashtra (GOM) in India.

Some of the very early pioneers who arrived in the UK as economic migrants in the 1950s were from Punjab, and this state continued to be the single most important region for the Dalit diaspora to the UK. The foreign travel of Dalits from Punjab was made easy and attractive, at least at first, by the British Nationality Act 1948 Act, which gave Commonwealth citizens free entry to Britain. The Commonwealth Act 1968 changed that and introduced stricter immigration controls, and the wives and children of the migrants joined them.[5] After 2000, highly educated Ambedkarites arrived in the UK as skilled workers, working in information technology, engineering and medicine, for example. A growing number now run their own businesses, with a focus on forward-looking intellectual activities and social mobility. Overall, British Indians account for over 1.4 million (2.3 per cent) of the British population (2011 Census). Without a specific census category for Dalits or Ambedkarites, it is difficult to pin down the exact numbers in Britain. Doaban Jat Sikhs dominate the Punjabi diaspora in the UK, but recent research has suggested that probably around 10 per cent of the Doaban Punjabi population in the UK is of Scheduled Caste (Dalit) origin, being dominated especially by Chamars and Ravidassis, although the community is very mixed.[6]

Ambedkar visited Punjab three times during his lifetime. The first time was in 1932, to Lahore, the then capital of Punjab. He was on an official fact-finding mission as a member of the Indian Franchise Committee under the chairmanship of the Marquess of Lothian, the Parliamentary Under Secretary of State for India.[7] During this visit, from 31 March to 1 April 1932, Ambedkar took evidence from official and non-official witnesses, including from members of the Depressed Classes of Punjab represented by the Ad Dharm Mandal and the Dayanand Dalit Uddhar Sabha.[8] The second visit was to address the 'Sikh Mission' Conference on 13–14 April 1936 in Amritsar. This followed Ambedkar's aborted meeting of the Jat-Pat-Todak Mandal, which he had been invited to preside over in the Easter of 1936 in Lahore, but which had been delayed until May 1936. The organisers withdrew Ambedkar's invitation after reading an advance copy of his speech, which he later self-published as *Annihilation of Caste*. In Amritsar, he reiterated his intention to renounce Hinduism. Ambedkar's third and final visit to Punjab was in October 1951—this time to Independent India's Jalandhar, Ludhiana and Patiala. He had been eagerly awaited in Punjab for decades. Ramesh Chander, a retired Indian diplomat, records from his contacts in his hometown of Jalandhar the 1951 visit during which Ambedkar addressed an audience of 600,000–700,000 in Jalandhar's 'Bootan Mandi' on 27 October.[9] The celebrated progressive and activist Dalit poet Gurdas Ram Alam, whose 1976 visit to London inspired the London-based Dr Ambedkar Buddhist Association, wrote the poem 'Aj koun ayia savere savere' ('Who has come so early this morning, this morning') to welcome Ambedkar to Jalandhar.[10] This poem is regularly recited and sung by many Punjabi Ambedkarites during Ambedkar's birth anniversary celebrations around Britain and wherever the Ambedkarite diaspora has settled.

Amongst the many people Ambedkar met in Punjab were the young Lahori Ram Balley and Kishan Chand Sulekh. Balley later founded *Bheem Patrika*, the long-running magazine and publishing house on Ambedkarism, in 1958, and his visits to Britain from the 1970s onwards played a part in energising the Ambedkarite movement. Sulekh, who also had links with Ambedkarites in Britain, fondly recollects his time with Ambedkar during his 1951 visit. At the time, Sulekh was the General Secretary of the Punjab branch of the All-India Scheduled Castes Federation, founded by Ambedkar to campaign for the rights of the Dalit community. 'I was managing the conferences as the General Secretary and stage secretary. At that time, there used to be a very big Bute car belonging to Seth Kishan Dass. We travelled in that car for three days together. Dass, Savita Ambedkar and Dr Ambedkar sat on the back seat. The driver and I in the front. After the conferences in Jalandhar, Ludhiana and Patiala, we talked in our spare time and shared our feedback with Babasheb

Ambedkar,' Sulekh said in an interview on 26 October 2019 at his home in Chandigarh, India.[11] Sulekh recalled how Ambedkar later included him on a list of prospective parliamentary candidates for India's 1952 general election. Sulekh declined: 'I was six months underage. The eligibility for election was 25,' he said with a hint of a smile, touched that Ambedkar had considered him worthy.[12]

Ambedkar's 1951 visit to Punjab inspired and re-energised the Ambedkarite movement and the assertion of Dalit rights in Punjab, with Jalandhar at the heart of it. Ishwar Das Pawar, a Dalit, was an Under Secretary at the Departments of Partition, and of Commerce and Industry in India in October 1952. He also took over the regional passport department. In his autobiography *My Struggle in Life* (2015), Pawar describes how he allotted plots of land to new entrepreneurs and businesses at various industrial estates set up by India's government, including ones in Jalandhar. It was there Pawar became well known to the Dalit community. They approached him for support with their applications under the scheme and also raised with him the difficulties they encountered with their passport applications to travel abroad. Untouchability was still rife then, and it was Pawar's official and personal interventions that helped deal with some of the bias, discrimination and red tape that helped Dalits from Punjab secure passports. 'In those days, there was no visa system as far as UK was concerned. It was introduced later,' Pawar recalled.[13] So it is no surprise that many of the educated Dalits who migrated to the UK in the early 1950s came from Punjab's villages in the Doaba region (the area between two rivers, Sutlej and Beas) in the Jalandhar, Hoshiarpur and Kapurthala districts. Like the Dalit diaspora in Bedford, Bedfordshire, a majority of the migrants were from the Ravidassia and Valmiki community and were from modest and landless labouring backgrounds.[14]

As the Dalit communities from India settled in Britain and their families later joined them, some turned their minds to social activism and social justice. A number of Ambedkarite groups and organisations were formed in the early 1960s and 1970s, located in the areas where the early migrants settled. Many of these organisations, some under new names, have continued to be active in the twenty-first century. The next sections explore, in turn, the key people behind the setting up of these organisations, their activism and their links with their communities in India and more globally.

### *The Indian Welfare Association, the Bhartiya Buddhist Cultural Association, and the Babasaheb Dr Ambedkar Buddhist Association*

Karam Chand Leal, an ex-British Indian Army man who had served in the Second World War, arrived in Britain in 1955. Inspired by Ambedkar, Leal converted to Buddhism in 1951 and met Ambedkar several times. He wrote:

> My last meeting with Ambedkar was at his home at 26 Alipur Road, Delhi, in 1953 when I asked him to write an article for the *Ujala Weekly*, an Urdu periodical which I edited. I was also at the time General Secretary of the Punjab Provincial Scheduled Castes Federation, appointed by Babasaheb Ambedkar himself. I was to have interviewed Babasaheb but instead he interviewed me, covering with great expertise and authority the area I proposed to concentrate on. It was yet another remarkable illustration of his great ability to anticipate the nature of problems both of local and universal interest.[15]

When Leal migrated to England, he first lived in Birmingham and later settled in Hornchurch, in Essex. In the 1950s and 1960s, most of the Ravidassia and Valmiki diaspora tended to support India's Congress Party and in 1960 formed the Indian Welfare Association (IWA) in Birmingham.[16] 'As the followers of Ambedkar followed the Republican Party of India (RPI), they parted from this [the IWA] and the group led by Leal and Sansari Lal founded the Bhartiya Buddhist Cultural Association (BBCA) in 1960,' recalls Fakir Chand Chauhan, a founding member of the IWA.[17] Sansari Lal, who arrived in Britain in 1957, later formed a number of other groups, including the Babasaheb Dr Ambedkar Buddhist Association.[18] The BBCA organised the first Buddha Jayanti (birth anniversary) celebration in Birmingham on 19 May 1963. Leal later successfully lobbied for a portrait of Ambedkar to be displayed permanently at the India High Commission (IHC) in London. This was unveiled on 6 December 1970.[19]

### *Indian Buddhist Society London and the Ambedkar International Mission UK*

One of the very early Ambedkarites from the state of Maharashtra, India, to arrive in London was Vishwanath Tanbajee Hirekar in 1958. He and his wife, Maadhuri Hirekar, an inspiring Ambedkarite, had converted to Buddhism at the same time as Ambedkar in Nagpur in 1956 and were very proud of this connection. Hirekar became an employee of the IHC in London and was one of the first Ambedkarites to host a celebration to mark Ambedkar's birthday in London. In April 1962, Maharashtrians including Hirekar, Shekhar Bagul and Krishna Gamre set up the Indian Buddhist Society, London (IBS London).[20] One notable guest this Society invited to the UK in 1964 was Advocate Bhaurao Dewaji Khobragade from India. Khobragade was also the General Secretary of the Republican Party of India at the time, and his visit helped energise the Ambedkarite movement in England. As more and more Dalits from Punjab joined the IBS London, some found the organisation's name was too religiously specific. So in 1974 members decided to change the Society's name to the Ambedkar International Mission UK (AIM UK). In the same year, they opened the first Ambedkar-related Buddha Vihara[21] at Dacre Road, London, E13. This was registered in the name of four trustees—Rattan Lal Sampla, from Birmingham, Darshan Ram Jassal (known as Abbipassano after he became a Buddhist monk) from Wolverhampton, Shyam Khobragade (Advocate Khoragade's brother) and Mehanga Ram from London.[22] The Dacre Road building was sold in 2014 and the AIM UK purchased a new building at Westminster Gardens, Barking, Essex in 2016. The AIM is registered with the Charity Commission for England and Wales and has six trustees—Subash Chander Jassal, Sat Pal Muman, Prem Chand Mann, Ramji Banger, Surinder Mehmi and Shammi Leal.[23] It caters to the religious needs of the Buddhist Community primarily in East London, but also has affiliates in other cities and town, and is founded on Ambedkar's life and mission.[24] In 2019 Sat Pal Muman gave a third-party witness statement to the Public Inquiry into 10 King Henry's Road (see Chapter 7). Muman is also active in the campaign to outlaw caste discrimination in Britain as chair of CasteWatchUK.

*Republican Group of Great Britain and the Dr Ambedkar Mission Society, Glasgow*

When Advocate Khobragade visited London in 1964 he also met Ambedkarites and Dalit activists in the Midlands where he set up the Republican Group of Great Britain (RGGB).[25] This group was very successful in attracting new people to the movement—including from the Ravidassia and Valmiki diaspora. Key members included activists Chanan Ram Ghoug (former President of RPI Punjab Branch), Khushi Ram Pardesi, Chanan Chahal, Hans Raj Ginda, Bishan Dass Bains, Sohan Lal Gindha, Fakir Chand Chauhan and Bishan Dass Mahay.[26] Bishan Dass Bains, who arrived in Britain in 1963, later became involved in politics and became the first Asian Mayor of Wolverhampton in 1986.[27] They spread Ambedkar's vision and social activism and, in meetings, helped raised awareness of the plight of Dalits in India. RPI leaders and Indian politicians were invited to address these meetings and gatherings. This helped attract more and more members to the movement. Ambedkarite activists Harbans Lal Virdee, Chanan Chahal, Arun Kumar, Fakir Chand Chauhan, Bhagat Ram Sampla, and others used this platform to distribute and share Ambedkar-related literature, and also their articles and translations in vernacular languages. Sampla, from Punjab, who settled in Aldershot, Hampshire, has many books to his credit in Punjabi, Hindi and English. In the 1960s and 1970s, Sampla was a sought-after speaker at Ambedkarite-related events.[28] Sampla's father, Chanan Ram, was particularly active in Punjab after meeting Ambedkar in 1951, and the Sampla family, including Balram, Ratan Lal, Hans Raj in England, and a cousin, Sohan Lal Sampla in Germany, continue to be very active in the movement. When the RPI in India split in 1966, the RGGB also disintegrated.[29] Ginda moved from Wolverhampton to Scotland in 1973. With the help of the Ravidassia and Valmiki community there, he set up the Dr Ambedkar Mission Society, Glasgow. In 1982 Ginda established the Ambedkarite Aid Society[30] to support activists in Punjab. He also set up the International Buddhist Mission Trust and its religious wing—the Budh Prachar Smiti (an organisation that preaches Buddhism)—and has also helped build several Buddha Viharas in India. Ginda also helped to establish the Bodhisattva Ambedkar Public Senior Secondary School in the village of Phool Pur Dhanal in Jalandhar in 2000.[31]

### *The Babasaheb Ambedkar Buddhist Association and the Dr Ambedkar Memorial Committee of Great Britain*

Sohanal Shastri, a writer and close associate of Ambedkar in his later years, visited Birmingham in 1973. It was during this visit that Sansari Lal and others set up the Babasaheb Ambedkar Buddhist Association (BABA). On 3 June 1973 they organised a large conversion of Dalits to Buddhism in West Bromwich, near Birmingham, which Shastri presided over.[32] The other group led by Fakir Chand Chauhan—the Dr Ambedkar Buddhist Society—later merged with BABA to become the Dr Ambedkar Buddhist Organisation, Birmingham (DABO, Birmingham). Devinder Chander, one of the founding members of DABO, continues to be very active. He is the Chief Editor of *Samaj Weekly*, a Punjabi, English and Hindi newspaper that has a large circulation around the UK and online. Chander, together with Bishan Dass Bains, also regularly appears on the British community TV channel Kanshi TV to discuss issues affecting the Dalit community, and spreads information about Ambedkar's life and mission.

Although the Ambedkarite movement was largely initiated in Birmingham, Wolverhampton soon became the hub for activities in the Midlands. With active members of the RGGB there, in July 1969 they established the Dr Ambedkar Memorial Committee of Great Britain (DAMC GB).[33] This Committee pursues and delivers practical initiatives that have helped raise awareness of Ambedkar in the diaspora and to a wider non-Ambedkarite audience. On 25 September 1973, the DAMC donated a portrait of Ambedkar to LSE.[34] The following year, it donated a portrait to Gray's Inn. This was unveiled by the Inn's Treasurer, Hugh Francis QC, on 6 July 1974.[35] Two years later, on 16 September 1975, the DAMC donated another portrait—this time to Columbia University, New York.[36] These initiatives have enhanced Ambedkar's profile and reinforced his connection with the three seats of learning that played a significant role in his life in the West. The Punjab Buddhist Society UK (PBS UK), based originally in Wolverhampton, was established on 28 March 2004. It is registered with the Charity Commission of England and Wales to work at a local, national and international level to advance the Buddhist faith around the world, by promoting the establishment and support of Buddhist monasteries.[37] On 10 October 2006 the PBS UK opened the Takshila Maha Buddha Vihara in Ludhiana.[38]

In 1976, the DAMC GB, with donations from Ambedkarites around Britain, bought and converted a small house into a Buddha Vihara on Lea Road, Penn Fields, Wolverhampton.[39] The Committee's ever-expanding membership and activities soon outgrew this building, and for the centenary of Ambedkar's birth in 1991, the DAMC secured and opened a much larger purpose-built Buddha Vihara, and the Dr Ambedkar Community Centre[40] on Upper Zoar Street, Wolverhampton. Ms Mayawati, the Indian politician and leader of Bahujan Samaj Party (BSP), inaugurated the Centre on 14 October 2000.[41] Mayawati had by then been the former Chief Minister of Uttar Pradesh twice. She later went on to hold the position twice more, from 2002 to 2003, and again from 2007–12. Mayawati was the first Dalit woman and Ambedkarite to achieve such a high and powerful political position in India. She and the BSP have supporters all over the world, including in the UK.

In 2003, the DAMC GB opened the Ambedkar Museum[42] in the Buddha Vihara in Wolverhampton. This has on display some of Ambedkar's personal belongings donated to the DAMC GB by Siddharth Rattu, the son of the late Nanak Chand Rattu, who was a personal secretary to Ambedkar in his later years. In the courtyard of the building there are statues of Ambedkar and the Buddha. The activities of the organisation in the UK are also linked to activities in India. For example, on 14 October 2006, the DAMC GB opened the Dr Ambedkar Buddhist Resource Centre on Behram-Mahilpur Road, Banga, Punjab. Six years later, on 15 September 2012, the DAMC opened the Dr Ambedkar Public School on the Banga site.[43] As part of its outreach activities in the UK, the DAMC Committee has regular weekly slots under the banner 'Lotus TV' on Kanshi TV. Members and trustees use this valuable platform to promote and spread the teachings of Ambedkar and Buddha. Dashran Ram Jassall, one of the founding members of DAMC GB, was the first Punjabi Buddhist monk, Abbipassano. He built a peace pagoda on the banks of the river Sutlej, in Ludhiana, that enables devotees to immerse the ashes of their loved ones in the river in line with Buddhist tradition. Tarsem Lal Chahal, also from Wolverhampton, set up a Vishav Bodh Sangh (World Buddhist Federation) to support the building of Buddha Viharas in Punjab too.

### *Ambedkar Mission Society, Bedford*

Punjabi Dalits also settled in the large market town of Bedford, enticed by the prospect of easily finding work in the brickyards, including the London Brick Company that met the increased demand for bricks after the Second World War. Later, when their families joined them, they made plans for places to socialise and worship. Many towns with an Indian diaspora set up places of religious worship to meet this spiritual and social need. Ambedkarites Chanan Chahal and Dhanpat Rattu both began their social activism at the Sri Guru Ravidass Sabha Bedford, established in 1969.[44] They were the early pioneers of the Ambedkarite movement in Bedford, with Chahal already active in the RPGB since 1964. In 1972 Chahal founded the Bheem Association which published and disseminated Ambedkar-related material to the wider community. The Bheem Association was renamed the Ambedkar Mission Society (AMS) Bedford in 1983.[45] The AMS continued the work and also published material on the life and teachings of Ambedkar Guru Ravidass and other Dalit icons. In 1984, Chahal set up the Kirti Publication Trust that published a weekly newspaper, *Kirti Weekly*, from Jalandhar from 1984 to 1987.[46] Like many other Ambedkar-related organisations in Britain, the AMS Bedford also reached out to help their community in India by setting up free medical camps for marginalised communities and supported children in Punjab with books and computers.[47]

The AMS Bedford was one of the first organisations whose members raised awareness of and exposed caste discrimination in Britain. In 1976 Chahal led a protest against an offensive article by Liz Brown in *The Bedfordshire Times*, in which she had described

'Untouchables' as 'subhumans' when discussing religions in Bedfordshire.[48] Since then, it has campaigned to outlaw caste discrimination in Britain. In the 1980s AMS Bedford supported Bhagwan Das, an advocate in the Supreme Court of India, a scholar and a research assistant to Ambedkar, with his World Conferences on Religion and Peace in Kenya, Korea and Australia.[49] They also helped Das attend the 36th Session of the United Nations (UN) Commission on Prevention of Discrimination of Minorities in Geneva, in August 1983. Like Dr Laxmi Berwa from the USA the year before him, Das was able to raise with the UN the reality of the atrocities and discrimination against Dalits in South East Asia. The AMS published and circulated Das's 1983 speech at the UN widely in the UK and in India.[50]

In 2004 the AIM donated a bronze bust of Ambedkar to Simon Fraser University in Vancouver that has been on display in the Bennett Library since 14 October 2004. This has become a place of pilgrimage for Ambedkarites who happen to live in or visit Vancouver. To mark Ambedkar's 125th birth anniversary, the AMS collaborated with Bedford Borough Council to hold an exhibition of photographs of Ambedkar and his key messages at the Bedford Central Library and the Corn Exchange in Bedford. Pirithi Kaeley and Arun Kumar of the AIM curated this.[51]

### *Dr Ambedkar Memorial Trust, London and the Dr Ambedkar Buddhist Association (now known as the Buddha Dhamma Association)*

In London, the movement that had begun in the early 1960s also saw the formation of two more Ambedkarite and Buddhist-related organisations. The Dr Ambedkar Memorial Trust, London (DAMT) was established in 1972 in East London, and the Dr Ambedkar Buddhist Association was founded in 1976 in West London. Gautam Chakravarty (commonly known as C. Gautam) leads on much of DAMT's activities.[52] The Trust was formally registered with the UK's Charity Commission in 1973, with its aim of helping needy students and propagating the Ambedkar mission in the UK.[53] The DAMT was the only organisation established in the 1970s, with its initial membership mostly from the diaspora from Gujarat. The

Trust now also has members from the Punjabi and Marathi diaspora, including Sohan Ginda and Surjit Kaur Birdi from Punjab. Like other Ambedkarite organisations in Britain, the Trust's members have also promoted school-age children's education in India—this time in a remote village in Valod, in the district of Tapi, Gujarat, with a population of mostly Adivasis, India's tribal people. The Trust continues to publish and propagate Ambedkar's work and mission locally and nationally.

The Dr Ambedkar Buddhist Association (DABA), based in Southall, West London, was founded in 1976 by Harbans Lal Virdee, who came to England as a fifteen-year-old in 1966 from Punjab with his father Ujagar Virdee.[54] DABA was founded at Virdee's home during a dinner reception for the poet Gurdas Ram Alam from Jalandhar. DABA is now known as the Buddha Dhamma Association (BDA). Virdee remains a very active Ambedkarite and a committed Buddhist. He has tirelessly promoted Buddhism in India and helped set up a number of Buddha Viharas there, including one in Phagwara, Punjab, and one near Pondicherry, in Tamil Nadu. In 2012, Virdee bought some land in Shravasti, a district in Uttar Pradesh, and set up a Bhikkhuni training centre for female Buddhist monks.[55]

In 1993, the DAMT purchased the house at 12 Featherstone Road, Southall at an auction. It was a derelict building badly damaged by fire. The DABA really wanted to buy the house at auction but just could not raise the funds. Virdee recounted how DABA had 'sweet-talked' C. Gautam (who had a thriving business at the time) and the DAMT into buying house: 'We offered, and the DAMT agreed, to pay for the property and for DABA to take over from the DAMT within a year. We just didn't manage this. The DAMT even gave us another year but we were unable to raise sufficient funds from donations'.[56] The house is now known as the Buddha Vihara, and is looked after and managed by the DAMT, while the BDA carries out its Buddhist activities from the building. On 14 April 2000, the DAMT unveiled the newly built Ambedkar Hall attached to the building.[57]

The Buddha Vihara provides short-term accommodation for students embarking on studies in the UK, as well as Ambedkarites just passing through London, and those attending meetings and conferences. The Vihara and the Ambedkar Hall has a steady stream of visitors and dignitaries and has nurtured a number of young Ambedkarites. CasteWatchUK, a charity that monitors and works to remove caste discrimination, was conceived at a meeting of activists at the Buddha Vihara in 2003 (see Chapter 8). Over the years, the Bahujan Samaj Party's UK supporters have held their meetings in the Ambedkar Hall, and which has also been used to host talks by visiting academics, Dalit activists, and Ambedkarites. Waman Meshram of BAMCEF,[58] academics Dr Anand Teltumbde and Dr Vivek Kumar, the social activist Dr R. S. Praveen Kumar and Padma Shri Kalpana Soroj, Lahori Ram Balley, writer Arundhati Roy, and the artist Pradymumna Kumar Mahanandia have all given talks at the Ambedkar Hall.[59]

*The Federation of Ambedkarite and Buddhist Organisations UK*

As more and more Ambedkar- and Lord Buddha-related organisations formed and grew in number in the UK, the need for coordination on Dalit and other issues became evident. The Ambedkar Buddhist Council UK (ABC UK) was formed in 1982 to fill this gap, and Fakir Chand Chauhan became the President with Swaran Chand Suman the General Secretary.[60] In 1985, the ABC UK sponsored an International Conference, 'The Right Path for the Salvation of Dalits' in West Bromwich.[61] Kanshi Ram, the social reformer and founder of the BSP, was the chief guest.[62] During his visit, Kanshi Ram toured around a number of cities in the UK to meet Ambedkarites and social activists. It was during a meeting in Letchworth in 1986 under the Chairmanship of Sohan Lal Shastri, that the ABC UK was renamed the Federation of Ambedkarite and Buddhist Organisations UK (FABO UK) to allow for a wider participation of Buddhist and non-Buddhist organisations.[63] The Federation is the central body that strengthens organisations within its membership, including loose or informal associations. Since 1986, FABO UK's presidents have been V. T. Hirekar, Harbans Virdee, Chanan Chahal, Sohan Lal Ginda, Dr N. Sirinivasan, Ram Murti Suman, and since 2013, Santosh Dass MBE—the Federation's first woman president. The general secretaries have been Gurdial Bangar, Dhanpat Rattu, C. Gautam and, since 2013, joint secretaries C. Gautam and Arun Kumar.

FABO UK has been demonstrably active on many fronts. In 1970 the IHC was persuaded by Ambedkarites to celebrate Ambedkar's birth anniversary. The IHC had already been celebrating the birth of Guru Nanak[64] and Gandhi, and religious and cultural festivals including Diwali[65] and Vaisakhi,[66] but until then had ignored Ambedkar. British politicians, academics, human rights activists and followers of Ambedkar continue to participate in these annual receptions. Tony Benn MP, Dr Christophe Jaffrelot, Professor Dr Kevin Brown, Chief Justice Balakrishnan and Somnath Chatterjee, the former speaker of the Indian Parliament, have been some of the keynote speakers in the past. FABO UK has been at the forefront of the annual receptions at the IHC, working closely with organisations including the Sri Guru Ravidass Sabha UK, Europe and Abroad, and the Valmiki organisations.

In 1992, FABO UK donated a bronze bust of Ambedkar to the IHC.[67] This was unveiled on 14 April by Chief Eleazar Chakwuemeka Anayaoku, the then Commonwealth Secretary General. Michael Foot MP, former leader of Labour Party, who attended the unveiling, described Ambedkar as 'a giant amongst giants'.[68] The IHC later named the hall where the bust is displayed as the Ambedkar Hall. A few years later, FABO UK donated a bronze bust of Ambedkar to LSE. This was unveiled by Dr John Ashworth, Director of LSE, on 14 April 1994; he described Ambedkar as 'one of the most prominent social reformers and thinkers of twentieth-century India'.[69] He also referred to the words in a letter written in 1930 by his former teacher, Professor Edwin Cannan, to the then Director, Sir William (Lord) Beveridge, in which he said 'Dr Ambedkar was by far the ablest Indian we ever had in my time'.[70] C. Gautam and C. Chahal, of FABO UK, were instrumental in delivering this initiative. FABO UK's relationship with LSE continued with them jointly hosting the conference 'Dalits' Politics of India' on 22 October 1994. Ambedkarites continue to lobby for an 'Ambedkar Chair' at LSE.

In 1995, FABO UK donated a bust of Ambedkar to Columbia University. This was unveiled on 24 October 1995 in the presence of Savita Ambedkar—Ambedkar's second wife, who travelled to New York at FABO UK's invitation.[71] The bust is displayed in the Lehman Library. Since 2003, FABO UK has spearheaded an annual peace walk from 10KHR to the LSE via the British Library to mark Ambedkar's birth and death anniversaries. This enables Ambedkarites to experience the walk Ambedkar made almost daily from 10KHR to the British Library and LSE. When 10KHR came on the market in 2014, it was Harbans Virdee of FABO UK, who at the end of August 2014 emailed Ambedkarites around the world calling on them to lobby the Government of Maharashtra (GOM) to buy the house and turn it into a memorial. Santosh Dass pursued this on behalf of FABO UK. After a year of intense lobbying with the support of Ambedkarites in India, GOM finally bought the property. Two members of FABO UK, Dass and C. Gautam, later formed the seven-member Dr Ambedkar Memorial Advisory Committee, announced by Mr Raj Kumar Badole, the Cabinet Minister for the Department of Social Justice and Special Assistance, GOM, on 2 February 2017.[72] The campaign for the Ambedkar Museum in London is discussed in more detail in Chapter 7.

In 2016, for the 125th anniversary of Ambedkar's birth and the centenary of his first visit to the UK to join LSE and Gray's Inn, FABO UK marked the anniversaries at 10KHR, LSE, the House of Lords, and at the IHC.[73] It also organised a conference 'Dr Ambedkar's Relevance Today and in the Future' in the Old Theatre at LSE. This was in collaboration with LSE's Inequality and Poverty Research Programme, in the Department of Anthropology and India Observatory, LSE, with professors Dr Ruth Kattumari and Dr Alpa Shah's support. The conference was chaired and hosted by Dass on 16 June 2016 and brought together academics, economists, equality champions and women activists from India, UK and the USA.[74] Professor Amartya Sen, Nobel Laureate, and Bharat Ratna, economist and philosopher, were the chief guest speakers. Among the speakers were Dr Alpa Shah (LSE), Professor David Moss (SOAS University of London), Dr Clarinda Still (University of Oxford and LSE), Vidya Bhushan Rawat, human rights defender (India), Dr Radha D'Souza (University of Westminster), Dr Harshadeep Kamble, Commissioner of the Food and Drug Administration for Maharashtra, Dr Virander Paul, the Deputy Indian High Commissioner, Ravi Kumar of the Anti Caste Discrimination Alliance (ACDA) and Dr Anand Teltumbde, the academic and writer.[75]

Since 2015, FABO UK has organised and hosted a regular annual conference at the House of Lords to mark Ambedkar's birth anniversary. Lord Harries of Pentregarth, of the All Party Parliamentary Group for Dalits, chairs these events, which are hosted by Santosh Dass. This has helped revive the participation of UK politicians, academics, and women in the campaign to raise awareness of Ambedkar in Parliament on a regular basis. This is also a useful platform to discuss developments on caste discrimination law in Britain and the plight of Dalits in India.

Towards the end of 2014, Dass began lobbying Gray's Inn for another fitting memorial to Ambedkar since the portrait donated by the Dr Ambedkar Memorial Committee of Great Britain in 1974. A second portrait of Ambedkar in his barrister's robes, by the portrait artist Hazel Morgan, was donated to Gray's Inn on 6 December 2016 by the Indian government. With the valuable support of Tony Harking, the Under-Treasurer of The Honourable Society of Gray's Inn, the Inn agreed that a room be named after Ambedkar, but the refurbishment work required and the unveiling were delayed, in part due to the Covid-19 pandemic. In 2020, FABO UK commissioned a new portrait of Ambedkar for this new room by the artist David Newens, based on a 1946 black-and-white photo by the American journalist Margaret Bourke-White. Describing the new portrait and Bourke-White's photo, Ken Hunt the writer notes, 'Unlike his usual formal patrician poses, her photo shoot captured him in relaxed mood. He is at home at 26 Alipur Road, Civil Lines, Delhi on his veranda with a cascade of bougainvillea beside him.'[76] The portrait was unveiled on 30 June 2021 at Gray's Inn on the same day as the Ambedkar room was opened to be used for training barristers and for holding meetings at Gray's Inn.[77] The Master Treasurer of the Inn, Ali Malek QC, Santosh Dass, Lord David Alton of Liverpool, and Sujat Ambedkar (Ambedkar's great-grandson) were the speakers at the unveiling.[78] Invited guests at the unveiling included Harshal and Shalaka Ahire, Bishan Dass, Davinder Chander, Rajesh Chavda, C. Gautam, Sohan and Rahul Ginda, William Gould, Ken Hunt, Arun Kumar, David Newens, Rampal Rahi, Balram Sampla, Dr Prena Tambay, Pratap Tambe, Harbans Virdee, and Dr Suraj Yengde.

*Ambedkar Centenary Celebration Committee, UK*

To mark the centenary of Ambedkar's birth, the then Prime Minister of India, Vishwanath Pratap Singh, declared 1990 the year of social justice in India, to conclude on 14 April 1991. In the UK, celebrating Ambedkar's birth anniversary is one of the highlights of the year in the diary of all the Ambedkarite organisations. As the centenary approached, many Ambedkarite and Buddhist organisations got together and decided to mark this significant anniversary in a coordinated way. FABO UK took the lead and the Ambedkar Centenary Celebrations Committee UK (ACCC UK) was established under its auspices.

FABO UK wanted to celebrate this important anniversary by bringing Ambedkar's life and messages to a new audience and remove him from the pigeonhole of being described as just a leader of the Untouchables. Work began at a meeting in London in 1988 to formulate a strategy, during which the ACCC UK was established. Bhagwan Das from New Delhi, Kenneth Griffiths, the actor and documentary film-maker, and Richard Houser, a sociologist and human rights activist, were amongst the attendees. Dr Indraprastha Gordhanbhai Patel, the then Director of LSE, and Dr Bhikhu Parekh (now Lord Parekh) became honorary Presidents of the Committee. Lord Home of the Hirsel and Lord Callaghan of Cardiff (both former UK Prime Ministers), Lord Bottomley, Former Secretary of State for UK in India, Lord Grimond, Countess Mountbatten of Burma, Dr Swraj Paul (now Lord Paul), Prakash Ambedkar (grandson of Dr Ambedkar), and Sharad Pawar, the then Chief Minister of Maharashtra, became the ACCC's patrons. The organising committee of the ACCC was comprised of Chanan Chahal (President), Dr Chaman Lal Maman (Vice President), C. Gautam (General Secretary), M. S. Bahal (Publicity Secretary), and Sohan Lal Gindha (Treasurer). An executive committee of UK Ambedkarites supported them.[79]

Though there were a number of Ambedkarite activists involved in the ACCC UK, the hands-on activism of C. Chahal and C. Gautam helped make the celebrations a great success. They led on the publicity material and fostered relationships with academic circles around the world for the key events. C. Gautam, at the time a businessman, converted a warehouse adjoining his large shop in London into a boardroom for the Committee meetings. He also personally employed a part-time assistant to handle the endless correspondence during this period and for the commissioning of articles and messages for the souvenir publications. A key element of the ACCC UK's strategy was to reach out to those who had worked with Ambedkar during British rule to obtain and catalogue first-hand accounts. Lord Bottomley and Lord Woodrow Wyatt, Baron of Weeford, came on board quickly. Bottomley was a member of the Parliamentary delegation of the Labour government under Prime Minister Clement Attlee to discuss the transfer of power in India in 1946. Bottomley was actively involved in the trade union movement in Britain at the time and keen to meet Ambedkar, who was a member of the Viceroy's Council dealing with industrial matters. Woodrow Wyatt also met Ambedkar when Wyatt was a personal assistant to Sir Stafford Cripps during their visit to India in 1946 to discuss the framing of India's constitution.

The ACCC UK was formally launched in the Jubilee Room at the House of Commons on 14 April 1989.[80] One of the organisations present was the British Organisation of People of Indian Origin (BOPIO). Its president, Sinna Mani, later became involved in the ACCC UK's activities too.

Ambedkarites in Britain celebrated the centenary over four years from 1989 to 1992. This involved talks, seminars, conferences, cultural programmes and exhibitions.[81] The ACCC published four souvenirs that contain historical documents, photographs and articles by scholars and people who had personally known or had worked with Ambedkar. A quarterly journal *New Era* continued to provide information in a similar way after these celebrations. Together, these are a valuable resource for research on Ambedkar and his movement. Encouraged and supported by the ACCC UK, TV documentaries *In the Footsteps of Ambedkar* (1989), *Caste at Birth* (1990), *It's My Belief* (1990), *Encounter* (1991) and *The World this Week* (1991) examined the issue of untouchability in India, its migration abroad, and Ambedkar's concept of a just society.

In London, the Committee organised a lavish conference and reception at the Royal Commonwealth Society, Commonwealth Hall in London on 14 April 1990. The Chief Guest was Lord Bottomley and also present were Dr Sathyawani Muthu, former Minister of Union of India, Bhagwan Das, Dr Berwa and Ambedkarites from India, USA and Europe. Countess Mountbatten, Baroness Shreela Flather, and Dr L. M. Singhvi, the Indian High Commissioner, were amongst the key speakers. The day ended with a reception at the IHC in London at which Lord Templeman, the British judge and Lord of Appeal, addressed the gathering. The Committee also held a conference jointly with Gray's Inn on 21 February 1991 at which Lord Goff of Chieveley described Ambedkar as 'The Moses of India'.[82]

During this period, a number of notable public exhibitions were organised to raise awareness of Ambedkar. These exhibited photographs, illustrations, and key messages from his writings. Arun Kumar of AMS Bedford, with Bedfordshire County Council and the ACCC UK organised a two-week exhibition at the Bedford Central Library, Harpur Street from 7 to 19 January 1991.[83] From 5 to 26 April 1991, the ACCC together with the London Borough of Hackney hosted a similar exhibition at the Homerton Library, East London. The Dr Ambedkar Buddhist Association hosted an exhibition at the Dominion Centre, Southall from 17 to 23 June 1991. This concluded with a seminar on caste-based discrimination on 23 June 1991.[84] The concluding exhibition was held at Holborn Library, London on 6 December 1991 to coincide with Dr Ambedkar's death anniversary. Councillor Jim Turner, the Mayor of Camden, inaugurated this exhibition. Later that day, Roy Hattersley MP (the then Deputy Leader of the Labour Party) unveiled a commemorative blue plaque at 10KHR in the presence of the Mayor of Camden, the actress Glenda Jackson MP and Ambedkarites. The blue plaque had been purchased and installed by the ACCC UK with the full knowledge of English Heritage and Camden Council. C. Gautam described how work on this had started in 1974 and had involved discussions with numerous landlords and residents of the property and the then Greater London Council.[85]

The ACCC UK had invited India's Prime Minister Vishwanath Pratap Singh and Ram Vilas Paswan, a former Union Minister to the UK to attend the celebrations.[86] By the time Singh and Paswan arrived on 20 May 1992, they were no longer in post. Nevertheless, their meetings and interactions with Ambedkarites in London, Southall, Birmingham, Bedford, Letchworth and Wolverhampton helped secure Singh's commitment to implement the recommendations of the 1980 'Mandal Commission' report.

During the centenary celebrations, it became apparent that more research on Dalit issues, leadership training and forging links with established humanitarian organisations around the world were required. The International Ambedkar Institute (IAI) was established in May 1990 to deliver this agenda. Professionals, social activists, and supporters from various fields became involved with the Institute with Kenneth Griffith (the Welsh actor) as the Chair.[87] Griffith wanted to make a film about the life of Ambedkar and his planning was well advanced. After weeks of prevarications, on 25 January 1989, the Indian government told him he would not get a visa to return to India to make the film.[88] Griffith later produced a documentary *The Untouchable—the Story of Ambedkar*. This was broadcast on BBC Two on 12 October 1996. Griffiths often described himself as an honorary Untouchable as he travelled far and wide to promote Ambedkar and his ideology.[89] On 3 April 1996, Griffith presented Ambedkar's collected works *Writings and Speeches* to both the University of British Columbia and the Simon Fraser University in Canada. The IAI disbanded soon after Griffith's death in 2006.

Sir Richard Attenborough's 1982 Oscar-winning film *Gandhi,* funded by the Indian government, received great critical and public acclaim. Airbrushed from the three-hour-long film, however, was even a walk-on part for Ambedkar. Naturally, this outraged Ambedkarites, who called for a film to be made on the life of Ambedkar too. The Government of India's Ministry of Social Welfare and Empowerment and the GOM finally funded a film over a decade later and engaged Dr Jabbar Patel to direct it. Patel had already made a seventy-one-minute documentary called *Dr Babasaheb Ambedkar* in 1991. He made a number of visits to London to finalise his schedule for the filming, and C. Gautam transported him around to the various locations for the shoot and to other meetings. A change of government in India saw the film's budget cut drastically. To help reduce the overhead expenses, FABO UK members provided the ten-member cast and crew with accommodation, transport and evening meals during the two-week shoot in 1996 in London. The film *Dr Babasaheb Ambedkar* was released in 2000 and toured many film festivals and received praise. It was not released in the UK, however, so FABO UK screened it privately at the Safari Cinema in Harrow, north London, and the Princess Cinema in Smethwick, Birmingham soon afterwards.

### *Protests against Atrocities*

Ambedkarites in Britain are not silent when it comes to protesting against injustices. They have raised their voice and banners against human rights violations and atrocities against Dalits for decades by staging and supporting protests around the country. These have included, for example, the protest about caste discrimination and atrocities against Dalits in India during a visit by Prime Minister Morarji Desai to Southall on 7 June 1978.[90] This led to Desai having to respond to media questions on the issue of untouchability in India. More recently, Ambedkarites have protested against Prime Minister Narendra Modi during his official visits to London in 2015 and 2018. Ambedkarites have stood in solidarity with their community in India when they have faced atrocities. For example, in June 1992 they protested against the massacre of Dalits in Kumher village, Rajasthan. In July 1997 they protested against India's Special Reserve Police's killing of Ambedkarites in a movement against the desecration of a statue of Ambedkar in Maharashtra on 11 July 1997. On 25 January 2016, Ambedkarites took part in the candlelit protest outside the IHC London against the death of a young Dalit scholar Rohith Vemula, who committed suicide at the campus of Hyderabad Central University after being excluded from his course by what he believed to be his casteist professors. On 21 January 2019, Ambedkarites and the Dalit community joined protests in London against the arrests and violence against Ambedkarites in the aftermath of the Bhima Koregaon arrests of academics, social and human rights activists, including that of Dr Anand Teltumbde.[91] Since 2010, Ambedkarites have also come out regularly in large numbers in London in support of caste discrimination being outlawed in Britain.

*Ambedkarites on the Global Stage*

Over the decades, the Dalit diaspora has shown it is not limited just to activities in the UK. Its members have reached out to spread Ambedkar's message of equality, liberty and social justice to many other countries too. C. Chahal of FABO UK presented a paper 'A Peaceful Revolution' at the Conference of the International Association of Buddhist Studies at UNESCO, Paris in August 1991.[92] C. Gautam and M. S. Bahal participated in the First World Dalit Conference in Kuala Lumpur from 10–11 October 1998. Babu Kanshi Ram, Ram Vilas Paswan, Phoolan Devi (the child bride kidnapped, turned bandit, and a former Indian MP, whose life is depicted in the 1994 film *Bandit Queen*), and Advocate Bhagwan Das shared the stage there.

As a director of the British chapter of US-based Ambedkar Centre for Justice and Peace, V. T. Hirekar travelled to many countries to lobby UN agencies to raise awareness of the plight of Dalits in India. Balram Sampla also led a delegation that included Devinder and Rani Chander to the UN World Conference against Racism (WCAR) in Durban, South Africa from 31 August to 8 September 2001.[93] This was the first conference of international Dalit delegates to jointly raise the issue of caste discrimination and atrocities against Dalits. In May 2003, Ambedkarites from the UK also participated in the International Dalit Conference in Vancouver.[94] C. Chahal and Arun Kumar played a significant role in the planning and framing of the Vancouver Declaration that made a number of demands, including calls for a proportionate number of Scheduled Castes and Scheduled Tribes to sit in India's national institutions, access to wealth and capital; and for the UN and NGOs to recognise Dalits as a special group with separate Dalit divisions within these organisations to be managed by the Dalits.[95] D. Rattu, C. Gautam and M. S. Bahal also attended this conference. The Chetna Association of Canada founded by Jai Birdi and Surinder Ranga, in partnership with University of British Columbia, Simon Fraser University, and the Dr Hari Sharma

Foundation, later set up the Annual B. R. Ambedkar Memorial Lecture in Vancouver.[96] Santosh Dass was the guest speaker in 2018. The previous lectures were delivered by Dr Anand Teltumbde in 2016, Dr Vivek Kumar in 2017 and Dr Suraj Yengde in 2019.[97]

In 2014, British Ambedkarites participated in the Dr Ambedkar International Convention held in Paris from 3–5 July. Organised by the French chapter of the Ambedkar International Mission, it was led by the dynamic Ambedkarite Raj Kumar Kamble from the USA. The Guru Ravidass Sabha in Paris, with financial contributions from, and the participation of, key committee members of the Shri Guru Ravidass Sabha UK, Europe and Abroad hosted the conference. The conference brought together Ambedkarites and social activists from around the world. Santosh Dass and C. Gautam addressed the conference on behalf of FABO UK. A year later, on 10 September 2015, Ram Pal Rahi, Vice President of FABO UK, took part in the unveiling ceremony of Dr Ambedkar's statue at the Koyasan University in Japan.

### *Campaign against Caste Discrimination in the UK and More Recent Developments in the Movement*

Ambedkar's name is synonymous with the struggle against caste oppression, so it is only natural that his followers, and organisations in his name, take a stand against caste-related atrocities or discrimination. Some of the early campaigners even faced criticism from their own community, who wanted to forget about caste in Britain, or not be outed as Dalits. Others accused them of giving a bad name to the Indian diaspora by exposing caste divisions, and called them 'anti-national'. Ambedkarites have stood shoulder to shoulder with organisations campaigning to outlaw caste discrimination in Britain for decades now. In the face of opposition from the Hindu community, C. Chahal, the then President of FABO UK, wrote and published *The Evil of Caste—The Caste System as the Largest Systemic Violation of Human Rights in Today's World* report. FABO UK released this report jointly with the Dalit Solidarity Network UK (DSN UK) at the House of Commons on 19 January 2009. This, along with the reports by the DSN UK and the ACDA, have been valuable in the campaign. Ambedkarites have organised and participated in discussions and conferences nationally and internationally at which they have called for caste discrimination to be outlawed in the UK. Those publicly speaking out have included barrister Saunvedan Aparanti, Dr Shrikant Borker, Dr Raj Chand, Santosh Dass, Ram Dhariwal, Pirthi Kaeley, Tarsem Kalyan, Arun Kumar, Ravi Kumar, Sat Pal Muman, Lekh Raj Pall, Davinder Prasad, and Dr Prena Tambey.

The Ambedkarite movement continues to develop in terms of their campaign focus and the communities they serve. It has seen followers of Guru Ravidass and Bhagwan Valmiki, and supporters of the Bahujan Samaj Party in Britain revere and celebrate Ambedkar in increasing numbers. In September 2021, the Ravidassia community in Derby renamed their Guru Ravidass Community Centre the Dr B. R. Ambedkar Community Centre.

In Coventry, Councillor Ram Prakash Lakha OBE, who arrived in Britain in 1977 at the age 28 from Punjab, and was the Lord Mayor of Coventry for 2005/2006, has actively lobbied for 14 April—Ambedkar's birthday—to be marked as Equality Day by the Council. The first of these celebrations took place in 2014. On 14 April 2022, Coventry Council marked Equality Day at its Council House with Santosh Dass as the keynote guest speaker.[98] FABO UK too has been calling for 14 April to be recognised as International Day of Equality since 2015, in support of the former Indian Ambassador Ramesh Chander's campaign for this.[99] Proclamations to mark 14 April as the Dr B. R. Ambedkar Day of Equality have already been made in Canada by the City of Burnaby in 2020 and British Columbia in 2021 after lobbing by the Chetna Association of Canada.[100] In 2022 similar proclamations were made in the USA by the state of Colorado, which proclaimed 14 April 2022 as 'Dr B. R. Ambedkar Equity Day'; and the Indian State of Tamil Nadu also announced 14 April as a day of equality.

In the twenty-first century, highly educated Ambedkarites have migrated and settled in the UK as skilled workers, operating in information technology, engineering and medicine. A growing number now run their own businesses with a focus on forward-looking intellectual activities and social mobility. Pratap Tambey, an IT professional from Maharashtra, remarked 'every house in the community has multiple graduate degrees and this progress continues into next generation. The next generation of the community is emerging as a role model for the UK and India. The fierce focus of parents to ensure grammar or private school education is unparalleled.'[101] The focus of this community is to nurture the younger generations as well as deepening and spreading Dhamma theory and practice in their community. Tambe noted: 'There are multiple subgroups of people who are loosely connected under the banner of Buddhist Ambedkarites and the Maitree Sangha, and they support students and new migrants not only financially where they can, but also help them solve local problems and find employment'.[102] This focus is not too unlike that of the early Ambedkarites in Britain who continue to be active. Maharashtrians, too, get together to celebrate, hold discussions on key Buddha and Ambedkar anniversaries and actively organise special programmes for young children.

Outside of Ambedkarite community circles, too, there continues to be a steady interest in Ambedkar. In 2016, the BBC's *History* magazine featured an article 'My Hero' in which the British actor, comedian, musician, novelist and playwright Nigel Planer talked about his hero 'Babasaheb'. Planer described how he became aware of Ambedkar in the 1970s and later discovered how extraordinary he was. 'There are few people who you can say were great in terms of both their achievements and willpower,' said Planer.[103] On 11 May 2022, Planer was one of the guest speakers at the Ambedkar Jayanti celebration at the House of Lords. In 2017, a new play *Untouchable* was staged at the RADA festival, in London from 30 June to 8 July 2017. Written by the playwright Peter Oswald, and directed by Kathryn Hunter, a theatre director and film actor, this radical play chronicled the life of Ambedkar.

### *Conclusion*

The Ambedkarite movement that began soon after the early pioneers arrived in Britain in the late 1950s has become a firm feature of the Dalit diaspora in Britain. The organisations these early pioneers established, energised by the activists they invited, who had a close association with Ambedkar, have stood the test of time, and adapted in name and membership to a changing environment. Ambedkarites continue to apply Ambedkar's vision of a more equal society in the way they work and in their demands for equality in the law when they experience caste discrimination in the UK. Although many of the very early pioneers in Britain are no longer with us, there is a new generation of young Ambedkarites continuing to emerge, with more girls and women gaining greater visibility and making a real difference. The children and grandchildren of Ambedkarites, including C. Gautam's granddaughters Sanchi and Shil, regularly give speeches and recite Buddhist verses with growing confidence at Ambedkar's birth celebrations. Outside of the Indian Dalit diaspora, Ambedkarites' hard work on raising awareness of the life and works of Ambedkar has seen growing numbers of admirers, including in both Houses of the UK Parliament. In 2017, two young speakers of British and Czech descent—David Orsulik (aged 14) and Adam Orsulik (aged 12)—came to the House of Lords to mark Ambedkar's birthday. They inspired the attendees with their heartfelt speeches in which David compared Ambedkar's battle against caste to Václav Havel and the Velvet Revolution bringing down Czechoslovakia's communist regime in 1989. This comparison was refreshing to hear. Adam Orsulik, like many Ambedkarites, called for Ambedkar to be made part of the school curriculum in citizenship classes. It may be only a matter of time before the movement will see British schoolchildren learn about Ambedkar in the same way they do about Gandhi, Martin Luther King, and Nelson Mandela.

7

# THE AMBEDKAR MUSEUM, LONDON

*Santosh Dass and Jamie Sullivan*

In a beautiful tree-lined street in a village like-area in North London is a museum dedicated to Dr Bhimrao Ambedkar. Located in a four-storey terraced house at 10 King Henry's Road, London (hereafter 10KHR), that we now know Ambedkar lodged at from 1920 to 1922 (see William Gould's Chapter 1). The house is a short walk from Primrose Hill—a highly desirable area that boasts panoramic views over Regent's Park and beyond, and on which once lived the poets Sylvia Plath, Ted Hughes and Dylan Thomas. The Ambedkar Museum in London is the first official museum in Dr Ambedkar's name outside of India. What makes this so special is that it is located in the house where Ambedkar lodged and worked.

The Museum took nearly six years to become a reality. First there was a written proposal on 1 September 2014 from the Federation of Ambedkarite and Buddhist Organisations UK (FABO UK) to the Government of Maharashtra (GOM) in India that they give a one-off grant of £4 million to FABO UK to buy 10KHR so they could turn it into a memorial. This was followed by a year's worth of lobbying of the GOM by FABO UK, Ambedkarites, and politicians in India. FABO UK's written proposal—submitted weeks before the announcement of the state election in Maharashtra—proved extremely timely.

This helped secure commitments and public announcements by politicians, and others, to the media on an issue that may otherwise have been dragged out by GOM. A year later in September 2015, within two months of being handed the keys to 10KHR, the High Commission of India (IHC) in London readied the ground floor, complete with a photo exhibition about Ambedkar, for the GOM and for India's Prime Minister Narendra Modi's inauguration of the memorial on 14 November 2015. A few years later, Camden Council refused museum status for the memorial developed by the Dr Babasaheb Ambedkar Memorial Advisory Committee London. This was the background to the drama of the two-day Public Inquiry into the appeal in 2019, replete with impassioned statements by local residents, Ambedkarites, and activists.

In this chapter, Santosh Dass MBE, President of FABO UK, and Jamie Sullivan MRTPI, Director of Planning at Iceni Projects, share their accounts of the lobbying involved in securing 10KHR for the public; the house's refurbishment; and the painstaking preparation for the Public Inquiry into GOM's appeal against Camden Council's planning decision. This account, based on personal recollections, correspondence, and media reports, gives a taste of the drive, determination, and lessons learnt in believing in an idea and making it a reality. It is not possible to mention every single person or organisation that *may* have lobbied GOM in India, or supported the Public Inquiry—but an attempt has been made to recall as many of the key players in this narrative as possible. Finally, discussed here are the opportunities that should be seized upon to make the Ambedkar Museum something really special and long-lasting. It has the potential to become a beacon for generations of visitors whether they are Ambedkarites or not.

### *Santosh Dass: First Time Ever I Saw ...*

The first time I saw 10KHR was on 6 December 2013. I was invited to lead a peace walk from the house to the London School of Economics (LSE). This was only a few months after I became President of FABO UK, but the walk had been a regular feature organised by FABO UK since 2003. 10KHR had already been known as the 'Dr Ambedkar House' in Ambedkarite circles for decades, and many Ambedkarite visitors to the UK marked this on their itinerary to visit. It helps to have a blue commemorative plaque outside the house that reads 'Dr Bhimrao Ramji Ambedkar, 1891–1956, Indian Crusader for Social Justice lived here 1921–1922'. The plaque was purchased and installed by the Ambedkar Centenary Celebrations Committee UK, and unveiled on 6 December 1991 by the Mayor of Camden, Councillor Jim Turner. It had taken Ambedkarites two decades to get to this point. Chanan Chahal, President of FABO UK, described in a press release for the unveiling the many hurdles involved:

> Since 1974, we have been trying to install this memorial plaque. We have had great difficulty in reaching this day. When we gained permission from the landlord, the occupiers declined a request. We tried to convince them but then the landlords changed. In the course of this to-and-fro process, the GLC [Greater London Council] was abolished in 1985, and the English Heritage have a long waiting list of applications for installing plaques. Due to the cooperation of the present occupier and the landlord, as well as the local council, we have at last succeeded in having this commemorative plaque installed during the year of the birth centenary of Babasheb Ambedkar.[1]

Roy Hattersley MP (the then Deputy leader of the Labour Party) unveiled the commemorative blue plaque at 10KHR in the presence of the Mayor of Camden, the actress Glenda Jackson MP and Ambedkarites.[2]

10KHR is a ten-minute walk from Chalk Farm underground station. When I arrived at the house, there was already a group of smiling people, young and old, waiting outside on the pavement, with others busy taking photos of themselves making sure they captured the blue plaque. Compared to the neighbouring houses on the street, the front of 10KHR was in a sorry state. Years of obvious neglect had resulted in flaking paint, old windows, pollution-ridden external brickwork, and an overgrown front garden. The privet hedge was so overgrown, it almost covered the black-and-white road sign. We paid our respects to Ambedkar in hushed tones. I longed to see the inside of the house. Just before we left, I recall remarking to Mr Gautam Chakravarty (who is better known as C. Gautam), the current Joint Secretary of FABO UK, how wonderful it would be if we were able to buy this house and turn it into a memorial. Gautam said he didn't expect houses like this one to come up for sale, and if this one did there would be little likelihood of us being able to afford it. We were only outside the house for about ten minutes and proceeded on our three-mile walk to LSE via the British Library. Some latecomers joined us on the way. We chatted and reflected on Dr Ambedkar. For me it was good to walk and speak with some of the younger generation and children in the group. There is a desire amongst Ambedkarites for a personal connection with Ambedkar. The annual walk from 10KHR is one way of doing this.

Nearly nine months after that walk, on 29 August 2014, an email landed in my in-tray from Harbans Virdee, of the Buddha Dhamma Association. Virdee, a staunch Ambedkarite from Punjab, is also a member of FABO UK's executive team. In the email to hundreds of Ambedkarites around the world, Virdee called on 'Sisters and Brothers in Dhamma to request the Indian Government or Maharashtra Government to buy this [10KHR] and make the Memorial of Baba Sahib Dr. Ambedkar.'[3]

I am a firm believer that everything happens for a reason. Chance meetings are an example. In July 2014, I attended the 3rd Global Ambedkarite Conference, held from 4 to 6 July in Paris, organised by the late Rajkumar Daulatrao Kamble—the very dynamic and dedicated Ambedkarite from Maharashtra who lived in Texas, USA.[4] The conference was hosted beautifully by Parminder Singh, the General Secretary (who kindly put me up at his family home in Paris for the night) and Harmesh Lal, the President of the Shri Guru Ravidass Gurdwara, La Courneuve, Paris. The Sri Guru Ravidass Sabha UK, Europe and Abroad (SGRS UK), with Tarsem Lal Balu and Desraj Bunger at the helm, supported this Ambedkar-related conference with a financial donation and by attending the conference with members of the SGRS UK, including Mr Ram Kishan Mehmi, the Labour Party Councillor for Walsall Borough Council at the time of writing. Kamble had heard about our campaign to outlaw caste discrimination in Britain and insisted I give a talk about it. He was keen others should learn from the Anti Caste Discrimination Alliance's (ACDA) experience. It was at this conference I first met Mr Ram K. Gaikwad (a retired Commissioner in the Social Welfare Department at GOM), Mr Ramesh Katke, Dr Vijay Kadam, Padma Shri Kalpana Soroj (the rags-to-riches Indian entrepreneur and millionaire Dalit businesswoman), and the Indian politician Mr Ramdas Athawale, who is also the President of the Republic Party of India. I returned to London within a day of my arrival and speech there. Most of the international delegates stayed on and took in the sites after the conference before their onward journeys or return home.

Katke was the first of the Paris delegates to get in touch with me, as soon as he arrived in London, and we met in Isleworth. A civil servant working on the Scheduled Caste (SC) and Scheduled Tribes (ST) scholarship scheme and other projects in the GOM, Katke was keen to hear about my ideas for projects for the SCs in India. My focus was access to education for Dalit girls in India. A week later, on 22 July 2014, Soroj, Manan Gore, Gaikwad, and Gautam came to visit me and Ken Hunt for tea at our home in Hounslow. In passing, they mentioned that they had been to see 10KHR earlier that day. When Virdee's email arrived a month later, I was really excited to hear that 10KHR was on the market. The first thing I did was email the estate agents Goldschmidt and Howland of Maida Vale, London to establish if 10KHR was still available. It surprised me to hear it had been on the market since April 2014—in a highly sought-after area. The estate agent, Adam French, informed me that an offer of £2.9 million on the £3.1 million asking price had been received but the owners had rejected that.

We had a quick discussion at FABO UK about the prospect of raising funds and soon came to the conclusion the sums involved were too great, even if we could muster up the ten per cent (£310,000) for the deposit. It was then I remembered Katke and decided to sound him out on possible funding from GOM as floated by Virdee. He was very enthusiastic about the idea and agreed to speak with Gaikwad and Kadam straight away. He also agreed to consult Ambedkarites and sympathetic local politicians in Maharashtra. Within twenty-four hours I prepared and shared a draft FABO UK proposal in readiness to send to Mr Prithviraj Chavan, the then Congress Chief Minister

(CM) of GOM. The aim was to use this document's contents to mobilise people in Maharashtra early on. FABO UK wrote to the CM on 1 September 2014. Katke informed us that the Maharashtra state elections were scheduled in October, and the election Code of Conduct was imminent. Once published, funding requests would be paused during the run-up to a new government's formation. So we had no time to spare.

Within days of us speaking, Gaikwad and Katke had spoken with Siddharth Kharat, the private secretary to Dr Nitin Raut, a Cabinet Minister in GOM. It helped to have Gaikwad on board. He had been a senior civil servant at GOM and built up an excellent network of contacts and relationships during his time as Commissioner. This enabled him to liaise at ease with relevant officials and ministers in the GOM cabinet. He arranged a meeting with Dr Raut for 2 September 2014 to lobby him to take a delegation of Members of the Legislative Assembly (MLAs) in GOM, along with FABO's proposal submitted to the CM. Minister Raut immediately understood the importance and urgency of the request and wrote a letter of support.[5] He met the Chief Minister of GOM on 3 September 2014. 'With reference to the historic proposal received from Santosh Dass, President of (FABO) UK,' Dr Raut stressed, 'it is a golden opportunity for Got [Government] of Maharashtra to pay respect to the great son of the soil Dr Babasaheb Ambedkar. It is in need of the hour to protect and propagate the thoughts and values of greatest humanitarian produced by our nation. This historical site can be utilised for strengthening international relations between UK and India.'[6] MLAs Dr Milind Mane and Dr Santosh Tarpe also supported the proposal.[7]

I arranged to view 10KHR on 4 September 2014. Ken Hunt came along too. He already knew the house because he had seen the blue plaque in 2007 on the way to visit Bonnie Dobson, the Canadian singer and songwriter, who lives nearby. Adam French, the estate agent, showed us around. The four-storey house was divided into two flats—each one with its own separate entrance. We entered the front door to the top-floor three-storey flat first. It was in very poor condition. Bits of the ceilings were missing, and the wallpaper and paint on the walls was falling off. Added to this was the damage to the ceiling and walls from a water leakage on the top floor. The carpets were old and dirty, and the kitchen and bathrooms were outdated and falling apart. I reacted emotionally to being inside the house. By the time I had moved to the second floor, I was weeping. The house aroused such an emotional response in me. The only explanation for this was the reality of Ambedkar having moved around in these rooms and the gardens.

A week passed without even an acknowledgement from GOM. Then things changed on 11 September 2014 when two encouraging news stories appeared in the UK's *Daily Telegraph* and the *Indian Express*.[8] In the articles, Dr Raut confirmed the Congress-led GOM had agreed to buy the house in response to FABO UK's proposal.[9] Dean Nelson, the journalist at the *Daily Telegraph* called me just before he published his story. He suggested the money could be better spent on other needy projects. I replied 10KHR was 'more than bricks and mortar' for the Ambedkarites. The excitement of 11 September was short-lived, however. The following day, Katke shared with me the timetable for the GOM state elections. Voting would take place on 15 October, with the vote count to begin on 19 October 2014. As expected, this delayed matters. On reflection I believe FABO UK's proposal's timing was perfect. This was an attractive Ambedkar-related proposal to get behind, and one with which to woo the Ambedkarite and Dalit community during the election period. Our friends in Maharashtra continued to build the support of the Ambedkarites, and lobbied Indian officials and prospective MLAs looking for votes. They also engaged Ravindra Ambekar, chief editor of *Mi Marthi* news channel, and Sunil Nimsarker, an Ambedkarite reporter in New Delhi, to cover stories.[10] In the UK, Raj Bangar helped provide regular updates on the community channel Kanshi TV, and Arun Kumar of FABO UK regularly wrote articles to rally the Ambedkarite diaspora in the UK and abroad for support.

It occurred to me around this time that I hadn't copied the IHC London into any correspondence. Ranjan Mathai, the Indian High Commissioner in London, had been very warm to my very first speech at India House on 14 April 2014 to mark the Ambedkar birth anniversary a few months after I became President of FABO UK. I expected the IHC would need to be involved with helping

GOM purchase the property. I raised the matter with Mathai on 18 September at an event I had been invited to. He was already aware of FABO UK's proposal that had hit the news, and seemed excited about it. He and Dr Virander Paul, the Deputy High Commissioner (DHC), both offered to assist all they could, but stressed they needed clear instructions from India's Ministry of External Affairs (MEA) to make an offer on the house. On 21 September 2014, the *Times of India* referred to 10KHR again: 'While he [Dr Raut] wants the state to spend around Rs 40 crore for the 10, King Henry's Road property, Raut is indifferent on converting Hotel Shyam into an Ambedkar memorial.'[11]

A day later, the estate agent informed me there was another potential buyer. It was then the team in London and Maharashtra discussed the next course of action. We agreed FABO UK should write to the Prime Minister of India because the election code for Maharashtra did not apply to the business of the Indian national government. FABO UK did this on 23 September 2014. Gaikwad, Katke and I also finalised the draft 'Letter of Intent' setting out GOM's intent to buy 10KHR, to be sent to the estate agent. To increase the pressure, Gaikwad arrived at the PM's private office in New Delhi on 24 September to lobby the Secretary to the Cabinet.[12] In the meantime, the person who had made the latest offer on 10KHR had a buyer for his home, which put him in a strong position to begin the legalities to buy. I sent another email to the PM's office, copied to the IHC in London stressing the need to take urgent action on this within 48 hours.[13] Gaikwad was still lobbying in New Delhi when on 25 September he sent me the following note on WhatsApp: 'The Secretary to PM has discussed [10KHR proposal] with PM. For final decision PM took the file with him while proceeding on America tour. One senior Ambedkarite officer in External Affairs ministry at New Delhi is pursuing the matter. The senior officer also suggested that Ambedkarite persons should also meet the PM in America. The senior officer, Mr Gondane Joint Secretary is good friend of Mr Raju Kamble in America. Please speak to Mr Raju Kamble to expedite matters.' I called Kamble immediately and he suggested we approach Ramdas Athawale MP too. I also sent Kamble some briefing on the proposal, and suitable questions his press contacts in the USA could pose to PM Modi to make progress on 10KHR. As Gautam of FABO UK knew Athawale well, he spoke with him on 28 September. Athawale helpfully sent a very supportive letter to PM Modi on 30 September 2014 with a request that a letter of intent be sent to the IHC and the estate agents in response to FABO UK's proposal.[14]

On Sunday 5 October, I met up with Dr Paul, DHC at the India High Commission, at a community event he was presiding over at the Paul Robson Theatre in Hounslow's Treaty Centre. His office had phoned me and invited me to come along to allow the DHC to have a word with me about progress on 10KHR. Paul offered to ring PM Modi's office for an update and suggested I write to the IHC too to get my request for support in the system. I wrote on 7 October and pleaded with the High Commissioner to do everything he could.[15] I continued to update the estate agent on developments on a near-daily basis. During this period, I remember watching endless media reports about the Maharashtra election results. The Bharatiya Janata Party's (BJP) Mr Devendra Fadnavis finally formed a coalition government and became Maharashtra's new CM on 31 October 2014.

Lobbying for 10KHR did not deter me from the campaign to get the UK government to implement the law against caste-based discrimination in Britain, or from the other human rights activities I gave my time to on a voluntary basis. Around this time, S. Anand of Navayana Publishing invited me to take part in a panel discussion with the writer Arundhati Roy in London. She had written an introduction chapter titled 'Dr and the Saint' (2014) to Dr Ambedkar's *Annihilation of Caste*. I agreed. I had met Roy in London, and she came for lunch at our home in June 2011, to which I had invited colleagues campaigning for caste discrimination to be outlawed in Britain. I also accompanied her to meet Ambedkarites at the Ambedkar Hall in Southall. The panel discussion took place on 25 November 2014 at the Purcell Room, on the South Bank in London. Tariq Ali, the British political activist and writer joined us on the panel. Interestingly, Ali talked about caste discrimination in Pakistan too. I took the opportunity there to stress the importance of public ownership of 10KHR. Straight after the discussion, Ken

Hunt and I went to the Jackson Browne concert at the Royal Albert Hall. Backstage I was able to give Browne a copy of *Annihilation of Caste* that Roy had signed for him. I use every opportunity to spread Ambedkarism!

The following day, 26 November, I sent another stalling email to the estate agents. I felt the house was slipping away from us. So when I received a call from Gautam a few weeks later while he was visiting India, I felt a ray of hope. Kalpana Soroj had invited Gautam to accompany her to meet PM Modi in New Delhi on 31 December 2014. Gautam agreed to take a copy of our 10KHR proposal along too. When they arrived, PM Modi was not in the office. On the way out, Gautam said he noticed Ajit Doval's name on a door and looked in to say hello and greet him. Gautam knew Doval from his time in London when he was at the IHC in the 1990s. They discussed FABO UK's proposal with him instead. This seemed to do the trick because on 5 January 2015, out of the blue, I received a phone call from a Mr P. Jain, who introduced himself as a joint secretary at the Ministry of Culture in New Delhi. He spoke beautifully in English and enquired about 10KHR's availability and how much time we had. For the first time in months, I felt there might actually be a firm result on this. I updated Adam French, the estate agent. He called me a few days later. No one had been in touch with him apart from an Indian TV station. I advised he refrain, like I did, from interacting with the media at this delicate stage. He confirmed the owners still wanted to sell to GOM because they loved the idea of a memorial to Ambedkar, but five months on, they really needed something more concrete by way of an offer. The press started picking up on the story again on 7 January 2015 and quoted Mr Mulkiat Singh Bahal, a London-based Ambedkarite: 'It is shameful that the Indian government need to be petitioned to preserve the country's heritage.'[16] Mr Prakash Ambedkar, Dr Ambedkar's grandson, asked that the house be 'preserved and turned into a hostel for students' in the same article. P. Ambedkar's sentiments were very much in line with FABO UK's original proposal to GOM that part of the house be used to lodge Dalit students on scholarships from India. A few days later, the BJP made some positive noises to the media about wanting to buy the house.[17] On the same day, the estate agent informed me another offer from an investor with the necessary finances ready had been received and this would be accepted the next day unless they heard from GOM.

By then a new Minister for Social Justice, Mr Rajkumar Badole, was in post. I was hopeful since Minister Badole was a Dalit, a staunch Ambedkarite and a Buddhist. I wrote to him on 14 January, and again to the CM of GOM: 'The only thing that will now stop this house from being sold to the private investor is a formal communication (a Letter of Intent) from the GOI via the IHC, London by 12.00 (UK Local Time) 15 January, to the owner via the Estate Agent'. I added: 'The formal written communication needs to confirm that funds are available from the GOI to purchase the house and that 10 per cent (GBP 310,000) of the asking price will be released as a deposit with a view to purchasing the House within two months of the date of the Letter of Intent.'[18] Gaikwad suggested I speak with Minister Badole too. The minister was quietly spoken and listened carefully to me in my broken Hindi laced with English. Kalpana Soroj also lobbied Minister Badole and the new CM of GOM. Gaikwad, in the meantime, travelled to New Delhi expecting to meet Jain. He suggested I speak with the CM of GOM. I called and called without success and became irritated with the delays, so I called Jain instead. He took my call immediately and indicated that a report supportive of FABO UK's proposal on 10KHR had been sent to PM Modi. He also mentioned he was going to meet Gaikwad at 4.30 p.m. India time. In the meantime, HC Ranjan Mathai informed me he was getting his team on the case straight away to chase GOM.

Nearly five months after it all started, the tide turned. Gaikwad had been trying without success to meet Minister Badole at Mantralaya, the administrative headquarters of GOM in Mumbai. As a last resort he and Katke decided they would try the Minister at the temporary accommodation he was lodging in whilst his official residence was being prepared. They both met Minister Badole on 22 January 2015 in the evening. It was during that meeting that the Minister sent the letter of intent for the estate agent via the IHC London with a copy to me.[19] This was a real game changer. On the same day, I received a phone call from a man who said he was the personal assistant to GOM's new Education Minister, Vinod Tawde.

The Minister was in London and wanted to meet me the next day—before he flew back to Mumbai. We had a cordial meeting the following morning in the reception lobby of the hotel he was staying at in Charing Cross, London. He invited me to talk him through the 10KHR proposal, and as soon as I had finished he informed me that GOM had agreed to buy the house.[20] I knew this already. Minister Tawde was keen to view 10KHR, but I couldn't get hold of the estate agent at such short notice. We decided to go to the house anyway. A meeting at the IHC followed where we met Ranjan Mathai, Mr Sukhdev Sidhu, the Minister for Coordination, and Pritham Lal, the First Secretary, to discuss the process involved with buying a house in London. We expected things to move at a faster pace after that. To my dismay, they didn't.

It had taken nearly five months to get to this point, and naturally the owners were keen to see action from GOM. GOM finally appointed Seddons Solicitors of 5 Portman Square, London in early February to manage things. Simon Ross, the solicitor at Seddons, wrote to me on 4 February indicating that the property was still under offer to an alternative buyer.[21] Alarmed, I chased GOM and the IHC. A few days later, on 9 February, Minister Badole met Mrs Sushma Swaraj, then MEA in New Delhi and secured her support for the IHC to act on behalf of GOM. Ujjwal Uke and Dinesh Dingle from Minister Badole's office, Gaikwad and Katke also took part in this important meeting. 'She has given her approval orally. IHC R. Mathai is in New Delhi. Tomorrow, Swaraj will direct Mathai to do next action,' wrote Gaikwad.[22]

Until then I had no idea of Ujjwal Uke's connection with Ambedkar was already strong. His father, Narayan Gomaji Uke, met Ambedkar in Nagpur in July 1942. N. G. Uke and barrister Bhaurao Dewaji Khobragade, who helped energise the Ambedkarite movement in the UK (see Chapter 6), later became Chairman and General Secretary of the reception committee for Ambedkar's meeting at 4 Downside Crescent, London, NW3 in 1946, with students sent by Ambedkar on scholarships to England.[23] This meeting is recorded in a black-and-white photo (displayed at the Ambedkar Museum) of Ambedkar seated with sixteen students. N. G. Uke is standing on the far left and Khobragade is standing on the far right in the photo. Neither N. G. Uke, nor Khobragade took up the scholarships arranged by Ambedkar. Uke had already been selected in the All-India General Scholarship, and Khobragade's father paid for his son's passage and fees. 'They were the only two who took up the Ambedkarite movement after their return. The others built their own careers,' said U. Uke.[24] Ambedkar later attended N. Uke's wedding to Kamal on 8 May 1949. He had known her since she was six years old, through her father Raisab Meshram, at their home, in Nagpur.[25] Ujjwal is proud of the history that Ambedkar was a signatory on his parents' marriage certificate.

Ujjwal Uke was instrumental in ensuring all the relevant files and paperwork on the 10KHR proposal were watertight for GOM's cabinet meetings that took place in March to agree the budget for the 10KHR and follow-up actions. For this, Katke asked me to provide FABO UK's estimated running costs for the property for ten years. I had already given some thought to this in October 2014, in between chasing and motivating everybody, and keeping the estate agent at bay. FABO UK had applied for a one-off grant of £4 million from GOM on 1 September 2014 to cover the cost price of the property, legal costs, taxes, and costs for minor refurbishment for year one. The original proposal included setting up an Ambedkar Foundation Trust and allowing some students on government scholarships to lodge in a self-contained section of the memorial to generate revenue towards the future running costs of the memorial. Our rough estimated projected running cost (including cost of a salary for one administrator) was £309,897 for ten years and £832,368 for twenty years. This factored in inflationary increases and revenue generated through students' rent.[26]

On 3 March 2015, Seddons Solicitors copied me into an email to GOM and IHC about another buyer on the scene for whom a contract was being drawn up by the owner's solicitors. The solicitors for GOM were concerned all had gone quiet on GOM's front and didn't want to lose out to this new buyer. I was in India at the time and chased Minister Badole and Uke. I also called Lahori Ram Balley of *Bheem Patrika,* in Jalandhar, whom I knew well, for support. He helped apply pressure directly on GOM, and via his Ambedkarite contacts in Punjab and Maharashtra. From 23 to 28

April 2015, Minister Badole and Uke visited London to meet the High Commissioner. I was in Hong Kong by then—so they met FABO UK colleagues C. Gautam, Rampal Rahi and Arun Kumar at the IHC in London. A Mr M. P. Singh, Head of Protocol, then took over additional responsibilities and became the point of contact between the IHC, GOM, the solicitors, and me on 10KHR. When I would chase the IHC and GOM about the delays, both sides would point me to the other. We had put too much time and energy into this, for too long, for the proposal to fail at the last hurdle. Minister Badole and his team made their next visit to London in August 2015, during which the formalities for the exchange of contracts were completed.[27] I met Minister Badole for the first time during this visit when he visited the Buddha Vihara in Southall on 30 August 2015. He was very quiet, genuine, and a very gentle man, and I liked him straight away. Singh at the IHC finally received the keys to 10KHR on 25 September 2015 on behalf of GOM. We all breathed a sigh of relief!

Very soon after this, there was talk of the Prime Minister of India inaugurating 10KHR during his delayed first official visit to the UK from 12–15 November 2015. It was evident the house required immediate and urgent attention. GOM's CM's office took the lead with getting it ready for the inauguration. Dr Caterina Corni, a curator from Italy, was appointed to get an exhibition ready in the few of the rooms on the first floor that were being quickly redecorated. She got in touch with me as soon she arrived in London at the end of October 2015, and we had several conversations on the phone about the exhibition and the key messages that needed to be conveyed about Ambedkar. She was receptive and did a splendid job with the exhibition.

In the lead-up to PM Modi's inauguration, a number of key people involved with the lobbying for 10KHR arrived in London, including R. Athawale, K. Soroj, R. K. Gaikwad, R. Katke, and Dr Vijay Kaddam. There was an expectation that they would be invited inside the house when PM Modi inaugurated it. It was Athawale who on 14 November 2015 joined PM Modi, CM Fadnavis, Minister Badole and the politician Mrs Sulekha Kumhare.[28] A crowd stood outside across the road eager to go inside 10KHR, and also protestors against PM Modi too. I had decided to stay away and have tea with Bonnie Dobson instead, and arrived after everyone had left, including PM Modi and the CM of GOM. Those waiting outside, including the visitors from India, were able to enter the newly inaugurated Ambedkar Memorial by then. For the same evening, FABO UK had already organised a conference at the Buddha Vihara in Southall to celebrate the successful campaign for 10KHR. Gautam invited CM Fadnavis, R Athawale, and Minister Badole to Southall out of courtesy when he met them as they posed for photos after PM Modi had left. I had already published an open letter to PM Modi, embargoed until 14 November, on India's equality and human rights atrocities.[29] It proved an interesting evening in Southall to say the least.

Things went quiet for many months again after the inauguration. Should I be surprised? No. We received no end of enquires from people keen to visit the memorial, but beyond the ground floor prepared for PM Modi's inauguration, the rest of the house remained in the same sorry state. I wrote to GOM and IHC several times about the lack of progress. On 23 June 2016, I wrote to the CM Fadnavis: 'It is essential that 10KHR is developed, and managed transparently, and with full accountability in order to deliver the purpose it was bought for. This includes the accommodation of two–four students on a GOM funded scholarship to LSE'.[30] We pressed for a committee to be set up to take things forward. Nothing materialised until Minister Badole arrived in the country with his team, including Dingle, for a four-day visit in February 2017. On 2 February 2017, he announced the formation of the Dr Babasaheb Ambedkar Memorial Advisory Committee London. The Committee's chair was the Indian High Commissioner, Yashvardhan Kumar Sinha. Members of the Committee included Surendrakumar Bagde (Secretary, Department of Social Justice, and GOM), Sunil Kumar (IHC), C. Gautam, Jograj Ahir (President, Shri Guru Ravidass Sabha and Southall), Sukhdev Hira, and Santosh Dass.[31] We welcomed Sunil Kumar's appointment to take over responsibility for 10KHR from Singh. Kumar was very passionate about it, and believed in the project. By 9 February I had submitted to the Committee what I considered to be the key components required for the refurbishment. This still factored in converting the basement flat into accommodation for at least two students on GOM scholarships. The flat element for students was later abandoned by GOM. Just over a month later, on 22 March 2017, Kumar, the Indian High Commissioner, wrote to the Committee:

> I am glad to inform you that the renovation works of the two-storey heritage building at 10 King Henry's Road, London (Dr Babasaheb Ambedkar International Memorial) has already commenced. As suggested by Santosh Dass, in the first meeting of the Advisory Committee viz. landscaping of the front and backyard of the Memorial, building a small conservatory for meditation facility to the visitors, making disabled-friendly access to the Memorial, providing furniture, bookshelves for Library-cum-Sitting Hall on the first floor and developing a multimedia room on the second floor for visitors to know about the life and messages of Dr Babasaheb Ambedkar, etc., tender process in this regard will be initiated soon.[32]

The IHC appointed a building contractor, Pradeep Kumar, to carry out the works and secure the necessary planning permissions from the Council. Sima Amini, an interior designer, was appointed later. She and I worked closely on choosing the fixtures, fittings, furniture, and even choosing the wallpapers and the colour of paint for the different rooms in the house. We tried our best to keep the original period features in place, and instructed repairs be carried out sensitively. The external brickwork was cleaned and repointed, restoring its integrity. Sunil Kumar also suggested, and the Committee agreed, that we install wood panelling for part of the first-floor entrance hall and along the stairs leading up to the top floor. Kumar was a delight to work with. He was so efficient and made constant progress. There remain two areas of disappointment for me with the refurbishment. First, the lift the Committee suggested be installed in the house was installed outside in front of the house. This remains an eyesore. Second, we were not able to refurbish the room where we believed Ambedkar lodged on the top floor in keeping with the period. This was something we agreed to pick up at a later stage. The IHC handled the tendering process for the works required and all the expenditure details with GOM directly. This was not shared with Ahir, Hira, Gautam and myself. Nevertheless, the four of us put in a lot of time voluntarily for the refurbishment, and we personally met all our travel and other expenses associated with the Committee meetings and developing the memorial. We were proud to do our bit for the Ambedkar mission.

August 2017 brought another chance meeting and friendship. BBC Radio 4's 'Beyond Belief' invited me to appear live on 14 August 2017 on their programme at their Manchester Studios to discuss Dr Ambedkar's legacy. This was to mark seventy years of India's independence. Also on the panel were Professor William Gould from Leeds University, and Dr Ananya Vajpeyi, Fellow and Associate Professor at the Centre for the Study of Developing Societies, New Delhi.[33] Gould and I hit it off straight away and have remained in contact ever since. The following year, I invited Gould and his colleague Jesús Cháirez-Garza to give a talk at the House of Lords on 30 April 2018 to mark Ambedkar's 127th birth anniversary. Little did I know I would call on William Gould to help with the Ambedkar Museum Public Inquiry two years later and we would work on a book together!

During the refurbishment of 10KHR, FABO UK donated a life-sized bronze statue of Ambedkar to the Ambedkar House. FABO UK had been looking for a suitable place to install it, and we agreed it would look good in the back garden of 10KHR. P. Kumar, the building contractor, organised the collection and associated costs of transportation of the statue from the Buddha Vihara in Southall to 10KHR and the installation of it in March 2018. PM Modi was due to make a short visit to the memorial the following month on 19 April but this never materialised. People protested outside the memorial against PM Modi in anticipation of the visit whilst others waited inside to hand him a petition about India's human rights.

As the refurbishment continued apace, the Committee decided it should try and apply for permission for museum status to regularise the memorial's use. P. Kumar handled the communication with Camden Council, with some input from the Committee. The Council refused the planning application and GOM appealed. By then, Sunil Kumar, the HC, had been posted elsewhere. Kiran Khatri took over responsibility for the house from him.

When stories appeared in the newspapers about the possibility of the Ambedkar House being closed down, Khatri and I met at India House.[34] The HC appointed solicitors Singhania and Co to act on behalf of GOM, and began a campaign to save the Ambedkar House. Ambedkarites and Dalit organisations lobbied their MPs and Members of the Lords to write letters in support of the Museum to Camden Council. Many did this. I worked closely with Khatri, Janeevan John of Singhania and Co, Jamie Sullivan, a town planning expert, and barrister Steven Gasztowicz QC, who had been appointed by them to prepare for the Public Inquiry. I suggested Gould also became a key witness alongside me at the Inquiry. His confident, no-nonsense persona was what I believed was required. My friend Bonnie Garnett, also known as Bonnie Dobson, who lives in the area, had seen the news stories about a disgruntled neighbour who complained about 'coachloads' of visitors to the Ambedkar House. She phoned me with an offer of support and also agreed to speak at the Inquiry. Around the same time, Sally Roach, who lived on the street, Alex Sunshine, who had visited the house, and Leena Dhingra, the actress and author and also daughter of Madam Lal Dhingra, the Indian revolutionary, phoned me and offered their support. This lifted the project team's spirits. By the time the Public Inquiry took place I had also enlisted the support of the writer Ken Hunt, Raj Banger of Kanshi TV, and the Venerable Bhante Vijithavansa to give their third party interests statements to the Inquiry. On both days, C. Gautam, FABO UK, Sat Pal Muman of the Ambedkar International Mission and a few of his colleagues also attended the hearing. Muman, like many others, was able to make a helpful contribution to the Inquiry about the significance of Ambedkar. The Public Inquiry is discussed by Sullivan in this chapter.

## *Conclusion*

The campaign by key individuals highlighted in this chapter in the history of the Ambedkar Museum has involved many twists and turns, but should inspire others to go for what they believe in and never give up. With the Museum, there is the potential to raise Ambedkar's profile in the UK in particular, but also to spread his ideas and message far and wide. The Museum should not be limited to visits by dignitaries and Ambedkarites on Ambedkar Jayanti or other milestones, during which they say a few words and garland the statues. In 2019, FABO UK organised a lecture 'Common Struggles: The Benefits for African-Americans and Dalits from Comparing Their Struggles', delivered at the Memorial by Professor Kevin Brown of Indiana University Maurer School of Law (see Chapter 9). There is scope for more lectures and talks at the Museum by academics on wide-ranging themes, as well as themes related to Ambedkar. Links with universities should also be explored, as well as visits to the Museum by university students and schoolchildren linked to South Asian Heritage Month and Black History Month in Britain. I believe this can only really be done without political and bureaucratic interference from India. The very committed administrator, Haja Fahad, who reports directly to the IHC, has almost single-handily looked after the Museum and the visitors to it since 2018. Now it is time for GOM to consider transferring the Museum to a trust or a foundation comprised of British Ambedkarites, academics, and patrons, with interim funding for five years to secure it for future generations of visitors. This would not be out of keeping with FABO UK's original proposal to GOM in September 2014.

***

*Jamie Sullivan: The Public Inquiry into the Ambedkar Museum*

At an initial impression, the planning application for the Ambedkar Museum, London, and its refusal by Camden Council might not seem like the most intriguing of subjects for a chapter in this book. For me personally, it was one of the most interesting and unique projects I have been involved with in my fifteen-year career in town planning in Britain. It is also relevant in the history of Dr Ambedkar's connection with London.

What made this application so exciting was that the proposal did not fit neatly within the existing planning system. Homes in Inner London are not generally bought to create new museums. The acute housing pressure in the capital means the planning system is set up to protect and significantly grow the existing housing stock. The proposal to take a valuable residential property in a sought-after area, Primrose Hill, and turn it into a free-to-enter museum was completely contrary to the ebbs and flows of development within London. As a result, it got caught up and jammed the gears and cogs of the planning system designed to manage and direct development in the ways we expect it to.

The Public Inquiry was also of considerable interest because of the format and the international attention it attracted. I doubt I will ever work on a project where a Buddhist Sri Lankan monk appears in full robes, or a well-known singer-songwriter like Bonnie Dobson comes and speaks so passionately in favour of one of my projects. As a planning consultant, it is more usual to have a procession of local residents speaking out *against* a proposal, but in this case a stream of individuals from very different walks of life came in person to *support* the planning application. The key points they made at the Public Inquiry featured in the final Inspector's Report (which set out the decision and reasoning) are included later in this chapter.

### *How the Planning System Works—An Overview of the Relevant Principles*

The planning system in the UK can appear very complex and opaque, but it is based on some fairly simple principles. An application is determined in accordance with planning policy, unless there are good reasons (or 'material considerations' in legal parlance) to depart from what policy directs. In London, there are three layers to planning policy: a national policy, that is very strategic and high level in the form of the National Planning Policy Framework (NPPF)—this sets out the government's overarching objectives for England and how these are expected to be applied; the London Plan, produced by the Mayor of London, that provides more detailed policy, building on the NPPF; and finally, Local Authorities write their own set of even-more-detailed policies in their own Local Plan. In this case, the local authority concerned was Camden Council.

When assessing a planning application, these national and local policies will direct the decision-maker to give weight to different elements of a proposed scheme. For example, you can't build a waste incinerator in the middle of a residential area, because the planning policy directs the decision-maker to attach significant harm to development that would give rise to harmful impacts on the local residents' amenities. A range of policies direct waste incinerators to industrial locations, unless there was a good reason that overrode all these safeguards.

*Planning Appeals*

The local authority decides whether to approve or refuse the application in the first instance (with some exceptions that didn't apply in this case). If a local authority decides to refuse a proposed scheme, the applicant can appeal to the Planning Inspectorate—an Executive Agency of what was at the time the Ministry of Housing, Communities and Local Government. This inspectorate is an independent decision-making body that maintains complete separation and impartiality from the local authority.

The Planning Inspectorate is also independent of ministerial influence, but the Secretary of the State responsible for local government, does have the power to 'recover' specific appeals and make his/her own decision on the planning application based on the recommendations of the Planning Inspectorate. This happens for only a relatively very small number of appeals each year.

The application for the Ambedkar Museum involved changing the use of a building from two residential properties to a museum. Camden Council therefore required planning permission as it considered this to be 'development'. The Ambedkar House project also involved some minor external changes to the property. These were relatively minor and uncontroversial, and I have not discussed these further.

The change of use from residential to a memorial museum had already begun in preparation for the Prime Minister of India's inauguration of the Ambedkar House on 14 November 2015, within two months of its purchase by the GOM. There had been some publicity and media attached to PM Narendra Modi's inauguration of the Ambedkar memorial and a public expectation that the house could be visited by the public—in particular the followers of Dr Ambedkar. The retrospective application to regularise the position was submitted as the building was being refurbished to make it secure and safe. Such applications are not unusual where there has been a misunderstanding. This application was subsequently refused (for reasons I will go into later) and an Enforcement Notice served. An appeal had been submitted to the Planning Inspectorate to quash Camden Council's Enforcement Notice.

It was at this point that I, as an employee of Iceni Projects, became involved with the Appeal. While there are some differences between an appeal to quash an Enforcement Notice and an appeal against the decision of the local authority to refuse a planning application, in this case they were very technical, and had limited bearing on the case. Essentially, the situation was that the Council decided the change of use to museum was contrary to their planning policy on protecting the existing residential stock in the Borough. They considered no overriding factors existed to indicate it should be granted permission. If the Appeal was successful, then it would be granted planning permission and could remain open to the wider public in the way desired by the applicants.

The Council's shorthand justification for seeking to return the property to a residential use was set out in the Decision Notice to refuse the retrospective application. The 'Reason for Refusal' was 'The proposed change of use to a museum, by reason of the unjustified loss of residential floor space, would be detrimental to the amount of permanent residential floor space provided in the borough.' Despite the media coverage of the Council's decision, that honed in on the potential impact from coachloads of visitors descending on the Museum, and the perceived noise impact on residential amenity, this was not part of the reason permission was refused. The Council's decision all came down to the loss of two residential properties and their efforts to retain as much of the existing residential stock in the Borough as possible. On the face of it, the proposal to turn just two residential flats into a museum to celebrate the life of one of India's greatest sons would appear to be a positive move. The planning system is set up to ensure that development delivers public benefits, and given that we already have lots of houses in London, it may appear perverse to refuse an application on this basis.

To understand the justification for this decision, therefore, we need to look at the policies that directed the Council to make this decision. The London Plan and Camden Council's Local Plan both direct decision-makers to seek to resist the net loss of all residential floor space. There are some exceptions to this. This includes consolidating smaller flats to deliver family housing where these might be more in demand. These exceptions, and others, did not apply in this case. Camden Council's Local Plan makes self-contained residential properties the priority land use within the Borough. Delivering significant levels of housing is one, if not the main, objective of the Local and London Plans. The driving force behind this is the housing crisis in London. Inner London boroughs had seen a fivefold increase in house prices over twenty years, [35] with the average house price in Camden rising to twenty-three times the median gross household income in Camden at £36,053.[36]

One of the few policy levers local, regional and national government have available to them to address the housing crisis in London is to set very challenging housing targets for each local authority. In Camden that figure was 1,120 new dwellings per annum.[37] To put the scale of this increase in perspective, the Council was delivering around 600–800 additional dwellings for much of the 2010s. As this shows, achieving this target is challenging for the Borough. Of course, when drafting these policies, the Council and the Mayor cannot consider every conceivable form of development and make provision for it within their policy. Local Plans already run to hundreds of pages. Seeking to cover every eventuality would make the Plans too unwieldy. These policies are drafted on the basis of the understanding of local trends to marshal decisions, so that, overall, any new developments should deliver on the objectives and targets set out by the Council.

The development of Ambedkar House was so philanthropic in nature that, in policy terms, it was against the grain of development in the Borough and the local and regional policy. The purchase by a state government of India (in this case Maharashtra) of an Inner London property containing two flats in order to turn it into a memorial, with the expectation that people would want to want to visit it for free, ran completely contrary to all trends in the market. Lack of availability of finance generally meant if a group wanted to open a museum, they would usually be restricted to a very limited number of properties that would be affordable. These do not usually include very expensive residential properties in a sought-after residential area in central London. The ebbs and flows of capital within London meant that policy was rather silent on this unique form of development. Residential properties usually needed to be protected from higher-value uses. For example, the trend of 'escape rooms' could be accommodated in a residential property or other leisure uses. Conversely, community projects such as museums are usually at risk from being converted to residential uses, rather than vice versa.

The conversion of residential property to a not-for-profit community museum was so rare as not to be considered by policy. Given the lack of a specific policy for the Ambedkar Museum scenario, and the 'direction of travel' in the Local and London Plans that sought to protect housing, Camden Council's starting position was that the development was unacceptable due to the loss of residential floor space. They set this out in the Officer's Report and Decision Notice when they came to refuse the application. At the time of the decision, the Council did not consider that material considerations that might suggest ignoring planning policy had been demonstrated.

The material considerations presented were that, first, the property was sufficiently historically significant (by virtue of Ambedkar having lived there for several years); second, a museum had to be located at that property; and third, the benefits of this new facility as a whole outweighed the harm of the loss of the two residential units.

The material considerations became the main battleground for this appeal, and exploring the historical significance made it unique. The role of the project team of which I was part was to demonstrate that this museum was needed, would provide a significant benefit to the community, and could not be located elsewhere. To do this, we needed to draw on a wide range of experience from a host of different people.

*Preparing for the Appeal*

The Team

The IHC who acted on behalf of the State of Maharashtra during the purchase of 10KHR instructed Singhania and Co. as the solicitors. Together, the solicitors and the IHC brought the team together to prepare for the Appeal's Public Inquiry Hearing. Janeevan John and Ravindra Kumar of Singhania and Co. acted as liaison with the IHC. They provided input on a range of matters. They appointed me on the project team. One of the first people to be invited on the project by the IHC was Santosh Dass, a human rights and equality campaigner. She was a crucial part of the group that campaigned to secure property so it could be turned into a memorial. She was brought on board to provide an additional insight on Dr Ambedkar, his relationship with the property, and the grassroots campaign to purchase and refurbish 10KHR.

Santosh Dass suggested William Gould be appointed to provide historical expertise on Dr Ambedkar's time in London. She believed his wider historical expertise to help demonstrate the historical connection between Ambedkar and the property was crucial to the case. Also appointed was Steven Gasztowicz, of Cornerstone Barristers. The format of the appeal was a Public Inquiry and meant that a barrister was usually appointed as an advocate who could undertake the cross-examination of witnesses on each side (see boxed text on the format of the appeal).

There were three witnesses from each side. For our team it was me, Dass and Gould. Camden Council's three witnesses were Mr N. Baxter (Senior Conservation Officer), Mr M. Candler (Manager of Camden's Arts Development Team) and Mr R. Yeung (Planning Officer). Each witness had to produce a Proof of Evidence in writing prior to the Public Inquiry Hearing scheduled for 21 September 2019. At the end of the cross-examination, additional questions from the original barrister can be posed to draw out any points raised during cross-examination, before the Inspector asks the witness any questions they may have. The Inspector (who is appointed by the Planning Inspectorate) can step in during questioning at any time. Their role is similar to a court judge. At the end of the Public

Inquiry, the Inspector produces a report that sets out their decision (or their recommendation if the appeal is recovered by the Secretary of State—as it was in this case).

It is unusual for the appeal to be heard in the Public Inquiry format when the scheme is for the conversion of two flats into a community museum. Usually, a development of this size would be heard via written representations (where each party sends its case in writing to the Planning Inspectorate and decision is reached remotely) or through an informal hearing (where a round-table discussion of various points and clarifications led by the Inspector takes place). What made this case special was the international dimension. While Ambedkar is not particularly well known in the UK, he is a huge a figure in India both historically and in contemporary times, and followed by millions of people in India and the diaspora. The potential impact on diplomatic relations meant a Public Inquiry would help ensure that a full, detailed, independent and transparent assessment of the case had taken place.

A further unusual step for a development of this size was that the Secretary of State (for the Department of Housing, Communities, and Local Government), Mr Robert Jenrick MP, decided to 'recover' the appeal on 20 September—just a few days before the Public Inquiry began. 'The reason for this direction is that the appeal relates to proposals for development of major importance having more than local significance'.[38] Mr Jenrick, therefore, had the final say based on the Inspector's report and recommendations. The project team welcomed this move, but we did not relax in preparing our case for the hearing.

I am not aware of a scheme of this size having been recovered previously, although there may well have been other examples. This is usually reserved for larger or more controversial schemes. For example, in 2019 (the year of the decision) seventeen other schemes were recovered.[39] These included residential schemes of up to 1,600 homes, a strategic rail freight interchange, a new motorway service station, supporting infrastructure for the rail development HS2, fracking developments, and gravel extractions schemes. The Ambedkar House scheme was very much the odd one out in terms of scale and impact. I suspect the reason for the decision to recover the appeal was that it would cause a significant international impact on Anglo-Indian relations in the build up to Brexit and future trade relations if it failed. While I do not think for one second that there was any impropriety here, I do not believe the Secretary of State, and other government departments, would have wanted such an internationally significant decision with political implications to be left solely to the Planning Inspectorate. This is not to say that the British government did not have confidence in the Planning Inspectorate to reach the correct decision in planning terms, but some appeal decisions can be very subjective, including the level of weight to be given to different impacts of a scheme. I believe that the Secretary of State wanted to reserve the right to ensure that if the decision was made to refuse the scheme, then this was absolutely robust.

## Developing the Case

As soon as the project team had been established and briefed, we moved to develop the case we needed to put forward with regard to 'Proofs of Evidence'. The nub of the case was to argue why Ambedkar House had to be located at this particular property. This involved demonstrating a clearer link between Ambedkar and the house, the length of his time in London whilst he was studying, and his wider achievements. We also needed to demonstrate that locating this museum elsewhere would not have the same significance. The Council suggested other locations within the 'Museum Mile' closer to Central London. The Officer's Report had already stated that a clear link between Ambedkar and his time at 10KHR had not been made.

We were very reliant on Santosh Dass to set out what we already knew about the connection, on the basis of her previous campaigning. Gould was then able to provide further insight and carried out additional research, unearthing new correspondence that connected Ambedkar to 10KHR for a longer period. It was not just a matter of stating that Ambedkar had lived at 10KHR for a significant period; we had to link this to his achievements too. For example, the thesis he wrote for LSE whilst he lodged at the house was important because this work resulted in the Reserve Bank of India being set up on 1 April 1935 to respond to economic troubles after the First World War. His links to the Fabian Society and his ability to view the caste system through the prism of another country was also important in his development and future input in the 1930s Round Table Conferences which formed the background to India's later freedom from the British Raj.

It was also important that our team explained who Ambedkar was to an audience who had very limited knowledge. Before this project, I had never heard of Dr Ambedkar. I suspect this is not unusual for a British person of non-Indian background. I recall an incident very early in the preparations for the Public Inquiry Hearing when I started to understand the importance of Ambedkar to the Indian community. I was at a cricket match with a number of work colleagues and was speaking to Nairita Chakraborty from our Heritage Team. Nairita is an Indian-born British national and we were chatting about our current projects. When I told her, 'You might be interested in one thing I'm about to start working on, it's a museum dedicated to Dr…errr…Ambedkar?'—still very unsure how to pronounce the name Ambedkar correctly—she replied 'What, Dr Ambedkar? You mean *the* actual Dr Ambedkar?' She was extremely impressed and went onto explain exactly why Ambedkar is so important to Indian people, and how he was an inspiration to her and her family. She offered to help pro bono, in whatever way she could. Eventually, she wrote a letter of support for the Ambedkar Museum that was referenced by the Inspector's report after the Public Inquiry. This was the first, but certainly not the last, time I witnessed the passion Ambedkar invoked in people. This passion and reverence was so crucial in the success of the appeal.

The final part of our argument for the Museum was to demonstrate how much Ambedkar meant to people and how it might benefit those who did not know much about his life. This was probably one of the easiest parts of the project because there was so much support for him and the Museum by those who took an interest in his life. This section contains extracts from the Inquiry, with people talking about their involvement in the appeal in their own words. I would add that one of the most powerful pieces of evidence we provided was a stream of personal and moving comments left in the guest book at 10KHR that Mr Haja Fahad, the caretaker/receptionist had encouraged visitors to leave. This feedback on visits was in different Indian languages, which the project team had translated. This was a very useful piece of evidence in the Public Inquiry.

Santosh Dass, who had decades of experience on better regulation and Regulatory Impact Assessments of government policies at the Department of Health, suggested we add to our case that Camden Council had not fully considered the regulatory impact of their decision. There is a duty on decision-makers to consider the equality impacts of their policies and decisions. As 'caste' featured in the Equality Act 2010, Camden Council denying a museum would negatively impact on people who shared a relevant protected characteristic—the Dalits and Buddhists. This also helped our case and was referred to in the Inspector's Report.[40] The support of Rebecca Anderson (my colleague at Iceni) with this case was invaluable She liaised on a day-to-day basis with the solicitors, our QC, the IHC, Santosh and William, and assisted in drafting the Proof of Evidence. She helped make everything run very smoothly for the project team.

### *The Public Inquiry Hearing 24 September 2019 and 11 October 2019*

The Public Inquiry began on 24 September 2019. In the lead-up there was significant press coverage of the appeal. This was unusual: at most an application I work on might make it into the local newspaper, but the Ambedkar House appeal had coverage in national newspapers in both the UK and India, including the BBC, who ran a story on their website. There was even a demonstration against Camden Council's decision outside a police station in Mumbai. So I was not all that surprised that there was a TV crew from *India Today* outside the Council Chamber where the Inquiry was being held. There were also a large number of followers of Ambedkar who turned up to the hearing. In addition, there were a range of people who lived on the street who had approached Dass to support the Museum, and others who wanted to speak in support. This, and the volume of evidence provided on both sides, resulted in a second day being allocated for the Inquiry on 11 October 2019.

A community project such as this one will only be successful if there is demand for it and people who are passionate about it. Lord Harries of Pentregarth's letter to Camden Council about the Museum was very powerful. He is, at the time of writing, the co-chair of the All Party Parliamentary Group for Dalits. He considered Ambedkar to be an inspirational figure to the more than 260 million Dalits worldwide. He argued the Museum would be invaluable to them and to everyone interested in human rights, equality and justice. Lord Harries regularly cited Dr Ambedkar's work in parliamentary debates on discrimination and saw the Museum as a valuable potential resource for schoolchildren. There were of course other parliamentarians, Ambedkarites and Dalit organisations who also wrote in support.

During the hearing on 24 September, any interested parties were invited to speak by the Inspector, Mr Keri Williams. Ms Sally Roach, Mr Alex Sunshine, Ms Garnett (better known as Bonnie Dobson, the singer-songwriter), Mr Ken Hunt, and Mr Sat Pal Muman gave excellent and impassioned contributions. Extracts of their contributions are included in the *Report to the Secretary of State for Housing, Communities and Local Government* by Mr K. L. Williams BA, MA, MRTPI, an Inspector appointed by the Secretary of State.

> *Ms Roach, local resident* (paragraph 35, page 9)
> Ms Roach has recently visited the museum. It fits into the area well. She was astonished by Dr Ambedkar's achievements for the Untouchables and for women and struck by his relevance to our current situation. Dr Ambedkar lived in the house and a museum to him is a positive addition to the area. Many residents were unaware of the museum and Ms Roach has not heard any objections from her neighbours. She has not seen buses full of people arriving or any traffic problems caused by the museum.

> *Mr Sunshine, London resident* (paragraph 36, page 9)
> Mr Sunshine has worked in India with the Dalit community. They would be deeply offended if the museum had to be removed and the property returned to a house. Dr Ambedkar is revered

in India as a very important figure, his birthday being a public holiday. There would be widespread negative press coverage. It would be regarded as petty and mean spirited. There would be harm to Anglo-Indian relations at a time when good bi-lateral relations are needed. Many visitors request to visit the museum. It closes at 5 p.m. and does not attract buses full of people.

*Ms Garnett, local resident* (paragraph 37, page 9)
Ms Garnett knew about the museum from the blue plaque. It is open to all and welcomes people from the local community and beyond. There is scope to develop links between the museum and local community organizations. We live in polarized times with immense inequality. Primrose Hill is a wealthy area but there is a food bank nearby. We need a place like this museum. Dr Ambedkar was a remarkable man and the museum gives an opportunity for all to learn about him. Ms Garnett has spoken to other local residents. They were in favour of the museum.

*Mr Hunt, London resident* (paragraph 38, page 9)
Mr Hunt is a music historian and writer, with involvement with Indian music and the culture of the sub-continent. He says that Dr Ambedkar is a hugely important figure, although less well known to westerners. He was a social justice and human rights champion of world-class status. The importance of this museum is still emerging. Living in London in this house gave Dr Ambedkar a period of stability and time to study. He used to walk to Gray's Inn, LSE or the British Museum. He would have witnessed suffering and emancipation going on around him and studied the writings of, for example, William Morris and John Ball. This experience shaped him and he went back to India to start his struggle. Dr Ambedkar's place in the *Dictionary of National Biography* is fully justified as someone who influenced our culture and society. There is no more suitable place in Britain than no. 10 King Henry's Road. Lord Avebury, another human rights champion, wrote in 2015 that 'The presence of an Ambedkar Centre in the house where he lived in London should help us all to confront the evil of caste prejudice, as we did against racism a generation ago.'

*Mr Sat Pal Muman, Secretary of the Ambedkar International Mission* (paragraphs 39, 40, page 10)
Dr Ambedkar is regarded as the emancipator and liberator of the Untouchables of India. No.10 King Henry's Road has special importance for millions of people as the place where he lived in 1921–22 while studying at LSE. He had previously studied at Columbia University. His stay at no.10 helped form his thinking and it has a spiritual connection to Dr Ambedkar. Mr Narendra Modi, the Prime Minister of India, inaugurated the Museum in 2015. Retaining it will enable visitors to pay their respects to the memory and legacy of Dr Ambedkar. Dr Ambedkar was born into the Untouchable caste but through his intellect and character he rose to challenge social and religious prejudices. He became the first Law Minister of India. In the 1930s he had a role in conferences and commissions on the future of the subcontinent. He was pivotal in the independence movement and the chief architect of the Indian constitution. He left a legacy to the people of India. He is widely celebrated and was voted the greatest Indian in a poll in 2015. In addition to the large Dalit community in the United Kingdom the museum reaches out to people of different faiths who are inspired by Dr Ambedkar. It would be disproportionate if the museum were required to close.

After the interested parties had spoken, proceedings moved on to the cross-examination of the key witnesses by the QCs. I would add at this stage that cross-examination of witnesses could at times be brutal. Usually a barrister goes easy on non-experts, such as local residents, but this is not the case when it comes to consultants, members of the Local Authority, and expert witnesses. As a planning consultant, I find it is certainly one of the most intimidating elements of my job. I have seen a witness being given a particularly torrid time under cross-examination in the past. There is also a certain air of the theatrical when it comes to cross-examination. The barrister will often look to the Inspector after a particular response with a raised eyebrow to note the importance of a response. Unsettling the witness is also a key tool used, with tutting and sighing often used early in the cross-examination to make the witness lose confidence at the start. Our QC Steven Gasztowicz, who had been inspired by the case, was calmly forensic.

Camden Council's witnesses came first and much of the discussion was about Ambedkar's link to the property. Ambedkar had stayed at two other properties during his time in London. The Council did not have the benefit of a historian or a local campaigner who had been involved in lobbying for the purchase of the property and who understood the significance of Ambedkar and his link to the property. As we have discussed, firm evidence demonstrating Ambedkar's link to 10KHR was uncovered in letters from archives, and from additional research conducted by Gould as we prepared for the Public Inquiry. In hindsight, Camden Council cannot be blamed for the absence of understanding Dr Ambedkar's connection to 10KHR, which seemed to have contributed to them arriving at their initial decision.

One of the other key moments of the appeal came in the afternoon of 24 September 2021 during cross-examination of the Council's Manager of the Arts Development Team. Our project team had submitted all the comments left in the visitors' book at the Ambedkar House, in some places translating them. Steven Gasztowicz took the witnesses through a variety of comments in which they said they had been inspired by their visit. There was a moving comment from an engineering student who stated that the visit to the house where Ambedkar had carried out such a significant part of his education had inspired the student to complete his own studies. In the face of such overwhelming support for the proposal that had a personal connection with Dr Ambedkar, it was very difficult for the experts from Camden Council to sustain their argument for the scheme to be located elsewhere. For example, the Council suggested that a room at LSE would provide a similar benefit without losing residential floor space.

The second day of the Public Inquiry hearing took place a couple of weeks later on 11 October 2020. A number of other interested parties had the opportunity to speak in favour of the proposal. Raj Bangar, a human rights activist and founder of Kanshi TV, a community channel, and a Sri Lankan Buddhist monk, The Venerable Vijithavansa Thero, voiced their support. A summary of their points is included in the Inspector's report to the Secretary of State on 4 December 2019:

> *Mr Raj Bangar* (paragraph 41, page 10)
> In considering Dr Ambedkar's achievements, the plight of Dalits before then must be considered. When at school, Mr Bangar's father was not allowed in the classroom but had to sit outside. He was not provided with pencil or paper and not allowed to drink from the shared urn. Many pupils were beaten to death for not complying. Later generations, including Mr Bangar and his wife, did not have to suffer this thanks to Dr Ambedkar's work. His experiences in the USA and the UK shaped Dr Ambedkar, who went on to emancipate millions of Indians. Mr Bangar has visited other places in India associated with Dr Ambedkar, but nowhere else does he feel the connection with him that he experiences at No.10 King Henry's Road.

> *The Venerable Vijithavansa Thero* (paragraph 42, pages 10 and 11)
> The Venerable Vijithavansa Thero is a Buddhist monk from Sri Lanka. The monks have great respect for Dr Ambedkar, as does the wider community in Sri Lanka. He revived Buddhism in India so that there are now over 23 million Buddhists there. He was also one of the greatest academics, the chief architect of the Indian constitution, the first post-independence Law Minister and the greatest champion of rights for Dalits and for women. Closure of Ambedkar House would be seen as a negative action by the British government against Buddhists. It would not be good for trade relations between Britain and Sri Lanka at a time when Britain is going through Brexit and needs to refresh trade relations with other countries. The museum should be allowed to continue to enable the unique achievements of Dr Ambedkar's great contribution to humanity to be remembered.

A Mr Bobhakar, an Ambedkarite, is also listed as a third-party 'local resident' in the inspector's report (page 16). During the hearing, Mr Bobhakar informed the Inspector and handed over a book to Ms C. Daly QC, Camden Council's barrister, that drew attention to a few letters published in the book from the landlady 'Fanny/Frances' to Dr Ambedkar.

It was then the turn of the appellant's witnesses to be appear. William Gould was first, setting out the historical importance of Dr Ambedkar, his time in London, and the links to the property. He was given some fairly difficult questions to start with, but I don't think that I had ever seen someone enjoy giving evidence—as he obviously did—on their debut at a Public Inquiry. I can remember being a total bag of nerves for my first cross-examination. I hated every moment of it. In contrast, I saw a smile break across Gould's face several times.

Next up was Santosh Dass. Despite her submitting a written lengthy Proof of Evidence explaining Ambedkar's links to London and how much the property meant to her and the Ambedkarite community, the cross-examination was relatively short. I suspect this was because the document submitted was thorough, and there was limited benefit to the Council in exploring these themes. For example, Dass provided first-hand testimony of the walks that she and other members of the Ambedkarite community took on Dr Ambedkar's birthday and anniversary of his death. These walks always started at 10KHR and finished at LSE. She also recalled to the Inspector how emotional she got when she went to the view the inside of the house in September 2014, a few days after submitting a proposal to the GOM that they buy the property before it went into private ownership again.[41]

For my own cross-examination, the main focus was to demonstrate that the loss of residential units would be greatly outweighed by the community benefits. The witnesses and interested parties had made my job very straightforward. They had set out what Ambedkar meant to them and the wider community and his clear link to this property. The cross-examination was fairly technical around land supply, but the main point I was able to argue in summary was that while two homes would be lost, this amounted to only 0.0001 per cent of the Council's supply of homes over the Camden Local Plan period. I argued this was a price worth paying for a cherished community facility, when we are talking about two units within an overall supply of over 6,000 homes across a five-year period.

For all the drama that can happen at a Public Inquiry, there was relatively little in the cross-examinations. The aim for both sides at these Inquiries is to get their side of the argument across to the Inspector without having to concede too much. If the case is particularly strong on either side, the cross-examination is unlikely to win the day. In my view, we put forward a very strong case without conceding much ground. In fact, the various interested parties who spoke up in favour further enhanced our case. Equally, I don't think the Council would have been disappointed with how the Public Inquiry went. The issue for them was that at the Public Inquiry the very compelling link between 10KHR and Ambedkar was more clearly put forward due to the presence of expert witnesses (William Gould and Santosh Dass) who developed the case significantly (with material that wasn't available at the time the Council refused the application). In addition, different voices from the community added passion to the case.

We had to wait a few months for the Inspector to write his report and make a recommendation to the Secretary of State. He did this on 4 December 2019. We were absolutely delighted to hear that the appeal had been allowed and Ambedkar House would remain open. The report of the Secretary of State and the Inspector, available on the government's website,[42] were both in agreement and relatively concise. They were satisfied that the Museum would provide a significant community benefit and this would outweigh the harm of the loss of two residential units. Personally, I learnt a lot from this historic case. I was honoured to be part of the project team that successfully demonstrated the historical importance of one of the most extraordinary social reformers in history. Preparation for the case with Mr Steven Gasztowicz, Santosh Dass and William Gould, and harnessing the passion of Dr Ambedkar's followers, was key to the case's success.

8

# THE CAMPAIGN TO OUTLAW CASTE DISCRIMINATION IN BRITAIN

*Santosh Dass*

In his paper *Castes in India* (1916), Dr Ambedkar describes India's caste system as having features that include hierarchy, endogamy, graded occupation and restrictions on temple worship. Twenty years later, in his *Annihilation of Caste* (a speech he never got to deliver), directed at Hindus and Hindu reformers in pre-independence India, he continued his call for social reform of the caste system. In the speech, he examined 'caste' in the context of other societies—Roman, Greek and Irish—and quoted from William Morris's poem 'A Dream of John Ball', paraphrasing the priest's preachings and sermonising which fed the Peasants' Revolt of 1381: 'The great treading down the little, And the strong beating down weak, Cruel men fearing not, Kind men daring not, And wise men caring not.'[1] Ambedkar saw potential in Morris's words. The poem illustrates what it meant to live under the weight of feudalism, whether via caste or a kind of social apartheid. We could view it as Ambedkar finding transferability.

The campaign to highlight experiences of caste discrimination in the UK began in the 1970s, with some far-sighted, committed and politically savvy Ambedkarites. In this chapter, I describe with personal insights and recollections, as a founding member of CasteWatchUK and the Anti Caste Discrimination Alliance (ACDA), the ongoing campaign, for nearly two decades, to outlaw caste-based discrimination in Britain. I discuss the notable early successes; the resistance from the Hindu (and also, in part, Sikh) groups; and the key organisations, activists, academics, and British politicians involved in the campaign. I discuss the drive in the UK to challenge the attitudes of the imperial age that has become a feature of the equality movement since George Floyd's murder in America in 2015, and the rise of the Black Lives Matter (BLM) movement. The caste law campaign is now part and parcel of such campaigns dealing with millennia-old attitudes and discrimination. Finally, I share the progress made in the public and private sector to deal with caste-based discrimination cases in Britain in the absence of the clarity in the law on caste discrimination that was agreed by the British Parliament in April 2013.

At its root, the campaign is based in personal and biographical experiences. In February 1968 I migrated to London as a small girl from a village in Punjab, India with my mum Raj Mohinder and brother to join my dad, Hans Raj Sidhu. Dad arrived in Britain from Jalandhar, Punjab on 28 October 1963—just over a month after securing his first passport. An educated man, fluent in English, Hindu, Punjabi and Urdu, he had left a respectable job as a bank inspector in what mum described as a Cooperative Society bank, to move to Britain for an even better life abroad. He was not new to starting a new life. As an eleven-year-old, he and his family had already moved from Lyallpur (now known as Faisalabad in Pakistan) to Jalandhar during the 1947 Partition. In England, he first settled with family in Birmingham and then moved to London and secured employment at the British Overseas Airways Corporation at Heathrow Airport, where he worked until he retired. Through hard work my father managed to save and borrow enough money to buy a three-bedroom house in Cranford, in the London Borough of Hounslow in West London, for us to move into when we arrived. He still continued to support his extended family in India, as well as sending money to support a few bright Dalit students with their college fees in Punjab. Dad firmly believed, like Ambedkar, in the power of education and good academic qualifications for social progression. The Education Aid Society, based in Southall in the 1970s, formalised the fundraising that my father, and uncles, including Harjit Raihal and Ram Prakash Rahl, were so passionate about. The Society often invited inspiring activists and politicians from India to address their meetings and social gatherings. Stories of atrocities against Dalits in India were shared at these family events. They shocked us children. Sometimes I would overhear my dad tell my mum about the caste discrimination he faced at work. He would talk about the harassment and the well-deserved promotions and bonuses that should have gone to him but which the so-called higher castes awarded to work colleagues of their caste. It pained me to hear this. But like many child migrants of my generation and those born soon after, including my youngest brother, I was busy learning English, assimilating and adapting to a new life—and also coping with the everyday overt racism we faced in those early years. We weren't spared the name-calling, abuse and harassment that was openly common then. It wasn't until I learnt in school about the international campaign against South Africa's apartheid regime, and the Black American freedom struggle against segregation after the abolition of slavery in the United States that I could relate this to India's caste system and what had raised its head in London too. When I read Ambedkar's *Annihilation of Caste* speech, and his other writings in my teens with encouragement from dad, I really got a measure of caste and its pernicious impacts.

At the time of writing this chapter, I am aware there are similar campaigns calling for caste discrimination to be outlawed in other countries where the South Asian diaspora populations have settled. In recent years the caste-based discrimination lawsuit against Cisco in the USA, and another in Canada that has not been publicised, are signs that the utter negativity of caste as a force for social and societal conditioning is unrelenting—even its subtlest form.[2] Caste benefits the privileged few at the top. The caste system justifies keeping swathes of the South Asian community—and diaspora—reminded about knowing their place. The open resistance to any change to this status quo is loud and clear. In Britain this resistance has been in the well-organised opposition to caste discrimination law. In the USA, it was visible in January 2022 when over eighty faculty members of the California State University (CSU) opposed the move by the CSU to add 'caste' to their anti-discriminatory policy.[3] More recently, in June 2022, in the US, it was reported that Google invited, and then uninvited, the Dalit activist and executive director of the US-based Equality Labs, Thenmozhi Soundararajan, to talk to Google News employees for Dalit History Month, when some Google employees objected and called her anti-Hindu in emails.[4]

*Dr Ambedkar in Parliament and Equality Laws in Britain*

There are copious references to Ambedkar in British Parliamentary debates in London that appeared in the official record *Hansard* long after his appearance at the Round Table Conferences (RTCs) in the early 1930s. These form one historical context or background to the legislative moves to add caste to equality laws in the UK. Ambedkar's name has been regularly cited in discussion of such topics as equality, human rights, modern-day slavery, and, more recently, in debates on the calls to outlaw caste discrimination in Britain. An early reference in *Hansard* to Ambedkar's assertion for those blighted by India's caste system occurred during a debate on the future of India on 18 March 1931. Lord William Peel, the former Secretary of State for India, repeated Dr Ambedkar's words: 'I saw the other day that Ambedkar, the representative of the 40 millions of the depressed classes, indignantly asked: Is that Committee [the Structural Committee for the RTCs] going to meet and have no representative of the depressed classes upon it?'[5] Another British parliamentarian sympathetic to Ambedkar's robust calls for a voice for his community during the 1930s conferences was Eleanor Rathbone MP. On 28 March 1933, she also referred to Ambedkar's calls for action to improve the lives of the depressed classes before the British quit India: 'You have been in India for a century and a half. You found us a depressed class. You leave us a depressed class. What have you done for us?' Rathbone added, 'this question might be asked also about the women of India. In what condition did we find the women of India? In what condition are we leaving them?'[6]

For the Dalit diaspora, Ambedkar has become a beacon and a uniting force for their campaign to outlaw caste discrimination in Britain which has been imported with the South Asian diaspora since the 1950s. Equality laws in Britain are designed to combat racial and other forms of discrimination and prejudice. Not only do they provide legal redress for the discrimination a person may face, they also promote equality of opportunity and treatment regardless of protected characteristics. When it came to race equality law, one of the leading figures was Lord Anthony Lester of Herne Hill, QC. A barrister and member of the House of Lords, Lord Lester was directly involved in the drafting of the race relations laws in the 1960s and 1970s. He also supported the campaign and the calls for caste discrimination to be outlawed in Britain. In his book *Five Ideas to Fight For—How Our Freedom Is Under Threat and Why It Matters* (2016), Lord Lester noted the Conservative Party's reluctance to outlaw caste-based discrimination 'For obscure political reasons, the Conservatives in the coalition were less keen to tackle another invidious form of minority oppression: caste discrimination. It is an ancient problem imported into this country as a result of the migration and settlement of British Asians.'[7]

Lester and Geoffrey Bindman's book *Race and Law* (1972) provides a really useful background to how the race laws came about in Britain. The book concludes with a cautionary tale: 'Race relations cannot be properly understood in contemporary Britain without an awareness of the inheritance of racial attitudes from the imperial age.' Lester and Bindman added, 'There are extreme instances of the use of the law as a declaratory gesture rather than an effective instrument of individual justice and social change; and they teach a lesson in the evasion and abuse of the law.' These far-sighted cautionary words are not so far removed from Ambedkar's in his final speech presenting the draft Constitution in the Constituent Assembly on 25 November 1949: '...however good a Constitution may be, it is sure to turn out bad because those who are called to work it, happen to be a bad lot'.[8]

### *The Word 'Caste' and the 'Caste System'*

Defining what the word 'caste' means as it is added to, or clarified in, Britain's equality legal framework has become a matter of obfuscation, heated debate and a topic for reports for nearly two decades. In July 2013, the Conservative and Liberal Democrat coalition government even commissioned research into whether and how caste should be defined in the legislation as part of its 'Caste legislation introduction—programme and timetable'.[9] The word 'caste' can mean different things to different people and communities depending on their place (or no place) within the caste hierarchy. Its meaning lies also in the lived experience of being 'outcaste' or regarded as 'Untouchable' within the caste system.

Sue Penney's book *Hinduism* (2005 edition) in the Discovering Religions series available for British schoolchildren allows those outside of the South Indian diaspora to learn about caste as something far removed from Britain. Penney discusses *varna*, *jati*, the caste system, and the Hindu holy books, including the laws of Manu. Teenage schoolchildren, who may also have read George Orwell's thought-provoking book *Nineteen Eighty-Four* as part of their coursework, for example, won't have easily connected it to the caste system. But the connection is certainly there, not least because Orwell himself for a time worked as a police officer in British India (in Burma). Bhagwan Das,[10] who worked as Ambedkar's research assistant in the final few years of Ambedkar's life, warned, 'To a serious student of Hindu Society, the horrible picture drawn in the *1984* (*sic*) of George Orwell or in Huxley's *Brave New World* looks like a childish imitate [sic] of Hindu Society based on Manu's Law.'[11] Orwell in his essay 'The English People', published in 1947, wrote of 'the subtle grading of the class system—with an inherited knowledge impossible to a foreigner'.[12] If we substitute class with caste in this specific context, western societies may begin to have an appreciation for the complexities for defining caste.

In 2008, in their report 'Caste in the UK', the Hindu Forum (HF) of Britain described caste as follows: 'the four main *varnas* or occupational classes stated in the *Rig Veda* and *Bhagavad-Gita* were: 1. Brahmanas (scholars and priests); 2. Kshatriyas (soldiers, administrators and warriors); 3. Vaishyas (merchants, artisans and cultivators); 4. Shudras (workers).'[13] These tiers are typically depicted as a hierarchical pyramid showing the Brahmins at the top and the Shudras at the base. For the group of humanity beneath and outside the four main *varnas*, labelled as Untouchables, now known as Scheduled Castes or Dalits, caste is, however, best described in their experience of it.

Dr Suraj Yengde, the author and activist, describes it powerfully in *Caste Matters* (2019) through the lived experience of his paternal grandmother: 'Her soft palm had seen everything—the horrors of Untouchability, the traditions of imposed inferiority, and her resolution to labour to build her family's life by working in farms and fields as a landless labourer, the servant at someone's house or in the mill. She represents the traditions of unknown yet so great people. The people made outcasts by the Hindu religious order, deemed despicable, polluted, unworthy of life—beings whose mere sight in public would bring a cascade of violence upon the entire community.'[14] Yet alongside this personal experience there are also ways in which the forms of hierarchy that caste creates are transferred elsewhere, and are clearly larger and more lasting than at first appears. Isabel Wilkerson in *Caste—The Lies That Divide* (2020) describes caste from an African-American perspective as 'an artificial construction, a fixed and embedded ranking of human value that sets the presumed supremacy of one group against the presumed inferiority of other groups on the basis of ancestry and often immutable traits, traits that would be neutral in the abstract but are ascribed life-and-death meaning in a hierarchy favouring the dominant caste whose forebears designed it.'[15]

At the same time, we also need to take care to be clear on the distinctiveness of caste, compared to other social hierarchies. There are those who dilute the caste system as being a class system. There may be some similarities but caste and class are very different social dividers. Class is generally connected to an individual's education, wealth or occupation, and there is an element of social mobility. Caste on the other hand is connected to an individual's birth and descent. It ranks people accordingly on a perceived scale of ritual purity which, among other things, determines who is touchable or untouchable in a wide range of social interactions. Whereas Gandhi proposed the caste system on the grounds of labour, Ambedkar argued the caste system was not merely a division of labour, but also a 'division of labourers'.[16]

The narrative around the meaning of the word 'caste' and the caste system's origins, then, has no doubt become a matter of considerable debate. The National Council of Hindu Temples, for example, asserted in a report *Caste, Conversion and a Thoroughly Colonial Conspiracy* (2017) that the caste system is a Western, colonialist, missionary construction and has never existed in India.[17] This approach is taking advantage, probably cynically, of a development in recent social science literature, which explores the colonial contribution to the politicisation of caste. But even if we accept the arguments of this research, this does not change or remove the realities of the lived experiences of caste discrimination in the modern world.

### *The Campaign to Outlaw Caste Discrimination in Britain*

Ambedkar warned that if Hindus migrate to other regions on earth, Indian caste would become a world problem.[18] Caste has migrated to Britain since the 1950s with people from India, Pakistan, Bangladesh, Nepal and Sri Lanka—all of which have aspects of caste. Since the 1980s, caste has also migrated with high-skilled Indians to Britain. It is evident in the names of places of worship like Gurdwaras (Sikh temples) and Mandirs (Hindu and other temples), which serve specific castes around Britain. For example, if you walk around Southall, London, you can find within walking distance the Shree Ram Mandir, Bhagwan Valmiki Mandir, Sri Guru Singh Sabha, Shri Guru Ravidass Temple, and the Ramgarhia Sabha Southall. In 2021 there were six UK charities registered with the UK's Charity Commission with the word 'Brahmin' in their title under organisations working with specific castes.[19] So-called matrimonial sites make it possible to find a potential bride or groom in the UK sifted according to particular castes.[20] Together, South Asians form five per cent of the total UK population and many still follow their culture and festivals. With these cultural activities come aspects of caste practices passed down from previous generations

The campaign to raise awareness of the reality of the caste system in India and caste discrimination in Britain as an equality issue began in the 1970s. Ambedkar too was very keen to identify the means by which Dalit rights could be protected in law and in India's constitution, and in this sense, the range of movements are following this method of campaigning around changes in the statutory rights and protections of these communities.

Ambedkarites living in Britain, including the late Chanan Ram Chahal and Arun Kumar of the Ambedkar Mission Society, Bedford, were optimistic they had escaped caste when they migrated to Britain. They soon found they had not. In 1976, a journalist called Liz Brown perpetuated the offence and slight of caste and caste discrimination by describing 'Untouchables' as 'subhumans' in her article in *The Bedfordshire Times* about religions in Bedfordshire: 'The caste system in India is thousands of years old and was designed by the Hindu priests—the Brahmins. And even though the idea of a sub-human class is repellent to us today its foundation was fairly practical. They decided that if the depressed, poverty-stricken class was to prostrate itself and kiss the floor of the temple everyone else was likely to catch whatever they were carrying. So The Untouchables were born and banned from practicing the religion.'[21] The word 'subhuman' resonated with the Nazi term *Untermensch*, that word's literal translation. Dalits and Ambedkarites expressed their outrage by protesting in the streets and boycotting the local Hindu shop owner quoted in Brown's article. After this incident, campaigners continued to share their experiences of caste discrimination with the media, the government and equality organisations. 'The Untouchables are no longer placidly accepting their hereditary inferiority and are determined to assert themselves,' observed the journalist Maurice Weaver in a 1990 *Daily Telegraph* article, 'I thought I would escape the name but it has followed me like a dark cloud.'[22] Weaver reported on offensive graffiti with a four-letter expletive and the words 'chamal on the block' found by locals in Bedford who frequented the Gardiners Arms pub. The word *Chamar* (classified as Scheduled Caste, and a usage used as a pejorative for Dalits) was misspelt 'Chamal' in the article. The graffiti essentially identified the people who frequented the pub as

*Chamars*, with the implication that so-called high castes might want to avoid it. Weaver observed, 'In the workaday heart of England it is a sign that the Hindu caste system, so often described as India's shame, is flourishing in Britain.'

The campaign against caste discrimination in Britain became particularly robust around the turn of the millennium as activists organised themselves and formed new organisations to campaign to outlaw it. In 1998 the Rev. David Haslam, a former executive member of the Anti-Apartheid Movement and War on Want, founded the London-based Dalit Solidarity Network UK (DSN UK). Together with Jeremy Corbyn MP, he successfully brought together activists and organisations to campaign specifically on the issue of caste discrimination and interacted on caste issues more globally. DSN UK is affiliated to the Denmark-based International Dalit Solidarity Network (IDSN) founded in 2000. Meena Varma was the long-serving Director of DSN from 2007 and Gazala Shaikh took over in 2022.[23]

In 1999 Eugene and Irene Culas founded the Voice of Dalit International (VODI) in Grimsby, the port town in north-east Lincolnshire. Within a year, on 7 June 2000, they organised a seminar on 'Caste and Human Rights' at Grimsby College.[24] David Haslam gave a keynote speech there. VODI later based itself in London, where it has remained. There they continued to meet key people around the country from the Sri Guru Ravidass Sabha UK Europe and Abroad (SGRSUK), Ambedkarite Buddhist organisations, and the Valmiki community to raise awareness of their work, and also learn about issues that concerned these communities. These interactions motivated VODI to organise the first two-day 'International Conference on Dalit Rights' in London from 16–17 September 2000.[25] This brought together representatives from various Dalit and Ambedkarite communities under one roof. One notable paper delivered there was 'Caste in Britain' by Sat Pal Muman.

The larger campaign to have caste recognised in UK's discrimination law was energised following the broadcast on 1 April 2003 of a BBC Radio 4 documentary 'The Caste Divide' by Naresh Puri.[26] VODI had input to this and it featured people from around Britain talking about their experiences of caste discrimination.

Councillor Ram Lakha from Coventry, who later became Lord Mayor of Coventry for 2005–2006, described the caste discrimination he faced during his election campaign. There were accounts of children being harassed and abused at school, and caste discrimination in the workplace. When I heard about this radio broadcast a little later, at a DSN meeting chaired by David Haslam, I volunteered to transcribe the content for wider written circulation. Eugene Culas came to my home with a copy of the cassette recording. We ended up talking for hours over lunch in my back garden. The transcript, and the actions I identified that needed taking forward to tackle the discrimination identified, were circulated to DSN and VODI, and this spurred on a number of activists to meet at the Buddha Vihara in Southall, West London, soon afterwards. Eugene Culas, C. Gautam, Ken Hunt, Sat Pal Muman and Harbans Virdee were amongst the attendees discussing the actions to be taken forward, which included regulatory and non-regulatory measures. It was during this meeting that we also discussed a suitable name for an organisation that could take the work forward. Ken Hunt, who had experience in 'branding', suggested we have a name along the lines of BBC's *Crimewatch* programme and proposed 'CasteWatch'. Eugene Culas was keen for this new group to meet other activists in VODI's sister organisation Voice of Dalit UK (VOD UK). Davinder Prasad hosted the meeting at his home in Coventry, at which we all met Pashori Lal and Jagdish Rai. VOD UK was formally subsumed into CasteWatchUK (CWUK) at that meeting, and Pashori Lal was appointed Chair with Davinder Prasad as the General Secretary. CWUK was formally launched on 3 July 2004 at St Mary's Guildhall, Coventry. Ken Hunt, one of the panellists at the launch that we all attended, introduced CWUK to the world in his article 'Reaching the Untouchables' in the *New Humanist* in summer 2004. The chair of CWUK at the time of writing is Sat Pal Muman.

CWUK's meetings and seminars in the early years attracted academics, activists, politicians and the media keen to learn more about caste discrimination. Victims were encouraged to share their personal experiences at these seminars. I recall Jasvinder Sanghera CBE, the author and campaigner against forced marriages, gave a talk at CWUK's conference at the Sandwell Conference Centre on 15 July 2007 soon after the publication of her book *Shame* (2007).[27]

She spoke about her own experience of caste discrimination when she ran away as a sixteen-year-old in the early 1980s with her friend Avtar's brother Jassey, a Dalit, to flee a forced marriage. Describing her relationship with Avtar, who was very independent, Sanghera writes, 'If my mum had known this she would never have let me be friends with her, but she didn't so all she had to worry about was a fact that Avtar's family were much lower caste than us. They were chamar. Mum had never let us have chamar friends. Years before I'd challenged her on that. I asked her why, if our chamar neighbour went to the same gurdwara why I wasn't allowed to play out with her kids. Mum beat me for that, but I never got an explanation.'[28] Sanghera's family and her community shunned and disowned her after she ran away with Jassey.

CWUK and other organisations, including DSN UK, VODI and the Federation of Ambedkarite and Buddhist Organisations UK (FABO UK), continued to campaign for the law by raising awareness of caste discrimination and mobilising academics and politicians at meetings and conferences. In 2004 Rena Dipti Annobil (née Prasad) and Reena Jaisiah (née Bhatoa), formed Caste Away Arts, CWUK's arts wing. By 2006 they had scripted a play based on the experiences of a British schoolboy who had been subjected to bullying and harassment because of his caste. Jagdish Rai's daughter Ravina Rai joined Caste Away Arts, and in 2007 they directed and successfully screened the play *The Fifth Cup* at the Drum Arts Centre in Birmingham.[29]

As the calls increased for caste discrimination to be outlawed, so did the demand from British politicians for evidence of discrimination to support any new law.[30] In July 2006, DSN UK published the evidence in its report *No Escape—Caste Discrimination in the UK*.[31] The first of its kind, this report contained examples of caste discrimination based on a survey. The same year, the International Dalit Solidarity Network published 'Ambedkar Principles' that contains excellent employment principles and additional principles to address economic and social exclusion of Dalits in South Asia.[32] This guidance is also useful for UK companies that operate in, and/or have a workforce in, India for example. In 2008 the Hindu Council UK produced its own counter-report,

*Caste in the UK*—a summary of the consultation with the Hindu community in Britain. This included a lengthy section on the origins of the caste system. The Hindu Council UK claimed its consultation found no caste discrimination, and if it did occur, it may only be limited to intercaste marriages, and relationships.[33] That year, the Hindu Forum of Britain (HF) also published a report, *The Caste System*, with similar findings. Chanan Chahal, the then President of FABO UK provided a robust response to the Hindu Council UK's report in *The Evils of Caste* (2009). This report was launched jointly by FABO UK and DSN UK.[34]

Nearly five years after CWUK was formed, some of the team, including Pashori Lal, Ravi Kumar, Ken Hunt and I, left the organisation because of differences of opinion, focus and direction. Together with activists Lekh Raj Pall, Onkar Sangha and Amarjit Singh of the Indian Workers Association, Dr Raj Chand from Letchworth, and other Dalit activists from the Midlands, Bedford and London, in 2008 we formed the Anti Caste Discrimination Alliance (ACDA). Pashori Lal became Chair, and Lekh Raj Pall the General Secretary. At the time of writing, the ACDA has had two more Chairpersons in its twelve years—Dr Raj Chand and me since 2018—with Ravi Kumar as the current General Secretary. ACDA's particular strength is its alliances with other like-minded organisations, connections with grassroots Dalit communities and parliamentarians in the UK, and its written briefings and communications. As the caste law campaign has grown, other organisations, including the Shri Guru Ravidass Sabah UK, Europe and Abroad, the Valmiki organisations, National Secular Society with Keith Porteous-Wood, and the South Asia Solidarity Group with Amrit Wilson, have similarly supported the calls for the new law.

Initially, campaigners found it a struggle to get their voice heard in the mainstream media. Without connections and opportunities it was, and continues to be, difficult. More recently, *The Guardian* and *The Times*, for example, have written on the topic. British TV channels such as the BBC, ITV, Channel 4, and the community channel Kanshi TV now report on caste discrimination, albeit not as regularly as the campaign would like. Both sides of the debate make good use of platforms in universities to debate the issue.[35] In 2010 the All

Party Parliamentary Group (APPG) for Dalits was established with DSN UK's support.[36] This informal group of House of Commons MPs and members of the House of Lords draws attention to the discrimination of Dalits wherever it occurs.

### *Successive Governments and the Caste Law*

In the lead-up to the Single Equality Bill in 2008, the policy of successive governments was to deal separately with issues of discrimination, according to Lord Avebury: 'Prior to that, it was the *custom* to treat them as if they were separate issues.'[37] Politicians were later convinced, and recognised that there were common features of discrimination. The pro-caste law campaigners believed these common features applied equally to caste discrimination. The Labour Government had remained silent on outlawing caste discrimination for over a decade despite robust lobbying by organisations. Its first public statement on the issue was on 17 July 2008 in response to the public responses to its consultations on the Single Equality Bill: 'While recognising that Caste discrimination is unacceptable, we have found no strong evidence of such discrimination in Britain, in the context of employment or the provision of goods, facilities or services. We would, however, consult the Equality and Human Rights Commission about monitoring the position.'[38] We found out almost two years later that the government had ignored the voice of Dalits, choosing instead to listen to the Hindu Forum and the Hindu Council.

Campaigners continued to put masses of time and energy into lobbying the government, Shadow Cabinet members, and the media in the lead-up to the Single Equality Bill's introduction in Parliament in 2009. The number of supportive parliamentarians from all the main political parties continued to grow. Cross-party support came from Jeremy Corbyn MP (also Honorary Chair of DSN UK), John McDonnell MP, Rob Marris MP, Seema Malhotra MP, Kate Green MP, Lyn Featherstone MP, Dr Evan Harris MP, Baroness Warsi, Richard Fuller MP, Lord Harries of Pentregarth, Lord Eric Avebury, Lord Lester of Herne Hill, Lord Alton of Liverpool, Baroness Flather, and Lord Singh of Wimbledon. Others supporting the calls for the law as governments changed, or were won over, included Baroness Thornton, Lord Cashman, Lord Deben and Mohammad Yasin MP.

When the Equality Bill was introduced in Parliament on 24 April 2009, there was no mention of caste discrimination. Campaigners didn't lose heart. They lobbied the Equality Bill Scrutiny Committee looking at the content of the Bill. CWUK submitted a memorandum 'Caste Discrimination in the UK—Evidence Paper' and the ACDA wrote to each member of the Scrutiny Committee calling on them to table an amendment on caste to the Bill.[39] This lobbying proved successful. It was during the Parliamentary discussions on the Bill on 11 June, regarding the amendments to the Bill on caste, that the government's then Solicitor General—Vera Baird MP–informed the Committee that the government had consulted a variety of predominantly Hindu groups and some Sikh and Muslim groups.[40] She said the decision to not outlaw caste discrimination had been based on those consultations.[41] Not a single Dalit organisation had been consulted directly by the government. John Mason MP of the Scottish National Party asked why there was such opposition to the law. Alarmingly, Vera Baird MP replied, 'Because it is socially divisive to have legislation against something that is not happening and is needed by no one.'[42] On reflection, the government response, informed by the Hindu Forum and Hindu Council, did have an echo of the resistance to Ambedkar's demands that the Depressed Classes have rights and be able to represent themselves on the discussions on the future of India in the 1930s. Ambedkar's demand was opposed by Gandhi, who saw this as a British attempt to split the Hindus.[43]

It was the outcome of the Bill Committee's discussion of 11 June 2009 that inspired the ACDA to conduct its own research during the Parliamentary recess from July to October 2009. The aim was to quickly explore the existence and new evidence of caste discrimination in the areas covered by the Equality Bill, namely employment, provision of services, and education. For this study, ACDA published and promoted an online questionnaire for feedback from the community and conducted focus groups around Britain. This was carried out with helpful advice and steers, and in collaboration with Professor Stephen Whittle OBE (University of Manchester), Professor Annapurna Waughray (Manchester

Metropolitan University), Professor Dr Roger Green (University of Hertfordshire) and Professor Gurharpal Singh (University of Birmingham). The ACDA published its research findings in their report *A Hidden Apartheid—Voice of the Community* (2009).

Over 300 people participated and fed their experiences into ACDA's research. It elicited evidence of people missing out on promotion, of being underpaid, and having been neglected in a domiciliary care setting. A few representative examples give a sense of the texture and seriousness of the responses: there were instances of children subjected to bullying at school because of their caste; there was the experience of a very old and vulnerable Indian woman in Derby whose care had been neglected by her 'higher-caste' female carer; there was a bus company manager in Southampton who had to completely reorganise the shift pattern so a lower-caste bus driver's shifts didn't coincide with a 'higher-caste' inspector's shifts. ACDA launched its report in the House of Lords on 11 November 2009 at a meeting hosted and chaired by Lord Eric Avebury.[44] This report gave the community a voice that had hitherto been ignored and denied by the British Government. This report, and Waughray's *Modern Law Review* article 'Caste Discrimination: A Twenty-First Century Challenge for UK Discrimination Law?' (February 2009), gave the caste amendments tabled to the Equality Bill the kudos that had been lacking until then.

Waughray described the two key moments when the campaign's fortunes changed. One was ACDA's report, and the second was a meeting of pro-caste lobby groups on 4 February 2010 in the House of Lords with Baroness Thornton, the Equalities Minister in the Lords.[45] The meeting gave the Dalit and Ambedkarite groups an opportunity to discuss the evidence, the case for law, and ways in which it could be drafted. Waughray, who was at the meeting, remarked later, 'At this meeting "behind the scenes", Government support (or at least non-opposition) was secured for an amendment to section 9 of the Bill, adding an enabling provision allowing for the future inclusion of caste in the definition of race.'[46] The United Nations Committee for the Elimination of Racial Discrimination (CERD) had issued a general recommendation in 2002 to all states party to the Treaty affirming that *descent* included caste. CERD later made a specific recommendation to the UK in 2003 that it introduce a legal prohibition of descent-based discrimination. To this the UK in 2005 responded stating there was no evidence of caste discrimination and therefore legislation was not required. Descent, however, is an existing legal category in a binding international instrument—9I CERD—to which the UK has been party since 1969.

During this period the ACDA lobbied members in both Houses of Parliament. It organised and led a number of protests in Parliament Square to coincide with key debates in Parliament during the passage of the Equality Bill when the amendment on caste was scheduled for discussion. The first of these protests took place on 11 January 2010.[47] This attracted fewer than 100 people. Later demonstrations organised by ACDA, CWUK with the support of Kanshi TV, the Sri Guru Ravidass Sabha UK, Europe and Abroad, and the Valmiki organisations saw thousands of people arrive in coachloads to protest in solidarity in Parliament Square. In April 2010 the British Government finally conceded, and introduced a power in the Equality Act 2010—in Section 9(5) a. This power could be used by a Government Minister to insert 'caste' as an aspect of Race in the Equality Act 2010 in the future. The Equality Act 2010's Explanatory Notes describe caste as:

> The term 'caste' denotes a hereditary, endogamous (marrying within the group) community associated with a traditional occupation and ranked accordingly on a perceived scale of ritual purity. It is generally (but not exclusively) associated with South Asia, particularly India, and its diaspora. It can encompass the four classes (varnas) of Hindu tradition (the Brahmin, Kshatriya, Vaishya and Shudra communities); the thousands of regional Hindu, Sikh, Christian, Muslim or other religious groups known as jatis; and groups amongst South Asian Muslims called biradaris. Some jatis regarded as below the Varna hierarchy (once termed 'untouchable') are known as 'Dalit'.[48]

We campaigners thought, 'Job done!' Little did we know that over a decade later we would be campaigning to retain this hard-won law.

In addition to the 'power' on caste law in the Equality Act in April 2010, the Labour Government announced it would commission research to underpin the future law. The National Institute for Economic and Social Research (NIESR)—one of the leading independent research bodies in the UK—was commissioned to undertake this. A month later, on 6 May 2010, Britain held a general election. With no overall majority, the Conservative Party formed a coalition government with the Liberal Democrats. This proved to be a huge setback for our campaign. NIESR's report *Caste discrimination and harassment in Great Britain* (2010) confirmed the existence of caste and caste discrimination in Britain.[49] While the government considered NIESR's findings, some caste-related Employment Tribunals (ETs) proceeded in the British courts. The first of these was in August 2011—*Begraj v Heer Manak Solicitors*. Vijay Begraj alleged he had been discriminated against because he, a Dalit, had decided to marry a Sikh colleague at the law firm where he worked. This case collapsed because the judge recused herself after a thirty-six-day hearing.[50] In 2012, the ET rejected a claim for caste discrimination in the case of *Naveed v Aslam and others* for two reasons.[51] Firstly, the government had not yet exercised its power to amend the Equality Act to include caste, and secondly, the claimant's caste was the same as the caste of the respondent.

At the UN level, DSN UK and IDSN submitted a joint shadow report to UN's CERD's 79 Session held from 8 August to 2 September 2011, at which Britain and Northern Ireland's performance on equality was examined.[52] The ACDA and the Odysseus Trust (set up by Lord Lester) also made submissions to CERD on the issue.[53] Dr Raj Chand from ACDA, Ravi Kumar representing SGRS Birmingham, Sam Kalyan from the Bhagwan Valmiki Sabha Bedford, Ram Kishan Mehmi from SGRS Darlaston, and Ajit Nahar from Bhagwan Valmiki Sabha in Southall also arrived in Geneva to lobby CERD in person. This was the first time this group of people had attended such a meeting. The submissions and the face-to-face lobbying proved fruitful. In September 2011, CERD called on the British Government to implement the 2010 caste law. To increase the pressure on the government, the ACDA organised a meeting on 28 November 2012 in the House of Lords to discuss the 2010 NIESR report and share new cases of caste discrimination. It was at that meeting that Baroness Glenys Thornton was inspired to make an amendment on caste to the Enterprise and Regulatory Reform Bill (ERR Bill) advancing in the House of Lords at that time. Her amendment would make the 'power' on caste in the Equality Act 2010 a 'duty' on government to make caste a protected characteristic in law.

The Alliance of Hindu Organisations (AHO) argued caste law was a backward step, and would institutionalise caste. They stonewalled, saying caste would not be an issue over time. They were also concerned such a law would result in individuals applying for work or places to study in the UK being forced to 'identify themselves by caste for equal opportunities monitoring purposes'.[54] This was never something the pro-equality law lobby advocated. The AHO representative trotted out similar arguments when I appeared on behalf of ACDA on BBC Two's *Newsnight* on 15 April 2013 to discuss caste discrimination in Britain. Jeremy Paxman hosted this flagship late evening news and current affairs programme. Hours before a critical parliamentary debate and the vote on caste law the next day, I was debating the need for the law on a live television broadcast with millions of viewers. It was my first time on television—only weeks after leaving the civil service—a move that had freed me to do this. The AHO's representative on the show, Arjan Vekaria, of the Hindu Forum, argued NIESR's 2010 report had not established the extent of caste discrimination in Britain. He advocated an educational approach package—*Talk for Change*—which the government had already announced on 4 March 2013.[55] Was a purely educative approach for race or gender discrimination ever successfully introduced in the UK? Of course it wasn't. The campaign's televised arguments in support of the law were very well received. Within minutes of coming of the air, I received calls from Richard Fuller MP, Baroness Thornton, and the folk singer and songwriter Peggy Seeger. On 16 April 2013, the Government Minister in the House of Commons again expressed concerns she said had been raised with them by the Hindu and Sikh communities that, if implemented, the new law could increase caste stigma. This very similar category of arguments was used in mid-twentieth-century Indian debates about the implementation of constitutional protections for 'Scheduled Castes' in India, as Jesús Cháirez-Garza has explored in this volume.[56] As expected, the government voted against the law in the House of

Commons. This vote was however, overturned in support of the law in the House of Lords.[57]

The government finally agreed an amendment (Section 97) on caste to the ERR Bill on 23 April 2013, which came into force on 25 June 2013. We were pleased, to say the least. However, the amendment also included a 'sunset clause' in the legislation called for by the anti-law lobby. This requires the law to cease to have effect after a specific date unless further legislative action is taken to extend the law. In the case of caste law, the government stated five years. This was a first in Britain. There had never been a sunset clause included in discrimination law.

### *The Lobby against the Implementation of the Law*

The lobby and factions against the legal duty on government to add caste as a protected characteristic in equality law began to mobilise their community against the law agreed by Parliament in 2013. They called meetings and set up the website mycasteishindu.org to share their point of view under the AHO banner. This peculiarly soon-vanished website issued a press release entitled, 'Hindu Community Called To Action' on 23 May 2013.[58] In it, they repeated their concerns about the consequences and practicality of such legislation and about the impact it may have on communities living within the UK.

The pro-equality legislation lobby, meanwhile, continued to press the British Government to publish a timetable for implementation of the law. Groups advised that the law could be implemented within a year, factoring in a twelve-week public consultation on the draft law. The AHO on the other hand continued stalling tactics, calling for 'a full and proper consultation period of at least two years with the affected communities.' Perhaps not by coincidence, the government's timetable published in July 2013 kicked the law into the long grass for two years, timed right up to the 2015 general election.[59]

In the face of the government's 'world-leading' procrastinations on the law, the ACDA invited Ms Navi Pillay, the UN High Commissioner for Human Rights, to attend their meeting in the House of Lords. Key representatives from the Dalit community, pro-caste law organisations, and parliamentarians including Jeremy Corbyn MP attended the meeting on 6 November 2013, hosted by Lord Eric Avebury. Pillay called for 'strong, swift implementation' of the law to wipe out the 'insidious stain' of caste-based discrimination.[60] Further research was forthcoming.

In 2014 the results of the 'Caste in Britain: Socio-legal Review' and 'Caste in Britain—Experts Seminar and Stakeholders' workshop reports by Meena Dhanda, David Mosse, Annapurna Waughray, David Keane, Roger Green, Stephen Iafrati and Jessie Kate Mundy were published. Commissioned by the government via the Equalities and Human Rights Commission (EHRC) as part of the British Government's timetable, this research also confirmed the existence of caste in Britain and peoples' understanding of caste in empirical terms. By then, the campaign *against* the pro-equality law had gathered strength. In addition to the AHO, the Anti Caste Legislation Committee (ACLC) had been formed. Additionally, an All Party Parliamentary Group for British Hindus was set up to support and promote the interests of British Hindus to Parliament, with Bob Blackman MP, one of the MPs very vocal against the law, as the Chair. Dr Prakash Shah argued, 'The caste system is one of the most prevalent and powerful markers of Indian culture and society. It is associated with Hinduism and seen as hereditary, hierarchical and oppressive, particularly for those at the bottom of the system. This image is founded on Christian theological polemic that saw Indian religion as false, the secularised version of which has strongly influenced subsequent debates, scholarship and law making on caste.' Plugging his own recent book, *Against Caste in British Law*, he said 'the UK should not be enacting legislation on such a basis.'[61]

The government's stalling tactics became more and more evident in their replies to Parliamentary Questions on the law. On 24 December 2014, *The Times* reported that David Cameron—the then Prime Minister—halted the consultation document on the law at a Cabinet meeting, owing to pressure from the Hindu lobby.[62] For over two years, the government stalled, citing an ongoing employment tribunal case as a reason for the delay. This was the *Tirkey v Chandok and another* case. The respondents argued for the case to be thrown out because they said there was no law on caste in Britain. The tribunal considered the definition of 'ethnic origin' within the meaning of the Equality Act 2010, and decided in 2014 it was wide enough to include caste. This allowed the case to go forward. The tribunal's judgement, delivered on 17 September 2015, found Ms Tirkey had been a victim of unlawful harassment on the grounds of race (not direct discrimination on grounds of race). This judgement had no binding authority as a precedent on how legislation is interpreted in the courts because it didn't make a general or definitive statement that caste is covered by ethnic origins in British law. Cynics might say that the government knew that already. The robust lobbying against the law was particularly evident in the lead-up to the 2015 general election. The *Dharma Seva Purva Puksha* published what the law campaigners saw as a divisive and offensive leaflet distributed in the Harrow East constituency.[63] It depicted an Indian woman holding a small child with the word 'caste' in capitals stamped on her and the child's foreheads.

*The Government's Consultation on Caste Law and the Outcome*

The public consultation on caste law finally began in March 2017. The pro-legislation organisations argued that the tone and bias in the consultation document was clearly framed to support non-implementation of the law. On 23 July 2018 Penny Mordaunt MP, the then Minister for Women and Equalities, announced that the government would not implement the law but instead allow case law to develop. She said, 'The consultation received over 16,000 responses, showing the importance of this issue for many people in particular communities. About fifty-three per cent of respondents wanted to rely on the existing statutory remedy and repeal the duty.' On that basis, the government announced it would repeal the legal 'duty' on caste agreed by Parliament in 2013, and publish short guidance to 'ensure that people know their rights and what sort of conduct could be unlawful under the Equality Act'.[64] This was an unprecedented move to repeal a yet-to-be-implemented aspect of equality law based on a consultation the pro-equality groups said was flawed and biased. This government decision entirely erased the Dalit voice. What is telling is that little attempt appears to have been made to look deeper into the significance of the response to question 10 of the consultation, which asked 'Which is your preferred option to tackle caste discrimination?'[65] In total, 2,879 supported the implementation of the law, with only 94 stating they supported case law; 4,722 stated they didn't know. To the pro-legislation lobby the government's decision was the equivalent of saying, 'We're not going to introduce legislation on race discrimination because white communities might object to it' or 'We're not going to have legislation on gender because men didn't like it'. Yet in effect that's exactly what the UK Government appears to have done.

The government has required that any future caste-related case law would need to demonstrate discrimination had been because of the claimant's descent (and thus their ethnic origins). Dalits, with their identity spanning different jatis and castes, have multiple and varying ethnic identities which criss-cross different languages, religions and cultures. Discrimination can occur within and between ethnic groups and religions. This is a legal minefield. The pro-caste equality law lobby argue that the British Government appears to have caved in to pressure from Hindu groups (and some Sikh groups) on the law, when it comes to votes. The need for a post-Brexit trade deal with India may also be a factor.

On a positive note, the UK's independent EHRC continues to support the case for the law. They argue that victims of caste discrimination will only have 'limited legal protection' and the government's decision 'is inconsistent with the UK's international obligations'. Furthermore, the EHRC stress the government has 'taken a step back to repeal the duty to include Caste as an aspect of race in Equality Act'.[66]

### *While We Wait for Clarity on Caste Law in Britain*

Since 2018, there have been three ET cases with a caste element that the ACDA has been involved with. Two (one in England and one in Scotland) settled out of court and will therefore never count as case law unless the government waives the non-disclosure agreements in these cases. One case did go to court in 2019—the ET in *Ms A Agarwal and Mr R Meshram v Tata Consultancy Services Ltd and Others*.[67]

This found constructive redundancy in the case of Meshram. This case was heard in London over seventeen days from 10 July to 5 August 2019, together with another complaint made by a member of Meshram's team. With no funds or financial support from the EHRC, both claimants, with no legal training, had no choice but to represent themselves to get some form of justice.

The calls for caste discrimination to be outlawed continue in Parliament. In June 2019, the Chair of Parliament's Joint Committee on Human Rights, Harriet Harman MP, wrote to Penny Mordaunt MP, and asked her to implement the caste discrimination law after ACDA raised the matter with the Committee.[68] The government's position remained unchanged. However, the caste law 'duty' has also had its impact on issues surrounding culture and heritage. At the Ambedkar Museum Public Inquiry hearing in 2019 (covered in Chapter 7), the Inspector factored into his decision-making the adverse impact on the Dalit groups if the Museum was not allowed.[69]

The health sector has also been affected, in the area of language use, for example. In 2020, the ACDA challenged a large National Health Service (NHS) hospital trust's guidance published on the chaplaincy section of their website about treating a Hindu patient.[70] NHS organisations quite rightly have a duty of care to their patients and staff to ensure both are treated equally with respect and dignity. ACDA's issue was the words 'Harijan', 'Untouchable', 'low Caste' and the lumping together of 'menstruating women and mourners' and Dalits as 'ritually unclean and therefore untouchable'. The latter was, to say the very least, an unfortunate juxtaposition. India banned the use of word 'Harijan' in the 1980s, and in March 2017, India's Supreme Court ruled the use of the word 'Harijan' in a caste discrimination case was an insult.[71] The NHS trust concerned swiftly removed the guidance from their website. They could not explain who had drafted the document or whether a consultation had taken place on the content. Without clarity in the law, there may well be more documents in Britain where the institutionalisation of caste and untouchability creeps in.

When it comes to hate speech, Twitter, YouTube and Facebook all recognise caste-related hate speech.[72] But the UK's Law Commission in its report 'Hate Crimes Laws—Final Report' (December 2021) has recommended to the government that the definition of 'race' be retained in its current form. This is a missed opportunity that casts a cloud over caste-related hate crimes and their reporting in Britain. For example, in 2020 the ACDA and the Ravidassia community campaigned for months before the Crown Prosecution Service finally agreed to prosecute a Sikh man who had produced and posted a video on TikTok that referred to Guru Ravidass in an offensive way. The man received a twelve-week suspended prison sentence with conditions attached for five years. The absence of clarity in the law meant there is no reference to caste discrimination or harassment in the charge sheet in this case, and therefore no associated publicity to deter others.

Those who oppose the law continue to argue it is an attack on Hindu and Jain communities in Britain, and the discrimination can be dealt with without the law. The law is about dealing with caste discrimination in the way other forms of discrimination are dealt with in the UK. Furthermore, introducing a law against caste discrimination in Britain would not be setting a precedent. Several national constitutions, including those of India, Nepal, Pakistan, Bangladesh and Sri Lanka, explicitly refer to caste in their non-discrimination provisions.[73] Furthermore, some governments have more recently enacted specific anti-discrimination laws, which prohibit and criminalise caste discrimination. Burkina Faso, for example, includes caste in the list of prohibited grounds of discrimination in the first article of its 1997 Constitution.[74] And Australia's Racial Discrimination Act 1975, which implements the International Racial Discrimination Convention, defines racial discrimination as any act involving a distinction, exclusion, restriction or preference based on race, colour, descent, or national or ethnic origin.

### *Conclusion*

The anti-equality law lobby argues, as it has done for decades, that caste will disappear over time. This was a common trope of the mid-twentieth-century reformist agenda in India—very much part of the debates in the Constituent Assembly, and in such areas as 1950s Civil

Service reform in India. But we know that's not the case. In Britain, the BBC documentary 'Hindus: Do We Have a Caste Problem?' (2020) confirms second- and third-generation British-born Hindus still identify with caste. The *2018 British Sikh Report* (2018) found nearly 50 per cent of respondents believed in the caste system, and 13 per cent considered caste to be important or very important. When it came to intercaste marriages, *The Times* (February 2020) carried an article on the dating website Shaadi.com and its use of algorithms based on caste. This resulted in prospective partners who had declared their caste, no matter how perfectly matched, were not being introduced to each other because of where they were in the caste hierarchy. Caste discrimination is not just confined, of course, to the UK. In the USA in 2020, the California Department of Fair Employment and Housing filed a caste discrimination lawsuit against the US multinational Cisco using sections of the Civil Rights Act. The following year, another federal law case in the USA accused BAPS, a prominent sect, of exploiting low-caste labourers from India in New Jersey.[75]

The decades-long campaign for justice and equality in respect of caste discrimination has seen a measure of success in Britain, albeit faced with robust resistance. There is a law ready and waiting for implementation supported by the EHRC. Since 2010, three successive governments have acknowledged the existence of caste discrimination in Britain, but the Conservative government has indicated it still intends to repeal the yet-to-be implemented law. The case law route offered only prolongs the pain at a high, if not prohibitive, financial cost to victims. At some point, a British government will have to listen and provide clarity on the law by listening to the voice of those affected by caste in a negative way. Bringing about anti-caste discrimination law in the UK won't annihilate caste. But it is one way of dealing with the discrimination many continue to face.

9

# AMBEDKAR IN LONDON AND THE AFRICAN-AMERICAN COMMUNITY

*Kevin Brown*

## *Introduction*

My first trip to India, and hence introduction to the Dalit liberation struggle and the work of Dr Ambedkar, occurred at the beginning of my time as a Fulbright Scholar from December 1996 to May 1997. Before spending most of that time as a visiting scholar at the Indian Law Institute in New Delhi, I was initially assigned to the National Law School of India University in Bangalore. There my office was next to the former Vice-Chancellor of Bengaluru Central University Dr S. Japhet, who was then the only law professor of Dalit descent on the faculty. Dr Japhet introduced me to the connection between the Dalit struggle against caste discrimination based on untouchability and the African-American struggle against race discrimination. On the second weekend of my stay in Bangalore, he took me to a Dalit rally in the coastal city of Mangalore, where he was one of three principal speakers. The rally was held in a soccer stadium and attended by over 80,000 people. It would have such a profound impact on me that it changed both my life and the direction of my scholarship.

As an African-American, two aspects about the assembly stood out. There was just one sign over the speaker's podium and it was the iconic slogan from the Civil Rights struggle of African-Americans in the 1960s, 'We Shall Overcome'. For African-Americans of that time, this slogan was our rallying cry, and for me it was the title to the liberation song that I had sung every Sunday at my all-Black church in Indianapolis, Indiana when I was young. The second aspect of the assembly that caught my attention was the speech of the second of the three speakers. He started his address by saying, 'I am a Dalit Panther, we take the name Panther from the Black Panther part of the African-Americans in the United States because we are one with their struggle.'[1] Even as an African-American scholar whose research had focused on the liberation struggle of my people for the past decade, it never occurred to me that our struggle could have a potential impact on the struggle of Dalits halfway around the world. This was true even though I had spent the prior eighteen months studying the history, religions and cultures of India in preparation for my Fulbright stay.

Since that Fulbright stay, I have participated in dozens of conferences, workshops and meetings with activists, politicians, community organisers and intellectuals fighting against caste discrimination based on untouchability in India, the United States, the UK and Japan. I have had the honour of speaking at celebrations of the life of Dr Ambedkar in Bangalore, New York, London, Mumbai, New Delhi, Patna, and Varanasi. I have also had the privilege of paying my respects to Dr Ambedkar at the final resting place of his ashes in Mumbai, one of the houses where he lived in Mumbai, and the printing press that he used for so many years to convey his messages. I should note that I also have a rare personal connection to Dr Ambedkar. All who have followed his remarkable work are familiar with the mass conversion of Dalits to Buddhism that Dr Ambedkar led two months before his death on 14 October 1956. By some estimates, as many as 500,000 Dalits converted on this occasion.[2] As it turns out, if you adjust for the time difference between my hometown of Indianapolis, Indiana and Nagpur, I was actually born the day the conversion took place.

The genesis for this piece was my visit in August 2019 to the Ambedkar House in London located at 10KHR. Dr Ambedkar stayed there in 1921 and 1922, and during that time he was called to the Bar at Gray's Inn. I was at the Ambedkar House to deliver a talk at the request of Santosh Dass, the President of the Federation of Ambedkarite and Buddhist Organisations UK. In many of my interactions with activists and academics concerned about the caste-based oppression of Dalits, I have encountered a persistent question: 'Why don't African-American intellectuals know more about Dr Ambedkar?' This is a fair question given the fact that African-Americans have compared our struggle against racial oppression to the Indian caste system for nearly 200 years. As I toured this remarkable structure in honour of Dr Ambedkar, I resolved to study this very important issue. However, I also knew that one of the major obstacles to African-Americans fully appreciating the accomplishments of Dr Ambedkar is the high esteem African-Americans have for the man we call Mahatma Gandhi. As it turned out, my study revealed that a part of the answer to the above question is tied to Dr Ambedkar's time in London, specifically the Round Table Conferences (RTCs) and their aftermath.

Anyone who does transnational inequality scholarship quickly learns that oppression and subordination are local. Each group that is struggling for liberation is responding to the unique circumstances and situations impacting that group's struggle for justice. And no one can deny that the history and cultures of India are vastly different from those of the United States. As a result, there can be little question that the struggle of the African-Americans against racism in the United States is qualitatively different from the Dalits' struggle against caste discrimination based on untouchability.

Despite the fact that Dalits and African-Americans encounter different forms of oppression, there are a number of very significant benefits that those committed to African-American and Dalit liberation can derive from engaging in this cross-cultural comparison and dialogue about the nature of their different forms of oppression and their different strategies, policies and programs to fight against it.[3] No doubt some of the benefits of this comparison may occur to both groups, but due to the differences in the socially constructed nature of each group's oppression, it is critical to note that the benefits will be unique to each group. Indeed, it could very well mean that a strategy, policy, or approach that will advance the interest of African-Americans in the United States may harm the interest of Dalits in India. The reverse could also be true. One place where this becomes apparent is in answering the question of 'Why don't African-Americans intellectuals know more about Dr. Ambedkar?' In answering that question, one of the vivid realisations is the different ways in which Ambedkar's 'splendid speech' at the first RTC in London and the aftermath of the second RTC in London, which led to the Poona Pact, were understood by the activists of the Dalit community and the African-American community. The Poona Pact was an agreement between Ambedkar and Gandhi to reserve a number of electoral seats for members of the Depressed Classes—see also Chapter 4. While the events above helped to propel knowledge of Ambedkar among Dalits in India, in the United States they led to heightening the respect and knowledge of Gandhi and his role in the independence movement.

By the early 1830s, anti-slavery societies in New England compared the treatment of Black people to the Hindu caste system.[4] It is logical to believe that a detailed analogy of the African-American situation in the USA to the caste system on the Indian subcontinent would eventually produce direct comparisons of the conditions of African-Americans to the conditions of Dalits and an appreciation of the extraordinary work of Dr Ambedkar. However, for the early activists against racial oppression in the USA, who set the tone for so many others to follow, it was enough to make the general point that racism in the USA functioned, like the caste system, to treat a group, white people, as superior and a different group, Black people, as inferior. Generally, they did not delve deeply into the operation of the caste system, nor do a direct comparison of the oppression of Black people to any of the five principal castes or to the Dalits, or the caste groups most negatively impacted by that system.

Typically, when activists and scholars speak of knowledge of African-Americans about Dr Ambedkar, they point to the exchange of letters in 1946 between Dr Ambedkar and the legendary African-American intellectual W. E. B. Du Bois. To this day, Du Bois is considered the greatest intellectual we as African-Americans have produced. He is also viewed as the father of Black Internationalism.[5]

The most powerful civil rights organisation in American history is the National Association for the Advancement of Colored People (NAACP). From 1910 to 1934, Du Bois had editorial control of its official publication, *The Crisis*—possibly the most influential magazine for the Black community of all time. By 1918, the NAACP's monthly magazine already claimed a circulation of over 100,000.[6]

The exchange of letters was not the first time that Du Bois indicated his knowledge about Dr. Ambedkar. The chapter in this volume by Jesús Cháirez-Garza discusses how Ambedkar was covered by the American media, particularly *The New York Times*. Surely, the important black leadership of the time would have been aware of this coverage. However, Ambedkar's attendance at the first RTC was also noted in an article written by Du Bois that was published in the 31 January 1931 edition of *The Crisis* magazine. In it, Du Bois complemented the 'splendid speech of Mr. Ambedkar.' Du Bois noted that Ambedkar criticised the British occupation of India because Dalits were in a loathsome condition when the British came 150 years earlier and nothing had changed for them—they were just as badly off in 1931 as they were before British rule. In order to comprehend how Black intellectuals and activists received this coverage of Ambedkar's speech at the first RTC and other coverage of Ambedkar in the Black press resulting from the second RTC, it is necessary to understand how discrimination in South Asia was viewed by the Black community within the historical context of its struggle against white supremacy at that time.

During the fifteen years prior to the first RTC, the Black community in the USA increasingly identified its struggle with that of Indian freedom fighters. For the Black community, the struggle of Indian freedom fighters fit nicely into an emerging twentieth-century concept of a global fight of people of colour against white supremacy, or as Nico Slate calls it 'Color Cosmopolitanism'.[7] Thus, for the Black community, it was fighting a battle against white supremacy in the form of segregation and disenfranchisement while the Indian freedom fighters were fighting a battle against white supremacy in the form of British colonialism. But these were simply local battles in a global struggle of people of colour against white supremacy. However, conditioned by the long use of the caste analogy, as renowned black historian Gerald Horne put it, 'The question of "Untouchables" was the hallmark of relations between Black America and India.'[8] Most African-American leaders at the time believed that the Indian freedom fighters were seeking a dual victory: overcoming white supremacy and eradicating the curse of untouchability. For African-Americans, the dual victory made the cause of Indian independence an incredibly honourable one. By supporting it, African-Americans were not only backing a fight against white supremacy, but also the eradication of one of the most extreme forms of oppression—caste oppression—that the world has ever known. And this was a form of oppression the Black community had identified with for nearly a century.

Reporting Ambedkar's criticism of the British during the first RTC, Du Bois played into the belief in the dual victory that many leaders of the Black community thought would result from the victory of the Congress-led independence movement. These understandings were reinforced by the coverage by the Black press of the second RTC, and more importantly, the aftermath that led to the Poona Pact. The interpretation of Gandhi's 'fast unto death' against separate electorates for 'Depressed Classes' that produced the Poona Pact was understood by Black leaders against the background of the concept of the dual victory. Reports in the Black press of Gandhi's fast saw him as engaged in a self-sacrificing hunger strike in order to further the cause of maintaining the unity of those in South Asia as they sought to prevent the British from delaying Indian independence. And Dalits would be major beneficiaries of this unity and subsequent independence. Therefore, the Black community viewed Gandhi as engaging in the fast, in part, on behalf of the Dalits.

In the aftermath of the fast unto death, by the mid-1930s Gandhi's reputation among Black leaders led several of the most prominent and influential among them to visit him in India. These were no ordinary leaders of the Black community. They were individuals who would mould the thinking of those Black leaders at the forefront of the Civil Rights Movement a generation later. Thus the coverage of Ambedkar at the first and second RTCs and the aftermath that led to the Poona Pact, and its particular focus on Gandhi, may provide a partial explanation for why Ambedkar is still not well known among African-American scholars today.

Part I of this essay will discuss how African-Americans analogised their struggle against white supremacy in the USA to discrimination on the Indian subcontinent. As the twentieth century unfolded, the Black community had two different lines of thought about comparing its struggle against oppression based on white supremacy in the US to oppression on the Indian subcontinent. One line of reasoning derived from the caste analogy, where the condition of African-Americans was compared to the caste system. The other line of thought saw the struggle of African-Americans in the USA as part of a global struggle against white supremacy. Part II will discuss how the Black community viewed the Indian freedom fighters, led, in their view, by Gandhi, before the RTC. By the time of the RTC, the Black community viewed the Indian freedom fighters as seeking a dual victory. Having set the context of the Black community before the RTC discussions, Part III will discuss how the article that Du Bois wrote about Ambedkar's speech at the first RTC and the aftermath of the second RTC fit within the way that the African-American community increasingly viewed issues of oppression on the Indian subcontinent. With the understanding of how the Black community viewed the struggle for Indian independence before the first RTC in place, Part IV will discuss how the 1931 speech by Dr Ambedkar fitted into that understanding. It will go on to discuss how issues surrounding the aftermath of the second RTC, including the agreement for the Poona Pact, were thought about by the Black press.

### *I. African-Americans and Dalits in the Indian Subcontinent: A Comparative Struggle*

Before we can comprehend the Black press's coverage of Dr Ambedkar's participation in the first RTC and the aftermath of the second RTC, it is necessary to understand how the Black community saw the relationship between its struggle against white supremacy in the USA and discrimination on the Indian subcontinent. That understanding centred on two different lines of reasoning. One was based on the caste analogy and the second on the concept of an alliance of people of colour against white supremacy.

### A. Employing of the Caste Analogy in the Struggles of African-Americans against White Supremacy

Even though South Asians did not arrive in the USA in significant numbers until the 1850s, knowledge of the caste system preceded them.[9] By the early 1830s, anti-slavery societies in New England tied the issue of southern slavery to the denial of equal civil liberties of Black people in the North.[10] To help demonstrate that both slavery and discrimination against free Black people were contrary to core principles of American society, some abolitionist proponents of Black equality, including Frederick Douglass, Thomas Dalton, William Lloyd Garrison, Harriet Beecher Stowe and Charles Sumner, compared the treatment of Black people to the caste system in South Asia.[11]

Perhaps the most thorough and complete discussion of the caste analogy to the condition of Black people before the US Civil War occurred as part of the legal arguments in the first major school segregation case in American history. The opinion was delivered in 1849 by the Supreme Judicial Court of Massachusetts, the oldest continuously functioning appellate court in the Americas and one of the most influential courts of the time of the *Roberts* decision. In *Roberts v Boston*,[12] Sarah Roberts sought to attend the nearest school to her home, which at the time excluded Black people. Sarah was represented by the Black attorney Robert Morris and Charles Sumner, who would go on to become one of the most influential leaders of the Radical Republicans in the Senate during the US Civil War and Reconstruction.[13] In his arguments before the Court, Sumner fully developed the analogy of the treatment of Black people to the caste system in India. Nevertheless, the Massachusetts Court ruled against Sarah.[14]

As Swedish social scientist Gunnar Mrydal pointed out in his epic book about American race relations entitled *The American Dilemma*, the Emancipation Proclamation stopped the common practice in the USA of referring to Black people as slaves.[15] Instead, the terms 'freedmen' and 'ex-slaves' came into popular use. In addition,

Americans needed a term to describe the still inferior status of Black people.[16] As a result, the use of the term 'caste' increased significantly in the 1860s.[17] Evidence of this process comes from the Congressional debates over the passage of the Civil Rights Act of 1866, Congress's first anti-discrimination measure, and adoption of the Fourteenth Amendment. The Fourteenth Amendment is the most important Amendment to the US Constitution and includes the equal protection clause, which is the Constitutional requirement for equal treatment by government.[18]

The caste analogy would remain central to the arguments regarding the treatment of Black people until the end of the nineteenth century. Perhaps the best example of the legal importance of the caste analogy after Reconstruction is in the arguments advanced by the plaintiff, Homer Plessy, in the Supreme Court's 1896 decision in *Plessy v Ferguson*.[19] This decision was agreed to by eight of the nine justices and set the USA on its path of *de jure* segregation, also known as the 'separate but equal' era, which lasted in the USA until the 1950s. The brief in the case filed on behalf of Plessy by James Walker and Albion Tourgee argued that slavery was a caste system because it tended 'to reduce the colored people of the country to the condition of a subject race' and imposed upon them the inequality of rights. Segregation has the same effect. The effect of the law that distinguishes citizens based on race is to legalise caste; as such, it is inconsistent with the concept of one equal citizenship for all of the United States and each state.[20] The US Supreme Court, however, upheld the segregation statute presented to it in *Plessy*. Virtually all American lawyers, law students and most American people who have a vague understanding of equality law in the USA know that Justice Harlan wrote a separate dissenting opinion in *Plessy*. In what may very well be the most renowned passage from any opinion ever written by a justice of the US Supreme Court, Harlan wrote:

> [I]n view of the constitution, in the eye of the law, there is in this country no superior, dominant, ruling class of citizens. *There is no caste here*. Our constitution is color-blind, and neither knows nor tolerates classes among citizens. In respect of civil rights, all citizens are equal before the law [emphasis added].[21]

The point of the discussion in this section is to demonstrate how significant the caste analogy was in conceptualizing the treatment of African-Americans throughout the nineteenth century. It was advanced during the nineteenth century at the most consequential political and legal disputes that occurred, segregation of public schools, the most comprehensive Civil Rights legislation to date, the passage of the Fourteenth Amendment that contains the equal protection clause, and the Supreme Court opinion that constitutionalised *de jure* segregation. It is logical to believe that a detailed analogy of the African-American struggle against white supremacy in the USA to the struggle of Dalits against caste discrimination based on untouchability would eventually produce a direct comparison of the condition of African-Americans to the conditions of Dalits. However, as the twentieth century dawned, a new line of thinking about the connection of the African-American struggle in the US to oppression on the Indian subcontinent emerged.

### B. The Rise of Color Cosmopolitanism and the Interaction of African-American Leaders with Indian Freedom Fighters

The caste analogy would continue to be important in the advocacy of equality for African-Americans throughout the twentieth century. Between 1903 and 1905, Du Bois emerged as the second most prominent living Black person behind Booker T. Washington.[22] Du Bois frequently used the caste analogy. For example, prior to the initial meeting of the Niagara Movement in July 1905, Du Bois proposed eight objectives, which were eventually incorporated as the listed objectives in the Constitution of the Niagara Movement. The fourth objective said that the Niagara Movement stands for the 'abolition of all *caste* distinctions based simply on race or color'.[23]

Six years later, the mission of the Niagara Movement was taken up by a new organization, the NAACP. The original charter for the NAACP expressed its mission as follows:

> To promote equality of rights and to *eradicate caste* or race prejudice among the citizens of the United States; to advance the interest of colored citizens; to secure for them impartial suffrage; and to increase their opportunities for securing

> justice in the courts, education for the children, employment according to their ability and complete equality before law [emphasis added].[24]

Even today, many scholars, activists and members of the Black community still refer to the treatment of Black people in the USA as a manifestation of caste. However, as the nineteenth century was coming to a close, African-Americans began to focus more on international affairs in light of the Berlin Conference in 1884–5, which sparked the Scramble for Africa by European powers, and the Spanish American War of 1898. As late as 1870, only ten per cent of the African land mass was colonised, but by 1900 over ninety per cent of Africa was under European control.[25] The European countries based their view of international law on the notion that people of colour could not legally oppose their will because they were 'backward races'.[26] Only the Europeans constituted the civilised world. Thus, as the 'superior race', they had the right to lay claim to the land, the labour and the wealth of these backward races because they were civilising the barbarians.[27] The brief war the USA fought with Spain ended with a peace treaty that compelled Spain to relinquish claims on Cuba, and to cede sovereignty over Guam, Puerto Rico and the Philippines to the United States. Since the USA now held colonies populated by people of colour, 'the spread of US imperialism to Cuba, Puerto Rico, and the Philippines did the most to crystallize the thinking of Black commentators about their relationship to subject peoples elsewhere'.[28] In addition, unrelated to the conflict with Spain, but in the same year as the war, the United States also took formal control of Hawaii.

The greater global consciousness of African-Americans helped to generate a new form of internationalism based on the concept of an alliance of people of colour against white supremacy, sometimes referred to as Color Cosmopolitanism.[29] As pointed out by Robin Kelley, this new perspective on the African-American struggle was the result of 'a particular historical convergence—the expansion of US and European empires, settler colonialism, an increasingly industrialized racial capitalism, and their attendant processes: expropriation, proletarianization, massive migration, urbanization, rapid technological development, and war'.[30] As with many corresponding movements throughout the world, during this time African-Americans were trying to understand their place in an interconnected, rapidly industrialising capitalist world that was increasingly turning towards war to resolve international disputes. In this new form of Black internationalism, the African-American struggle against segregation and disenfranchisement in the USA was viewed as a local aspect of a global struggle of people of colour against white supremacy. It is the emergence of this new Black internationalism that also helps to explain why more detailed comparisons of the experiences of Black people resisting racial oppression with the experiences of Dalits resisting caste oppression based on untouchability did not occur during the time Ambekdar was fighting for the extinction of untouchability.

The catalyst for the emergence of this new perspective of the twentieth century within the Black community in the USA was the triumph of Japan over Russia in the Russo-Japanese War of 1904–1905. While the crucial battle was a naval one, at the time Russia had the largest standing army in the world.[31] As the new form of Black internationalism was beginning to take shape, Japan's triumph encouraged Black people in the USA to believe that victory by people of colour in a global struggle against white supremacy was possible, if not inevitable. Even though Black leaders were divided in their approaches to the current problems facing the Black community, they were united in their estimate of the significance of Japan's rise to power. The fact that a nation of people of colour defeated a mighty European power instilled a sense of pride in African-Americans. In a rare display of Black unity at the time, the Black press and a number of African-American leaders, including Du Bois, Booker T. Washington, Mary Church Terrell and Marcus Garvey, to name but a few, cheered the victory as if Black people in the USA were the ones responsible. In the eyes of the Black community, almost overnight, the Japanese were turned from an improvident, ignorant and superstitious people into a courageous, fearless nation.[32] Before the war, Japan was criticised as heathen. Now, its hostility towards Christian missionaries could be explained as a rejection of 'all the ludicrous follies of the white man'.[33] Furthermore, Black leaders and the press began increasingly to see Japan not in the way that mainstream American society saw her, but from a racialised lens of the leading nation among people of colour.[34]

A great example of the enthusiasm in the Black community regarding the Japanese victory and what it meant for the future for people of colour was Du Bois's famous passage about the colour line. Du Bois enthusiastically wrote that since Charles Martel beat back the Saracens at Tours in 732, the white races have had the hegemony of civilization to such a great extent that 'white' and 'civilized' have become synonymous in everyday speech to the point where people have forgotten where civilisation started. Du Bois goes on to write:

> [F]or the first time in a thousand years a great white nation has measured arms with a colored nation and has been found wanting. The Russo-Japanese war has marked an epoch. The magic of the word 'white' is already broken and the Color Line in civilization has been crossed in modern times as it was in the great past. The awakening of the yellow races is certain. That the awakening of the brown and black races will follow in time, no unprejudiced student of history can doubt. Shall the awakening of these sleepy millions be in accordance with, and aided by, the great ideals of white civilization or in spite of them and against them? This is the problem of the Color Line.[35]

### *II. African-Americans and Indian Freedom Fighters before the Round Table Conferences*

In the twenty-five years following the Japanese victory over Russia, Black commentators in the USA increasingly followed and embraced the efforts of Indian freedom fighters advocating independence from British colonial rule. The first section of this part will discuss the growing awareness of the Black community of the struggle for independence on the Indian subcontinent. African-Americans also observed that, like themselves, those from South Asia were victims of racially discriminatory treatment in the USA. The second section will discuss some prominent aspects of this discrimination. The Black community, via the publicity received from colonial India, believed that Indian freedom fighters were seeking a dual victory.

Supporting these anti-colonialists would accomplish the goals of both the black struggle against white supremacy, and oppression on the Indian subcontinent. This third section will discuss the view of the Black community about the Indian freedom fighters as the RTCs took place.

In the time after the Japanese victory over Russia, African-American leaders increasingly became aware of the struggles against British colonialism in India. Seeking American support for the Indian independence movement, several Indian intellectuals and freedom fighters came to the USA. Of these, Lajpat Rai, known as the 'Lion of the Punjab',[36] deserves special attention. Rai, who was a lawyer and President of the Bar Association of India, founded the India Home Rule League of America to advocate for self-rule for India.[37] Though Taraknath Das, Syed Hossain, Kumar Gohsal and Haridas T. Muzumdar would follow,[38] Rai was the first major Indian freedom fighter to establish close ties with African-American leaders.[39] Rai visited the USA in 1905 and again from December 1914 to December 1919.[40] Touring the country, Rai made a point of studying the American racial situation. He became personally acquainted with the most significant leaders of the African-American struggle, including Booker T. Washington, John Hope (the first African-descended president of Morehouse College and later Atlanta University), and Mary Ovington.[41] Rai also developed a close friendship with Du Bois, primarily based on the notion of analogising Indian independence and black equality. Up to the point of meeting Rai, Du Bois had not devoted much attention to the anti-colonial struggles on the Indian subcontinent.[42] However, Du Bois would go on to dedicate to Rai his 1928 novel *Dark Princess*, which is an allegorical story about a Hindu princess who weds an African-American man to unite black and brown people.[43]

As the number of South Asians in the USA increased, so did their independence activities against British rule. Their labours culminated in the USA with the efforts of members of the Ghadar Party to spark a rebellion against British rule in India during the First World War. These activities eventually led American officials to put the leaders of the Ghadar Party in California on trial from November 1917 to April 1918 for violation of America's neutrality during the early part of the war. The Ghadar Party Conspiracy trials were the most expensive trials in US history to that point, and introduced many Americans to the Indian independence movement. The Ghadar Party Conspiracy also became a subject of debate in the Black community. For example, *The Crisis* commented that the NAACP found the criminal convictions of Party members were unjust because the Indians were struggling to free their country from a foreign power. A 1921 edition of the pro-communist African-American magazine *The Crusader*[44] wrote, 'it is essential to the early success of our cause that the Negro seek cooperation with the Indian nationalists ... and all other peoples participating in the common struggle for liberty and especially with those peoples whose struggle is against the great enslaver of the darker races—England'.[45]

One potential obstacle to an alliance between the African-American community and the high castes who dominated the Indian freedom fighters was the Aryan Origin Theory. This theory was the subject of much litigation in the US federal courts in the first quarter of the twentieth century. Not long after the ratification of the US Constitution, Congress passed its first restrictive citizenship measure—the Naturalization Act of 1790.[46] This measure limited naturalised citizenship to 'free white persons'. From 1909 to 1923, there were a series of naturalisation cases brought by South Asians who asserted that they were white and, accordingly, eligible for naturalised citizenship. In doing so, they rested their assertion that they were Caucasian on the Aryan Origin Theory. According to Taunya Banks, a superficial review of these cases indicates that the courts were confused about how to handle the racial status of South Asians, initially granting their petitions.[47] The US Supreme Court, however, delivered the final legal word on the race of South Asians in its unanimous 1923 decision *US v Thind*.[48] The Court noted that in attempting to determine the meaning of the original framers of the 1790 statute for the words 'white persons', that meaning must be taken from common ordinary speech and not scientific origin. Thus, '[i]t may be true that the blond Scandinavian and the brown Hindu have a common ancestor in the dim reaches of antiquity, but the average man knows perfectly well that there are unmistakable and profound differences between them to-day'.[49]

Despite some awareness of the Aryan Origin Theory, most Americans did not consider people from the Indian subcontinent to be white. Thus, the Black community was able to observe that South Asians were also victims of race discrimination in the US.[50] For example, the Asiatic Exclusion League, which was formed in 1905 through a merger of the Japanese and Korean Exclusion Leagues, raised an alarm about the huge numbers of 'Hindus' coming into the country. In addition, in 1910 a widely published report by the chief investigator of the Immigration Commission on the Pacific Coast found that South Asians were 'universally regarded as the least desirable race of immigrants thus far admitted to the United States'.[51] Although we do not know whether he commented on these events and this legislation, they coincided with Ambedkar's period of study in the USA. In 1917, Congress passed a new immigration act that was primarily directed at excluding South Asians from the country. By this time, the Chinese Exclusion Acts had prevented further immigration from China, and the 1907 Gentlemen's Agreement with Japan already in place significantly reduced immigration from that country. The 1917 bill did not specifically mention Indians by race, but rather banned anyone born within a geographical area called the 'Asiatic Barred Zone' from immigrating to the USA. The Barred Zone covered an area of land that stretched from the Arabian Peninsula and Afghanistan across most of China, British India, French Indochina, portions of Central Asia and the Polynesian Islands. Given that immigrants from China and Japan were already victims of immigration reforms, in practice, the only current stream of immigrants from Asia that the Act prevented from coming to the USA were from South Asia. To clarify the rationale behind the 1917 Immigration Act, the Governor of California at the time, William Stephens, stated that 'the Hindu ... is the most undesirable immigrant in the state. His lack of personal cleanliness, his low morals and his blind adherence to theories and teachings [so] entirely repugnant to American principles makes him unfit for association with American people.'[52]

The leadership of the Indian independence movement in the interwar years, although mainly high caste, fit within the growing connection between that movement and the African-American fight against segregation and disenfranchisement. It is also important to note that, regardless of practice, Rai, the Sikhs and the Ghadar Party all followed religious doctrines that rejected untouchability. Most African-American leaders at the time believed that the Indian freedom fighters were seeking a dual victory, namely overcoming white supremacy and eradicating the curse of untouchability. For African-Americans, the dual victory made the cause of Indian independence an easy one to embrace.

The first African-American Christian denomination, the African Methodist Episcopal (AME) Church published the influential *AME Church Review*. Reverdy Ransom, a highly regarded socialist bishop and a member of the Niagara Movement, was the editor of the *Review*. He published an editorial in 1921 that reflected the awe of Gandhi that many in the Black community were beginning to embrace: 'From the ranks of the myriad millions of India has recently sprung a new messiah and saint. Gandhi, the new "Light of Asia", would deliver his countrymen from the rule of British imperialism, not by violent resistance, but through the peaceful method of non cooperation.'[53]

Marcus Garvey's organization the United Negro Improvement Association, which was the largest ever mass movement organisation of the African-American Community, published a magazine titled *Negro World*. *Negro World* printed a brief statement by Gandhi on the front page of its 31 May 1924 edition. The first line of Gandhi's statement was 'Removal of the curse of untouchability among Hindus'. As if to recognise that the feelings of inadequacy that Dalits could have about untouchability may also exist among Black people due to slavery, in July 1929, Gandhi wrote 'Message to the American Negro' that was published in *The Crisis* magazine. In the text, he urged the 12-million-strong community not to be ashamed of being the grandchildren of slaves, and that there was no dishonour in being slaves—the dishonour was in being slave owners.[54] The Black press also continued to point out how Gandhi abhorred the treatment of the Untouchables.[55] While the Black press did not cover Ambedkar leading the temple entry agitation at the Kala Ram Temple at Nashik, it did cover the Gandhi-led 240-mile Salt March to the Arabian Sea in the spring of 1930.[56] It is likely that Gandhi's powerful international publicity strategies enhanced his message by comparison to Ambedkar's. There were dissenting voices among Black commentators, especially from George Schuyler. However, as the 1930s progressed, it was 'not uncommon for African-American journals and newspapers to present Gandhi to their readers as one of the foremost sages and seers of human history, comparing Gandhi to the Buddha, Mohammed, and Jesus Christ and lauding the moral leadership in world affairs which Asia was taking.'[57]

### *III. Coverage by Du Bois of Ambedkar's Speech at the First Round Table Conference*

One of the few times that I have found Dr Ambedkar referred to by name in the Black press may very well have been the first time Du Bois wrote about him. This was an article that Du Bois wrote in the 31 January 1931 edition of *The Crisis* magazine about Ambedkar's participation in the first RTC, which was held from November 1930 to January 1931:

> There is the splendor of India in London. Prince and Untouchable, Muslim and Hindu, all standing shoulder to shoulder, when England counted upon disunion and mutual jealousies and hatreds to perpetuate her tyranny in India. *That was a splendid speech of Mr. Ambedkar.* He said when the British came to India 150 years ago, 'We were in a loathsome condition. We could not draw water at the village wells; we could not enter a temple; we could not serve on the police force; we could not serve in the army.' And what happened, he said. Nothing. We are just as badly off now as we were before the English came. It was precisely what the English planned. From no country which they dominate do they propose to remove the internal friction which helps to keep it in subjection. Magnificent India, to reveal to the world the inner rottenness of European imperialism. Such a country not only deserves to be free, it will be free [emphasis added].[58]

In this article in *The Crisis*, Du Bois echoed several long-held sentiments of many in the Black community of the time. First, Du Bois made the point that Indian independence is furthered by uniting the different Indian factions who demand independence from British rule. One of the core cultural values of the African-American community is that unity among us is strength. As a result, our community tends to believe that a principal method that whites use to maintain the subordination of Black people in the USA is through pitting them against each other in an effort to weaken our collective struggle. For the African-American community, this is a belief that goes all the way back to the transatlantic slave trade. After all, the overwhelming majority of Black people who were enslaved were sold to Europeans by other Black people on the continent. It was the lack of Black unity that was the source of how African-Americans found their way to America.

By pointing to the British 'divide and conquer' strategy, we can see Du Bois drawing an analogy, with the behaviour of white supremacy that Black people encounter in the USA being replicated by white supremacy in its desires to combat the efforts of Indian freedom fighters. Secondly, the British were no friends of the Dalits—Ambedkar had stated that their condition did not improve under British domination. Thus, the British imperialist support for the Dalit cause was not motivated by an interest in assisting Dalits. Rather it was motivated by the British desire to divide the Indian people into a number of factions in order to weaken the Indian independence movement and maintain British dominance over South Asia. Distrusting the British was also a deeply held belief in the Black community. To use the words of Malcolm X, 'We [Black people] didn't land on Plymouth Rock, Plymouth Rock landed on us.'[59] And it was the British colonists who dropped the Rock on our collective heads. Third, Du Bois implies that the elimination of caste discrimination based on untouchability would have to wait until Indian independence. Since the British were concerned with maintaining control, not eradicating discrimination based on untouchability, British control of India would hinder the ability of Indian freedom fighters to do so.

### *IV. Understanding the Coverage of Ambedkar in the Aftermath of the Second Round Table Conference*

Understanding Du Bois's report in *The Crisis* against this background of the interaction between the African-American community and the

Indian freedom fighters that had existed for fifteen years prior to the first RTC helps us to put in perspective how the Black community processed Ambedkar's 'splendid speech' at the event. But reports of Ambedkar in London in the Black press do not end there. While the Congress Party and Gandhi had refused to participate in the first RTC, they did participate in the second RTC that occurred from September to December 1931. Ambedkar also attended and once again presented himself as the main spokesperson representing the Dalits. During these deliberations, Gandhi claimed that the Congress Party alone represented the political interest of all in India. He rejected the notion that Ambedkar represented the Dalits, and asserted that the Dalits were Hindus, and thus should not be treated as a separate 'minority'.

Two weeks after the second RTC ended in failure, *The New York Age*, 'distinguished black newspaper of opinion' under the leadership of Fred Moore, a close associate of Booker T. Washington until the latter's death, published a letter to the editor by Dr Madha Singh on 26 December 1931. Singh's letter discussed Ambedkar's claim to represent the Dalits and his opposition to Gandhi. The author noted the very statements of Ambedkar that Du Bois pointed out in his 31 January 1931 *Crisis* article. He went on to state that Ambedkar's presence at the first RTC 'was not to represent the "Untouchables", but the British Government, at whose request he went there, and he certainly was loyal to them [and] in a well-planned scheme the Government tried to usurp the power of Gandhi as the representative of the "Untouchables."'[60] Singh noted that Gandhi and the Congress Party were 'working earnestly to abolish not only untouchability, but the idea of the caste system in India, which the Government has been encouraging since the British became rulers of the land'. On 9 July 1932, the *New York Age* published an instalment from its special correspondent in India that covered the Hindu–Muslim riots in Bombay.[61] This article also asserted that Ambedkar was an agent of British imperialism pursuing his own selfish ends by misleading his own ignorant followers, who become ready tools in his hand.

With this background of the coverage of Ambedkar and Gandhi at the RTC came the reports in the Black press of the Poona Pact. In order to prevent the Communal Award (which would have granted separate electorates to 'Depressed Classes' on 18 September 1932, Gandhi announced he was going on a hunger strike to the death. In Dalit circles, however, this hunger strike was understood as a statement by Gandhi that 'I will give my life if Untouchables are granted their rights.'[62] As the days elapsed, all of India was increasingly concerned about Gandhi's health. At the beginning of Gandhi's fast, Ambedkar remained firm that he was not willing to curtail the rights of the Dalits in any manner. However, Gandhi's strike put a great deal of pressure on Ambedkar and other Dalit leaders to come to an agreement that would preserve Gandhi's life. Open threats were made to Ambedkar with a warning about genocidal consequences for Untouchables should Gandhi die.[63] An entire gamut of public perception was created around the morality of the fast, and as the pressure mounted on Ambedkar, a meeting was arranged between him and Gandhi. The result of the meeting was the Poona Pact announced on 24 September 1932.

A sharp contrast existed, however, between the views of many Dalit activists regarding Gandhi's fast that forced Ambedkar into the Poona Pact and how the Black press of the time covered the fast. For example, the *Washington Tribune* stated 'The dramatic "Fast Unto Death" undertaken by Gandhi on behalf of India's "forgotten men" the 60,000,000 Untouchables came to an end Monday evening with the British and Indian Governments approved a settlement of the Hindu problem.'[64] In an article in the November 1932 issue of *The Crisis*, Du Bois stated that the purpose of Gandhi's fast was to force the British government to reach an agreement with all Hindus of all castes that would lead to the termination of control by the British and would not strengthen the caste barriers in India.[65]

Given the experiences of the Black community with political rights, it may not have appreciated the difference between separate electorates and legislative reservations for the Dalits. This lack of appreciation is understandable. When Prime Minister Ramsey MacDonald made his proposal that included communal awards, Black people made up 9.7 per cent of the American population,[66] but had virtually no political representation in local, state or federal elected bodies. Over seventy-five per cent of them still lived in the south of the country,[67] where white legislators had disenfranchised the overwhelming majority of potential black voters since the beginning of the twentieth century. There were no black state-wide elected officials in the USA, including governors, lieutenant governors, secretaries of state and treasurers. There were no Black people serving in the upper house of Congress. And, after having no Black person in the lower house of Congress from 1901 to 1929, at the time of the Poona Pact there was only one Black out of the 435 members of the US House of Representatives. Thus, given the political reality of African-Americans at the time, the significance of the debate between the political advantages of separate electorates as opposed to legislative reservations was not readily apparent.

### *Conclusion*

The question of why African-American intellectuals are not more familiar with the extraordinary work of Dr Ambedkar is a legitimate one. African-Americans have analogised their struggles against white supremacy in the USA to the caste system of South Asia for nearly 200 years. No one has done more to liberate Dalits and the Dalit mind from the oppressive mentality presented to it by the caste discrimination based on untouchability than Ambedkar. As Dalit activist Anand Teltumbde put it, for the Dalit masses, Ambedkar is everything together: a first-rate scholar, a Moses who led his people out of bondage, a Bodhisattva in the Buddhist pantheon—he is like a God.[68] One important Dalit slogan epitomises Ambedkar's significance: 'We Are, Because He Was.'[69] Given these realities, one would think that African-American intellectuals would be familiar with Ambedkar.

Any scholar comparing liberation struggles of different groups in different countries quickly realises that liberation fights are local. While there are probably some points of similarity, each given group is struggling against the conditions it faces at a given place during a given time. Thus, each subordinated group struggling for liberation is responding to the unique circumstances and situations impacting that group's struggle for justice. The struggles that African-Americans have in the USA against white supremacy are qualitatively different from the struggles of Dalits against caste discrimination based on untouchability. Thus, it is possible that a strategy, policy, or approach that advanced the interests of African-Americans in the USA may have harmed the interests of Dalits in India and vice versa. This is apparent when answering the question: 'Why don't African-Americans intellectuals know more about Dr. Ambedkar?'

In answering that question, one of the vivid realizations is the different ways in which Ambedkar's 'splendid speech' at the First RTC in London and the aftermath of the Second RTC in London, which led to the Poona Pact, were understood by the activists of the Dalit community and the African-American community, half a world away. For the Black community, these events were understood within the context of how the Black community had come to analogise its struggle against racial oppression in the USA to various forms of subordination on the Indian subcontinent. In that regard, African-Americans had developed two different lines of reason for comparing their struggle to oppression on the Indian subcontinent. Under one line of thinking, the oppression of Black people was analogised to caste oppression. Under the other, Indian freedom fighters were viewed as fighting white supremacy in the form of British colonialism, while African-Americans were fighting white supremacy in the form of segregation and disenfranchisement. However, due to the interaction of the Black community with Indian freedom fighters in the fifteen years before the first RTC, the Black community believed that the Gandhi-led Congress were seeking a dual victory—firstly to obtain independence from the British, and secondly to eradicate the curse of untouchability. This dual victory made it easy for the Black community to support the Gandhian Congress because this advanced both analogies of the struggles of Black people in the USA to oppression on the Indian subcontinent. Thus, while the events above helped to propel knowledge of Ambedkar among Dalits in India, in the USA, they led to heightening the respect and knowledge of Gandhi and his role in the Indian independence movement.

# CONCLUSION

*William Gould*

Bhimrao Ramji Ambedkar is celebrated or memorialised today in multiple ways in India and elsewhere, and arguably, as a single historical figure, his wider political significance is unmatched. Throughout India today, there are probably more statues, roads and parks being created or named after him than any other personality in South Asia. Because of this laden iconography and the political changes in the development of the Dalit movement worldwide, followers and scholars alike sometimes find it difficult to separate the man from the wider processes that came in the wake of his life; to distinguish Ambedkar from Ambedkarism. In some cases, this has led to a kind of deification that Ambedkar himself would probably have strongly eschewed and discouraged. What is also remarkable (as some of the chapters in this volume suggest) is that Ambedkar was often misunderstood or deliberately marginalised in his own times, mainly (but not only) as a result of the structural forms of discrimination which underpinned his core message. This book has tried to present Ambedkar in a period of his life when these later challenges and symbolic representations had not begun to fully form, and to examine some of the foundational experiences of his years as a student, and their wider historical and global effects. It is also, at another level, a book that examines how the emotional effects of Ambedkar continue to exist in particular places within London and the UK.

The period of Ambedkar's study in the USA and in London, covering broadly the First World War and its aftermath, have been covered by most accounts of Ambedkar's life as a brief prelude to the important and central parts of his political and intellectual career from the early 1930s. During the Public Inquiry to re-establish Ambedkar House as a museum / memorial, which inspired the writing of this book, the legal team representing Camden Council picked up on this point. Their argument was that a London-based memorial to Ambedkar could not be justified at 10 King Henry's Road, since this was in any case a relatively insignificant phase of his life, before his politics had formed and before his most important intellectual contributions. The central motifs of his life are considered to include the following episodes: the Round Table Conferences (RTCs) in the early 1930s and his confrontation with Gandhi; the publication of his radical intervention, *The Annihilation of Caste*; and his pivotal role in the both the development of Dalit parties in the 1940s and the legal and constitutional foundations of the Indian republic.

But what happened in the early 1920s is crucial to all of these areas in two respects, as the chapters in Part 1 of this volume suggest: firstly, the early 1920s in London position Ambedkar's intellectual contributions in the longer term. Ambedkar's powerful principles and strategies for Dalit representation and keen sociological approaches to Indian inequality that characterise his mature phase can only be fully explained in relation to his longer-term intellectual contributions. In his early writings this included the politics and governance of space, the nature of the colonial economy, the idea of the rule of law, and the wider context of political power in interwar India. All of these themes were central to his research and training while in London. Secondly, as the chapters by Cháirez-Garza and Jaffrelot in this volume argue, Ambedkar's experiences within, and connections to, London, especially around the early mobilisation of 'Depressed Classes' via education and reform, were significant as a strategic background to his later more radical ideas about caste. Indeed, the very fact of his study in London helped him to better set out the importance of space and transnationalism to the problems of social segregation and the inherent subjection of the pariah.

This book has explored the role of education in Ambedkar's life in some detail. Its importance was not just because of London itself—the key site for his most intense period of self-development via LSE and Gray's Inn, but also because education became a key index for the wider Dalit movement. Establishing his own qualifications through a second doctoral project on India's currency, and training as a barrister were, at one level, part of a larger strategic move whose consequences are obvious when we examine his early career. Ambedkar's financial sponsors rightly viewed his further education as a means to gaining a more secure foothold in India's political mainstream—to be taken seriously as an internationally qualified figure capable of challenging both the colonial government and high-status Indian politicians. Ambedkar became the best-qualified Dalit leader in any representative role in the interwar period, for example, when he gained a seat on the Bombay Legislative Council from 1927. As Chapter 2 by Donnelly and Payne and Chapter 3 by Gasztowicz in this volume show, the instrumental value of his postgraduate work in London also lay in the range of networks and interconnections he was able to make with other intellectuals and political influencers.

There were other, less tangible reasons why education was so pivotal to Ambedkar's later career and also in the subsequent Ambedkarite movements worldwide. John Dewey, who met Ambedkar at Columbia and whose books were later purchased and annotated by him, was perhaps the most important influence on his formulation of the pivotal role of education and social reform. As Chapters 1 and 5 by Gould and Jaffrelot explore, education therefore became of central importance to Ambedkar's early experiments in Dalit institution building, social mobilisation and as a basis for thinking about social transformation. These principles continued into the 1950s and beyond with the LSE scholarships sponsored towards the end of his life. Education was also persistent as a project in the Ambedkarite movement in the UK and beyond, as explored in Chapter 6 by Santosh Dass and Arun Kumar, for example in the activities of the Buddha Vihara in London.

Just as Ambedkar's ideas have had their own long-term legacies in Indian politics, his influence is lasting and arguably of growing importance in London and other parts of the UK too. What his experiences in London show both in the early 1920s and the early 1930s, when he returned to represent the 'Depressed Classes' at the RTCs, is his keen spatial contextualisation of the power of caste discrimination. For contemporary Ambedkarite activists, this principle is at the root of their movements when it comes to their drive to have caste discrimination acknowledged in anti-discrimination legislation in the UK. In juxtaposing Chapter 8 by Dass in this volume with Chapter 4 by Cháirez-Garza, we also come to a unique realisation about how important and relevant Ambedkar's own London history is to this contemporary struggle. There are some important parallels between the early 1930s battles by Ambedkar and those fought by Ambedkarites in contemporary Britain. For both Ambedkar in 1931 and organisations like FABO UK in the 2000s, the struggle is about overcoming quite entrenched and systemic obstructions that are generated by a social elitism, whose beneficiaries are unable to recognise the structural advantages they have historically enjoyed. London provided a different kind of strategic space for these struggles in the acknowledgement of caste discrimination in both historical moments.

In this sense, our study of Ambedkar in London is one lens through which to explore the internationalisation of his politics. Intellectuals and leaders of Ambedkar's stature inevitably produced effects that travelled both directly in movements and people, and indirectly in shared principles, around the globe. The international networking that clearly started for Ambedkar at least from his time in London in the early 1920s was, however, in many ways deliberate and instrumental. There is no doubt that he took opportunities to make headway in promoting the cause of Dalits outside India, and like other Indian publicists, sought to correspond with a range of sympathetic and powerful figures worldwide, some of whom may have held quite contrasting political positions. In a more theoretical or cerebral register, his ideas always seemed to acknowledge that systems of social apartheid, and other structural forms of inequality, were common to a range of global contexts. In theory too, they could be challenged with a similar logic. Gould, Cháirez-Garza and Brown in this volume all explore the possibilities, but also the limitations in the international movement of Ambedkar's ideas. For

Cháirez-Garza, Ambedkar's use of London contacts could be both advantageous and politically limiting or subordinating. As Brown shows, for Black internationalists in the interwar period, the dangers of associating with a particular logic of social inequality in India ran the risk (at least in the minds of many figures) of losing sight of larger anti-colonial battles or struggles against white supremacy.

What is really beyond dispute, however, is the emotional power of Ambedkar for millions of Dalits worldwide, and one of the key motivations for this book is how we see this power potentially focusing in on very particular spaces—even in single houses where Ambedkar spent his life. In the Public Inquiry around 10 King Henry's Road, one of the most important pieces of evidence presented by us, the appellants, was the visitors' book to the new museum, which contained entries detailing visitors' reactions to the house. The importance of Ambedkar and his legacy to so many people who had often made very long pilgrimage-like trips to the house was palpable. In reading these comments, written in multiple languages, we can gain a sense of how transformative Ambedkar's ideas have been for such large numbers of people who continue to fight against entrenched injustices. In Chapter 7 of this book, Jamie Sullivan and Santosh Dass narrate the ways in which the 10KHR Public Inquiry assumed not just a national, but an international gravity. The house, therefore, can never just be a museum, or a building which holds a blue plaque—another historical curiosity among the many famous sites of the city. It also holds a place among a number of other sites, mainly in India, associated with Ambedkar. Perhaps most appropriately, it is likely too that the house will also be a location for the kinds of work and activities that the man himself would have commended. This could include educational visits, the hosting of scholars from India, and the holding of some research materials and resources, as well as hosting talks and other events. What better opportunity could there be to fulfil the adopted motto of Bhimrao: 'Educate, Organise, Agitate!'

# NOTES

## INTRODUCTION

1. See, for example, Part I of Suraj Yengde and Anand Teltumbde, eds, *The Radical in Ambedkar: Critical Reflections* (Gurgaon: Penguin, 2018), pp. 3–106; see also Jesúus Cháirez-Garza, 'B. R. Ambedkar, Partition and the Internationalisation of Untouchability', *South Asia: Journal of South Asian Studies*, 42, 1 (2019), pp. 80–96.
2. The most important recent chapter which explores this history is Rohit De, 'Lawyering as Politics: The Legal Practice of Dr Ambedkar, Bar At Law' in Yengde and Teltumbde, eds, *The Radical in Ambedkar*, *op. cit.*, pp. 134–50.
3. Association for the Improvement of the Condition of Victims of Social Ostracism.
4. For an exploration of how the Constitution often served (and was driven by) rights movements from marginalised communities, see Rohit De, *A People's Constitution: The Everyday Life of Law in the Indian Republic* (Princeton: Princeton University Press, 2018).
5. See Vivek Kumar, 'Understanding Dalit Diaspora', *Economic and Political Weekly*, 39, 1 (3–9 January 2004), pp. 114–16. Kumar differentiates the earlier indentured labour migration in the nineteenth century from the later 'professional' post-independence Dalit diaspora, but argues that caste discrimination was still carried with most communities globally.
6. Nicolas Jaoul, 'Beyond Ambedkar: Ambedkarism, Multiculturalism and Caste in the UK', *Samaj*, 27 (2021).
7. Most of the work on Dalits in the UK explores larger themes of identity and education, and does not generally focus on the

Ambedkarite movements. See for example, Paul Ghuman, *British Untouchables: A Study of Dalit Identity and Education* (London: Routledge, 2011). There is also a literature exploring religious conversion in the UK, e.g. Steve Taylor, 'Religious Conversion and Dalit Assertion among a Punjabi Dalit diaspora', *Sociological Bulletin*, 63, 2 (2014), pp. 224–46; Julie Leslie, *Authority and Meaning in Indian Religions: Hinduism and the Case of Valmiki* (London: Routledge, 2003).

8. See, for example, Vivek Kumar, 'Dalit Diaspora: Invisible Existence', *Diaspora Studies*, 2, 1 (2009), pp. 53–64; Meena Dhanda, 'Anti-Casteism and Misplaced Nativism: Mapping caste as an aspect of race', *Radical Philosophy*, 192, (July 2015), pp. 33–43.

## 1. AMBEDKAR THE ACTIVIST

1. See, for example, S. Ambirajan, 'Ambedkar's Contribution to Indian Economics', *Economic and Political Weekly*, 34, 46/7 (20–26 November 1999), pp. 3280–5; Manak Singharia, 'Dr B. R. Ambedkar: As an Economist', *International Journal of Humanities and Social Science Invention*, 2, 3 (March 2013), pp. 24–7. A few examples stand out in clearly establishing a strong connection between his thought in economics and his political philosophy, for example Anand Teltumbde, 'Economics of Babasaheb Ambedkar', in Gummadi Srivedi, ed., *Ambedkar's Vision of Economic Development for India* (London: Routledge, 2020).
2. For a detailed examination of this complex chronology in Ambedkar's transition between the USA and London, see J. Krishnamurthy, 'Ambedkar's Educational Odyssey, 1913–1927', *Journal of Social Inclusion Studies*, 5, 2 (2020), pp. 147–57. This cites correspondence between Ambedkar and Seligman, found in Seligman Collection, Box 23, Correspondence Sent 1919–1924, Columbia University Library. The letter admitting his loss of the manuscript is contained in a letter sent to Seligman from Ambedkar (addressed from 10 King Henry's Road) on 16 February 1922.
3. Vijay Mankar, *Life and Movement of Dr B. R. Ambedkar: A Chronology* (Nagpur: Blue World Series, 2009), p. 12.
4. Arun P. Mukherjee, 'B. R. Ambedkar, John Dewey, and the Meaning of Democracy', *New Literary History*, 40, 2 (2009), pp. 345–70.
5. Jesús Cháirez-Garza, 'B.R. Ambedkar, Franz Boas and the Rejection of Racial Theories of Untouchability', *South Asia: Journal of South Asian Studies*, 41, 2 (2018), pp. 281–96.

6. 'Journey to England from the USA of British subject Bhimrao, alias Brimvran Ambedkar', 1916, IOR/L/PJ/6/1443, File 2349. India Office Records, British Library (hereafter IOR).
7. 'Ambedkar's Attendance Record at LSE 1916-1917', LSE Student File, available at https://www.lse.ac.uk/library/whats-on/exhibitions (last searched 15 July 2021). See also Chapter 2 in this volume.
8. Ambedkar's editorials for *Mooknayak* ('The Leader of Voiceless') dealt with caste affairs in the months before his departure for London. This fortnightly publication was dedicated specifically to the exploration of grievances of Untouchables, and to examine the bases of their powerlessness and lack of education. Specifically, it was set up to represent Untouchables in the absence of other such journals. See *Mooknayak*, 31 January 1920, *Da. Babasaheb Ambekdaranche Bahishkrit Bharat ani Mook Nayak* (Vol 2, p. 346), cited in Hemant Devasthali, 'Portrait of a Scholar and Activist: Ambedkar as a Young Man', *The Beacon*, 30 December 2018, available at https://www.thebeacon.in/2018/12/30/potrait-of-a-scholar-and-activist/.
9. Eleanor Zelliot, 'Experiments in Dalit Education: Maharashtra, 1850–1947', in Sabyasachi Bhattacharya, ed., *Education and the Disprivileged: Nineteenth and Twentieth Century India* (Delhi: Orient Longman, 2002), pp. 38–41, 44.
10. Christophe Jaffrelot, *Dr Ambedkar and Untouchability: Analysing and Fighting Caste* (London: Hurst, 2005).
11. Zelliot, 'Experiments', *op. cit.*, p. 41.
12. Rozina Visram, *Asians in Britain: 400 Years of History* (London: Pluto Press, 2002), p. 90.
13. *Report of the Committee of Indian Students 1921–22: Part 1, Report and Appendices* (London: His Majesty's Stationery Office, 1922), p. 36.
14. Dhananjay Keer, *Dr Ambedkar Life and Mission*, 3rd edn (Bombay: Popular Prakasan, 1971), p. 45, quoting from Prabhar Padhye, *Prakashatil Vyakti* (p. 30).
15. *Report of the Committee of Indian Students 1921–22, op. cit.*, p. 17.
16. For a detailed account of Indian student experiences in the UK in this period, see Sumita Mukherjee, 'Mobility, Race and the Politicisation of Indian Studies in Britain before the Second World War', *History of Education* (London: Routledge, 10 February 2022, e-publication).
17. Seligman to B. R. Ambedkar, 5 January 1921, in the Seligman Collection, Columbia University Library. This previously unreported letter was unearthed for the 2019 Public Inquiry hearing into the GOM's appeal against Camden Council's rejection of museum status for 10KHR.

18. B. R. Ambedkar to the Director of the British Museum, 27 June 1921. This letter asks for admission to consult records around economics and finance at the British Museum.
19. The 1921 Census, Find My Past in Assocation with the National Archives, available from https://www.findmypast.co.uk/1921-census?ds_kid=43700056080490730&gclid=Cj0KCQjwvZCZBhCiARIsAPXbajtAZK1jPhr6kX-_z1Kfap6dUClsiirDKjH7b7arPfkKDM06H7Y7ca8aAhVGEALw_wcB&gclsrc=aw.ds
20. Ambedkar had written to the University of Bonn, again from 10 King Henry's Road, on 25 February 1921, sending a short CV and asking to be supervised by Prof. Hermann Jacobi. See Maren Bellwinkel-Schempp, 'Dr Ambedkar in Germany', *Velivada*, available at https://velivada.com/2015/01/18/dr-ambedkar-in-germany/.
21. See, for example, Keer, *Dr Ambedkar*, *op. cit.*, pp. 41–5.
22. See, for example, Little Pal to Bhim, 15 May 1924, and Fx to Bhim, 11 March 1925, in Surender Ajnat, *Letters of Ambedkar* (Jalandhar: Bheem Patrika Publications, 1993), pp. 134–6.
23. There is no doubt, as Ananya Vajpayi has suggested in discussions with the author, that Ambedkar did have a very close relationship with 'F', which at the very least was based on a close intellectual connection.
24. Ajnat, *Letters of Ambedkar*, *op. cit.*, pp. 134–6.
25. Nanak Chand Rattu, *Little Known Facet of Dr Ambedkar* (New Delhi: Focus Impressions, 2001).
26. See, for example, the film made about Ambedkar's life by Jabbar Patel, *Dr Babasaheb Ambedkar* (2000).
27. Gail Omvedt, *Ambedkar: Towards an Enlightened India* (London: Penguin, 2004), p. 30.
28. Email, Kate Brolly, Camden Local Studies and Archives Centre, to Santosh Dass and William Gould, 10 June 2021.
29. The surviving marriage records for Frances and Gaston Proust give her maiden name as Fanny Brooks. Source Information—FreeBMD. England & Wales, Civil Registration Marriage Index, 1837–1915 [database online]. Provo, UT, USA: Ancestry.com Operations, Inc., 2006, available at https://www.ancestry.co.uk. We would like to thank Kate Brolly at the Camden Local Studies and Archives Centre for her invaluable assistance in locating these sources on Fanny Proust and her family (Emails dated 8–15 June 2021).
30. Metropolitan Borough of Hampstead general rate books 1918–41, Ward 3 (held at Camden Local Studies and Archives Centre).
31. Source Citation–The National Archives: Kew, London, England; 1939 Register; Reference: RG 101/240A. Source Information Ancestry.

com. 1939 England and Wales Register [database online]. Lehi, UT, USA: Ancestry.com Operations, Inc., 2018, available at https://www.ancestry.co.uk.

32. 'Search probate records for documents and wills (England and Wales)', available at https://www.gov.uk/search-will-probate.
33. Metropolitan Borough of Hampstead general rate books 1918–41, Ward 3 (held at Camden Local Studies and Archives Centre).
34. Brant Moscovitch, 'Harold Laski's Indian students and the power of education, 1920–1950'. *Contemporary South Asia*, 20, 1 (2012).
35. See also Ben Zachariah, *Developing India: An Intellectual and Social History c. 1930–1950* (Delhi: Oxford University Press, 2005), pp. 55–6.
36. See Chapter 2 in this volume.
37. Brant Moscovitch, 'Harold Laski's Indian students', *op. cit*.
38. Vakil's PhD resulted in a publication entitled *Our Fiscal Policy* (Bombay: Taraporevala, 1923). See also C. N. Vakil and S. K. Muranjan, *Currency and Prices in India* (Calcutta: Longmans, 1927). Later on, Vakil also contributed to work on industry and trade—C. N. Vakil, S. C Bose and P. V. Deolalkar, eds, *Growth of Trade and Industry in Modern India* (Bombay: Longmans, 1931).
39. See, for example, C. N. Vakil, *Economic Consequences of Divided India—A Study of Economy of India and Pakistan* (Bombay: Vora and Co., 1950); C. N. Vakil, *Poverty and Planning* (Bombay: Allied Publishers, 1963).
40. 'Autumn Leaves', memoir, Mss Eur F341/147, Oriental and India Office Collections, British Library.
41. 'Miss Mithan Ardeshir Tata, The First Indian Lady Barrister', *The Times of India*, 20 January 1923, p. 15; also cited in Yi Chen and Yi Li, 'Seeking "A Fair Field" for Women in the Legal Profession: Pioneering Women Lawyers from Burma of 1924–1935', *Britain and the World*, 14, 2 (2021), pp. 105–27.
42. Ratan Chand Rawlley, *Mr John Bull Speaks Out* (Bombay: Thacker and Co., 1943).
43. Hira Metharam Jagtiani, *The Role of the State in the Provision of Railways* (London: P. S. King, 1924).
44. *British History Online—University of London: The Historical Record*, available at https://www.british-history.ac.uk/no-series/london-university-graduates/269-270.
45. *Ibid*. The papers of Edith How-Martyn are available at Women's Library Archives, GB 106 7EM.
46. See Mildred Wretts-Smith, 'The English in Russia During the Second Half of the Sixteenth Century', *Transactions of the Royal Historical*

*Society*, 3 (1920), pp. 72–102. Wretts-Smith went on to publish *The Business of the East India Company 1680–1681* (1963).

47. Susan Hogan and Heather Radi, 'Campbell, Persia Glendoline (1898–1974)', *Australian Dictionary of Biography*, available at https://adb.anu.edu.au/biography/campbell-persia-gwendoline-9682.
48. Aristide R. Zolberg, 'Herman Finer', *Political Science and Politics*, 2, 2 (Spring 1969), pp. 199–200.
49. William A. Orton Papers, Smith College Archives, Northampton, MA.
50. William A. Orton, *The Liberal Tradition: A Study of the Social and Spiritual Conditions of Freedom* (New Haven: Yale University Press, 1945); *The Economic Role of the State* (Chicago: University of Chicago Press, 1950).
51. G. E. Wilson, 'Robert MacGregor Dawson, 1895–1958', *The Canadian Journal of Economics and Political Science / Revue canadienne d'Economique et de Science politique*, 25, 2 (May 1959), pp. 210–13.
52. Keer, *Dr Ambedkar*, *op. cit.*, p. 47.
53. Sachin Roy, *Anthropologists in India* (New Delhi: Indian Anthropological Association, 1970). See also T. N. Madan, 'The Search for Synthesis: The Sociology of D. P. Mukerji', in Patricia Uberoi, Nandini Sundar and Satish Seshpande, eds, *Anthropology in the East: Founders of Indian Sociology and Anthropology* (Ranikhet: Permanent Black, 2007).
54. The classic points of reference here are the late nineteenth century- and early twentieth-century 'nationalist' economic histories written by Dadabhai Naoroji and R. C. Dutt.
55. For a study of this change financial and fiscal governance, see Eleanor Newbigin, *The Hindu Family and the Emergence of Modern India: Law, Citizenship and Community* (Cambridge: Cambridge University Press, 2013), Chapters 1–2.
56. B. R. Ambedkar, *The Evolution of Provincial Finance in British India: A Study in the Provincial Decentralisation of Imperial Finance* (London: P. S. King and Son, 1925). The final Part IV of the text contains the most detailed criticism of the flawed logic underlying dyarchy, and the problem (among many others) of how Indian ministers would potentially end up having their budgets reallocated for 'reserved' expenditures, for which they are not responsible.
57. Gail Omvedt, *Ambedkar: Towards an Enlightened India*, *op. cit.*, p. 35; see also Ben Zachariah, *Developing India*, *op. cit.*, p. 177, on the effects of work with Seligman on this form of anti-colonialism situated in economic analysis.
58. Ambedkar, *Evolution of Provincial Finance*, *op. cit.*, p. 261.
59. *Ibid.*, pp. 279–80.

60. 'Statement concerning the state of education of the Depressed Classes in the Bombay Presidency submitted by Dr Bhimrao R. Ambedkar, Member of the Legislative Council, Bombay on behalf of the Bahishkrita Hitakarini Sabha (Depressed Classes Institute of Bombay) to the Indian Statutory Commission', 29 May 1928, in Hari Narke, ed., *Dr Babasaheb Ambedkar: Writings and Speeches*, Vol. 2 (New Delhi: Dr Ambedkar Foundation, 2014), pp. 407–28.
61. See B. R. Tomlinson, *The Indian National Congress and The Raj: The Penultimate Phase* (London: Macmillan, 1976), pp. 7–31; B. R. Tomlinson, 'Britain and the Indian Currency Crisis', *Economic History Review*, xxxii (1979), pp. 88–99.
62. Niranjan Rajadhyaksha, 'Ambedkar, rupee and our current troubles', *Livemint*, 14 April 2015, available at https://www.livemint.com/Opinion/rMImvbuYNDk4RvWGfcMtQO/Ambedkar-rupee-and-our-current-troubles.html.
63. This was most clearly set out in John Maynard Keynes, *Indian Currency and Finance* (London: Macmillan, 1913).
64. B. R. Ambedkar, *The Problem of the Rupee: Its origin and its solution* (London: P. S. King and Son, 1923), pp. vi–vii.
65. *Ibid.*, p. xiii.
66. *Ibid.*, Chapters 1 and 2.
67. *Ibid.*, pp. 87–90.
68. *Ibid.*, pp. 66–7.
69. *Ibid.*, p. 91.
70. *Ibid.*, pp. 96–8.
71. *Ibid.*, pp. 113–17.
72. *Ibid.*, p. 186. See also the series of essays by Arun Bannerji, 'Revisiting the Exchange Standard, 1898–1913: II Operations', *Economic and Political Weekly*, 37, 14 (6–12 April 2002), pp. 1353–62.
73. Another detailed exploration of this process can be found in *ibid.*, and in Arun Bannerji, 'Revisiting the Exchange Standard', *op. cit.*, 37, 43 (26 October–1 November 2002), pp. 4455–65.
74. *Ibid.*, pp. 201–15.
75. *Royal Commission on Indian Currency and Finance Vol. IV: Minutes of Evidence Taken in India Before the Royal Commission on Indian Currency and Finance* (London: His Majesty's Stationery Office, 1926), pp. 313–22.
76. See Narendra Jhadav, 'Neglected Economic Thought of Babasaheb Ambedkar', *Economic and Political Weekly*, 26, 15 (13 April 1991), pp. 980–2.
77. Some accounts of Ambedkar's London studies suggest that he may have been assisted in his work by the elusive 'F' who subsequently wrote to

him from 10 King Henry's Road. See, for example, Omvedt, *Ambedkar: Towards an Enlightened India, op. cit.*, p. 30. However, there is no clear evidence that this assistance actually took place during the early 1920s.

78. B. R. Ambedkar, *Evolution of Provincial Finance, op. cit.*, Preface.
79. V. Geetha, 'Unpacking a Library: Babasaheb Ambedkar and His World of Books', *The Wire*, 20 October 2017, available at https://thewire.in/caste/unpacking-library-babasaheb-ambedkar-world-books (searched 30 Mar. 2021).
80. Ambedkar to Ramabai, 17 July 1920, cited in Vijay Mankar, *Life of the Greatest Humanitarian Revolutionary Movement of Dr B. R. Ambedkar—A Chronology*, 2nd edn, (Nagpur: Blue World Series, 2009), p. 27. Ambedkar expressed sorrow for leaving her behind with responsibilities and child care, but asked her to not let anyone touch his books.
81. Geetha, 'Unpacking a Library', *op. cit*.
82. We know that Ambedkar applied for a passport to travel to London in May 1916, and that Seligman wrote to Sydney Webb to recommend him on 23 May 1916, 'to finish up his dissertation' (cited in Krishnamurthy, *op. cit.*).
83. B. R. Ambedkar to The Director of the British Museum, 27 June 1921.
84. Changdeo Bhavanrao Khairmode, *Da. Bhimrao Ramji Ambedkar*, Vol. 1 (1992), p. 270, cited in Hemant Devasthali, 'Portrait of a Scholar and Activist: Ambedkar as a Young Man', *The Beacon*, available at https://www.thebeacon.in/2018/12/30/potrait-of-a-scholar-and-activist/.
85. *Ibid.*
86. *Ibid.*, cited from Dr Jaysinghrao Pawar, ed., *Rajarshree Shahu Smarak Granth* (Kolhapur: Maharashtra Itihas Prabodhini, 2001).
87. This idea is also firmly proposed by Cosimo Zene, 'Justice for the Excluded and Education for Democracy in B. R. Ambedkar and A. Gramsci', *A Journal of Economics, Culture and Society*, 30, 4 (2018), pp. 494–524.
88. See Shailaja Paik, 'Forging a New Dalit Womanhood in Colonial Western India: Discourse on Modernity, Rights, Education and Emancipation', *Journal of Women's History*, 28, 4 (2016), pp. 14–40.
89. Scott Stroud, 'What did Ambedkar Learn from John Dewey's "Democracy and Education"?' *The Pluralist*, 12, 2 (2017), pp. 78–103.
90. Ambedkar to Kohlapur, 2 February 1921, in Devasthali, *op. cit*.
91. Keer, *Dr Ambedkar*, *op. cit.*, p. 46.
92. Ambedkar to Kohlapur, 3 February 1921, cited in *The Beacon*.
93. This positioning of Ambedkar does not simply suggest that he was an uncomplicated exponent of liberal constitutional values. More importantly, he developed 'a unique moral and political framework for

public reasoning'. For more on the development of this idea, see Bidyut Chakrabarty, 'B. R. Ambedkar and the history of constitutionalizing India', *Contemporary South Asia*, 24, 2 (2016), pp. 133–48.

94. 'Evidence Before the Southborough Committee on the Franchise', in Anand Teltumbde, *Dr B. R. Ambedkar: Complete Works*, available at https://archive.org/stream/Ambedkar_CompleteWorks/07.%20Evidence%20before%20the%20Southborough%20Committee_djvu.txt.
95. For a good example of this larger body of work to the Simon Commission, see 'A Report on the Constitution of the Government of Bombay Province', in Narke, ed., *Dr Babasaheb Ambedkar: Writings and Speeches*, *op. cit.*, pp. 315–400.
96. 'Evidence of Dr Ambedkar before the Indian Statutory Commission on 23 October 1928', in *ibid.*, pp. 459–90. Ambedkar was, however, quite dismissive of the possibility that 'Criminal Tribes' might be considered in relation to the Franchise—'With regard to the criminal tribes, it might not be a good thing to give them adult suffrage, because by occupation they are a people who have more the interest of their own particular community in their mind, and they are not very particular as regards the means whereby they earn their living' (*ibid.*, p. 471).
97. See, for example, Seligman's foreword in *The Evolution of Provincial Finance* which starts with the sentence: 'The problem discussed by Mr. Ambedkar in his excellent dissertation is one that is arousing a growing interest in all parts of the world'.
98. Eleanor Zelliot, *Dr Babasaheb Ambedkar and the Untouchable Movement* (Sacramento: Blumoon Books, 2004).

## 2. A STUDENT IN LONDON

1. *LSE Yearbook, 1895–1896* LSE/Unregistered/27/2/1A, London School of Economics and Political Science.
2. *Ibid.*
3. See Sue Donnelly, 'Graham Wallas. The supreme teacher of political philosophy', available at https://blogs.lse.ac.uk/lsehistory/2018/01/24/graham-wallas-the-supreme-teacher-of-social-philosophy/.
4. See Sue Donnelly, 'An Unsung Heroine of LSE: Charlotte Shaw', available at https://blogs.lse.ac.uk/lsehistory/2014/01/24/an-unsung-heroine-of-lse-charlotte-payne-townshend/.
5. A full account of the foundation of LSE can be found in Ralf Dahrendorf, *LSE: A History of the London School of Economics and Political Science, 1895–1995* (Oxford: Oxford University Press, 1995).

6. Maud Pember-Reeves, *Round About a Pound a Week* (London: G. Bell and Sons Ltd, 1913) was an investigation into working-class household budgets organised by the Fabian Society Women's Group.
7. *Calendar for the Twentieth Session, 1914–1915*, LSE/Unregistered/27/5/1, London School of Economics and Political Science.
8. Unfortunately, not all student files have survived; some were lost due to a flood in a basement during the 1950s.
9. *Abridged Calendar for Twenty-second session, 1916–1917*, LSE/Unregistered/27/5/2, pp. 96–8.
10. LSE/Student File/Ambedkar, p. 62, available at https://www.lse.ac.uk/library/assets/documents/Ambedkars-LSE-student-file.pdf.
11. G. Lowes Dickinson, *The European Anarchy* (London: George Allen & Unwin, 1916).
12. G. Lowes Dickinson, *The International Anarchy* (London: George Allen & Unwin, 1926).
13. Professor Michael Cox, 'Goldsworthy Lowes Dickinson, LSE and the origins of International Relations', available at https://blogs.lse.ac.uk/lsehistory/2018/12/12/goldsworthy-lowes-dickinson-lse-and-the-origins-of-international-relations.
14. *Abridged Calendar for Twenty-second session, 1916–1917*, LSE/Unregistered/27/5/2, p. 56.
15. *Ibid.*, pp. 62–3.
16. Dahrendorf, *LSE: A History, op. cit.*, p. 103.
17. L. T. Hobhouse, *Liberalism* (London: Oxford University Press, 1911).
18. Dahrendorf, *LSE: A History, op. cit.*, pp. 104–5.
19. Keer, *Dr Ambedkar, op. cit.*, p. 32.
20. The fullest biography of William Beveridge is Jose Harris, *William Beveridge: A biography*, 2nd edn (Oxford: Clarendon Press, 1977).
21. Professor Michael Cox, 'A Beveridge Plan for an Unruly School? William Beveridge and LSE', available at https://blogs.lse.ac.uk/lsehistory/2018/03/14/a-beveridge-plan-for-an-unruly-school-william-beveridge-and-lse/.
22. 'Notes for address to new students', LSE/Beveridge/5/10/8.
23. 'Address to new students, annotated typescript, 9 October 1935', LSE/Beveridge/5/10/26.
24. 'Mair, Janet', LSE/Staff File/Mair Janet.
25. Director's Report 1924–1925, LSE/Unregistered/27/1/1, p. 3.
26. 'International Study Circle' in *Clare Market Review*, Michaelmas term, 1922, p. 10.
27. See Brant Moscovitch, 'Harold Laski's Indian Students', *op. cit.*, pp. 33–44.

28. V. Geetha, *Bhimrao Ramji Ambedkar and the Question of Socialism in India* (London: Palgrave, 2021), p. 230.
29. The LSE Calendar provides complete lists of full- and part-time LSE staff.
30. Sue Donnelly, 'Dr Vera Anstey—so absolutely sane, clear, quick, intelligent and safe', https://blogs.lse.ac.uk/lsehistory/2018/04/11/dr-vera-anstey-so-absolutely-sane-clear-quick-intelligent-safe/.
31. 'Admission application form for regular students', LSE/Student File/Ambedkar, p. 60.
32. 'Seligman to Foxwell, 23 September 1920', *ibid.*, p. 56.
33. *Ibid.*
34. Foxwell to Janet Mair, School Secretary, 10 November 1920, LSE/student file/Ambedkar, p. 54.
35. *Clare Market Review*, Lent Term, 1920, p. 19.
36. D. H. Travers, 'The Problem of Research Students', *Clare Market Review*, Summer Term, 1925, p. 103.
37. 'Indian Society', *Clare Market Review*, Summer Term, 1925, p. 94.
38. 'Tennis Club, Malden, June 1928', LSE/Image Library/902.
39. 'Ambedkar, B. R.', LSE/Student File/Ambedkar, p. 52.
40. Available at LSE Digital Library, https://lse-atom.arkivum.net/uklse-dl1pu01001001.
41. *Calendar for the Twenty-Eighth Session, 1922–1923*, LSE/Unregistered/27/5/2.
42. I. Bogle, '100 Years of the PhD in the UK', in *Proceedings of Vitae Researcher Development International Conference 2018*, Birmingham, UK. Careers Research and Advisory Centre (CRAC), available at https://discovery.ucl.ac.uk/id/eprint/10068565/.
43. *Calendar for the Twenty-Eighth Session, 1922–1923*, LSE/Unregistered/27/5/2, p. 169.
44. LSE/Student File/Ambedkar, p. 15.
45. Ambedkar, *The Problem of the Rupee*, *op. cit.*, p. ix.
46. Edwin Cannan, *Wealth* (London: P. S. King & Son, 1914).
47. Edwin Cannan, *A Review of Economic Theory* (London: P. S. King and Son, 1929).
48. Sue Donnelly, 'Edwin Cannan (1861–1935)—economist, local councillor and cyclist', 1 April 2015, available at https://blogs.lse.ac.uk/lsehistory/2015/04/01/edwin-cannan-1861-1935-economist-local-councillor-and-cyclist/.
49. *LSE Year book, 1895–1896*, LSE/Unregistered/27/2/1A, p. 2.
50. *London School of Economics and Political Science Register, 1895–1932*.

51. *Calendar for Eighteenth Session 1912–1913*, LSE/UNREGISTERED/27/5/1, p. 254, available at https://lse-atom.arkivum.net/uploads/r/lse-institutional-archives/6/4/5/64544b078d8e4faf17e9a7eb0988204ae31e3f301faceeb7bed50d43d1d739e9/00176099-1b1c-4310-bc70-569f8ad72582-UKLSE_DL1_PU01_001_001_0018_0001.pdf.
52. LSE Calendars, 1922, p. 222.
53. 'Tata, H', in LSE/Student File/Tata, H.
54. *London School of Economics and Political Science Register, 1895–1932*. All information about Ambedkar's fellow students comes from the LSE Register and student file.
55. Kyoshi Ogata, *The Co-operative movement in Japan* (London: P. S. King, 1923).
56. Cannan to Beveridge, 12 December 1932, in 'Ambedkar, B. R.', LSE/Student File/Ambedkar, p. 30.
57. *Ibid.*, p. 51.
58. 'B. R. Ambedkar to R. A. Butler, 29 July 1952', in LSE/Student file/Vithal Kadham, p. 1.
59. *Ibid.*, p. 1.
60. B. R. Ambedkar to Vera Anstey, 29 July 1952, LSE/Student File/Vithal Kadam, p. 41.
61. B. R. Ambedkar to W. S. Collings, 4 September 1952, LSE/Student File/Vithal Kadam, p. 14.
62. Vithal Kadam to Lionel Robbins, 11 April 1957, in 'General Correspondence', LSE/ROBBINS/3/1/15.
63. Professor Amartya Sen, 'India Week Listings', *The Beaver*, 24 January 2006, available at https://digital.library.lse.ac.uk/objects/lse:jug399yuy/read/single#page/28/mode/2up.
64. 'Presentation of Bust Statue of Dr B. R. Ambedkar to LSE', 14 April 1994, LSE/Student File/Ambedkar, p. 2.
65. See https://www.lse.ac.uk/library/whats-on/exhibitions/educate-agitate-organise.
66. The site had 15,000 page views within five days of launching.
67. See 'Ambedkar: Caste, Constitution, Gender', available at https://www.youtube.com/watch?v=43i7oMI1Kk8.

## 3. AMBEDKAR AS LAWYER

1. Particularly the work of Rohit De, which has been invaluable in considering much of his early legal practice. See Rohit De, 'Lawyering as Politics', *op. cit.*, pp. 134–50.

2. Quoted in the Biographical Notes of P. C. Beddingham, 'Souvenir Released by the Dr Ambedkar Memorial Committee of Great Britain' (13 March 1973). Available from Gray's Inn library.
3. The Regulations (as updated in May 1916) are set out in the Calendar of the Council of Legal Education for 1916–17, a copy of which is held in Lincoln's Inn library. The full form of the required certificate to be signed by the Secretary for Indian Students was as follows: 'I have caused enquiries to be made in India and this Country as to the character and position of [name and description of Applicant], and from the reports and other information I have obtained and as a result of a personal interview I have had with him I am satisfied that he is a gentleman of respectability and a proper person to be admitted as a Student of the Honourable Society of [name of Inn] with a view to being called to the Bar'.
4. Gail Omvedt, *Ambedkar: Towards an Enlightened India*, *op. cit.*, p. 27.
5. *Ibid.*, pp. 28–30.
6. He wrote to Prabhakar Padhye, 'The keeper of the boarding house was a harsh and terrible lady'. He described his evening meal as 'a cup of Bovril, biscuits and butter'. Keer, *Dr Ambedkar*, *op. cit.*, p. 45, quoting from Prabhar Padhye, *Prakashatil Vyakti, op. cit.*, p. 30.
7. For another account of the custom of dining at Gray's Inn, see Vivienne K. Gay, 'Courtesy and Custom in the English Legal Tradition: On Dining at Gray's Inn', *Journal of Legal Education*, 28, 181 (1976–77).
8. See footnote 6 above.
9. As published, for example, in the Calendar of the Council of Legal Education, 1922 (p. 32).
10. Visram, *Indians in Britain*, *op. cit.*
11. For a sense of the typical social background of this generation of law students, see H. A. C. Sturgess, ed., *South Asians at the Inns of Court: Middle Temple, 1863–1944. Register of Admissions to the Honourable Society of the Middle Temple* (London: Butterworth and Co. for the Hon. Society of the Middle Temple, 1949). There is an equivalent volume for Lincoln's Inn.
12. See Prabhat Patnaik, 'Obituary: Nirmal Kumar Chaudhury', *Social Scientist,* 42, 3–4 (2014), pp. 108–10.
13. Sayantani Adhikary, 'The Bratachari Movement and the Invention of a Folk Tradition', *South Asia: Journal of South Asian Studies,* 38, 4 (2015), pp. 656–70.
14. H. A. C. Sturgess, ed., *South Asians at the Inns of Court*, *op. cit.*, p. 83.
15. Sumita Mukherjee, 'Tata [*married name* Lam], Mithan Ardeshir', *Oxford Dictionary of National Biography* (15 February 2018),

available at https://www.oxforddnb.com/view/10.1093/odnb/9780198614128.001.0001/odnb-9780198614128-e-111939.

16. Relevant extracts from the Order Book can be found in the Biographical Notes of Beddingham, 'Souvenir Released by the Dr Ambedkar Memorial Committee of Great Britain', *op. cit*.
17. For more information on this Act, see https://www.gov.uk/government/news/the-sex-disqualification-removal-act-1919.
18. Edith Hesling—who was in fact admitted as a student member in October 1920 but chose to qualify slightly later.
19. Sumit Kataria, 'Ambedkar: A Jurist With No Equals', *Forward Press,* 13 July 2017, available at https://www.forwardpress.in/2017/07/ambedkar-a-jurist-with-no-equals/ (searched 17 Jan. 2022).
20. For examples of the elitism of this first generation of legally trained political figures in India, see John McLane, *Indian Nationalism and the Early Congress* (Princeton: Princeton University Press, 1978). See also, H. L. Levy, 'Lawyer-Scholars, Lawyer-Politicians and the Hindu Code Bill, 1921–1956', *Law & Society Review*, 3, 2/3 (Nov 1968–Feb 1969), pp. 303–16.
21. Rohit De, 'Lawyering as Politics', *op. cit.*, p. 136.
22. Keer, *Dr Ambedkar*, *op. cit.*, pp. 50–3.
23. Cited by Rohit De, 'Lawyering as Politics', *op. cit.*, p. 137.
24. Speech by Ambedkar at the AISCF rally at Jalandhar, 1951; Narak Chand Rattu, ed., *Reminiscences and Remembrances of Dr Ambedkar* (New Delhi: Samya Prakash, 2017), p. 77.
25. 'Ambedkar's Connection with Hyderabad Recalled', *The Hindu*, 20 January 2015.
26. V. B. Gaikwad, *Court Cases Argued by Dr Babasaheb Ambedkar* (Thane: Vaibhav Prakashan, 2012), p. 164.
27. *Ibid*.
28. *Ibid*.
29. *Ibid*.
30. Rohit De, 'Lawyering as Politics', *op. cit.*, p. 139.
31. Sumeet Mhaskar, 'Ambedkar's Fight Wasn't Just Against Caste: Scholars have overlooked his Labour Activism', *The Print*, 14 April 2020, available at https://theprint.in/opinion/ambedkars-fight-wasnt-just-against-caste-scholars-have-overlooked-his-labour-activism/401133/.
32. Sumeet Mhaskar, 'How a Strike 40 Years Ago Dismantled Workers' Claim Over Mumbai, Hastened Its Gentrification', *The Wire*, 18 January 2022, available at https://thewire.in/labour/great-textile-strike-mumbai-mill-workers.

33. Kataria, 'Ambedkar: A Jurist With No Equals', *op. cit.*
34. A detailed description of the case can be found in C. H. Rolph, ed., *The Trial of Chatterley: Regina v Penguin Books Limited* (London: Penguin, 1961). See also E. C. S. Wade, 'Obscene Publications Act 1959', *The Cambridge Law Journal*, 17, 2 (November 1959L, pp. 179–82.
35. Jeremy Hutchinson was the son of St John Hutchinson KC and was called to the Bar in 1939, having been educated at Stowe School and Oxford and been an officer in the Royal Naval Volunteer Reserve; Gerald Gardiner, called to the Bar in 1925, was the son of Sir Robert Gardiner, having been educated at Harrow School and Oxford and been an officer in the Grenadier Guards; see 'Who was Who' (Oxford: Oxford University Press, 2022), available at https://www.ukwhoswho.com.
36. Gail Omvedt, *Dalits and the Democratic Revolution: Dr Ambedkar and the Dalit Movement in Colonial India*, 11th edn, (New Delhi: Sage, 2011), pp. 138–41.
37. Eleanor Zelliot, 'Dr Ambedkar and the Mahar Movement', PhD thesis, University of Pennsylvania (1969), pp. 107–17.
38. Rohit De, 'Lawyering as Politics', *op. cit.*, pp. 141–3.
39. V. M. Ravi Kumar, 'History of Indian Environmental Movement: A Study of Dr B. R. Ambedkar from the Perspectives of Access to Water', *Contemporary Voice of Dalit*, 8, 2 (2016), pp. 239–45.
40. *Constituent Assembly Debates*, AD Vol. VII p. 320; Vol. VII, p. 227.
41. For a detailed account of the Assembly debates on the Hindu Code Bill and the conservative opposition to Ambedkar, see Reba Som, 'Jawaharlal Nehru and the Hindu Code: A Victory of Symbol over Substance?' *Modern Asian Studies*, 28, 1 (1994), pp. 165–94.
42. 'The Power of Change', *Graya News*, 27 (2016).
43. See 'Ambedkar Room and Portrait', at https://www.graysinn.org.uk/news/ambedkar-room-and-portrait/. The event was attended by Ambedkar's great-grandson, Sujat Ambedkar.

## 4. AMBEDKAR, LONDON AND THE FIRST ROUND TABLE CONFERENCE

1. For more on the conference, see R. J. Moore, *The Crisis of Indian Unity, 1917–1940* (Oxford: Oxford University Press, 1974); and the recent work of Stephen Legg, such as 'Political lives at sea: working and socialising to and from the India Round Table Conference in London, 1930–1932', *Journal of Historical Geography*, 68 (2020), pp. 21–32.

2. For more on Bhaurao Gaikwad, see Ramchandra Kshirsagar, *Dalit Movement in India and its Leaders* (Delhi: M.D. Publications Pvt. Ltd, 1994), pp. 214–17.
3. See for instance Kris Manjapra, *Age of entanglement: German and Indian intellectuals across Empire* (Cambridge, MA: Harvard University Press, 2014); Maia Ramnath, *Decolonizing anarchism: An antiauthoritarian history of India's liberation struggle* (Oakland: AK Press, 2011); and Ali Raza, Franziska Roy and Benjamin Zachariah, eds, *The internationalist moment: South Asia, worlds and world views, 1917–39* (New Delhi: Sage, 2014).
4. Shruti Kapila, ed., *An intellectual history for India* (NewYork: Cambridge University Press, 2010); Samuel Moyn and Andrew Sartori, eds, *Global intellectual history* (New York: Columbia University Press, 2013); Faisal Devji, *Muslim Zion: Pakistan as a political idea* (London: Harvard University Press, 2013); Faisal Devji, *The impossible Indian: Gandhi and the temptation of violence* (London: Harvard University Press, 2012); and Christopher Bayly, *Recovering liberties: Indian thought in the age of liberalism and empire* (Cambridge: Cambridge University Press, 2012).
5. Carl Bridge, *Holding India to the Empire: The British Conservative Party and the 1935 constitution* (New Delhi: Sterling Publishers, 1986); R. J. Moore, *Crisis of Indian Unity*, *op. cit.*
6. Luis Cabrera, 'Dalit cosmopolitans: Institutionally developmental global citizenship in struggles against caste discrimination', *Review of International Studies*, 43 (2016), pp. 280–301; Suraj Yengde, 'Ambedkar's foreign policy and the ellipsis of the "Dalit" from international activism', in Yengde and Teltumbde, eds, *The radical in Ambedkar*, *op. cit.*, pp. 87–106.
7. Stephen Legg, 'Imperial internationalism: The Round Table Conference and the making of India in London, 1930–1932', *Humanity*, 11 (2020), pp. 32–53.
8. For more on Rajah, see Kshirsagar, *Dalit movement*, *op. cit.*, pp. 302–4.
9. One of the best works about this period is S. K. Gupta, *The Scheduled Castes in modern Indian politics: Their emergence as a political power* (New Delhi: Cambridge University Press, 1985), Chapter 5.
10. On Ambedkar's background, see Zelliot, *Dr. Babasaheb Ambedkar and the Untouchable movement*, *op. cit.*; Omvedt, *Dalits and the democratic revolution*, *op. cit.*, Chapter 2.
11. Among the many committees and commissions that Ambedkar participated in were the Southborough Committee, the Simon Commission, the Indian Central Committee, and the Round Table

Conferences among many others. See Gupta, *Scheduled Castes*, *op. cit.*, Chapter 6.
12. Ambedkar letter to Bhaurao Gaikwad, SS Viceroy of India ,11 October 1930, in Narke, ed., *Dr Babasaheb Ambedkar: Writings and Speeches*, Vol. 21, *op. cit.*, p. 49.
13. Ambedkar to Bhaurao, 29 October 1930, in Narke, ed., *Dr Babasaheb Ambedkar:Writings and Speeches*, Vol. 21, *op. cit.*, p. 51–2.
14. Beatrice Barmby, 'Hope at Last- for the "Untouchables"', *The New York Times*, 30 November 1930, pp. 7, 21.
15. Charles A. Selden, 'Prince and Outcast at Dinner in London End Age-Old Barrier', *The New York Times*, 30 November 1930, pp. 1, 19.
16. *Ibid.*
17. *Ibid.*
18. Barmby, 'Hope at Last'. *op. cit.*, pp. 7, 21.
19. Selden, 'Prince and Outcast', *op. cit.*
20. *Ibid.*
21. Barmby, 'Hope at Last', *op. cit.*, pp. 7, 21.
22. Selden, 'Prince and Outcast', *op. cit.*
23. This was one of Ambedkar's most radical writings. See B. R. Ambedkar, 'Annihilation of caste', in Moon, ed., *Ambedkar writings*, *op. cit.*
24. Selden, 'Prince and Outcast', *op. cit.*
25. *Ibid.*
26. *Ibid.*
27. *Ibid.*
28. Ambedkar wrote this letter while staying at 42 Clifton Gardens, Maida Vale, London. See Ambedkar to Bhaurao Gaikwad, 17 November 1930, in Narke, ed., *Dr Babasaheb Ambedkar:Writings and Speeches*.
29. *Ibid.*
30. *Ibid.*
31. B. R. Ambedkar and R. Srinivasan, 'A scheme of political safeguards for the protection of the Depressed Classes in the future constitution of a self-governing India' (1930), India Office Records and Papers (IOR), 1st Session, Minorities Committee, IOR/Q/RTC/24, p. 3.
32. *Ibid.*
33. *Ibid.*
34. *Ibid.*
35. See Jesús Cháirez-Garza, 'Moving untouched: B. R. Ambedkar and the racialization of untouchability', *Ethnic and Racial Studies*, 2 (2022), pp. 216–34.
36. O. H. B. Starte, P. G. Solanki, B. R. Ambedkar, P. R. Chikodi, L. M. Deshpande, L. C. Burfoot, A. V. Thakkar, A. A. Thorat, Rao Saheb J. K.

Mehta, and D. A. Janvekar, *Report of the Depressed Classes and Aboriginal Tribes Committee* (Bombay: Bombay Presidency, 1930), p. 67.

37. Ambedkar and Srinivasan, 'Political safeguards', *op. cit.*, p. 5.
38. Ambedkar discusses this period at length in B. R. Ambedkar, 'What Gandhi and Congress have done to the Untouchables', in Moon, ed., *Ambedkar writings*, *op. cit*.
39. See Shabnum Tejani, *Indian Secularism: A social and intellectual history 1890–1950* (Bloomington: Indiana University Press, 2008), p. 202.
40. Ambedkar and Srinivasan, 'Political safeguards', *op. cit.*, p. 10.
41. *Ibid.*, p. 8.
42. *Ibid.*, p. 9.
43. *Ibid.*
44. *Ibid.*
45. *Ibid.*
46. Indian Round Table Conference, 12 November 1930–19 January 1931, Proceedings, p. 136. Gupta Scheduled Castes, *op. cit.*, p.267.
47. Report of the Sub-Committee no. III (Minorities) presented at Meeting of the Committee of the Whole Conference held on 16 to 19 January 1931, p. 333.

## 5. DR AMBEDKAR IN THE 1920S

1. M. S. Gore, *The Social Context of an Ideology*: *Ambedkar's Political and Social Thought* (New Delhi: Sage, 1993), p. 85.
2. E. Zelliot, 'Congress and the Untouchables—1917–1950', in R. Sisson and S. Wolpert (eds), *Congress and Indian Nationalism—The Pre-Independence Phase* (Delhi: Oxford University Press, 1988), p. 183–4.
3. 'Evidence before the Southborough Committee on franchise. Examined on 27th January 1919', in: *Ambedkar Writings*, *op. cit.*, Vol. 1 (Bombay: Government of Maharashtra, 1979), pp. 251–3.
4. *Ibid.*, p. 252.
5. 'Supplementary written statement of Mr. Bhimrao R. Ambedkar' in *Ambedkar Writings*, *op. cit.*, p. 271.
6. The difference between the two systems was nevertheless important. In the system of reserved seats, the candidate should only be an Untouchable in a certain number of constituencies (proportional or not to the demographic weight of the Untouchables). But Untouchables were never in a majority in any constituency. A coalition of high and intermediate castes could then elect an Untouchable of their choice, for whom the local Untouchables would not have voted. On the other hand, in the system of separate electorates, only the Untouchables

would vote for candidates who could only be Untouchables, again in a number of constituencies proportional or not to their demographic weight. The system of the separate electorates would have therefore allowed the Untouchables to endow themselves with their own representatives and to constitute themselves into a real political force, whereas the reserved seats left the possibility to upper-caste-dominated parties to co-opt Untouchables, to give them tickets at the time of elections and to elect them, even against the will of the local Untouchables.

7. This attitude is all the more surprising as, at the same moment, sixteen out of eighteen Dalit organisations consulted by the Simon Commission in Bombay Presidency had clearly expressed themselves in favour of separate electorates. For instance, the common testimony of the Depressed India Association and the Servants of Somavamshiya Society before the Simon Commission stipulated 'experience has shown during the last two decades that it has served as a powerful lever to raise our Muslim brethren who in consequence are making rapid headway and coming into line with more advanced sections'; see *The Servants of Somavamshiya Society, Bombay*, 9 July 1928, p. 2 in Private Papers of Ambedkar, reels 1/2.
8. B. Ambedkar, 'Report on the Constitution of the Government of Bombay Presidency', in *Ambedkar Writings*, *op. cit.*, pp. 338 and 400.
9. 'Evidence of Dr Ambedkar before the Indian Statutory Commission one 23rd, October 1928', *ibid.*, p. 465. Ambedkar justified this demand of universal suffrage for the underprivileged persons (who never could reach the tax quota for voting rights) because they were the first to need it to protect themselves from the dominant castes ('Report on the Constitution', *op. cit.*, p. 338). He added that in spite of their illiteracy, they are rather intelligent for it ('Evidence of Dr Ambedkar', *op. cit.*, p. 473).
10. *Ibid.*, p. 351.
11. *Ibid.*, p. 479.
12. *Ibid.*, p. 483.
13. The passage in which these words are found deserves to be quoted in its entirety: 'Having regard to the fact that the cancer of untouchability is before their minds every minute of their lives, and having regard to their being alive to the fact that political power is the only solvent of this difficulty, I emphatically maintain that the depressed class voter would be an intelligent voter' (*ibid.*, p. 477).
14. *The Bombay Chronicle*, 18 August 1930, in *Source Material on Dr Ambedkar, op. cit.*, p. 40. *Indian Round Table Conference*, 12 November 1930–19

January 1931, Proceedings, Government of India, Calcutta, 1931, p. 440.

15. This conversation—whose content and date are not fully ascertained—is reproduced in part in Keer, *Dr. Ambedkar*, *op. cit.*, p. 166–7.
16. *Ibid.*, p. 173.
17. E. Zelliot, 'Gandhi and Ambedkar—A study in leadership', in J. M. Mahar, ed., *The Untouchables in Contemporary India* (Tucson: The University of Arizona Press, 1972), p. 81.
18. Quoted in Gore, *Social Context*, *op. cit.*, p. 103.
19. Cited in Zelliot, 'Gandhi and Ambedkar', *op. cit.*, p. 83. This subcommittee included heavyweight conservatives such as Madan Mohan Malaviya, who had just revived the Hindu Mahasabha.
20. He 'used to listen to Phule addressing the soldiers at Poona military camps on Sundays' and there were large numbers of Mahars among these soldiers; P. Constable, 'Early Dalit Literature and Culture in late nineteenth—and early twentieth—century Western India', *Modern Asian Studies*, 31, 2 (1997), p. 318.
21. *Ibid.*, p. 322.
22. J. Gokhale, *From Concessions to Confrontation* (Columbia: South Asia Books, 1993), pp. 68–9.
23. Omvedt, *Dalits and the Democratic Revolution*, *op. cit.*, p. 109.
24. E. Zelliot, *From Untouchable to Dalit*, *Essays on the Ambedkar Movement*, 3rd end (New Delhi: Manohar, 2001), p. 65.
25. *The Indian and Pakistan Year Book and Who's Who—1948* (Bombay: The Times of India, 1948), p. 1182.
26. Quoted in Zelliot, *Dr Ambedkar*, *op. cit.*, p. 77.
27. Although he insisted on the fact that Untouchables were the real autochthonous and had inherited from a superior culture, Shinde dissociated himself from the non-Brahmin movement which, according to him, was 'detrimental to unity' of society (G. M. Pawar, *Vitthal Ramji Shinde*, *op. cit.*, p. 47).
28. Omvedt, *Dalits and the Democratic Revolution*, *op. cit.*, p. 142.
29. Gokhale, *Concessions to Confrontation*, *op. cit.*, p. 75.
30. Gore, *Social Context*, *op. cit.*, p. 77. In 1919 Ambedkar opposed Shinde, who claimed before the Southborough Committee that 'instead of having representatives of Untouchables from amongst themselves, their interests would be better safeguarded by caste-Hindus'—K. N. Kadam, *Dr Babasaheb Ambedkar and the significance of his movement* (Bombay: Popular Prakashan, 1991), p. 21.
31. Zelliot, *Dr Ambedkar*, *op. cit.*, *p.* 77.

32. Letter of D. Ramrao (sub-inspector to Mahuli) Commissioner of Police, Bombay (December 1925), *Source Material*, *op. cit.*, p. 4.
33. *The Bombay Chronicle*, 26 April 1926, p. 8.
34. Ambedkar took over an old demand following D. D. Gholap, who had become the first Untouchable to have been appointed to the Legislative Council of the Bombay Presidency in 1920, having already introduced a bill in this direction (Gokhale, *From Concessions to Confrontation*, *op. cit.*, p. 84).
35. Keer, *Dr Ambedkar*, *op. cit.*, p. 62.
36. *Source Material*, *op. cit.*, pp. 6–7. Ambedkar had founded caste associations in the mid-1930s, such as the Mahar Sabha and the Mahar Panchayat, albeit in a very specific context, while he was preparing the ground for conversion to a non-Hindu religion. According to him, such a move had to take place in the caste framework, with castes having to convert *en masse*. In 1938 Ambedkar's elder brother formed the Mahar Samaj Seva Sangha and he took over from him at the helm of this association in 1941. A. Jurane, *Ethnic Identity and Social Mobility* (Jaipur/Delhi: Rawat, 1999), p. 39.
37. Quoted in Zelliot, *Dr Ambedkar*, *op. cit.*, p. 122.
38. Appeal on behalf of the Depressed Classes Institute (1931) in Private Papers of Ambedkar, reels 1/2.
39. Swapna H. Samel, 'Mahad Chawadar Tank Satyagraha of 1927: Beginning of Dalit liberation under C.R. Ambedkar', *Proceedings of the Indian History Congress*, Vol. 60, Diamond Jubilee (1999), p. 723. https://www.jstor.org/stable/44144143.
40. Quoted in *ibid.*, p. 724.
41. On the Mahad Satyagraha, the best source is Anand Teltumbde (2016), op. cit.; see also the memories of Damodar Runjaji Jadhav in Jadhav, *Intouchable* (Paris: France Loisirs, 2003), p. 43. The author recalls that there were many Mahar ex-army men among the participants (*ibid.*, p. 46).
42. Cited in Samel, 'Mahad Chawadar', *op. cit.*, p. 725.
43. Bojja Tharakam, *Mahad: The march that's launched every day* (Delhi: The Shared Mirror, 2011), p. 39.
44. *Poisoned Bread*, pp. 225–7 and p. 233. Transcribed by Changdeo Khairmode and translated by Rameshchandra Sirkar, http://www.cscsarchive.org/dataarchive/otherfiles/TA001003/file.
45. Cited in Samel, 'Mahad Chawadar', *op. cit.*, p. 726.
46. Interestingly, Ambedkar then borrowed from Gandhi the notion of *satyagraha* (lit. 'grasp of truth'), which designated peaceful demonstrations.

47. K. N. Kadam, ed., *Dr. Babasaheb Ambedkar*, *op. cit.*, p. 24.
48. Quoted in G. Poitevin, 'Préface' in S. Kamble and B. Kamble, *Parole de femme intouchable* (Paris: Côté-Femmes, 1991), p. 17.
49. 'Notre Existence', in Kamble and Kamble, *ibid.*, p. 242.
50. Quoted in Keer, *Dr Ambedkar*, *op. cit.*, p. 109.
51. Zelliot, *Dr Ambedkar*, *op. cit.*, p. 196.
52. *Ibid.,* p. 99.
53. On the satyagraha of Nasik, see the memories of D. R. Jhadav, who emphasises the personalisation of the movement—there were bills showing Ambedkar and a temple everywhere in town—and its rather well-managed organisation by Ambedkarites (Jhadav, *Intouchable*, *op. cit.*, pp. 179–80).
54. Quoted in *ibid.*, p. 114.
55. Quoted in *ibid.*, pp. 116–17.
56. *Ambedkar Writings*, *op. cit.*, p. 489. At the same time, he took the case of Brahmins to illustrate the theory according to which 'Caste, to be real can exist only by disintegrating a group. The genius of caste is to divide and to disintegrate' (B. R. Ambedkar, 'The Curse of Caste', in *Ambedkar Writings*, op. cit., p. 211).

## 6. THE AMBEDKARITE MOVEMENT IN BRITAIN

1. Nicolas Jaoul, 'Beyond Ambedkar', *op. cit*. Also see Suraj Yengde, 'Iterations of shared dalit-black solidarity (2021)', www.india-seminar.com/2021/737/737_suraj_yengde.htm.
2. The Ravidassia diaspora are followers of the medieval Guru Ravi Dass, and the Valmiki diaspora followers of Bhagwan Valmiki who wrote the *Ramayana*.
3. V. B. Rawat and N. G. Uke, 'Remembering a True Humanist', *Countercurrents*, 10 November 2006, available at www.countercurrents.org/dalit-uk101106.htm.
4. WhatsApp, Ujjwal Uke to Santosh Dass, 20 January 2022.
5. Paul Ghuman, *British Untouchables*, *op. cit.*, p. 53. Also see Runnymede Trust, 'Oral Histories Commonwealth Immigration Act 1968', available at www.runnymedetrust.org.
6. Steve Taylor, 'Religious Conversion', *op. cit.*, pp. 224–46.
7. D. C. Ahir, *Dr Ambedkar and Punjab* (New Delhi: B. R. Publishing Corporation, 2103), p. 9.
8. *Ibid*.
9. Ramesh Chander, 'Oral History—Ambedkar's Visit to Jalandhar in 1951', 17 November 2012, http://diplomatictitbits.blogspot.com/2012/11/oral-history-ambedkars-visit-to.html?m=1.

10. *Ibid.*
11. Kishan Chand Sulekh, interview with Santosh Dass, 26 October 2019, filmed by Arun Kumar.
12. *Ibid.*
13. Ishwar Das Pawar, *My Struggle in Life* (Conneaut Lake: Page Publishing Inc., 2015), p. 110.
14. John Brown, *The Un-melting Pot—An English Town And Its Immigrants* (London and Basingstoke: Macmillan, 1970).
15. K. C. Leal, 'We lost our hero before the battle was won', in *Babasaheb Ambedkar, A Birth Centenary Commemoration Vol II* (London: Ambedkar Centenary Celebrations Committee UK, n.d.), p. 56. Available from fabo@ambedkar.org.uk.
16. Sohan Singh Barpaga, *Vatno Vilayat tak* (Jalandhar: Neelam Publishers, 2014), p. 106. The book's title translates to 'Homeland to UK'. The word 'Vilayat' was often used by the British people in India to describe their British homeland. The book provides a history of the Ravidassia community living in the Sandwell area of Birmingham from 1950 to 2014.
17. Arun Kumar interview with Fakir Chand Chauhan on 20 June 2021, available from fabo@ambedkar.org.uk
18. *Ibid.*
19. Ahir, 'Punjabi Ambedkarites and Buddhism in U.K', in *Dr Ambedkar and Punjab*, *op. cit.*
20. Arun Kumar, correspondence with Krishna Gamre in 2008, available from fabo@ambedkar.org.uk. In the late 1990s, the veteran Ambedkarite Shekhar Bagul moved from London to Manchester. There he worked closely with the Department of History and Economic History, Manchester Metropolitan University (MMU), and in 2001 this culminated in the setting up the Ambedkar Memorial Committee. The Committee, chaired by Dr Gervase Phillips, Head of History at MMU, organised an annual Ambedkar Memorial Lecture in memory of Ambedkar. Dr Annapurna Waughray at MMU was closely associated with this. This fizzled out after Shekhar Bagul died on 21 December 2010—see 'A great loss to Babasaheb Ambedkar's Mission: The sudden passing away of Babasevak Shekhar Bagul', *Ambedkarite Times*, available at www.ambedkaritetime.com/buddha.htm.
21. A Buddhist temple/monastery.
22. N. C. Kaul, *True Story of theVihara*, N. C. Kaul & Ambedkar International Mission, 27 April 1996.
23. 'Register of Charities', Charity Commission (searched 12 Jan. 2022), https://register-of-charities.charitycommission.gov.uk/charity-search/-/charity-details/275170/trustees.

24. *Ibid.*
25. Arun Kumar, *Ambedkarite Movement in the Western Hemisphere*, Dr Ambedkar 2nd International Convention, 2011, Kuala Lumpur, Malaysia, p. 16.
26. Arun Kumar, interview with Fakir Chand Chauhan on 20 June 2021.
27. Bishan Dass Bains, *Pride v Prejudice* (self-published 2015) ISBN 978-0-9575238.
28. Email, Balram Sampla to Santosh Dass, 22 December 2021.
29. Kumar, *Ambedkarite Movement*, *op. cit.*
30. Arun Kumar, interview with S. L. Ginda on 2 August 2021.
31. Bodhisattva Ambedkar Public Senior Secondary School, available at http://www.bapsss.org/.
32. *A Birth Centenary Commemoration*, *op. cit*.
33. DAMC GB website, www.drambedkar.org.uk/about-us (searched 20 Jan. 2022).
34. Sue Donnelly, 'No More Worlds Here for Him to Conquer', *Ambedkar at LSE: LSE History*, available at https://blogs.lse.ac.uk/lsehistory/2016/01/29/no-more-worlds-here-for-him-to-conquer-br-ambedkar-at-lse/ (search 27 Jul. 2022).
35. 'Gray's Inn in London unveils the Ambedkar Room and a new portrait', *Global Indian Stories*, www.globalindianstories.com.
36. Ahir, *Dr Ambedkar and Punjab*, *op. cit.*, p. 129.
37. A History of Punjab Buddhist Society UK, available at www.dokumen.tip/documents/a-history-of-punjab-buddhist-society.uk.html.
38. *Ibid.*
39. DAMC GB website, www.drambedkar. org.uk/about-us (searched 20 Jan. 2022).
40. *Ibid.*
41. DAMC GB website, www.drambedkar.org.uk/about-us (searched 20 Jan. 2022).
42. https://www.ambedkartimes.com/arun_kumar.htm.
43. 'Dr Ambedkar Memorial Public School, Soond', https://schools.org.in/nawanshahr/03060309104/dr-ambedkar-memorial-public-school-soond.html.
44. Guru Ravidass, or Raidas, was a medieval Indian mystic poet-saint of the Bhakti movement who opposed caste discrimination and stood for equality.
45. Arun Kumar, *Ambedkar Movement in Bedford* (Bedford: Ambedkar Mission Society, Bedford, 11 May 2014).
46. *Ibid.*

47. *Ibid*.
48. Liz Brown, 'Religion like Branches on a Tree', *The Bedfordshire Times*, 1976.
49. 'Bhagwan Das-a True Ambedkarite', 2011, available at https://bhagwandasatrueambedkarite.blogspot.com http://bhagwandasatrueambedkarite.blogspot.com/2011/.
50. Kumar, *Ambedkar Movement*, *op. cit*.
51. Arun Kumar, 'The History Of Ambedkarite Movement in United Kingdom', *Countercurrents*, 3 December 2016, available at www.countercurrents.org.
52. Arun Kumar, information given by C. Gautam on 27 January 2022.
53. https//www.charitychoice.co.uk/the.dr-b-r-ambedkarmemorial-trust-161029.
54. Vidya Bhushan Rawat, 'In Conversation with Mr Harbans Virdee', *The Asian Independent*, 4 August 2020.
55. *Ibid*.
56. WhatsApp, Harbans Virdee to Santosh Dass, 17 February 2022.
57. *Asian Voice*, 'Glowing Tributes to Dr Babasaheb Ambedkar', 22 April 2000, p. 18. Also see 'Opening Ceremony', *Ealing Times*, 20 April 2000, p. 1.
58. BAMCEF is the 'All-India Backward and Minority Communities Employees Federation'.
59. Per J. Anderson, *The Amazing Story of the Man Who Cycled from India to Europe for Love* (London: Oneworld Publications, 2017).
60. Ambedkar Buddhist Council souvenir published in 1985.
61. A pamphlet published in Punjabi, and YouTube interview in Punjabi with Fakir Chand Chauhan, https://www.youtube.com/watch?v=MrZcByJz1CI.
62. 'Bahujan' is a Pali term frequently found in Buddhist texts and refers to 'the many' or 'the majority'.
63. Arun Kumar's interview with Fakir Chand Chauhan on 27 January 2022.
64. First of the ten Sikh Gurus.
65. A major festival often referred to as the 'Hindu festival of light'. Sikhs celebrate Bandi Chhorh Divas (Prisoner Release Day) that happens to fall around the same time of the year as Diwali. It is a celebration of the release of the sixth Sikh Guru, Hargobind Sahib, from Gwalior prison in India along with fifty-two Indian princes in 1619.
66. Also pronounced Baisakhi, this is an annual festival to celebrate the solar New Year. In Punjab, it marks the harvest festival, and for Sikhs it

marks the birth of the Khalsa (founding of the faith of Sikhism) order by Guru Gobind Singh, the tenth Guru of Sikhism, in 1699.

67. 'Birth Centenary Celebration of Dr B. R. Ambedkar', *Asian Times*, 21 April 1992, p. 8.
68. *Ibid.*
69. 'Commemoration of Dr Ambedkar celebrates', *The Daily Awaz International*, 22 April 1994, p. 6.
70. 'Ambedkar birth anniversary commemorated', *India Weekly*, 22 April 1994.
71. *Columbia University Record*—3 November 1995, Vol. 21.
72. *Ambedkarite Times*, https//www.ambedkartimes.com/arun_kumar/htm.
73. 'Ambedkar's birth anniversary celebrated at new memorial in UK', *Deccan Chronicle*, 14 April 2016.
74. 'Dr Ambedkar's relevance today and in the future', available at blogs.lse.ac.uk/inequalityandpoverty/files/2014/03/Agenda-and-speakers.pdf.
75. *Ibid.*
76. 'Dr. Bhimrao Ambedkar (1881–1956)' booklet (2021) prepared by FABO UK for the unveiling of the portrait at Gray's Inn and for the Ambedkar Room, Gray's Inn.
77. *Gray News*, 37 (Autumn 2021), pp. 9, 29.
78. Graysinn.org.uk/news/ambedkar-room-and-portrait.
79. *Ambedkar Centenary Celebrations Committee UK* (1989), publication by the ACCC UK, available from fabo@ambedkar.org.uk.
80. 'Legacy of Babasaheb Ambedkar: Some Memorable Moments', *Ambedkar Birth Centenary Souvenir*, Vol. III (London: Ambedkar Centenary Celebrations Committee UK, 1991), p. 96.
81. *Ambedkar Centenary Celebrations Committee UK*, *op. cit*.
82. *Dr Ambedkar Birth Centenary Souvenir*, Vol. III, p. 11.
83. 'A symbol of revolt', *Bedfordshire on Sunday*, p. 13.
84. Arun Kumar interview with Harbans Virdee on 12 June 2021.
85. C. Gautam, *Dr Ambedkar Birth Centenary Souvenir*, Vol. IV (London: Ambedkar Centenary Celebrations Committee UK, 1992), p. 113.
86. *A New Era, An International Quarterly Journal*, April 1993, p.14.
87. G. S. Thind, *Our Indian Sub-Continent Heritage, from prior to 3200 B.C. to our time* (Burnaby: G. S. Thind, 2000), pp. 367–9.
88. Dr V. Annamalai, 'Why making a film on Dr Ambedkar denied by Indian Government', *Babasaheb Ambedkar, A Birth Centenary Commemoration*, Vol. II (1989), pp. 142–3.
89. *Ibid.*

90. YouTube, 'Synd 7 June 1978 Indian Prime Minister Desai Visits Southall', available at https://www.youtube.com/watch?v=UgrhvcE14Pw.
91. 'India arrests activist Anand Teltumbde over 2018 caste violence', *Al Jazeera*, 14 April 2020.
92. *Dr Ambedkar Birth Centenary Souvenir*, Vol IV, p. 75.
93. Arun Kumar, telephone interview with Balram Sampla on 19 September 2021.
94. Vivek Kumar, 'Dalit Diaspora Joins The Fight', *Indian Express*, 24 May 2003.
95. *Ibid.*
96. Chetna Association of Canada, www.chetna.ca.
97. The University of British Columbia, Vancouver Campus, 'Annual Dr B. R. Ambedkar Memorial Lecture', available at https://cisar.iar.ubc.ca/events/ambedkar-lecture/ (sourced 9 Feb. 2022).
98. Santosh Dass, Keynote Speech, Equality Day, Council House, Coventry, 14 April 2014.
99. 'Call to declare Ambedkar birthday as an International Day of Equality', *The Asian Independent*, 22 April 2022.
100. 'B. C. Government proclaims April 14 as Dr B. R. Ambedkar Day of Equality', *Voiceonline*, 7 April 2021, https://voiceonline.com/burnaby-proclaims-april-14-as-dr-b-r-ambedkar-day-of-equality/.
101. WhatsApp, Pratap Tambe to Santosh Dass, 2 January 2022.
102. *Ibid.*
103. https://www.historyextra.com/period/20th-century/my-history-hero-bhimrao-ambedkar-1891-1956/.

## 7. THE AMBEDKAR MUSEUM, LONDON

1. Press Release ACCC UK, C. Chahal, 6 December 1991.
2. *Ambedkar Times,* 4, 5, 18 July 2012, available at https://www.ambedkartimes.com/Ambedkar%20Times%20(July%202012).pdf.
3. Email, Harbans Virdee to Santosh Dass and many others, 29 August 2014.
4. For more information about Rajkumar Kamble, read Vinay Shende, *Tribute to Raju Kamble*, *Round Table India*, 25 August 2018, https://www.roundtableindia.co.in/tribute-to-raju-kamble/.
5. Letter from Dr Nitin Raut to Hon. Shri Prithviraj Chavan, Chief Minister, Maharashtra, 3 September 2014.
6. *Ibid.*

7. WhatsApp, K. Katke to Santosh Dass, 23 November 2021.
8. Dean Nelson, 'India to buy £4m London student home of independence hero', *Daily Telegraph*, 11 September 2014; Shubhangi Khapre, 'Maharashtra wants to buy Ambedkar's London home', *Indian Express*, 11 September 2014.
9. *Ibid.*
10. WhatsApp, R. Katke to Santosh Dass, 23 November 2021.
11. 'Politics over Ambedkar Memorial Its Nagpur v London', *The Times of India*, 21 September 2014.
12. WhatsApp, Gaikwad to Ambedkar Project Group, 23 September 2014.
13. Email, Santosh Dass to Prime Minister Modi, 23 September 2014.
14. Ramdas Athawale, Letter to Rt Hon. Prime Minister, New Delhi, 30 September 2014.
15. Email, Santosh Dass to High Commissioner, 7 October 2014.
16. 'Ambedkar House in London back on market as Indian Government sleeps', *Mumbai Mirror*, 9 January 2015.
17. 'BJP willing to buy B. R. Ambedkar's house', *Indian Express*, 12 January 2015.
18. Email, Santosh Dass to Raj Kumar Badole and CM GOM, 14 January 2015.
19. Letter, Rajkumar Badole, Minister for Social Justice and Special Assistance, to The High Commissioner, IHC, London, 22 January 2015.
20. 'Maharashtra Government gives nod to Ambedkar memorial in London', *Economic Times*, 25 January 2015; 'Maharashtra govt dispatches letter of intent to buy Ambedkar house in London', *Hindustan Times*, 28 January 2015.
21. Email, Simon Ross, Seddons, to Santosh Dass, 4 February 2015.
22. WhatsApp, Gaikwad to Ambedkar Project group, 9 February 2015.
23. V. B. Rawat and N. G. Uke, 'N. G. Uke: Remembering A True Humanist', *Countercurrents*, 10 November 2006. 1946 Photo at Ambedkar House.
24. WhatsApp, Ujjwal Uke to Santosh Dass, 20 January 2022.
25. Rawat and Uke, 'N. G. Uke', *op. cit*.
26. 'Dr Ambedkar Memorial Centre, 10 King Henry's Road, London, Ambedkar Foundation UK. Prepared by Santosh Dass MBE, President, FABO UK. 23 October 2014'.
27. 'Contract exchange in 2 days to buy Ambedkar's London house: Govt', *Deccan Chronicle*, 24 August 2015.
28. 'PM Modi, Fadnavis inaugurates Ambedkar's memorial in London', *Indian Express*, 15 November 2015.

29. Santosh Dass, 'An Open Letter To Narendra Modi, Prime Minister of India: Ambedkar Museum, London', *Countercurrents*, 14 November 2015, https://www.countercurrents.org/dass141115.htm.
30. Email, Santosh Dass to D. Fadnavis, CM Maharashtra, 23 June 2016.
31. 'Panel formed for Dr Ambedkar memorial in London', *Hindustan Times*, 2 February 2017.
32. Email, Sunil Kumar to the Dr Babasaheb Ambedkar International Memorial Advisory Committee, 22 March 2017.
33. Ernie Rea, 'Beyond Belief, Ambedkar', *BBC Radio 4*, 14 August 2017.
34. 'Ambedkar House: India's £3m property row with two London residents', *BBC News*, 27 August 2019, https://www.bbc.co.uk/news/world-asia-india-49411985.amp.
35. Land Registry, 'Average Mean House Prices by Borough, Ward, MSOA & LSOA', https://data.london.gov.uk/dataset/average-house-prices.
36. Camden Strategic Housing Market Assessment, Camden Council, 2016.
37. The New London Plan, GLA, 2021.
38. 'Report to the Secretary of State for Housing, Communities and Local Government by Mr K. L. Williams BA, MA, MRTPI, an Inspector appointed by the Secretary of State Date: 4 December 2019', para. 1, p. 2.
39. 'Planning Applications: called in decisions and recovered appeals', available at https://www.gov.uk/government/collections/planning-applications-called-in-decisions-and-recovered-appeals (searched 28 Jan. 2022).
40. 'Equality considerations', para. 33, page 8 of *Report to the Secretary of State*, *op. cit.*.
41. 'Report to the Secretary of State', *op. cit.*, p. 16.
42. 'Recovered appeal: land at 10 King Henry's Road, London, NW3 3RP (ref: 3219239 - 12 March 2020)', available at https://www.gov.uk/government/publications/recovered-appeal-land-at-10-king-henrys-road-london-nw3-3rp-ref-3219239-12-march-2020.

## 8. THE CAMPAIGN TO OUTLAW CASTE DISCRIMINATION IN BRITAIN

1. B. R. Ambedkar, *Annihilation of Caste, The Annotated Critical Edition* (New Delhi: Navayana, 2014), p. 257, para. 11.4.
2. 'California's Legal Ground Battling Caste Discrimination Takes Centre Stage in Historic Cisco Caste', *The Wire,* 10 March

2021, available at https://thewire.in/caste/cisco-case-caste-discrimination-silicon-valley-ambedkar-organisations.

3. Sriram Lakshman, 'California University Board unanimously votes to recognise protection from caste discrimination', *The Hindu*, 26 January 2022.
4. 'Google cancelled a talk on caste bias by Thenmozhi Soundararajan after some employees revolted', *The Washington Post*, 2 June 2022.
5. 'India', vol. 80, column 408, *Hansard*, House of Lords, 18 March 1931, available at www.hansard.parliament.uk/Lords/1931-03-18/debates/.
6. 'Indian Constitutional Reform', vol. 276, column 942, *Hansard*, House of Commons, 28 March 1933, available at www.hansard.parliament.uk/Commons/1933-03-28/debates.
7. Anthony Lester, *Five Ideas to Fight For—How Our Freedom Is Under Threat and Why It Matters* (London: Oneworld Publications, 2016), p. 92. Lester singled out the ACDA's campaign to include caste as a protected characteristic in the Equality Act.
8. 'Dr B. R. Ambedkar's speech in the Constituent Assembly, 25 November 1949, presenting the Indian Draft Constitution for approval', p. 122, available at http://mls.org.in/books/HB-2667%20CPA%20Speaches%20(Eng).pdf (searched 22 Jan. 2022).
9. *Caste Legislation introduction—programme and timetable*, 29 July 2013, available at https://assets.publishing.service.gov.uk/government/uploads/system/uploads/attachment_data/file/225658/130726-Caste-Discrimination.pdf.
10. S. Anand, 'Bhagwan Das: An Untouchable's Life in Politics—A Rare memoir centered around Ambedkar', *The Caravan*, 1 January 2010, available at https://caravanmagazine.in/caste/untouchables-life-politics.
11. Bhagwan Das, *Thus Spoke Ambedkar* (Jallandhar: Bheem Patrika Publications, 1968), pp. 6–7.
12. John Carey, ed., 'George Orwell', *Essays* (New York: Everyman, 1998), p. 613.
13. Ramesh Kallidai, Hindu Forum of Britain, *Caste in the UK*, 2008, p. 4, available at www.hfb.org.uk (searched 29 Jan. 2022).
14. Suraj Yengde, *Caste Matters* (London: Penguin, 2019), p. 1.
15. Isabel Wilkerson, *Caste—The Lies That Divide* (London: Allen Lane, 2020), p. 17.
16. B. R. Ambedkar, *Annihilation of Caste, The Annotated Critical Edition*, *op. cit*.

17. Pt Satish Sharma, *Caste, Conversion and a Thoroughly Colonial Conspiracy*, National Council of Hindu Temples UK (NCHT), 2017. This report is available in *Caste, Conversion A Colonial Conspiracy: What Every Hindu and Christian must know about Caste* (BBDS Publishing, 2021).
18. Dr Alexander Goldenweiser, *Castes in India: Their Mechanism, Genesis and Development*, 9 May 1916.
19. Register of Charities with the UK's Charity Commission, can be found at https://register-of-charities.charitycommission.gov.uk/charity-search (searched 26 Jan. 2022).
20. 'Matrimonialsindia', available at www.matrimonialsindia.com/nri/uk-matrimony.htm.
21. Liz Brown, 'Religion like Branches', *op. cit*.
22. Maurice Weaver, 'I thought I would escape the name…but it has followed me like a dark cloud', *Daily Telegraph*, 11 October 1990, p. 25.
23. 'Dalit Solidary Network—Who We Are', https://dsnuk.org/what-we-do/about-us/.
24. 'What We Do', Voice of Dalit International, available at https://vodintl.org.uk/internationally/ (searched 26 Jan. 2022).
25. *Ibid.*
26. 'Caste Divide in Britain', *BBC Radio 4*, April and May 2003. Transcript available at castewatchUK.org/resources.htm.
27. 'Caste Watch UK Conference on 15th July in Birmingham', *Ambedkar Times*, 6 July 2007.
28. Jasvinder Sanghera, *Shame* (London: Hodder and Stoughton, 2007), p. 52.
29. 'Play examining the caste system among British Asians to be staged in Birmingham', *Birmingham Live*, 11 December 2007 (revised 12 October 2012), available at https://www.birminghammail.co.uk/news/local-news/play-examining-the-caste-system-among-47579.
30. Legislative Scrutiny, *Equality Bill—Human Rights Joint Committee Contents*, Part 2, para 6, available at https://publications.parliament.uk/pa/jt200809/jtselect/jtrights/169/169we07.htm (searched 27 Jan. 2022).
31. Gina Borbas, Rev. David Haslam, and Balram Sampla, eds, *No Escape—Caste Discrimination in the UK* (2006), Dalit Solidarity Network, research by Savio Lourdu Mahimaidass and analysis by Dr Nidhi Sadana, available at www.dalits.nil/pdd/noescape.pdf.
32. International Dalit Solidarity Network, *Ambedkar Principles* (2006).
33. Hindu Forum, *Caste in the UK* (2008), available at https://www.academia.edu/Caste_in_the_UK.

34. Chanan Chahal, *Evils of Caste* (London: Federation of Ambedkarite and Buddhist Organisations UK, in association with the Dalit Solidarity Network UK, 2009).
35. 'Dr Prakash Shah debates the clause on caste discrimination in the Equality Act 2010', *Queen Mary University London*, 26 January 2016, available at https://www.qmul.ac.uk/law/news/2016/items/dr-prakash-shah-debates-the-clause-on-caste-discrimination-in-the-equality-act-2010.html (accessed 27 Jul. 2022).
36. Membership of the APPG can be found on https://www.parliament.uk/mps-lords-and-offices/standards-and-financial-interests/parliamentary-commissioner-for-standards/registers-of-interests/register-of-all-party-party-parliamentary-groups/ (last published 2021).
37. Ken Hunt, 'A conversation about social reform, equality, caste and absurdity with Lord Eric Avebury', 19 May 2013.
38. HM Government, The Equality Bill—Government Response to the Consultation, Cm 7454, July 2008, pp. 183–4.
39. https://publications.parliament.uk/pa/cm200809/cmpublic/cmpbequality.htm.
40. 'Public Bill Committee', column 178, *Hansard*, House of Commons, 11 June 2009, available at https://publications.parliament.uk/pa/cm200809/cmpublic/equality/090611/pm/90611s06.htm.
41. 'Session 2008–09 Publications on the Internet General Committee Debates', column 179, *Hansard*, 11 June 2009.
42. *Ibid.*
43. William Gould, 'The U. P. Congress and "Hindu Unity": Untouchables and the minority question in the 1930s', *Modern Asian Studies*, 39, 4 (2005), pp. 845–60.
44. Sam Jones, 'Asian caste discrimination rife in UK, says report', *The Guardian*, 11 November 2011, https://www.theguardian.com/society/2009/nov/11/caste-discrimination-uk-report.
45. Annapurna Waughray, *Capturing Caste in Law: The Legal Regulation of Caste and Caste-Based Discrimination* (London: Routledge, 2022), p. 225.
46. *Ibid.*
47. 'Equality Bill debate', *Hansard*, House of Lords, 11 January 2010, available at https://hansard.parliament.uk/Lords/2010-01-11/debates/10011130000341/EqualityBill.
48. *Equality Act 2010*, Explanatory Notes, Section 9, paragraphs 49 and 50, available at https://www.legislation.gov.uk.

49. Hilary Metcalf, *Caste discrimination and harassment in Great Britain* (London: National Institute of Economic and Social Research, December 2010).
50. Sam Jones, 'Employment tribunal hearing first claim for caste discrimination collapses', *The Guardian*, 14 February 2013.
51. *Naveed v Aslam and others*, Practical Law, ET/1603968/2011.
52. The DSN and IDSN's Shadow Report to UN CERD's 79 session is available at https://tbinternet.ohchr.org/Treaties/CERD/Shared%20Documents/GBR/INT_CERD_NGO_GBR_79_8868_E.pdf (searched 27 Jan. 2022).
53. The ACDA's joint shadow submission to UN CERD's 79 Session is available at https://tbinternet.ohchr.org/Treaties/CERD/Shared%20Documents/GBR/INT_CERD_NGO_GBR_79_8854_E.pdf.
54. 'Hindu groups class over anti-caste discrimination law', *Economic Times*, 16 April 2013, https://economictimes.indiatimes.com/nri/nris-in-news/hindu-groups-clash-over-anti-caste-discrimination-law/articleshow/19562947.cms?from=mdr.
55. 'New education package to help stamp out caste discrimination in communities', Department for Digital, Culture, Media & Sport, 4 March 2013, available at https://www.gov.uk/government/news/new-education-package-to-help-stamp-out-caste-discrimination-in-communities.
56. Kaka Kalelkar, *Backward Classes. Commission, Report* (30 March 1955).
57. 'Enterprise and Regulatory Reform Bill', Motion C, columns 1298–1320 Division Motion C, *Hansard*, House of Lords, 22 April 2013, available at https://publications.parliament.uk/pa/ld201213/ldhansrd/text/130422-0003.htm.
58. Alliance of Hindu Organisations press release can be found on www.hinducounciluk.org (searched 27 Jan. 2022).
59. 'Caste discrimination legislation timetable', 29 July 2013, https://www.gov.uk/government/publications/caste-discrimination-legislation-timetable.
60. 'Statement by UN High Commissioner for Human Rights Navi Pillay at the meeting on caste-based discrimination in the UK organised by the ACDA, House of Lords, London, 6 November 2013', UN Human Rights Office of the High Commissioner, available at https://newsarchive.ohchr.org/EN/NewsEvents/Pages/DisplayNews.aspx?NewsID=13973&LangID=E.
61. Prakash Shah, 'What lies behind the inclusion of caste in the UK Equality Act', London School of Economics Blogs, 11 October 2016, available at http://eprints.lse.ac.uk/76462/.

62. Marie Woolf, 'Cameron blocks ban on caste bias', *The Sunday Times*, 21 December 2014.
63. 'Why has this Labour candidate been the target of a "deeply divisive leaflet" which backs her Tory opponent?' Labour List, 5 May 2015, available at https://labourlist.org/2015/05/why-has-this-labour-candidate-been-the-target-of-a-deeply-divisive-leaflet-which-backs-her-tory-opponent/.
64. 'Statement made by Penny Mordaunt MP, Minister for Women and Equalities', *Government Response to Caste Consultation*, 23 July 2018, Statement UIN HCWS898.
65. 'Caste in Great Britain and equality law: a public consultation—Consultation analysis report for the Government Equalities Office', July 2018, p. 31, available at https://assets.publishing.service.gov.uk/government/uploads/system/uploads/attachment_data/file/727791/Caste_in_Great_Britain_and_equality_law_-_analysis_report.pdf.
66. 'Caste consultation: our response to the government statement', EHRC, 23 July 2018.
67. *Ms A Agarwal and Mr R Meshram v Tata Consultancy Services Ltd and Mr G Krishnaswami: 2202616/2018 and 2205035/2018*, HM Courts & Tribunals Service and Employment Tribunal, 29 October 2018, available at https://www.gov.uk/employment-tribunal-decisions/ms-a-agarwal-v-tate-consultancy-services-ltd-and-mr-g-krishnaswami-2202616-2018.
68. 'UK human rights body wants to revive caste law', *Hindustan Times*, 29 June 2019.
69. *Report to the Secretary of State*, *op. cit.*, p. 8.
70. ACDA correspondence with NHS Trust, January and February 2020.
71. S. Ramanathan, 'Calling Dalits Harijan SC Calls Term Abusive'. *The News Minute*, 27 March 2017, https://www.thenewsminute.com/article/stop-calling-dalits-harijan-sc-calls-term-abusive-we-remain-ignorant-and-insensitive-59315.
72. See 'Twitter, Rules and Policies, Hateful Conduct', available at https://help.twitter.com/en/rules-and-policies/hateful-conduct-policy (searched 28 Jan. 2022); see also YouTube, 'Hate speech policy' available at https://support.google.com/youtube/answer/2801939?hl=en-GB (searched 28 Jan. 2022); Facebook, 'Hate speech', available at https://transparency.fb.com/de-de/policies/community-standards/hate-speech/ (searched 28 Jan. 2022).
73. *Constitution of India*, article 15(1) [general prohibition against discrimination], *Constitution of the Kingdom of Nepal* (1990), article

11(2) and (3), *Constitution of the Islamic Republic of Pakistan*, articles 22(3) [concerning admission to any educational institution receiving aid from public revenues], 26(1) [concerning access to places of public entertainment or resort not intended for religious purposes only] and 27(1) [concerning appointment to public service]. See also article 38 [providing for an affirmative duty on the part of the State to secure the well-being of the people and to provide the basic necessities of life irrespective of, inter alia, Caste]. *Constitution of the People's Republic of Bangladesh*, articles 28(1) [general prohibition of discrimination by the State], 28(3) [concerning access to places of public entertainment or resort, and admission to educational institutions] and 29(2) [concerning appointment to public service]. *Constitution of Sri Lanka* (1978), articles 11(2)(a) [general non-discrimination provision], 11(3) [concerning access to shops, public restaurants, hotels, places of public entertainment and places of public worship] and 27(1) [non-discrimination in the context of derogations in times of public emergency].

74. *Constitution du Burkina Faso* (Loi No. 002/97/ADP du 27 janvier 1997), Article premier: '… Les discriminations de toutes sortes, notamment celles fondées sur la race, l'ethnie, la région, la couleur, le sexe, la langue, la religion, la Caste, les opinions politiques, la fortune et la naissance, sont prohibées.'
75. Annie Correal, 'Hindu Sect Known as BAPS is Accused of Using Forced Labor to Build New Jersey Temple', *The New York Times*, 11 May 2021.

## 9. AMBEDKAR IN LONDON AND THE AFRICAN-AMERICAN COMMUNITY

1. Kevin Brown, 'The Essence of African-American Culture is the Resistance to our Oppression', in Vidya Bhushan Rawat, *Contesting Marginalizations: Conversations on Ambedkarism and Social Justice*, Vol. 1 (Delhi: People Literature Publications, 2017), pp. 263–4.
2. B. R. Ambedkar, *The Buddha and His Dhamma* (New Delhi: Kalpaz Publications, 2017), p. 5; Eleanor Zelliot, *From Untouchable to Dalit*, *op. cit.*, pp. 207–8; see also Gail Omvedt, *Buddhism in India: Challenging Brahmanism and Caste* (Delhi: Sage, 2003), pp. 2–3.
3. There are many writings drawing comparisons between African-Americans and Dalits. See Gyanendra Pandey, *A History of Prejudice: Race, Caste and Differences in India and the United States* (Cambridge: Cambridge University Press, 2013); Mohan Dass Namishray, *Caste*

*and Race: Comparative Study of B. R. Ambedkar and Martin Luther King* (Delhi: Rawat Publications, 2003); Arvind Sharma, *Reservation and Affirmative Action: Models of Social Integration in India and the United States* (New Delhi: Sage, 2005); Laura Dudley Jenkins, 'Race, Caste and Justice: Social Science Categories and Anti-discrimination Policies in India and the United States', *Connecticut Law Review*, 36, 747 (2004); Cunningham, Clark D., 'After *Grutter* Things Get Interesting! The American Debate Over Affirmative Action Is Finally Ready for Some Fresh Ideas from Abroad', *Connecticut Law Review*, 36, 665 (2004); Smita Narula, 'Equal by Law, Unequal by Caste: The Untouchable Condition in Critical Race Perspective', Wisconsin International Law Journal, 26, 2 (2008); Kevin Brown and Vinay Sitapati, 'Lessons Learned from Comparing the Application of Constitutional and Federal Discrimination Laws to Higher Education Opportunities of African-Americans in the U.S. with Dalits in India', *Harvard Blackletter Law Journal*, 24, 3 (2008).

4. Daniel Immerwahr, 'Caste or Colony? Indianizing Race in the United States', *Modern Intellectual History*, 4, 2 (2007), pp. 275–301.
5. See, for example, Jonneke Koomen, 'International Relations/Black Internationalism: Reimagining Teaching and Learning about Global Politics', *International Studies Perspectives,* 20, 4 (November 2019), pp. 390–411.
6. Robin D. G. Kelley and Earl Lewis, *To Make Our World Anew: A History of African Americans* (New York: Oxford University Press, 2000), p. 380.
7. Nico Slate, *Color Cosmopolitanism: The Shared Struggle for Freedom in the United States and India* (Cambridge, MA: Harvard University Press, 2012).
8. Gerald Horne, *The End of Empires: African Americans and India* (Philadelphia: Temple University Press, 2008), p. 119.
9. Horne, *End of Empires*, *op. cit.*, p. 90.
10. J. Morgan Kousser, 'The Supremacy of Equal Rights: The Struggle Against Racial Discrimination in Antebellum Massachusetts and the Foundations of the Fourteenth Amendment', *Northwestern University Law Review*, 82, 4 (1988), p. 941, pp. 953–55.
11. Immerwahr, 'Caste of Colony', *op cit.*, pp. 275–7.
12. *Roberts v Boston*, 59 Mass. 198 (1849).
13. Brief of Charles Sumner in *Roberts v Boston* is available at file:///H:/INDIA.JOU/Comparison%20Book/Caste%20based%20analogy/Brief%20of%20Sumner%20in%20Roberts%20v%20Boston.pdf and https://www.blackpast.org/african-american-history/1849-

charles-sumner-equality-law-unconstitutionality-separate-colored-schools-massachusetts-2/.

14. *Ibid.*, pp. 16–21.
15. Gunnar Myrdal, *The American Dilemma* (New York: International Publishers, 1944), p. 667.
16. *Ibid.*
17. *Ibid.*
18. For a discussion of the use of the caste analogy during Congressional debates for the Civil Rights Act of 1866 and the Fourteenth Amendment, see Kevin Brown, Lalit Khandare, Annapurna Waughray and Kenneth Dau-Schmidt, 'Does U.S. Federal Employment Law Now Cover Caste Discrimination Based on Untouchability?: If All Else Fails There is the Possible Application of Bostock v Clayton County', *New York Review of Law and Social Change*, 46 (2022).
19. 163 US 537 (1896).
20. Brief of Albion Tourgee and James C. Walker filed in *Plessy v Ferguson*, 11, 14, and 36, available at 1893 WL 10660.
21. *Plessy v Ferguson* 163 US 537, 559 (Harlan J., Dissenting).
22. Elliott M. Rudwick, 'The Niagara Movement', *The Journal of Negro History*, 42 (July 1957), p. 177.
23. For the eight-point program see Rudwick, *op. cit.*, pp. 177, 179. See also George Padmore, *Pan-Africanism or Communism?: The Coming Struggle for Africa* (New York: D. Dobson, 1956), p. 112. For a copy of the text of Du Bois's proposals, see 'Key Documents of the Niagara Movement', available at http://scua.library.umass.edu/digital/dubois/312.2.839-01-15.pdf.
24. Kyle D. Wolf, 'The Niagara Movement of 1905: A Look Back to a Century Ago', *Afro-Americans in New York Life and History*, 32, 2 (2008), pp. 9–20.
25. Michael Tidy and Donald Leeming, *A History of Africa 1880–1914* (London: Hodder and Stoughton, 1980), pp. 110–77.
26. Ruth Gordon, 'Saving Failed States: Sometimes a Neocolonialist Notion', *American University International Law Review*, 12, 6 (1997), pp. 903–36.
27. See Basil Davidson, *Black Man's Burden: Africa and the Curse of the Nation State* (London: James Currey, 1993).
28. Marc Gallichio, *The African American Encounter with Japan and China: Black Internationalism in Asia, 1895–1945* (Chapel Hill: University of North Carolina Press, 2000), p. 11.
29. Slate, *Color Cosmopolitanism*, *op cit.*

30. Robin Kelley, 'Foreword and Introduction', in Davarian L. Baldwin and Minkah Makalani, eds., *The New Negro Renaissance Beyond Harlem* (Minneapolis: University of Minnesota Press, 2013).
31. Major James S. Sisemore, 'The Russo-Japanese War, Lessons not Learned', in Geoffrey Jukes, *The Russo-Japanese War 1904–5* (2002).
32. David Wright, 'The Use of Race and Racial Perceptions Among Asians and Blacks: The Case of the Japanese and African Americans', *Hitotsubashi Journal of Social Studies*, 30 (1998), pp. 135, 139.
33. *Ibid.*
34. Reginal Kearney, *African American Views of the Japanese: Solidarity or Sedition?* (New York: State University of New York Press, 1998); Gallicchio, *African-American Encounter*, *op cit.*, p. 14.
35. See Bill V. Mullen and Cathryn Watson, eds, *W. E. B. Du Bois on Asia: Crossing The World Color Line* (Jackson: University Press of Mississippi, 2005), pp. 33–4; see also W. E. B. Du Bois, 'The Color Line Belts the World', *Colliers Weekly* (20 October 1906), available at http://credo.library.umass.edu/view/pageturn/mums312-b207-i148/#page/1/mode/1up. While the 'problem of the color line' rises to prominence in the forethought of the *Souls of Black Folk* (1903), Du Bois also mentioned the concept in his closing remarks delivered on 25 July 1900 and the First Pan-African Convention held in Westminster Town Hall in London. In doing this, Du Bois is considering the problem of the colour line not as just a national issue, but as an international one. See J. R. Hooker, 'The Pan-African Conference 1900', *Transition* 46 (1974), pp. 20–4. For a copy of Du Bois's remarks, see https://www.blackpast.org/african-american-history/1900-w-e-b-du-bois-nations-world/. Du Bois introduced the concept of the colour line in a lecture at the third annual meeting of the American Negro Academy in 1900 in piece titled 'The Present Outlook for the Dark Races of Mankind', reproduced in *Sundquist* (1996), pp. 47–54.
36. Murali Balaji, 'Globalizing Black History Month: Professor and the Punjabi Lion', *Huffington Post*, 23 February 2015, https://www.huffingtonpost.com/murali-balaji/globalizing-black-history_b_6737948.html. He was also considered a great friend of the Dalits by Dr Ambedkar. See B. R. Ambedkar, 'Which is worse slavery or untouchability?' available at http://drambedkar.co.in/wp-content/uploads/books/category2/1which-is-worse.pdf.
37. Balaji, 'Globalizing BHM', *op. cit.*
38. Sudarshan Kapur, *Raising Up a Prophet: the African American Encounter with Gandhi* (Boston: Beacon Press, 1992), p. 16.
39. *Ibid.*

40. Horne, *op. cit*.
41. Lajpat Rai, *The United States of America: a Hindu's Impression and a Study* (Calcutta: R. Chatterjee, 1916). He thanked all of them in the preface of the book. A copy of the book can be found at https://ia802707.us.archive.org/35/items/unitedstatesofam00lajp/unitedstatesofam00lajp.pdf.
42. Balaji, 'Globalizing BHM', *op. cit*.
43. W. E. B. Du Bois, *Dark Princess* (San Diego: Harcourt Brace, 1928).
44. *The Crusader*, September 1920. *The Crusader* was founded as a black Communist magazine by Cyril Briggs, who had worked for the *Amsterdam News*. *The Crusader* published articles calling for African nationalism and was anti-colonial.
45. Horne, *op. cit*., p. 45 (citing *The Crusader*, August 1921).
46. Naturalization Act, Ch. 3, 1 Stat. 103 (1790).
47. For a discussion of these cases, see Tanyua L. Banks, 'Both Edges of the Margin: Blacks and Asians in Mississippi Masala, Barriers to Coalition Building', *Asian Law Review*, 7, 5 (1998), pp. 19–20.
48. US Supreme Court, *United States v Bhagat Singh Thind*, 261 US 204 (1923).
49. *Ibid*.
50. Cf. Vivek Bald, *Bengali Harlem and the lost histories of South Asian America* (Cambridge, MA: Harvard University Press, 2013), p. 7 (discussing the experiences of Bengali seamen in the USA and how they tended to live in integrated neighbourhoods with Black people, Puerto Ricans, and other minorities).
51. Immigration Commission, US Senate, *Reports of the Immigration Commission* 349 (1911); see also Sanjoy Chakravorty, Devesh Kapur, Nirvikar Singh, *The Other One Percent: Indians in America* (Oxford: Oxford University Press, 2017), p. 7.
52. Horne, *op. cit*., p. 48.
53. Kapur, *Raising up a Prophet*, *op. cit*., p. 28.
54. M. K. Gandhi, 'Message To The American Negro', *The Crisis*, 1 May 1929, available at https://www.mkgandhi.org/letters/unstates/amer_negro.htm. For example, see 'Negro World, Gandhi's Original Plea', 26 September 1931, p. 4.
55. *Ibid*.
56. Dennis C. Dickerson, 'Gandhi's India and Beyond: Black Women's Religious and Secular Internationalism, 1935–1952', *Journal of African American History*, 59 (2019), p. 66.
57. Kapur, *Raising up a Prophet*, *op. cit*., p. 45.

58. W. E. B. Du Bois, 'Postscript 29', *The Crisis* (January 1931). What Ambedkar said was, 'Before the British, we were in a loathsome condition due to our untouchability. Has the British Government done anything to remove it? Before the British, we could not draw water from a village well. Has the British Government secured us the right to the well? Before the British, we could not enter a temple. Can we enter now? Before the British, we were denied entry into the police force. Does the British Government admit us into the force now? Before the British, we were not allowed to serve in the military. Is that career now open to us? To none of these questions can we give an affirmative answer. All the wrongs have remained as open sores and they have not been righted although 150 years of British rule have rolled away.'
59. Malcolm X, *The Autobiography of Malcolm X* (New York: Ballantine Books, 1992), p. 201.
60. *The New York Age*, 4 (26 December 1931).
61. *The New York Age* (9 July 1932), p. 4.
62. Waman Meshram, 'Complete Puna pact explained by Waman Meshram' (BAMCEF), https://www.youtube.com/watch?v=2zSs6AMmwK4.
63. Raja Shekhar Vundru, *Gandhi, Ambedkar and Patel* (New Delhi: Bloomsbury, 2017).
64. 'Ministers Cable London in Behalf of M. K. Gandhi', *Washington Tribune*, 30 September 1932, p. 8.
65. Kapur, *Raising up a Prophet*, *op. cit*.
66. See Campbell Gibson and Kay Jung, *Historical Census Statistics on Population Totals by Race, 1790 to 1990, and by Hispanic Origin, 1970 to 1990, for the United States, Regions, Divisions, and States, at tbl.1* (United States Census Bureau, Working Paper Series No. 56, 2002).
67. *Bureau of the Census, The Social and Economic Status of the Black Population in the United States: An Historical View, 1790–1978: Current Population Reports, Special Studies*, Series P-23, No. 80, 13 tbl.5 (1979).
68. Anand Teltumbde, *Ambedkar in and for the Post-Ambedkar Dalit Movement* (Pune: Susana Prakashan, 1997). Teltumbde is the grandson-in-law of Ambedkar. See Parth MN, 'India Arrests Activist Anand Teltumbde over 2018 Caste Violence', *Al Jazeera*, 14 April 2020, https://www.aljazeera.com/news/2020/04/india-arrests-activist-anand-teltumbde-2018-dalit-event-200414112452191.html.
69. One can purchase such a bumper sticker today from Amazon, https://www.amazon.in/Ambedkar-because-Bumper-Decal-Blue/dp/B06XBVJ2PK (searched 4 Oct. 2021).

# SELECT BIBLIOGRAPHY


*Official Records and Private Papers*

B. R. Ambedkar and R. Srinivasan, 'A scheme of political safeguards for the protection of the Depressed Classes in the future constitution of a self-governing India' (1930), India Office Records and Papers (IOR), 1st Session, Minorities Committee, IOR/Q/RTC/24.

'Autumn Leaves', memoir, Mss Eur F341/147, Oriental and India Office Collections, British Library.

Du Bois proposals, 'Key Documents of the Niagara Movement', available at http://scua.library.umass.edu/digital/dubois/312.2.839-01-15.pdf.

'Journey to England from the USA of British subject Bhimrao, alias Brimvran Ambedkar', 1916, IOR/L/PJ/6/1443, File 2349. India Office Records, British Library.

LSE/Student File/Ambedkar, available at https://www.lse.ac.uk/library/assets/documents/Ambedkars-LSE-student-file.pdf.

LSE/Student file/Vithal Kadham.

*Calendar for the Twentieth Session, 1914–19*15, LSE/Unregistered/27/5/1 LSE.

*Abridged Calendar for Twenty-second Session, 1916–1917*, LSE/Unregistered/27/5/2.

*Calendar for the Twenty-eighth Session*, *1922–1923*, LSE/Unregistered/27/5/2.

'Address to new students, annotated typescript, 9 October 1935', LSE/Beveridge/5/10/26.

*Director's Report 1924–1925*, LSE/Unregistered/27/1/1.

Biographical Notes of P. C. Beddingham, 'Souvenir Released by the Dr Ambedkar Memorial Committee of Great Britain' (13 March 1973). Available from Gray's Inn library.

*Bureau of the Census, The Social and Economic Status of the Black Population in the United States: An Historical View, 1790 1978: Current Population Reports, Special Studies*, Series P-23, No. 80, 13 tbl.5 (1979).

*Calendar of the Council of Legal Education for 1916–17*, Gray's Inn Archive.

*Calendar of the Council of Legal Education for 1922*, Gray's Inn Archive.

Gibson, Campbell and Kay Jung, *Historical Census Statistics on Population Totals by Race, 1790 to 1990, and by Hispanic Origin, 1970 to 1990, for the United States, Regions, Divisions, and States, at tbl.1* (United States Census Bureau, Working Paper Series No. 56, 2002).

FreeBMD. England & Wales, Civil Registration Marriage Index, 1837–1915 [database online], National Archives, Kew.

Metropolitan Borough of Hampstead general rate books 1918–1941, Ward 3, Camden Local Studies and Archives Centre.

Seligman Collection, Box 23, Correspondence Sent 1919–1924, Columbia University Library.

Wills and Probate 1858–1996. Available at https://www.gov.uk/search-will-probate

### *Newspapers and Media*

Bheem *Patrika*.

*Clare Market Review* (London).

*Daily Telegraph* (London).

*The Guardian* (London, but formerly *The Manchester Guardian*).

*Mooknayak* (Bombay).

*The New York Times* (New York).

*The Sunday Times* (London).

*The Times* (London).

*Times of India* (New Delhi).

*Velivada*.

*The Washington Post* (Washington DC).

### *Official Publications*

Membership of the APPG can be found on https://www.parliament.uk/mps-lords-and-offices/standards-and-financial-interests/parliamentary-commissioner-for-standards/registers-of-interests/register-of-all-party-party-parliamentary-groups/ (last published 2021).

Brief of Charles Sumner in *Roberts v Boston*, available at file:///H:/INDIA.JOU/Comparison%20Book/Caste%20based%20analogy/Brief%20of%20Sumner%20in%20Roberts%20v%20Boston.pdf and https://www.blackpast.org/african-american-history/1849-charles-sumner-equality-law-unconstitutionality-separate-colored-schools-massachusetts-2/.

*The Bombay Chronicle*, 18 August 1930, in *Source Material on Dr Ambedkar*, *op. cit.*, p. 40. *Indian Round Table Conference*, 12 November 1930–19 January 1931, Proceedings, Government of India, Calcutta, 1931, p. 440.

Camden Strategic Housing Market Assessment, Camden Council, 2016.

'Caste discrimination legislation timetable', 29 July 2013, https://www.gov.uk/government/publications/caste-discrimination-legislation-timetable.

'Caste in Great Britain and equality law: a public consultation—Consultation analysis report for the Government Equalities Office', July 2018, p. 31, available at https://assets.publishing.service.gov.uk/government/uploads/system/uploads/attachment_data/file/727791/Caste_in_Great_Britain_and_equality_law_-_analysis_report.pdf.

'Caste consultation: our response to the Government statement', EHRC, 23 July 2018.

*Constituent Assembly Debates*, AD Vol VII, available at http://164.100.47.194/loksabha/writereaddata/cadebatefiles/vol7.html

*Caste in Britain: Experts' Seminar and Stakeholders' Workshop*, Equality and Human Rights Commission Research Report no. 92 (2014), Meena Dhanda, David Mosse, Annapurna Waughray, David Keane, Roger Green, Stephen Iafrati and Jessie Kate Mundy.

*Caste in Britain: Socio-legal Review Caste in Britain: Socio-legal Review*, Equality and Human Rights Commission Research report 91 (2014), Meena Dhanda, Annapurna Waughray, David Keane, David Mosse, Roger Green and Stephen Whittle, University of Wolverhampton.

*Dr Babasaheb Ambedkar Writings and Speeches*, Vol. *2* (Bombay: Government of Maharashtra, 1982).

*Equality Act 2010*, Explanatory Notes, Section 9, paragraphs 49 and 50, available at https://www.legislation.gov.uk.

'Evidence before the Southborough Committee on franchise. Examined on 27th January 1919', in *Dr Babasaheb Ambedkar, Writings and Speeches*, Vol. 1 (Bombay: Government of Maharashtra, 1979), pp. 251–3.

In the Court of R. L Yorke Esq, ICS, Additional Sessions Judge, Meerut, In the Case of *King Emperor V P Spratt and Others* (Meerut: Station Press, 1932).

*Hansard*, 'India', vol. 80, column 408, House of Lords, 18 March 1931, available at www.hansard.parliament.uk/Lords/1931-03-18/debates/.

———, 'Indian Constitutional Reform', vol. 276, column 942, House of Commons, 28 March 1933, available at www.hansard.parliament.uk/Commons/1933-03-28/debates.

———, 'Public Bill Committee', column 178, House of Commons, 11 June 2009, available at https://publications.parliament.uk/pa/cm200809/cmpublic/equality/090611/pm/90611s06.htm.

———, 'Session 2008–09 Publications on the Internet General Committee Debates', column 179, 11 June 2009.

———, 'Equality Bill debate', House of Lords, 11 January 2010, available at https://hansard.parliament.uk/Lords/2010-01-11/debates/10011113000341/EqualityBill.

———, 'Enterprise and Regulatory Reform Bill', Motion C, columns 1298–1320 Division Motion C, House of Lords, 22 April 2013, available at https://publications.parliament.uk/pa/ld201213/ldhansrd/text/130422-0003.htm.

HM Government, The Equality Bill—Government Response to the Consultation, Cm 7454, July 2008, pp. 183–4.

Legislative Scrutiny, *Equality Bill—Human Rights Joint Committee Contents*, Part 2, para 6, available at https://publications.parliament.uk/pa/jt200809/jtselect/jtrights/169/169we07.htm (searched 27 Jan. 2022).

London School of Economics and Political Science Register, 1895–1932.

Land Registry, 'Average Mean House Prices by Borough, Ward, MSOA & LSOA', https://data.london.gov.uk/dataset/average-house-prices.

Metropolitan Borough of Hampstead general rate books 1918–1941, Ward 3 (held at Camden Local Studies and Archives Centre).

'New education package to help stamp out caste discrimination in communities', Department for Digital, Culture, Media & Sport, 4 March 2013, available at https://www.gov.uk/government/news/new-education-package-to-help-stamp-out-caste-discrimination-in-communities.

Recovered appeal: land at 10 King Henry's Road, London, NW3 3RP (ref: 3219239—12 March 2020). Decision letter and Inspector's Report for a recovered appeal.

Register of Charities with the UK Charity Commission, available at https://register-of-charities.charitycommission.gov.uk/charity-search.

*Report of the Committee of Indian Students 1921–22: Part 1, Report and Appendices* (London: His Majesty's Stationery Office, 1922).

Report of the Sub-Committee no. III (Minorities) presented at Meeting of the Committee of the Whole Conference held on 16 to 19 January 1931.

'Report to the Secretary of State for Housing, Communities and Local Government by Mr K. L. Williams BA, MA, MRTPI, an Inspector appointed by the Secretary of State Date: 4 December 2019', para. 1, p. 2.

*Royal Commission on Indian Currency and Finance Vol. IV: Minutes of Evidence Taken in India Before the Royal Commission on Indian Currency and Finance* (London: His Majesty's Stationery Office, 1926).

Starte, O. H. B., P. G. Solanki, B. R. Ambedkar, P. R. Chikodi, L. M. Deshpande, L. C. Burfoot, A. V. Thakkar, A. A. Thorat, Rao Saheb J. K. Mehta, and D. A. Janvekar, *Report of the Depressed Classes and Aboriginal Tribes Committee* (Bombay: Bombay Presidency, 1930).

'Statement made by Penny Mordaunt MP, Minister for Women and Equalities', *Government Response to Caste Consultation*, 23 July 2018, Statement UIN HCWS898.

'Statement by UN High Commissioner for Human Rights Navi Pillay at the Meeting on caste-based discrimination in the UK organised by the Anti-Caste Discrimination Alliance, House of Lords, London, 6 November 2013', UN Human Rights Office of the High Commissioner, available at https://newsarchive.ohchr.org/EN/NewsEvents/Pages/DisplayNews.aspx?NewsID=13973&LangID=E.

The New London Plan, GLA, 2021.

*Published books, articles, reports and edited source collections*

Ahir D. C., *Dr Ambedkar and Punjab* (Delhi: B. R. Publishing Corporation, 2013), p. 9.

Ajnat, Surender, *Letters of Ambedkar* (Jalandhar: Bheem Patrika Publications, 1993).

Ambedkar, B. R., *Annihilation of Caste, The Annotated Critical Edition* (New Delhi: Navayana, 2014), p. 257, para 11.4.

———, 'Dr B. R. Ambedkar's speech in the Constituent Assembly, 25th November 1949, presenting the Indian Draft Constitution for approval', available at http://mls.org.in/books/HB-2667%20CPA%20Speaches%20(Eng).pdf (searched 22 Jan. 2022).

———, 'Poisoned bread', pp. 225–7 and p. 233. Transcribed by Changdeo Khairmode and translated by Rameshchandra Sirkar, available at http://www.cscsarchive.org/dataarchive/otherfiles/TA001003/file

———, 'Report on the Constitution of the Government of Bombay Presidency', in Vasant Moon, ed., *Dr Babasaheb Ambedkar: Writings and Speeches*, Vol. 2 (Bombay: Government of Maharashtra, 1982), pp. 338 and 400.

———, *The Buddha and His Dhamma* (New Delhi: Kalpaz Publications, 2017).

———, *The Evolution of Provincial Finance in British India: A Study in the Provincial Decentralisation of Imperial Finance* (London: P. S. King and Son, 1925).

———, *The Problem of the Rupee: Its origin and its solution* (London: P. S. King and Son, 1923).

———, 'Waiting for a Visa', in Vasant Moon, ed., *Dr Babasaheb Ambedkar: Writings and Speeches*, Vol. 12 (Bombay: Education Department, Government of Maharashtra, 1993), pp. 661–91.

Ambedkar Centenary Celebrations Committee UK, Birth Centenary Commemoration Volumes 1–4 (1992). Available from fabo@ambedkar.org.uk

Ambirajan, S., 'Ambedkar's Contribution to Indian Economics', *Economic and Political Weekly*, 34, 46/7 (20–26 November, 1999), pp. 3280–5.

Anand, S., 'Bhagwan Das: An Untouchable's Life in Politics—A Rare memoir centered around Ambedkar', *The Caravan*, 1 January 2010, available at https://caravanmagazine.in/caste/untouchables-life-politics.

Anderson, Per J., *The Amazing Story of the Man Who Cycled from India to Europe for Love* (London: Oneworld Publications, 2017).

Anti Caste Discrimination Alliance, 'A Hidden Apartheid—Voice of the Community' (2009).

Bains, Bishan Dass, *Pride v Prejudice* (self-published 2015) ISBN 978-0-9575238.

Balaji, Murali, 'Globalizing Black History Month: Professor and the Punjabi Lion', *Huffington Post*, 23 February 2015, https://www.huffingtonpost.com/murali-balaji/globalizing-black-history_b_6737948.html.

Bald, Vivek, *Bengali Harlem and the lost histories of South Asian America* (Cambridge, MA: Harvard University Press, 2013), p. 7.

Baldwin, Davarian L., and Makalani Minkah, eds, *The New Negro Renaissance Beyond Harlem* (Minneapolis: University of Minnesota Press, 2013). See Robin Kelley, 'Foreword' and 'Introduction'.

Bannerji, Arun, 'Revisiting the Exchange Standard, 1898–1913: II Operations', *Economic and Political Weekly*, 37, 14 (6–12 April 2002), pp. 1353–62.

Barpaga, Sohan Singh, *Vatno Vilayat tak* (Jalandhar: Neelam Publishers, 2014).

Bayly, Christopher, *Recovering liberties: Indian thought in the age of liberalism and empire* (Cambridge: Cambridge University Press, 2012).

'Caste Divide in Britain', *BBC Radio 4*, April and May 2003. Transcript available at castewatchUK.org/resources.htm.

Bellwinkel-Schempp, Maren, 'Dr Ambedkar in Germany', *Velivada*, available at https://velivada.com/2015/01/18/dr-ambedkar-in-germany/

Bhattacharya, Sabyasachi, ed., *Education and the Disprivileged: Nineteenth and Twentieth Century India* (Delhi: Orient Longman, 2002).

*Birmingham Live*, 'Play examining the caste system among British Asians to be staged in Birmingham', 11 December 2007 (revised 12 October 2012), https://www.birminghammail.co.uk/news/local-news/play-examining-the-caste-system-among-47579

British Sikh Report (2018), pp. 39–40.

Brown, Kevin, 'The Essence of African-American Culture is the Resistance to our Oppression', in Vidya Bhushan Rawat, *Contesting Marginalizations: Conversations on Ambedkarism and Social Justice*, Vol. 1 (Delhi: People Literature Publications, 2017), pp. 263–4.

Brown, Kevin, and Sitapati Vinay, 'Lessons Learned from Comparing the Application of Constitutional and Federal Discrimination Laws to Higher Education Opportunities of African-Americans in the U.S. with Dalits in India', *Harvard Blackletter Law Journal*, 24, 3 (2008).

Brown, Kevin, Lalit Khandare, Annapurna Waughray and Kenneth Dau-Schmidt, 'Does U.S. Federal Employment Law Now Cover Caste Discrimination Based on Untouchability?: If All Else Fails There is the Possible Application of Bostock v Clayton County', *New York Review of Law and Social Change*, 46 (2022).

Brown, John, *The Un-melting Pot—An English Town And Its Immigrants* (London and Basingstoke: Macmillan, 1970).

Brown, Liz, 'Religion like Branches on a Tree', *The Bedfordshire Times*, 1976.

Cabrera, Luis, 'Dalit cosmopolitans: Institutionally developmental global citizenship in struggles against caste discrimination', *Review of International Studies*, 43 (2016), pp. 280–301.

Cannan, Edwin, *A Review of Economic Theory* (London: P. S. King and Son, 1929).

Carey, John, ed., *Orwell: Essays* (London: Everyman's Library, 1998), p. 613.

Cháirez-Garza, Jesús Francisco, 'B. R. Ambedkar, Franz Boas and the Rejection of Racial Theories of Untouchability', *South Asia: Journal of South Asian Studies*, 41, 2 (2018), pp. 281–96.

———, 'B.R. Ambedkar, Partition and the Internationalisation of Untouchability', *South Asia: Journal of South Asian Studies*, 42, 1 (2019), pp. 80–96.

———, 'Moving untouched: B. R. Ambedkar and the racialization of untouchability', *Ethnic and Racial Studies*, 2 (2022), pp. 216–34.

Chakrabarty, Bidyut, 'B. R. Ambedkar and the history of constitutionalizing India', *Contemporary South Asia*, 24, 2 (2016), pp. 133–48.

Chakravorty, Sanjoy, Devesh Kapur and Nirvikar Singh, *The Other One Percent: Indians in America* (Oxford: Oxford University Press, 2017), p. 7.

Chander, Ramesh, 'Oral History—Ambedkar's Visit to Jalandhar in 1951', 17 November 2012, http://diplomatictitbits.blogspot.com/2012/11/oral-history-ambedkars-visit-to.html?m=1.

Chen, Yi and Yi Li, 'Seeking "A Fair Field" for Women in the Legal Profession: Pioneering Women Lawyers from Burma of 1924–1935', *Britain and the World*, 14, 2 (2021).

Chahal, Chanan, *Evils of Caste*, (London: Federation of Ambedkarite and Buddhist Organisations UK, in association with the Dalit Solidarity Network UK, 2009).

Correal, Annie, 'Hindu Sect Known as BAPS is Accused of Using Forced Labor to Build New Jersey Temple', *The New York Times*, 11 May 2021.

Cunningham, Clark D., 'After Grutter Things Get Interesting! The American Debate Over Affirmative Action Is Finally Ready for Some Fresh Ideas from Abroad', *Connecticut Law Review*, 36, 665 (2004).

Dahrendorf, Ralf, *A History of the London School of Economics and Political Science, 1895–1995* (Oxford: Oxford University Press, 1995).

Dalit Solidarity Network, 'No Escape Caste Discrimination in the UK', (2006) Research by Savio Lourdu Mahimaidass and analysis by Dr Nidhi Sadana. Written and edited by Gina Borbas, DSN.

Das, Bhagwan, *Thus Spoke Ambedkar* (Jalandhar: Bheem Patrika Publications, 1968).

Davidson, Basil, *Black Man's Burden: Africa and the Curse of the Nation State* (London: James Currey, 1993).

De, Rohit, *A People's Constitution: The Everyday Life of Law in the Indian Republic* (Princeton: Princeton University Press, 2018)

———, 'Lawyering as Politics: The Legal Practice of Dr Ambedkar, Bar At Law', in Suraj Yengde and Anand Teltumbde, eds, *The Radical in Ambedkar: Critical Reflections* (Gurgaon: Penguin, 2018).

Devasthali, Hemant, 'Portrait of a Scholar and Activist: Ambedkar as a Young Man', *The Beacon*, 30 December 2018.

Devji, Faisal, *The impossible Indian: Gandhi and the temptation of violence* (Cambridge, MA: Harvard University Press, 2012)

Dhanda, Meena, 'Anti-Casteism and Misplaced Nativism: Mapping caste as an aspect of race', *Radical Philosophy*, 192 (July 2015), pp. 33–43.

Dickerson, Dennis C., 'Gandhi's India and Beyond: Black Women's Religious and Secular Internationalism, 1935–52', *Journal of African American History*, 59 (2019), p. 66.

Donnelly, Sue, 'Edwin Cannan (1861–1935)—economist, local councillor and cyclist', 1 April 2015, https://blogs.lse.ac.uk/lsehistory/2015/04/01/edwin-cannan-1861-1935-economist-local-councillor-and-cyclist/.

DuBois, W. E. B., 'The Color Line Belts the World', *Colliers Weekly*, 20 October 1906, available at http://credo.library.umass.edu/view/pageturn/mums312-b207-i148/#page/1/mode/1up.

———, 'Postscript 29', *The Crisis* (January 1931).

Gaikwad, V. B., *Court Cases Argued by Dr Babasaheb Ambedkar* (Thane: Vaibhav Prakashan, 2012).

Gallichhio, Mar, *The African American Encounter with Japan and China: Black Internationalism in Asia, 1895–1945* (Chapel Hill: University of North Carolina Press, 2000), p. 11.

Geetha, V., 'Unpacking a Library: Babasaheb Ambedkar and His World of Books', *The Wire*, 20 October 2017, available at https://thewire.in/caste/unpacking-library-babasaheb-ambedkar-world-books.

Ghuman, Paul, *British Untouchables—A study of Dalit Identity and Education* (London: Routledge, 2016), p. 53.

Gokhale, J, *From Concessions to confrontation* (Columbia, MO: South Asia Books, 1993).

Goldenweiser, Dr Alexander, *Castes in India: Their Mechanism, Genesis and Development*, 9 May 1916.

Ruth Gordon, 'Saving Failed States: Sometimes a Neocolonialist Notion', *American University International Law Review*, 12, 6 (1997), pp. 903–36.

Gore, M. S., *The Social Context of an Ideology: Ambedkar's Political and Social Thought* (New Delhi: Sage, 1993), p. 85.

Gould, William, 'The U. P. Congress and "Hindu Unity": Untouchables and the minority question in the 1930s', *Modern Asian Studies*, 39, 4 (2005), pp. 845–60.

*Gray News*, 37 (Autumn 2021), pp. 9, 29.

Hindu Forum, *Caste in the UK* (2008), available at https://www.academia.edu/Caste_in_the_UK.

Horne, Gerald, *The End of Empires: African Americans and India* (Philadelphia: Temple University Press, 2008), pp. 90, 119.

Hunt, Ken, 'A conversation about social reform, equality, caste and absurdity with Lord Eric Avebury', 19 May 2013.

Immerwahr, Daniel, 'Caste or Colony? Indianizing Race in the United States', *Modern Intellectual History*, 4, 2 (2007), pp. 275–301.

International Dalit Solidarity Network, 'Ambedkar Principles' (2006).

Jaffrelot, Christophe, *Dr Ambedkar and Untouchability: Analysing and Fighting Caste* (London: Hurst, 2005).

Jaoul, Nicolas, 'Beyond Ambedkar: Ambedkarism, Multiculturalism and Caste in the UK', *Samaj*, 27 (2021).

Jenkins, Laura Dudley, 'Race, Caste and Justice: Social Science Categories and Anti-discrimination Policies in India and the United States', *Connecticut Law Review*, 36, 747 (2004);

Jhadav, Narendra, 'Neglected Economic Thought of Babasaheb Ambedkar', *Economic and Political Weekly*, 26, 15 (13 April 1991), pp. 980–2.

Jones, Sam, 'Asian caste discrimination rife in UK, says report', *The Guardian*, 11 November 2011, https://www.theguardian.com/society/2009/nov/11/caste-discrimination-uk-report.

Kadam K. N., ed., *Dr Babasaheb Ambedkar and the significance of his movement. A chronology* (Bombay: Popular Prakashan, 1993), p. 24.

Kalelkar, Kaka, *Backward Classes. Commission, Report* (30 March 1955).

Kallidai, Ramesh, Hindu Forum of Britain, 'Caste in the UK', 2008, p. 4, available at www.hfb.org.uk (searched 29 Jan. 2022).

Kapur, Sudarshan, *Raising Up a Prophet: the African American Encounter with Gandhi* (Boston: Beacon Press, 1992), p.16.

Kataria, Sumit, 'Ambedkar: A Jurist With No Equals', *Forward Press*, 13 July 2017, available at https://www.forwardpress.in/2017/07/ambedkar-a-jurist-with-no-equals/ (searched 17 Jan. 2022).

Kaul, N. C., *True Story of the Vihara*, N. C. Kaul & Ambedkar International Mission, 27 April 1996.

Keer, Dhananjay, *Dr Ambedkar Life and Mission*, 3rd edn (Bombay: Popular Prakasan, 1971).

Kelley, Robin D. G. and Earl Lewis, *To Make Our World Anew: A History of African Americans* (New York: Oxford University Press, 2000), p. 380.

Khapre, Shubhangi, 'Maharashtra wants to buy Ambedkar's London home', *Indian Express*, 11 September 2014.

Knot, Kim, *Hinduism—A Very Short Introduction* (Oxford: Oxford University Press, 1998).

Koomen, Jonneke, 'International Relations/Black Internationalism: Reimaginging Teaching and Learning about Global Politics', *International Studies Perspectives*, 20, 4 (November 2019), pp. 390–411.

Kousser, J. Morgan, 'The Supremacy of Equal Rights: The Struggle Against Racial Discrimination in Antebellum Massachusetts and the Foundations of the Fourteenth Amendment', *Northwestern University Law Review*, 82, 4 (1988), p. 941, pp. 953–55.

Krishnamurthy, J., 'Ambedkar's Educational Odyssey, 1913–1927', *Journal of Social Inclusion Studies*, 5, 2 (2020), pp. 147–57.

Kshirsagar, Ramchandra, *Dalit Movement in India and its Leaders* (Delhi: MD Publications, 1994).

Kumar, Arun, *Ambedkarite Movement in the Western Hemisphere*, Dr Ambedkar 2nd International Convention, 2011—Kuala Lumpur, Malaysia, p. 16.

Kumar, V. M. Ravi, 'History of Indian Environmental Movement: A Study of Dr B. R. Ambedkar from the Perspectives of Access to Water', *Contemporary Voice of Dalit*, 8, 2 (2016), pp. 239–45.

Kumar, Vivek, 'Understanding Dalit Diaspora', *Economic and Political Weekly*, 39, 1 (3–9 January 2004), pp. 114–16.

———, 'Dalit Diaspora: Invisible Existence', *Diaspora Studies*, 2, 1 (2009), pp. 53–64.

———, 'Dalit Diaspora Joins The Fight', *Indian Express*, 24 May 2003.

Leal, K. C., 'We lost our hero before the battle was won', in *Babasaheb Ambedkar, A Birth Centenary Commemoration Vol II* (London: Ambedkar Centenary Celebrations Committee UK, n.d.), p. 56.

Legg, Stephen, 'Political lives at sea: working and socialising to and from the India Round Table Conference in London, 1930–1932', *Journal of Historical Geography*, 68 (2020), pp. 21–32.

Lester, Anthony, *Five Ideas to Fight or—How Our Freedom Is Under Threat and Why It Matters* (London: Oneworld Publications, 2016).

Lester, Anthony and Geoffrey Bindman, *Race and Law* (London: Penguin, 1972).

Levy, H. L., 'Lawyer-Scholars, Lawyer-Politicians and the Hindu Code Bill, 1921–1956', *Law & Society Review*, 3(2/3) (November 1968–February 1969), pp. 303–16.

McLane, John, *Indian Nationalism and the Early Congress* (Princeton: Princeton University Press, 1978).

Malcolm X, *The Autobiography of Malcolm X* (New York: Ballantine Books, 1992).

Mankar, Vijay, *Life and Movement of Dr B. R. Ambedkar: A Chronology* (Nagpur: Blue World Series, 2009).

Mays, Benjamin, *Born to Rebel: An Autobiography* (Athens, GA: University of Georgia Press, 1987), p. 156.

Meshram, Waman, 'Complete Puna pact explained by Waman Mesham' (BAMCEF), https://www.youtube.com/watch?v=2zSs6AMmwK4.

Metcalf, Hilary, *Caste discrimination and harassment in Great Britain* (London: National Institute of Economic and Social Research, December 2010).

Mhaskar, Sumeet, 'Ambedkar's Fight Wasn't Just Against Caste: Scholars have overlooked his Labour Activism', *The Print*, 14 April 2020, available at https://theprint.in/opinion/ambedkars-fight-wasnt-just-against-caste-scholars-have-overlooked-his-labour-activism/401133/

Moon, Vasant, ed., *Dr Babasaheb Ambedkar: Writings and Speeches*, Vol. 12 (Bombay: Education Department, Government of Maharashtra, 1993).

Moscovitch, Brant, 'Harold Laski's Indian students and the power of education, 1920–1950', *Contemporary South Asia*, 20 (2012).

Mukherjee, Arun P., 'B. R. Ambedkar, John Dewey, and the Meaning of Democracy', *New Literary History*, 40, 2 (2009), pp. 345–70.

Mukherjee, Sumita, 'Mobility, Race and the Politicisation of Indian Studies in Britain before the Second World War', *History of Education* (London: Routledge, 10 February 2022, e-publication).

Mullen, Bill V. and Cathryn Watson, eds, *W. E. B. Dubois on Asia: Crossing The World Color Line* (Jackson: University Press of Mississippi, 2005).

Myrdal, Gunnar, *The American Dilemma* (New York: International Publishers, 1944), p. 667.

Namishray, Mohan Dass, *Caste and Race: Comparative Study of B. R. Ambedkar and Martin Luther King* (Delhi: Rawat Publications, 2003).

Narke, Hari, ed., *Dr Babasaheb Ambedkar: Writings and Speeches* (New Delhi: Dr Ambedkar Foundation, 2014).

Narula, Smita, 'Equal by Law, Unequal by Caste: The Untouchable Condition in Critical Race Perspective', *Wisconsin International Law Journal*, 26, 2 (2008).

Nelson, Dean, 'India to buy £4m London student home of independence hero', *Daily Telegraph*, 11 September 2014.

Newbigin, Eleanor, *The Hindu Family and the Emergence of Modern India: Law, Citizenship and Community* (Cambridge: Cambridge University Press, 2013).

Omvedt, Gail, *Dalits and the democratic revolution* (New Delhi: Sage, 1994).

———, *Ambedkar: Towards and Enlightened India* (London: Penguin, 2004).

———, *Buddhism in India: Challenging Brahmanism and Caste* (Delhi: Sage, 2003).

———, *Dalits and the Democratic Revolution: Dr Ambedkar and the Dalit Movement in Colonial India*, 11th edn (New Delhi: Sage, 2011).

Orton, William Aylott, *The Liberal Tradition: A Study of the Social and Spiritual Conditions of Freedom* (New Haven: Yale University Press, 1945).

Padmore, George, *Pan-Africanism or Communism?: The Coming Struggle for Africa* (New York: D. Dobson, 1956), p. 112.

Paik, Shailaja, 'Forging a New Dalit Womanhood in Colonial Western India: Discourse on Modernity, Rights, Education and Emancipation', *Journal of Women's History*, 28, 4 (2016), pp. 14–40.

Pandey, Gyanendra, *A History of Prejudice: Race, Caste and Differences in India and the United States* (Cambridge: Cambridge University Press, 2013).

Pawar, Ishwar Das, *My Struggle in Life* (Conneaut Lake: Page Publishing, 2015), p. 110.

Rai, Lajpat, *The United States of America: A Hindu's Impression and a Study* (Calcutta: R. Chatterjee, 1916).

Rajadhyaksha, Niranjan, 'Ambedkar, rupee and our current troubles', *Livemint*, 14 April 2015, available at https://www.livemint.com/Opinion/rMImvbuYNDk4RvWGfcMtQO/Ambedkar-rupee-and-our-current-troubles.html.

Ramanathan, S., 'Calling Dalits Harijan SC Calls Term Abusive', *The News Minute*, 27 March 2017, https://www.thenewsminute.com/article/stop-calling-dalits-harijan-sc-calls-term-abusive-we-remain-ignorant-and-insensitive-59315

Ramnath, Maia, *Decolonizing anarchism: An antiauthoritarian history of India's liberation struggle* (Oakland: AK Press, 2011).

Rankow, Liza and Howard Thurman, 'Spirituality and Social Change', Ella Baker Center of Human Rights, available at https://ellabakercenter.org/blog/2012/02/howard-thurman-spirituality-social-change.

Rawat, Vidya Bhushan, 'In Conversation with Mr Harbans Virdee', *The Asian Independent*, 4 August 2020.

Rawat V. B. and N. G. Uke, 'Remembering A True Humanist', *Countercurrents*, 10 November 2006, available at www.countercurrents.org/dalit-uk101106.htm.

Rudwick, Elliott M., 'The Niagara Movement', *The Journal of Negro History*, 42 (July 1957), p. 177.

Runnymede Trust, 'Oral Histories Commonwealth Immigration Act 1968', www.runnymedetrust.org.

Samel, Swapna H., 'Mahad Chawadar Tank Satyagraha of 1927: Beginning of Dalit liberation under C.R. Ambedkar', *Proceedings of the Indian History Congress*, Vol. 60, Diamond Jubilee (1999), p. 723. https://www.jstor.org/stable/44144143.

Sanghera, Jasvinder, *Shame* (London: Hodder and Stoughton, 2007), p. 52.

Shah, Prakash, *Against Caste in British Law: A Critical Perspective on the Caste Discrimination Provision in the Equality Act 2010* (London: Palgrave Macmillan 2015).

———, 'What lies behind the inclusion of caste in the UK Equality Act', London School of Economics Blogs, 11 October 2016, available at http://eprints.lse.ac.uk/76462/.

Sisemore, Major James S., 'The Russo-Japanese War, Lessons not Learned', in Geoffrey Jukes, *The Russo-Japanese War 1904–5* (Oxford: Osprey Publishing, 2002).

Slate, Nico, *Color Cosmopolitanism: The Shared Struggle for Freedom in the United States and India* (Cambridge: MA: Harvard University Press, 2012).

Sharma, Arvind, *Reservation and Affirmative Action: Models of Social Integration in India and the United States* (New Delhi: Sage, 2005).

Sharma, Pt Satish, 'Caste, Conversion and a Thoroughly Colonial Conspiracy', National Council of Hindu Temples UK (NCHT), 2017. This report is available in book form as *Caste, Conversion A Colonial Conspiracy: What Every Hindu and Christian must know about Caste* (BBDS Publishing, 2021).

Singharia, Manak, 'Dr B. R. Ambedkar: As An Economist', *International Journal of Humanities and Social Science Invention*, 2, 3 (March 2013), pp. 24–7.

Som, Reba, 'Jawaharlal Nehru and the Hindu Code: A Victory of Symbol over Substance?' *Modern Asian Studies*, 28, 1 (1994), pp. 165–94.

Sriram, Lakshman, 'California University Board unanimously votes to recognise protection from caste discrimination', *The Hindu*, 26 January 2022.

Srivedi, Gummadi, ed., *Ambedkar's Vision of Economic Development for India* (London: Routledge, 2020).

Stroud, Scott, 'What did Ambedkar Learn from John Dewey's "Democracy and Education"?' *The Pluralist*, 12, 2 (2017), pp. 78–103.

Taylor, Steve, 'Religious Conversion and Dalit Assertion Among a Punjabi Sikh Diaspora', *Sociological Bulletin*, 63, 2 (2014), pp. 224–46.

Tejani, Shabnum, *Indian Secularism: a social and intellectual history 1890–1950* (Bloomington: Indiana University Press, 2008).

Teltumbde, Anand, *Dr B. R. Ambedkar: Complete Works*, available at https://archive.org/stream/Ambedkar_CompleteWorks/07.%20Evidence%20before%20the%20Southborough%20Committee_djvu.txt

———, *Mahad: The making of the first Dalit revolt* (Delhi: Aakar Books, 2016).

———, *Ambedkar in and for the Post-Ambedkar Dalit Movement* (Pune: Sugawa Prakashan, 1997).

*The Indian and Pakistan Year Book and Who's Who—1948* (Bombay: The Times of India, 1948), p. 1182.

Thind, G. S., *Our Indian Sub-Continent Heritage, from prior to 3200 B.C. to our time* (Burnaby: G. S. Thind, 2000), pp. 367–9.

Tidy, Michael and Donald Leeming, *A History of Africa 1880–1914* (London: Hodder and Stoughton, 1980), pp. 110–77.

Tomlinson, B. R., 'Britain and the Indian Currency Crisis', *Economic History Review*, xxxii (1979), pp. 88–99.

Vakil C. N. and S. K. Muranjan, *Currency and Prices in India* (Calcutta: Longmans, 1927).

Visram, Rozina, *Asians in Britain: 400 Years of History* (London: Pluto Press, 2002).

Vundru, Raja Shekhar, *Gandhi, Ambedkar & Patel* (New Delhi: Bloomsbury, 2017).

*Washington Post*, 'Google cancelled a talk on caste bias by Thenmozhi Soundararajan after some employees revolted', 2 June 2022.

Waughray, Annapurna, *Capturing Caste in Law: The Legal Regulation of Caste and Caste-Based Discrimination* (London: Routledge, 2022), p. 225.

Weaver, Maurice, 'I thought I would escape the name ... but it has followed me like a dark cloud', *Daily Telegraph*, 11 October 1990, p. 25.

Wilkerson, Isabel, *Caste—The Lies That Divide Us* (London: Penguin Random House, 2020).

Wolf, Kyle D., 'The Niagara Movement of 1905: A Look Back to a Century Ago', *Afro-Americans in New York Life and History*, 32, 2 (2008), pp. 9–20.

Woolf, Marie, 'Cameron blocks ban on caste bias', *The Sunday Times*, 21 December 2014.

Wright, David, 'The Use of Race and Racial Perceptions Among Asians and Blacks: The Case of the Japanese and African Americans', *Hitotsubashi Journal of Social Studies*, 30 (1998), pp. 135–9.

Yengde, Suraj, *Caste Matters* (London: Penguin, 2019).

Yengde, Suraj and Anand Teltumbde, eds, *The Radical Ambedkar: Critical Reflections* (Gurgaon: Allen Lane, 2018).

Zachariah, Ben, *Developing India: An Intellectual and Social History c. 1930–1950* (Delhi: Oxford University Press, 2005).

Zelliot, Eleanor, *Dr Babasaheb Ambedkar and the Untouchable Movement* (Sacramento: Blumoon Books, 2004).

———, 'Congress and the Untouchables—1917–1950', in R. Sisson, S. Wolpert, eds, *Congress and Indian Nationalism—The Pre-Independence Phase* (Delhi: Oxford University Press, 1988), p. 183–4.

———, 'Gandhi and Ambedkar—A study in leadership', in J. M. Mahar, ed., *The Untouchables in Contemporary India* (Tuscon: The University of Arizona Press, 1972), p. 81.

———, *From Untouchable to Dalit*, 2nd edn (New Delhi: Manohar, 1996).

———, *From Untouchable to Dalit: Essays on the Ambedkar Movement* (New Delhi: Manohar, 2001).

Zene, Cosimo, 'Justice for the Excluded and Education for Democracy in B. R. Ambedkar and A. Gramsci', *A Journal of Economics, Culture and Society*, 30, 4 (2018), pp. 494–524.

Zolberg, Aristide R., 'Herman Finer', *Political Science and Politics*, 2, 2 (Spring 1969), pp. 199–200.

# INDEX

Note: Page numbers followed by "*n*" refer to notes